P9-CFJ-227

THE SCARLET THREAD

Evelyn Anthony

1817

HARPER & ROW, PUBLISHERS, NEW YORK

Grand Rapids, Philadelphia, St. Louis, San Francisco
London, Singapore, Sydney, Tokyo, Toronto

FIRST EDITION
Designed by Helene Berinsky

Library of Congress Cataloging-in-Publication Data

Anthony, Evelyn.
    The scarlet thread / Evelyn Anthony. — 1st ed.
        p.   cm.
    ISBN 0-06-016100-0
    I. Title.
PR6069.T428S3   1990
823'.914—dc20   89-46068

90 91 92 93 94 NK/HC 10 9 8 7 6 5 4 3 2 1

To Shirley and Tony Fanshawe
with my love

THE SCARLET THREAD

1

It was dark and cool inside the church. It smelled of incense and candle grease; there were statues of the Virgin with the Christ Child nestling in her arms, and of saints in ecstasy. The images were painted and gilded, with crowns and paste jewels glimmering in the dim light. It was the last place in the world she would have imagined in picturing her wedding day.

She held on to his arm as they walked up a side aisle, close to the altar. Marble and gilding surrounded a writhing Savior on his cross.

He said, "Sit down and wait here, sweetheart. I'll go find the priest."

She sat on a rickety wooden chair. There were no pews.

A woman was on her knees, polishing the floor.

They had driven up the steep hillside, over the narrow, rutted tracks that led to the village. It clung to the hill as if it had grown out of the rock. They left the jeep in the tiny piazza close to the church, and he had taken her by the hand and walked up cobbled streets to show her the house where his grandfather had been born. It was poor and mean, with tiny windows and a low door that no full-grown man could have passed through without stooping. Geraniums bloomed blood red from little pots and cracks in the walls. Someone's wash hung limply from an upper window.

It was blindingly hot, and the red Sicilian dust was in the air they breathed. "His name was Stefano too," he told her. "That's what we'll call our boy. Let's go to the church now."

The woman who had been polishing the floor straightened up, rubbing the small of her back to ease an old ache. As she turned and stared at Angela for a moment, her expressionless face was sallow and wrinkled like an old map. Picking up the tin of polish and stuffing her rags into it, she painfully went down on one knee before the altar and crossed herself with her free hand. It seemed a strange pantomime to Angela Drummond. She wondered whether Steven had found the priest. The old woman went out, and the door closed behind her. She ought to pray, Angela thought suddenly. Even in this alien place with its sickly smells and guttering candles, she should remember her upbringing and pray for God's blessing on her wedding day.

It was all so different from what she had imagined. She had thought the ceremony would be in the church at home in Sussex, where her mother helped with the flowers and her father dutifully read the lesson once a month. The vicar who had baptized her would marry her to some faceless young man, with a ribbon of bridesmaids behind them and the pews full of friends and relatives in neat suits and flowered hats, whom her brother had ushered in.

But that was before the war had broken out and all their lives had been changed. Her brother was dead, killed on a bombing raid over Germany in 1942. She'd done her nurse's training and gone overseas, and she'd seen a lot of other young men die.

She closed her eyes and tried to formulate some kind of prayer from her thoughts. *I love him; please let us be happy* was all that echoed in her mind.

The priest was seated. He had a spreading bald patch on the top of his head. His cassock was dusty and stained. He looked up at the American captain and said slowly, "Why do you come here? We're at peace now. We don't want you."

"That's not why I've come," was the answer. "I've come for myself."

"You've come to bring back the men of blood," the priest said. He removed his spectacles and wiped them on his sleeve. "There's nothing for the Falconis here," he said. "Nothing."

"You don't understand. You're not listening to me. Listen to me, Father."

"The word comes even to Altodonte," the priest said. "The Americans are bringing you back to prey on us, to bleed us, as you did in all the years before we drove you out. Altodonte is poor. You can't squeeze anything from us. You can't bleed a corpse. Tell your people that."

"I was born here." Steven Falconi spoke quietly. "I've come here to be married. You can't deny me that. That's all I want from you. Nothing else. I've brought my woman; she's waiting outside."

"No." The priest got up, and the rickety chair creaked with relief. "I won't marry you. There's blood on your hands."

"She is carrying my child," Steven Falconi said. "For the sake of honor I ask you to marry us."

"No," the priest repeated. He opened the sacristy door into the church. A young woman in a nurse's uniform was sitting in the shadows at the back. "I won't pardon your sin. Take your woman and leave my church."

Steven Falconi didn't move. "If you marry us, Father, we will forget Altodonte. You'll be left in peace. I guarantee you won't be troubled. Ever." He crossed to the door and closed it quietly. "You'll never see or hear from us again."

It was the tried and proved negotiating term. Do this favor, and I promise a favor in return. Refuse me . . . There was never any choice then. The priest knew there was no choice now.

"You swear this?"

"On my family's honor," was the answer, and the priest knew that oath was never broken. Like the oath of silence.

He sighed. "God forgive you. And me."

"I will wait outside for you," Steven Falconi said. "You've made a wise decision. You won't regret it."

"I remember your grandfather," the priest mumbled, not looking at him. "I was only a boy, but I remember him. He was a murderer."

"I'll wait five minutes, Father," Steven Falconi said. He went out of the sacristy into the nave of the church.

There had been nothing to warn Angela Drummond when she went on duty that day. It seemed a day like all the other days. The base hospital was set up after the Americans captured Palermo; Angela had joined it from Tripoli. Casualties were still coming in from the fighting around Messina, where the British were. American losses had been less light. The American boy she was tending had lost both legs when his tank hit a mine. He was unconscious, and from experience Angela knew that he was going to die. He lay as bloodless and still as if he were already dead. As she bent over, checking the failing pulse, she heard a voice say, "Nurse, is this Lieutenant Scipio?"

Angela straightened. "Yes, it is. I'm sorry, but you can't come in here. You'll have to go."

He was tall and very dark, with an infantry captain's bars on his uniform collar. "We grew up together," he said. "I heard he was brought in. How bad is it?"

"Very bad," Angela answered, her voice low. "He's lost both legs. Please, Captain, you shouldn't have been let in."

"I'll come back," he said. He stood staring down at the dying boy. "I'll come tomorrow. Take care of him."

"We take care of them all. Now, please . . ."

He nodded and turned away. She could see he was moved. If they had grown up together . . . She bent closer to the bed to see his chart: Alfred Scipio, Lieutenant, Tenth Armored Corps, age 23.

What a waste, Angela thought, as she had thought so often at so many deathbeds. A waste like her brother, blown to oblivion over a blazing German city.

"Nurse Drummond!" The head nurse's voice was sharp. "What are you supposed to be doing?"

"I'm sorry, Sister. I was just checking the patient's pulse. It's very weak."

"It doesn't take five minutes, Nurse, and that's how long you've been dawdling. Over here, please. Help me change this dressing."

When the American infantry captain came the next morning, there was another man in Scipio's place. He had shrapnel wounds, second-degree burns to the chest and arms. He would recover.

He came into the ward and straight toward her. "He's gone," he said. "Lieutenant Scipio's gone. Where is he?"

Angela had forgotten the captain would return. After a long day, she was always too tired to think of anything. Then she said, as she had many times before, "He died last night. I'm so sorry."

He looked over to the bed where Scipio had lain, and he said, "It's better for him. I knew him. He wouldn't want to live like that. Thank you, Nurse. Thank you for taking care of him."

"I only wish I could have done more. . . ." Suddenly she was overwhelmingly tired, saddened by the futile words. Her eyes filled with tears, which overflowed. "Poor boy," she said, and turned away. "Please go. I'll get in trouble if the ward Sister comes and finds you here."

"When do you come off duty?"

She answered without thinking, wiping the tears away. It was unforgivable to give way and cry. She was an experienced nurse, with the North African campaign behind her. "Seven-thirty." Then, collecting herself, she added, "Why?"

"I'll wait outside," he said quietly. "My name is Steven Falconi. I'd like to thank you for taking care of my friend."

She didn't mean to let him drive her into Palermo to have dinner. He seemed to know exactly where to get good Sicilian food.

"Where did you and that poor boy grow up?" she asked. "Where do you live in America?"

"New York City," he answered. "Scipio was two grades behind me in school, but his family knew my family. I graduated from college and joined the army. He'd already enlisted. His mother was crying to my mother for weeks. She didn't want him to go. Have some wine— it's good. Do you like the food?"

He spoke fluent Italian. The owner of the little café was never far away. It seemed to Angela that he was always watching Falconi.

Steven talked a lot about Scipio and how he'd promised his friend's mother to look out for him when they were overseas. Not that he'd expected ever to see him once they embarked, but the promise was a comfort to the family.

"We all grew up in the same neighborhood," he elaborated, in answer to a question of hers. "We come from the same background. That's important to us."

He leaned over and poured some wine for her.

"He was only a boy," he said. "No time to know what life was all about. After seeing him like that—both legs gone—I said to you it was better he died."

"I understand," Angela responded. "But I always hope against hope they'll get better, no matter what. I suppose it's part of being a nurse. You want to heal. Every time someone dies, it's a defeat."

He looked at her. "You feel things, don't you? You feel from the heart."

She smiled at him. "I think you do too. You were so upset this morning. It was hell when I first started nursing. I joined the hospital in North Africa, and there were so many casualties. . . . I used to cry myself to sleep. In the end, I just had to make myself accept it. Otherwise I couldn't have gone on. But you must have seen worse." She felt guilty about complaining.

"I haven't been in combat," he said quietly. "But before I'm through with my job here, I'm going to do my share. I've learned a lot since I joined the army. I learned to like some of the guys I trained with, to respect them. My family's very close. We weren't encouraged to make friends outside. Even at college I didn't get involved."

[5]

Angela said, "What about girls?"

He grinned slightly. "The girls I went with, you didn't bring home to your family. But the army was different. You had to mix in, you were part of something bigger than your neighborhood or your city. I found it hard at first. Now I think it was good for me."

"Are you from a big family?" she asked him.

He shook his head. "Just two of us. I have a brother, younger than me."

"Your parents?" She hoped he didn't mind the questions. She wanted to know about him. They hadn't made small talk from the first moment they met.

"My father's a strong man. We love him, but even now, if he says something, we don't argue. Everyone respects him. He's done well for us all." His expression softened. "My mother—she's very special. She's a good woman. She couldn't do a bad thing or a mean one. I don't know how I'm going to write her about Scipio. And then there's his own mother. . . . I promised to take care of him, but what could I do? Maybe if I wasn't stuck with this goddamned job . . ." He looked down, frowning.

On an impulse, Angela reached over and briefly touched his hand. "You weren't even in the same unit. Nobody could blame you. His family will understand."

"Of course they will," he said. "A man is born to die. We're brought up to accept that. Now why don't we talk about something else? I'm going to have some Strega. Will you try some?"

"Thank you, but I have to be on duty first thing in the morning. I have to have a clear head. But isn't it impossible to get?"

Steven half turned from her and signaled the proprietor. "I think he'll have a bottle somewhere," he said. And he was right.

They talked on, and the candle on the table burned down and had to be replaced. There was no sense of time. She told him silly incidents in her nursing career to make him smile. He didn't laugh much. He was a very intense man. He had the darkest eyes she'd ever seen, but they were fine and expressive, set well apart. His face was striking, with a handsome high-bridged nose. It was an arresting face, not easily forgotten.

He spoke softly, in a measured way, as if American was a language he had taken pains to learn properly. And sitting opposite him in the dimly lighted café, Angela felt a strange power coming from him, a

[6]

power of personality and, above all, an overwhelming sensuality that made her tremble.

She hadn't meant to stay so late, but they went on talking, and the time passed quickly. It was close to midnight when he drove her back.

"I'll come tomorrow," he said. "The same time?"

"I get off at three tomorrow," Angela said. "It's my rest day."

"We could go into the country if you like," he said.

They stood by the jeep, not touching, the air vibrating between them.

For something to say, she asked, "What about petrol?"

"I can get enough," he said. "I'd like to show you this part of the island. It's very beautiful. Do you like mountains?"

"I don't know," Angela answered.

"We can take a drive," he went on. "I'll bring some food and a bottle of wine. Would you like that?"

"It sounds wonderful," she answered. She held out her hand. He took it and came closer to her. "Thank you for dinner," she said.

"Thank you for coming. See you tomorrow."

"Yes." He still held on to her hand. "Good night," Angela said, and he let go. She glanced back as she turned the corner of the nurses' quarters, and he was standing there, watching her. She waved, and he made a gesture in return. The back door had been left unlocked by Christine, Angela's roommate. Angela closed and locked it. She hoped Christine would be asleep. For some reason, she didn't feel like answering questions about the evening.

But Christine was awake. She was a professional nurse, three years older than Angela. Theirs was an odd friendship, for they were opposites. Christine made no secret of her liking for men and her enjoyment of sex, and it had been a long time since she cried over a death in the ward. She thought of Angela as sweet-natured and in need of someone to look out for her. It was time she had a boyfriend. She took life much too seriously.

"You must have had a good time," she said. "It's after twelve. What did you do?"

"We had dinner and we talked." Angela undressed quickly. "Thanks for leaving the door unlocked."

"What's he like?" Christine persisted. "Typical Yank? Make a pass at you?"

"No." Angela smiled at her. "Not typical at all. We shook hands, believe it or not. It was rather old-fashioned."

"But you enjoyed it," her friend insisted. "You look as if you did. Seeing him again?"

"Tomorrow," Angela answered. She got into bed and settled down.

"That's quick," Christine remarked. "What's his name?"

"Steven Falconi," she murmured. "We've got to be up at five-thirty, and I'm dead tired. I'll tell you all about it tomorrow."

"I'm seeing my new fellow tomorrow," Christine said. She switched the light off. "I'll ask him if he knows him." Christine tended to mother her younger friends.

Angela had met Christine's latest boyfriend the month before. He was married, but all the nice ones were, Christine maintained. A lieutenant colonel, no less. Very generous and good fun. There were nylon stockings in her drawer and supplies of chocolate and whiskey for the asking.

His name was Walter McKie, and he was some big wheel in the military administration in Palermo. Details like that didn't interest Christine. She was intent on squeezing what fun she could out of the war, and one day, when it was all over, she might hook someone and settle down. But until then she played it strictly for laughs. Naturally, Christine was a very popular girl and never lacked admirers.

She wondered about this American. Christine tried to imagine any of the Americans she knew behaving in an "old-fashioned" way. There had been a distinctly star-struck look in Angela's eye when she came in. Christine had never seen it before, and there had been several young officers in Tripoli who had taken her out and one who had obviously fallen for her.

Angela lay awake in the darkness long after Christine had fallen asleep. It had been a strange evening. It wasn't something she could explain to Christine. She didn't fully understand it herself. But no man had ever made her feel like this before. There'd been a brief affair in Tripoli with a young Scot she had felt sorry for and persuaded herself that she loved. But he was a shadow, though he was her first lover, a fleeting memory of sentiment and transient sex. It wouldn't be the same with this man, if she ever let it get that far. She couldn't stop thinking about him, and about the trip into the mountains. It would be dawn soon, time to get up and begin the early round of the ward. She slept at last and seemed to be shaken out of sleep almost immediately. The red Sicilian sun was creeping up over the edge of the horizon.

They couldn't drive beyond a certain point. Not even the jeep could hold the twisting track up the mountainside. So he found a place with some shade. He'd brought food and wine.

He was always watching her; whenever she looked at him, he was considering her with that deep stare.

Finally, she said, "Why do you look at me like that?"

"You're beautiful," he said. "I like to look at you. Does it bother you?"

They were sitting in the shelter of a rock. She drained the last of her wine. "Yes, it does. I feel as if I've got a dirt mark on my face. And I'm not a bit beautiful. You don't have to say that."

"So what are you, then? What do other men say to you?" he asked as he took her empty cup and filled it.

"I don't want any more," Angela said. "It's too hot; I shall only go to sleep."

"You haven't told me," he reminded her. "What do other boy-friends tell you?"

"I haven't got any boyfriends," she answered. "You're the first person I've been out with since I left Tripoli. In the family they say I'm not bad-looking. That's about it."

"That's English understatement," he said slowly. "Tell me about your family, Angela. Where do you live? What kind of people are they?"

"Oh." She stretched and sighed. "It seems so far away. A million miles from this bloody war and all the misery. My home's in the country. A place called Haywards Heath, in Sussex. It's very gentle countryside, not dry and fierce like this. We haven't any mountains, only smooth rolling hills. It's green and cool, and everyone complains if it rains and worries about their gardens if it doesn't. My father is a doctor; so was my grandfather. He lived in the house and practiced in the town. My mother was born in India; her father was in the Indian army. We're very ordinary, Steven, nothing special about us."

"Brothers and sisters?"

"I had a sister, but she died when she was little, before I was born. I had one brother, Jack. He was in the RAF. He was killed. We were very fond of each other. I was closer to him than to either of my parents."

"I'm sorry," he said. "Why did you choose nursing? Because of your father?"

"No, not really." She paused. "It was mostly because of Jack being killed. I didn't want to go into the Waaf or the Wrens; I didn't want to be a wireless operator or a driver or anything connected with the fighting. I wanted to help, not hurt anyone. Not very patriotic, am I?"

He watched her for a moment. "It's a lousy war, but it'll be over someday soon. And then you'll go back home and forget all about this."

"And so will you," she said. "Isn't Falconi an Italian name? You speak it fluently."

"Sicilian," he corrected. "That's not the same thing. We're not Italians. We're descended from many different peoples: Arabs, Moors, Greeks, even Normans. Sicily was always being invaded. There's some Italian in us, but we're not the same people, not the same culture. My family came from a little village not so far from Palermo. Just in the hills to the north. My grandfather moved to America. We all speak Italian among ourselves. We keep the old traditions, go to church, eat pasta." He looked down at her and smiled. "Not like Haywards Heath," he said.

"Do you feel American?" Angela asked him.

"I'm a citizen. My father took out papers. I went to an American school and an American college. I graduated; I played football for the college; I joined the army. I'm American. But maybe Sicilian too."

They sat in silence for a while as the heat shimmered around them.

Angela said, "I've changed my mind. I'll have some wine if there's any left." It was heavy, and it didn't help her thirst. She tilted the cup and let the red stream out across the ground.

"Do you know what you're doing, Angelina?" His low voice resonated against her, making her lean closer to hear every next syllable. "That's a libation to the gods. We give something back of the good wine to the gods of Sicily so they won't ruin our harvest. Sicily has lots of gods, did you know that?"

She shook her head. The wine was soaking into the ground like blood.

"It's a pagan country," he went on. "The Church tried to civilize us by driving out the gods the Romans and Greeks had given us, but we kept them hidden. They're still here, all around us. Can you feel them?"

She didn't answer. She let him take her and pull her close and begin to kiss her, slowly and then fiercely. The ground was hard, and the rock dust clung to them as they lay entwined on the baking earth. Their passion swayed them to and fro out of the shadow of the rock above, and they made love, coming to their climax together in the molten glare of the sun.

As he dressed her in the shade, he said softly in Italian, *"Io ti amo, amore mio,"* and held her close to him.

"Do you?" she asked him. "You don't have to say it."

"I love you," he said in English. "Say it to me in Italian."

She stumbled over the words, and he repeated them until she followed him. *"Io ti amo, amore mio."*

It was the second time they were together and the first time they made love.

They spent every free moment together. He had hired a little room above the café where they had eaten dinner that first evening. It was bare and sparsely furnished, but there was a big brass double bed and a key that locked the door. They made love with a fierce abandon that amazed her, and yet he was always gentle. He was given to sudden changes of mood. Once he covered her naked body with fresh flowers, then removed them one by one until she lay exposed and longing for him. At other times he was urgent and demanding, begging her to love him, love him quickly. . . .

It was a time of ecstasy and madness, and a time of discovery. Because they talked together. He talked to her as he had never before talked to a woman or imagined that he could. He spoke of his love for her, his childhood, searching her eyes for answers to her past. And she gave them freely. She told him about her home and family, of a reserved, choleric father, a mother kind but vague, a household where decent reticence covered the gamut of human emotions, from happiness to sorrow, and the calm was never broken.

She told him of her love for her dead brother, the shy intimacy they shared as they grew up, and the aching sense of loss when he was killed.

"I minded so desperately that he couldn't be buried," she told Steven, her eyes full of tears. "It seemed so incomplete, being blown up and scattered over the sea." She had never put the thought into words before. And he understood. He talked more about his family, and she began to visualize them.

"You asked me, do I feel American? On the hillside, remember?"

"I remember," she said softly. Only a few weeks away, and yet it could have been a lifetime.

"I've thought about that," he said. "You make me think about things, Angelina, things that never bothered me before. Let me tell you. My grandfather came to America; he came on a ship where they packed the immigrants in like animals below the decks. He carried all he owned in a bundle on his back. When he got to New York he was hungry; he roamed the streets till he found some relatives. They took him in; they gave him work to do. He made a life and got a home for my grandmother to come to. She never learned to speak English. My parents followed, bringing me. My mother didn't want to leave Sicily, she told me once."

"Couldn't they have stayed?" Angela asked him.

"No," he said after a pause. "Things were bad for them. Like for my grandfather. They were hard times for people like us in Sicily. The landowners were trying to drive us out. A lot of men with pride in themselves got into trouble. I was a stranger; I was seven when we came to America. I had to learn to speak English, to change, to become someone I wasn't born to be.

"But always I had my family . . . and the other families, Sicilians like ourselves. They kept the old values, the old loyalties, alive. A lot of people didn't like it. We lived in a hostile world. We learned to fight back, to make our own way. Above all, to be loyal to each other.

"It was rough. I learned to use my fists; it was my father who taught me to use my brains. He believed in education; he sent me to college. He was proud of me, and he wanted me to do well. I owe him everything. My brother too. He didn't like school; he didn't go to college. But he served my father just as I did."

Served. It was an odd word. But as he'd said, English was his second language.

"You'd love my mother," he said suddenly. "You will love her, Angela, and she'll love you. Why do you blush like that? Don't you understand what I'm saying?"

"I'm not sure," Angela answered. They were walking, the clean wind off the sea stinging their faces in the cool of the evening. "What are you saying?"

He stopped and took her in his arms. He tilted her face up to his and kissed her gently on the lips. "I'm going to marry you," he said.

"Steven, we can't," she whispered. "Your army doesn't allow it."

"If we have to wait, then we wait. But we'll be married. There'll never be another woman for me but you. You know that, don't you?"

She closed her eyes, resting against him. She felt safe and loved, and everything seemed possible. Even the end of the accursed war. "I know it," she said. "And it's the same for me. I love you, Steven. I'll wait for you. I want to be with you so much."

He drove her back to the hospital. She was on night duty.

"I haven't a ring to give you," he said. "I gave my graduation ring to my mother. To keep till I got home. I'll write and ask for it. I'll tell her it's for you."

"No," Angela protested. "I don't need rings, Steven. Let her keep it for you. Now kiss me. I've got to go."

"I love you," he said, and took possession of her mouth.

"What happens when he's posted?" Christine demanded. "They're all going, as soon as the weather's right. Walt says it's going to be a bloodbath. He gets killed, and you're left with a brat! Angela, be sensible," she begged. "You can't go through with it. I'll help you. Look, you're only just over six weeks. It'll be a day off with a bad period. No one'll know."

Angela sat up. She had been violently sick in the lavatory and sent to the lounge to lie down. She felt dizzy, but the dreadful nausea had passed.

"I shouldn't have told you," she said. "I wish I hadn't said anything. Have you got a cigarette, Chrissie? I've run out."

"Here. Keep the packet. Thank God you *did* tell me. You can get away with throwing up once, but what are you going to say if it happens every morning? Don't you realize you'll be chucked out and sent home in disgrace?"

"He wants to marry me," Angela answered. She lit the cigarette. It tasted bitter.

"He can't, and he bloody well knows it," Christine retorted. "He'd never get permission. One mention about getting married, and they're posted within forty-eight hours. I wish you'd let me talk to him. Listen, if he loves you, he won't let you go through with this."

"You don't know him," Angela said. "I keep telling you, Steven isn't one of your Yanks. He's different; he'd want the baby. I just haven't told him yet. I wasn't even sure for the first couple of weeks."

"He's no different from any other man." Christine turned away impatiently. "Oh, I know—he loves you, he wants to marry you." She hesitated and then said, "I'm sorry, but I'm going to be cruel. You'll hate me for saying this, but I think it's all pie in the sky. He'll sail off with the invasion fleet, and that'll be the last you'll ever hear of him. And you'll have buggered up your life for nothing."

"I won't get rid of it," Angela said slowly. "You're not right, Christine, but even if you are, I won't kill my own child. So don't mention it again, will you? I'm seeing Steven tonight. I'll tell him."

"You do that," Christine said grimly. "And if you change your mind, just let me know. But it's got to be soon. I'd want nothing to do with it at three months. Now I'd better get back to the ward. I'll say you're asleep." She went out and closed the door hard. It was as near as she dared go to slamming it with frustration.

Angela stubbed out the cigarette. It wasn't a comfort anymore. She felt no sign of the change taking place in her body, just a sudden revulsion from the remembered stench in the lavatory and the acrid taste of tobacco in her mouth. For a moment she put a hand on her stomach. She wasn't afraid of what was to come. Tough, practical Christine couldn't understand that total lack of fear. She thought it was irresponsible, unrealistic.

"For Christ's sake," she'd insisted. "It's not a *baby;* it's not much bigger than a pinhead!"

Angela hadn't even tried to explain to her that this was not the point. It was Steven's child, conceived on the hillside or on the hard little bed in the room above the café. She didn't know, and it didn't matter. All that mattered was the intensity of her love for him and of his love for her. She had no doubts about that love. That he couldn't marry her didn't matter either. They'd find a way to be together when the war was over. The invasion of mainland Italy was very close. She didn't believe he would be killed. She lay back and closed her eyes for a moment. She would tell him. She would choose the moment when they lay together after making love.

She got up, put on her cap and apron and went back to the ward.

The head nurse looked up briefly as she reported back for duty. "You're sure you're better, Nurse? Good, there's plenty to do." She watched Angela while pretending to read through some charts on her desk. Actually, the ward was only half full now; the worst casualties had died or been sent to the base hospital. Angela had never been sick before. If it was food poisoning, she wouldn't have recovered so quickly.

Everyone knew about her affair with the American captain. He was always hanging around outside, waiting for her. She was a good nurse, and the Sister hoped she hadn't made a fool of herself.

He held himself above her; the single light bulb flared over their heads. His body glistened in the heat. Angela reached up and ran both hands from his shoulders to his belly and down to his thighs.

"I want you," she said. "I want you so much it hurts me. . . ."

"Cara bella, bella," he groaned, and came down on her. The love talk was silenced as her mouth reached up for his. Her cry was fierce and brought him to a turbulent climax that left him collapsed and emptied, his head cradled between her breasts.

Angela stroked his hair. *It'll be a dark child,* she thought, and smiled with happiness. His weight pressed on her, and she said softly, "You mustn't lie on me, darling."

"Why not? I like to feel you next to me. . . . You like it too."

Angela ran one finger down the side of his face, tracing the line of his brow, to the prominent cheekbone around the curve of his jaw. For a moment the tip of her finger teased his lips apart.

"It might hurt the baby," she said.

"I'm going to marry you." He had taken her out in the jeep and driven down to the quayside, where the sea breeze brought coolness.

It was dark, and they held each other close. *Christine,* she thought, *how very wrong you were.*

"I'm going to find a way."

"You can't," she told him. "After the war is over; we'll get married then."

"And have my boy a bastard?" He cursed in Italian.

Angela had never seen him angry. She was calm and happy and reassured. She teased him. "How do you know it's a boy?"

He frowned and said, "Because I know it is. Boy or girl, it's my child. Our child. Don't make a joke, Angelina. We'll get married. I'll find a way, even if I have to—" He stopped and eased her a little away from him. "You want to marry me, don't you?"

"I don't care," she said. "I love you; that's what's important. I'm so happy about the baby, I don't see that anything else matters."

He was silent for a moment. He *was* angry, and she realized it suddenly.

"You don't understand," he said. "It matters to me that my child is a Falconi, born into my family. And that they accept you. They will, *cara mia*. They'll love you and be happy for us. But not if the child is born in dishonor."

Dishonor! She said slowly, "Steven, you sound like something out of the Middle Ages. We can't get married because they won't give you permission. Everyone knows it's American policy to stop this sort of thing. There's nothing we can do about it except for me to have the baby. Then we'll get married and make it right as soon as we can."

"It won't be right for us," he answered. "You don't realize, people will disrespect you. Listen to me, sweetheart. You're happy and not making any sense. Let me decide what to do and how to do it. You must be protected. You must have my name. I'll think. I'll find a way. Now I'm taking you back. It's late."

He walked her to the nurses' quarters, stopped and took her in his arms. She had been quiet during their drive back. He had upset her. He had been a fool, forgetting that she wouldn't understand.

"Listen to me, my darling," he said. "You think it's just because of the baby? You don't think I care about you? I don't want our child to be a bastard. I'm not going to let it happen. But it's more; I won't have people disrespecting you—pointing at you. And do you think I'd let you have this baby without a husband to protect you, to see you through it? Without support, except some promise to marry you sometime after the war? I'll soon be sent away from here. And what happens to you when I'm gone? Just another girl who got herself knocked up by an American—that's how it would look. That's how you'd be treated. No. No, my Angelina. You will be married to me, and everyone will know it."

He held her close to him. She could have faced the future secure in his love and his promise. But what was possible for her was inconceivable to him. Dishonor. His family. She didn't understand, but she didn't doubt that he meant it.

"I'm so happy about the child," he said. "I want to be with you for the rest of my life. I'm going to take care of you, *cara mia,* you and the baby. There's only one way to make sure of that. Will you trust me? Will you do what I ask?"

She nodded, blinking back tears.

"Friday is your free day?"

"Yes," she said. He kissed her on one cheek, then the other, and lastly, with great tenderness, on the lips.

"I will have arranged something by then," he said. "I promise you."

They came out of the cool, dim church into the blinding sunlight. For a moment they paused, and he slipped his arm around her. The street outside was empty in the midday heat. No wedding party, no friends to greet them, not even a flower for her to carry. But his family would accept the marriage. Accept her and their child.

It had been a hurried ceremony, conducted swiftly in Italian. He had prompted Angela to answer in English. The priest was sullen; he refused to take Steven's offering. He didn't bless them or shake hands. He turned and hurried back into the sacristy, divesting himself of his stole as he went. But it was valid. It would be entered on the church register.

Steven looked down at her with tenderness. "Not much of a wedding for you, my darling," he said softly. "But I'll make it up to you."

"It was a beautiful wedding," she insisted. "Don't be silly. He just wasn't very friendly, that's all. I suppose it was because I'm not a Catholic."

He guided her down the street. The jeep was parked near the tiny piazza. He turned and lifted her up and placed her in it.

"Your bridal car," he said.

She laughed and held his hand. "No white ribbons and confetti, but it's the happiest day of my life."

"Wait till we get home to New York," he promised, as they drove. "We'll have such a party. You shall have everything to make up for this—a reception, a dance, all your family from England. We know how to celebrate a marriage. I'll buy you a diamond, a proper ring. My father will give you pearls for a necklace. And we'll get presents from all our friends. Very good presents. Enough to set up a whole house. Our people know how important it is to be generous——"

"Steven," she interrupted, "it all sounds lovely, but I don't really care. I'm married to you, and that's what matters."

"We'll have a honeymoon," he went on. "I'll take you anywhere you want to go. Florida, the West Indies . . . My uncle has a house in Palm Beach. We'll have one too."

"If you go on like this, I'll start thinking you're rich," she said.

He looked at her and smiled. "We're not poor," he answered. They were speeding along the road now toward Palermo. They passed a convoy of U.S. Army trucks. The GIs whistled at her, and she turned in her seat to wave to them.

"I wonder if making love will feel any different now that we're married," Angela said.

"It'll be better," he promised.

They had a few hours alone before she had to go back to the hospital. "I'll make it better for you than ever," he said. "Stop waving at those *ragazzi,* my darling. You belong to me now."

"That's a nice thing to call your own GIs," she protested. "It means ruffians, doesn't it?"

"From now on," he answered, "it means all other men."

"He's given her a watch," Christine announced. "Solid gold. She showed me. Walt, she pretty well hinted they'd gone through some kind of marriage service. She's been sick most mornings. I've managed to cover for her, but Sister Hunt's got her beady eye on her. I just don't know how long she's going to get away with it."

Walt McKie reached across the café table and patted her hand. He had grown fond of Christine. They dated regularly, and she didn't go out with anyone else. He had even begun to forget about his children, and his wife was out of mind except when he got letters from home, usually filled with complaints about the hardships of managing the house and the children on her own.

"Quit worrying about her," he advised. "This guy Falconi seems genuine. It sounds like he's just as crazy about her as she is about him. They'll work something out."

Christine shook her head. "You haven't met him. I went with them into Palermo for a drink. I said something about the baby. He looked at me, and I tell you, it was scary.

" 'You offered to help,' he said. 'Angelina told me. Do yourself a favor. Keep out of our business.' She didn't hear it and I didn't say anything, but it gave me the creeps, the way he said it. There's something funny about him; she always said he wasn't a typical Yank, and she's too right. Walt, could you find out about him?"

He said in surprise, "Find out what?"

"Whether he's married," Christine suggested. "That'd be in his records. If he is—if she knew he'd been lying to her—she might do the sensible thing and get rid of it. He *is* odd; I mean it."

McKie grinned at her. "Maybe he's just not your type," he said.

"You can say that again," she retorted. "I don't like Eye Ties anyway." She smiled at him. "I like my men fair and chunky, with nice blue eyes. Remind you of anyone?"

"Could be," he answered. He was really very fond of her, he thought, not at all alarmed. She'd love Cincinnati. He ordered them another drink and let his imagination run free. The pert young thing he'd married fifteen years before was a very dim memory now. The dissatisfied, self-pitying woman she'd become was a reality he could do without.

"Will you see what you can dig up?" Christine asked him.

"Okay, if it'll make you happier. I've a friend at HQ who'd have access to personnel records. But don't expect anything soon. We're going to be very busy in the next few days."

"Oh, God," Christine exclaimed. "You mean it's coming?"

"Any minute," he replied. "Everyone's on standby, waiting for the weather report."

"Thank God you won't be going," she said.

"You're not to say anything," he enjoined. "Not to your friend Angela, or anyone. It's going to be a hell of a fight. It was tough enough here, but they'll defend the mainland every inch of the way. You'll be busy up at the hospital, I guess. That'll take your mind off things."

"I suppose so." She sipped her wine. She didn't want to think about the invasion or the casualties that would come pouring back. The war was bloody awful, and getting what enjoyment you could while you could was the only way to keep going. "You will ask about Falconi, won't you? As soon as you can. He'll be shipped off too. Funny, Angela didn't say he was on standby."

"Maybe he didn't tell her. He'll be going. His division is scheduled to make up the second support force. Now let's forget it, shall we, Chris?"

"Let's," she agreed. "I'm hungry. How about eating?"

"Here or back at my hotel?"

"Here first, and back at the hotel for coffee," Christine suggested. "You know how much I like American coffee. Especially your brand." She squeezed his knee under the table.

The 10th Corps sailed for Anzio on September 9. Walter McKie was right when he had said the fighting would be hard and bloody.

The base hospital was crammed with the wounded. There was no free time for anyone in the aftermath of the landings. Angela worked until she fell exhausted into bed. But she was happy. Her fear that Steven would join his regiment in the assault was unfounded. By some miracle he had stayed behind in Sicily. He was needed by the military administration as liaison officer with the civilian authorities in the southern part of the island. They snatched brief meetings on the hospital grounds on odd days. He was anxious about her. She looked thin and pale and would burst into tears when too many of the wounded died.

"Why don't you give it up?" he asked her. "Apply for a discharge. They'll send you home when they know you're pregnant. You could injure yourself, working like this. You could lose the baby."

They were walking hand in hand under the trees on the hospital grounds. He stopped and took her in his arms.

"I could get you sent back to the States," he said. "I have friends who could fix it. My family will take care of you."

"If I went anywhere, I'd go home to England, wait for you there," she said.

He didn't seem to hear. "No, not England." He shook his head. "There are air raids. You wouldn't be safe. In America, you'd have the best doctors, everything you needed. I'd know you and the baby were safe—"

"I'm not going to argue about it, darling," she said, "because it's impossible! Nobody could arrange that."

"I could try," he insisted. "*Cara,* listen. I'll have to go to Italy eventually. They'll want me over there."

"You said you wouldn't," she protested.

"Not to Salerno," he said. "To Naples, when it's cleared of the Krauts. Same sort of job I've been doing here. I want you out of Sicily before I go. Will you do it? For me, for the baby?"

"I can't," she answered. "I can't leave while this is going on. I can't just walk out on the wounded and think of myself. I'll stay on at the hospital till I can't go on any longer. Don't ask me to do anything else."

"Let me see what I can do anyway," he insisted. "I won't commit you to going. Let me see if it would be possible."

"So long as this hospital is taking casualties, I'm staying, Steven. Nothing will happen to me or the baby. Now I have to get back. Try to understand. I have a duty too. It's here."

He walked back with her. She turned and waved as she hurried through the entrance. He didn't understand. He loved her too much to care about principles. Someone else would come in her place. She should think of herself and their child first and do what he wanted. There would be a way to get her a passage through to the States. There would be a way to make her change her mind. He had been taught that there was always a way.

By September 18 the city of Naples and the surrounding countryside were under Allied control. Italy had surrendered ten days earlier. The American invasion forces sailed across to make the assault on Salerno. By mid-September, the Eighth Army under Montgomery was racing eastward to divert German troops from the beleaguered American forces, pinned down after a long and bitter battle.

Steven Falconi arrived at military headquarters in Palermo with four other men in U.S. uniform. He was the only commissioned officer. They were shown into the office of a colonel who wore U.S. Intelligence insignia. He got up from his desk and shook hands with them one by one.

"I'm Colonel Harding, gentlemen. You all know each other, I expect?"

Falconi answered. "Our families are acquainted."

"Sit down, won't you?" The colonel was courteous, even friendly. He offered cigarettes and produced a bottle of whiskey. They watched him and each other with the dark wariness common to such men. "I guess we have achieved what we set out to do in Sicily," he said. "With your family backgrounds, you, Captain Falconi, Sergeant Brassano and Corporal Capelli, have provided a very necessary liaison with the civilian authorities here in Sicily. But southern Italy is going to be a much more important and difficult area for us to control. Sergeant Rumoranzo and Private Luciano have Neapolitan connections, and there are a number of U.S. Army personnel with Calabrian relatives and influence already over there. You will each be assigned certain sections of the civilian administration to whom to explain our point of view. We want you to get their cooperation. And just as important, to find out who might be unreliable, who could be working for the Fascists."

"We understand," Falconi said. "I think we can bring the people concerned into line."

The others nodded. Rumoranzo spoke, in the ugly twang of New York's Lower East Side. "We said we'd deliver. Don't worry about it,

Colonel. These guys know us, and they'll go along with us, which means they'll go along with you." He glanced at Falconi, and his expression showed a brief glower of dislike. Fuckin' officer, college and all that shit. He felt like spitting the saliva gathered in his mouth. The Colonel was not one of them, but he had a tough reputation.

Harding stood up. Falconi and the others followed.

"Gentlemen, the U.S. Government will be very grateful for the help you're giving us. Now if you go along to Major Thompson's office, he'll fill you in on the details. Goodbye and good luck."

Again he shook hands with each in turn and ushered them out. Closing the door, he poured himself a large Scotch. Rumoranzo had been released from San Quentin prison, his sentence for extortion and violent assault commuted in return for his special service to the U.S. Army in the Italian campaign. The silent Luciano was a murderer, reprieved from a life sentence for the same reason. Capelli was a known mobster and killer, without convictions but with a fraud case pending. Brassano was buying out a close relative, and Falconi had bargained his education and intelligence against a tax demand that would have kept the Falconis in litigation with the Internal Revenue Service for the next ten years, at a cost of a million dollars or more.

They were the scum of the earth, in the colonel's opinion, but they were needed if the Allies were going to govern Sicily and Italy and rout out any underground Fascist resistance. He swallowed his drink and consoled himself with the belief that they would all end up where they belonged when the war was won and they returned home. This was only a respite for those convicted or suspected of heinous crimes. He was on the telephone when Major Thompson came in. "Sit down, Jim," he said, and went on talking.

Finally, he hung up. "Goddamned transport; there's no military aircraft available. We'll have to send them over on a supply ship. Any problems?"

"No problems," Thompson said.

"Help yourself." Harding pointed to the bottle of Scotch.

They were friends who had worked together in civilian life and joined up together. Both were FBI veterans.

"What a bunch of shit," Thompson remarked. "You know the one that really sticks in my craw?"

"Falconi?" the colonel suggested.

"Yeah, Falconi. The college education, the nice manners. He even speaks good Italian. That's the kind of mobster we *don't* want back home. Capelli and the rest of 'em know what they are. But Falconi stayed on and put in a request."

"What kind of request?" the colonel asked sharply.

"Not the usual. He didn't want concessions for some sonofabitch relative over here or any of that crap. He wanted passage back to the States for some dame he's knocked up."

"You're kidding! She's Sicilian?"

"No. She's English, and she's a nurse at the hospital in Palermo."

"For Christ's sake—what did you say?"

"I said it couldn't be done. He didn't like that. He wouldn't take no. He just said he was doing a lot of work for us and he felt we should do him this favor. You know the score, Bill. It sounded just like they talk back home. You owe me. That kind of crap."

"So?" The colonel leaned forward. An English nurse. A Sicilian girl he could have understood, but not this. They never married outside their own people. He wanted to send her home to America. To his family, no doubt. The colonel scowled. It was an outrageous request, and the sheer nerve of it made him boil. Give them an inch and they took the whole rope.

"I said I'd see about it. I'd let him know, but it didn't look promising. I talked about the complications, the passage home, the immigration, illegal entry—you know the sort of stuff. He didn't give a goddamn. He just sat there and said, 'You fix it for me, Major. You can fix it.' Afterward, it clicked. Some colonel in the Legal Department was asking questions about Falconi. He told Personnel there was a nurse involved and he wanted to find out if this guy was on the level. Personnel stalled and came to me. I said, Tell him the guy's okay. No wife, no criminal record. What do I do, Bill? It can't be fixed, and he knows it. But if we say no, he'll find some way to shit on us. They always do."

"Get hold of this colonel. What's his name?"

"McKie," Thompson said. "He's a lawyer, from Cincinnati. I made a few inquiries about him when this stuff came up about Falconi. He's shacked up with another nurse up there. She's buddy-buddy with Falconi's girl. I guess that's why he was asking questions."

"Let's give him a few answers, Jim," was the reply. "This nurse may solve the problem for us when she knows what her boyfriend really is."

* * *

"Sit down, Miss Drummond. Cigarette?"

"No, thank you."

It was a small office in the municipal building in the center of Palermo. The Stars and Stripes hung from the flagpole over the entrance; the mayor and his officials had been moved out to make room for the American occupying forces. Walter McKie had driven her into the city.

Major Thompson took a Lucky Strike from the packet and lit it. Pretty girl, he thought, blond and blue-eyed; just the type these bastards went for. She looked apprehensive.

It had taken a lot of persuading to get her there. Even so, she didn't know why she was asked to come, just that it concerned Steven Falconi. McKie was no fool; he hadn't even hinted that there was anything wrong.

Thompson didn't feel sorry for her. She was lucky, only she didn't know it yet.

She said suddenly, "Major, has anything happened to Steven?"

He'd sailed for Naples three days before. There was still an ache in her breast, as if the parting had been a physical blow.

"No," he answered. "He landed, and he's busy right now, I guess. Miss Drummond, you're close friends, I understand?"

She flushed. "Yes . . . we are. Major, what is this all about? What have my private affairs got to do with you?"

"Before he embarked, Captain Falconi asked me to arrange a passage to America for you," he said.

His eyes were cold, and she felt as if he and she were antagonists.

"He did mention that," she admitted. "I told him I couldn't leave my post at the hospital."

"It would be strictly illegal," Thompson went on. "A forged passport, for example, official instruction to all kinds of people to look the other way. He knew all this, of course, but he still tried to pressure me. So I thought that before I went any further, I'd better talk to you."

She thought Steven was being accused, and she didn't hesitate. "I'm having a baby," she said. "That's why he asked; he's worried about leaving me alone. If anything happened to him, he wanted me to be where his family could look after us."

She had guts, Thompson decided. She wasn't going to let Falconi take any blame.

"How much do you know about Steven Falconi, Miss Drummond? How much has he told you about this family of his?"

"I don't understand you," she said. "Walter, what is this all about? Why did you persuade me to come here? I think I'd like to go."

McKie put a hand on her arm. "Listen to him, Angela. Don't walk out now."

"Miss Drummond." Thompson stubbed out his cigarette and stared at her. "Have you heard of the Mafia?"

"Mafia? I don't think so." McKie's hand was still on her arm.

"You've heard of gangsters in America? Seen movies about them?" He had such a flat, ugly voice; it was deliberately toneless.

"Major Thompson—"

"Your friend Falconi was born in Sicily. His family came from Altodonte."

For a moment she saw the pink-washed houses on the hillside and the church where they had been married.

"I know," she said. "I know they came from Sicily."

"A lot of people came to the States from here. And from Italy. They brought the Mafia with them. Murder, extortion, prostitution— every dirty vice and racket in the book. That's what they brought to America. And that's what Steven Falconi is; and that's why he's over here. I'd like to show you something, Miss Drummond. Read it." Thompson got up and handed a folder to her. He was surprisingly small and thickset without the shield of the desk.

Angela looked up at him. "What is this?"

"It's Falconi's criminal record," he said. "You'll see there are no convictions. They could never make anything stick. The Falconis are big-time racketeers on New York's Lower East Side. They're into every-thing: betting, vice, and especially the labor unions. You don't pay your dues, you don't work. You talk back, and you get beaten up the first time and murdered if you do it again."

The blue-covered folder was open in her lap. His photograph was in the top right-hand corner. Full face, profile. It was hard to recognize at first because the expression was flat and dead. But it was Steven.

"Take your time," she heard Thompson say.

The typescript blurred as she read, then it pitilessly came back into focus. Grandfather: Stefano Falconi. Emigrated to U.S. 1923 to escape conviction for three murders. Convicted for bootlegging, served jail sentence, released; rearrested on charges relating to unsolved murder of rival "family" boss. Released, lack of evidence. Founded Falconi "family" on Lower East Side. Died in hospital after assassination attempt, 1933. Father: Lucca Falconi. Mafia debt collector, Palermo. Suspected of two murders; not arrested, lack of evidence. Intimidation of witnesses in related case. Emigrated to U.S. 1925. Naturalized 1931. Head of Falconi "family" since 1933. No U.S. criminal convictions but indictments on charges of attempted murder, attempts to pervert the course of justice by bribery of witnesses in corruption charges against members of the Teamsters Union; currently under investigation by the Internal Revenue Service.

"Angela, are you okay?" she heard Walter McKie say. She looked around the room. The major was lighting yet another cigarette, and the blue folder was open at the last page on her knee.

"I don't believe this," she said. "It isn't true. I don't believe it."

"It is true," McKie said. "He's a mobster. That's his police record."

Grandfather, father and son. "My family." He had talked about them so often that she had formed a picture of them in her mind. Like other Italian families, a tribe of uncles and aunts and cousins. "We all speak Italian among ourselves . . . go to church, eat pasta. . . . My family will look after you . . . you and the baby . . ." His words were mocking her as she looked first at McKie and then at Thompson, impassive behind his desk.

"He's in the army," she managed to say. "He couldn't be in the army—"

"He's got no criminal conviction," Thompson interrupted. "Not that it matters with guys like him. We've let murderers out of jail to come back here. Don't ask me why, Miss Drummond, because I'm not proud of it. We need them, that's all I can tell you. You never asked Falconi what he was doing here in Sicily?"

She just shook her head.

"What did he tell you—administration?"

"Yes, something like that."

"Yeah, well, you could call it that. You see, people around here know that family. They're scared of guys like Falconi. It makes them cooperate with us. So now he's in Naples. You still want to go to the States, Miss Drummond? You want your kid brought up with the Falconis?"

Angela closed the dossier. She didn't want to see the photograph of him again. Dead-eyed, full face, profile. Gangsters. Yes, she'd seen it all in the movies. Murder, extortion . . . every vice in the book. The mean little house in the narrow street where his grandfather Stefano Falconi was born. He had murdered three men, that report said.

We'll call our boy after him, he had said.

She stood up; she drew away from Walter McKie as he tried to take her arm. She walked over and placed the dossier on the desk.

"I don't believe my Steven is the man in this," she said. "I know him, and he couldn't do these things. But I can't argue with the rest of it. I'd like to go now, Major, if there's nothing else."

"Would you like a drink?" he offered. "You look as if you could use one."

"No, thank you. I'd just like to go."

He rose and opened the door for her. "No passage to the States?"

"No," she said. She didn't shake hands with him. "We got married, you know. In the church in Altodonte."

Thompson nodded slowly. "I wondered about that. They don't mind murder, but they won't accept a bastard child. It's against their honor. You've had a lucky escape, believe me."

She walked past him through the door without answering. McKie didn't try to catch up with her till they were out in the street.

"You want to go back to the hospital right away?"

"Yes. I told Sister I wouldn't be away more than an hour."

Sitting in the jeep, she turned back her sleeve, and the elegant gold watch gleamed in the sunshine.

"He gave me this," she said slowly. She slipped her hand into the neck of her uniform and drew out a chain with a gold ring on the end of it. "And this. They came from the same jewelers. I passed there one day and the place was boarded up. How did he get the ring and the watch?"

McKie didn't like the look of her. He said, "What the hell does it matter? I'm sorry, Angela. I'm sorry you had to find out. Can Chris and I do anything to help?"

"I don't think so," she said quietly. "From now on I've got to help myself. Do you think I'll stop loving him?"

"Sure." He turned the jeep into the short drive up to the hospital forecourt. "Sure you will. What worries both of us is the baby. How are you going to manage?"

"I'll be all right," she said. She stepped down and looked at him. "I'll have some part of him in my life. That's something. Goodbye, Walter."

"I'll be seeing you," he called out.

She nodded and quickened her pace as she came to the entrance.

Sister Hunt checked her watch. She noticed that Nurse Drummond was a ghastly color and bit back the rebuke for being a few minutes late.

"Sister," Angela said, "when I come off duty, I'd like an appointment to see Matron."

Sister Hunt had been hoping she would go of her own accord. "Very well. I'll ask when she can see you, Nurse. Over there, bed number eight. He had a transfusion an hour ago. Pulse and respiration to be monitored."

"Oh, Angela! I'm going to miss you. But you're doing the right thing."

"I'll miss you too." For a moment they embraced, and she knew Christine was close to tears. She was close to them herself.

She hadn't cried, even when the supervisor had spoken of the disgrace she had brought on the nursing service and on her family. She had been calm, almost detached, throughout the interview. At the end, the older woman had taken a little pity on her.

"You're very young," she'd announced. "But you have your life ahead of you. You must think about adoption. I'm sure your parents will advise you that's the best course."

Angela had paused. "If they do," she'd said, "I shan't take any notice of them. Goodbye, Matron. And thank you. I'd like to go on with my duties till the last moment, if I may."

"You may." The tone was frigid. "But only because we're so short of trained nurses." Then she had turned away.

"You promise you'll keep in touch?" Christine was saying. "You'll write and let me know how you are, and about the baby, won't you?"

"I promise." Angela hugged her once more. "And give my love to Walter. Say I'm sorry I didn't see him to say goodbye."

"I'll tell him." Christine was grateful. "He had to do it. He couldn't let you walk into that, once he knew. You've been very good about it, Angie." She paused. "I'm fond of him."

"I know you are, and he's fond of you. It's been such fun working together, and you've been a real friend to me through all this. The last couple of weeks have been sheer hell—"

"They're a lot of cows," Christine declared, referring to the senior staff, who had been bearing down on Angela for the least infraction. Only Sister Hunt, renowned for her fierce adherence to the rules, had gone out of her way to be kind. "They can stuff themselves now. You'll be back home before you know it. And a sea voyage'll do you good. I wish I could have seen you off."

"Don't worry. I've got transport. I'd better go. I'll write, and you write back. Here, take this. It's a present." She thrust a little box into Christine's uniform pocket. "It'll stop you being late," she called out, and started quickly down the stairs.

Christine opened the box. Inside was the gold watch Steven Falconi had given Angela.

The hospital ship docked at Southampton. Angela had worked her passage among the wounded being repatriated from the Italian campaign. There had been no time to think and little time to feel. Feeling would come later, when the reality of what she had done sank in. She hadn't written to Steven, although his letters had arrived from Naples. She didn't open them. She didn't trust herself. Later, when she was safe in England and the last link between them was broken, she might read what he had said.

Southampton in late October was gray and chill in the early morning. A thin rain fell as they prepared to dock. Those able to had climbed on deck to cheer at the first sight of home. Leaning along the railing, beside the young airman she had helped climb up, Angela felt as sad as the morning. There was no one to meet her. They had only her letter explaining that she was coming home and would call when she arrived. She couldn't take the coward's way out by writing what had to be spoken face-to-face.

"Oh, Gawd," the boy beside her kept repeating. "Oh, Gawd. It's so good to be home. Aren't you glad, Nurse? Aren't you bloody glad?"

"Not as bloody glad as you," she said, and managed to smile at him. "Are you being met?"

"Mum and Dad," he announced. "They're down there somewhere. Can't bloody well see anything in this mist."

There was a cheer when they actually docked, and then the gangway rattled up and one by one the men on stretchers and in wheelchairs were helped off the ship. The rain had stopped by the time Angela went down to gather up her bag of belongings. In spite of her cloak, she shivered in the cold. There were long queues at the public telephones, until someone, seeing her waiting, called her and gave up his place. She didn't know how forlorn and tired she looked.

Her mother's voice sounded crackly and far away. Angela had only a few English coins to feed the coin box.

"Angela darling. Where are you?"

"I'm at Southampton. I'll catch a train home. No, no, I'm fine. How are you? How's Daddy? . . . I don't know. It depends when I can get a train. . . . No, don't keep anything hot for me; God knows when I'll get there. . . . Yes, longing to see you both too. . . . I'm running out of money. Bye, Mum darling."

She pushed the door open and an eager serviceman thrust past her. "Sorry, must phone the wife." For a brief moment he watched as she maneuvered her way out of the booth. He wondered what on earth she had to cry about.

"What do you mean there's no line? I know there's a goddamned line!"

The army telephone operator went red. She took off her headphones and stood up. Officer or no officer, she wasn't going to be talked to like that. And by a Yank. "I'm sorry, sir, but I've told you. There is no line to that number on the island. I'm closing the switchboard."

He moved a little nearer. He looked dangerous, as if he might do something violent. "It's the military hospital at Palermo," he said. "So don't give me that crap about no number. Try again."

He reached into his pocket and pulled out a wad of money. "How much will it take? Twenty U.S. dollars?"

The military hospital? Hadn't he heard? *I'd better be careful,* she thought. *I'd like to give him one in the eye, but I'd better not chance it.*

"Just wait a minute, please. I'll get someone." She hurried out of the office to find her sergeant. She wasn't about to give that nasty customer the bad news.

He had been busy for the past fortnight, meeting groups of partisans in the wild Calabrian countryside, cut off from all communication with Naples. There was no letter from Angela waiting for him, and he had sent off three in succession through army channels before he went upcountry.

No letter, no message from her, nothing. No civilian lines of communication were open, so he had naturally gone to the military telephone service. It was ten o'clock at night, and the offices were closed. Only the sullen English girl was on duty. He shouldn't have lost his temper with her. He should have kept calm.

"Evening, Captain. Can I help you?"

There was a hostile look in the man's eye. She'd gone in and complained, of course. He wouldn't get much cooperation from the sergeant either.

"I've got to get through to this number," he said. "It's very important. Your operator said there was no line. Telephone communication was established with Sicily over a week ago. So I know there's a line. Will you try it for me?"

The sergeant said flatly, "The military hospital at Palermo doesn't have a line, sir. It was bombed to the ground yesterday morning."

It was a freak, they told him. A German Heinkel, off course and limping away from the beachhead at Salerno, jettisoned its load over Sicily, and the hospital was hit. The plane crashed shortly afterward in the mountains. It was called an atrocity, though the most likely explanation was that the pilot didn't even see the Red Cross markings on the roof of the building. The way the Heinkel dived into the mountainside, he was probably wounded or dying at the controls.

Steven boarded a reconnaissance plane. When it landed, a jeep and a driver were waiting for him. No casualty lists were available yet. Nurses and patients were still being brought out of the debris. Some had been identified; others were crushed beyond recognition. A temporary morgue had been set up while the rescue work was going on. The driver told him all about it as they approached the devastated site. There was still a huge pall of dust hanging in the air. All the buildings had been destroyed, and fire had broken out in the rubble, adding a new dimension of horror. Water had turned the ground into areas of squelching mud. There was debris everywhere. He picked his way through it, looking for someone, anyone, who could tell him if Angela Drummond had been rescued.

"Eighty percent killed," the driver told him. "Probably more when they get the last lot of bodies out. Lousy bastards, bombing a hospital." One of the NCOs in charge of digging people out shouted across to him that there was a casualty list of sorts. It was down at the warehouse off the Via Presolli. They were taking the dead there for identification.

It was a meat-storage unit, and they had kept the temperature low. He went in, and the chill and the smell of death nearly turned his stomach. A medical orderly gave him a typewritten list.

"It's chaos," he admitted. "Half of the bodies will never be identified. Nurses, patients, Italians cleaning out the wards. Christ, Captain, it's worse than any combat I've been in."

Her name was not on the list. He heard the orderly say, "We've got personal effects over here. Do you want to take a look?'

There were stains on the gold watch—bloodstains—and the dial was shattered. Steven Falconi picked it out of the box.

The orderly looked at him. "You recognize it?"

There was no answer. He turned away, leaving the captain alone. Better to let him cry it out.

2

The damp mists of early morning had lifted. By afternoon it was a beautiful autumn day. Angela had forgotten the brilliant reds and golds that glowed in the sunshine. The air was clean and cool, with the fresh smell of rain lately fallen; she had breathed desert dust for so long, she had forgotten what English air was like.

It all looked so familiar and yet so strange. She got a lift from Sevenoaks station and walked the last half mile to the village near Haywards Heath. Her childhood and young life rose up to greet her. There was the little school where she and Jack had gone before they went away to what her father called their "proper schools." And there was the War Memorial in the center of the green, some faded flowers at its base. In memory of those who gave their lives for King and Country in the Great War, 1914–1918. "Their names liveth for evermore." She knew the words by heart. She wondered when they would put her brother's name there, and those of the others who fought and died in another war, 1939 till when?

The house was close to the green. There was the old eighteenth-century brick wall, with the iron gate and the slope of the red-tiled roof above it. The gate squeaked, as it had always done. Her father's polished brass plate shone in the sunshine. Inside the front garden, a wooden notice was staked firmly in the grass. SURGERY, it said in black letters, and an arrow pointed to the side of the house. Would he understand?

She rang the doorbell. It jangled inside the hall. The bell had been there during her grandfather's time. The surgery door had an electric buzzer. She lifted her bag and waited.

Then she heard the quick footsteps. She could imagine her mother hurrying to the door. She would understand, surely. The flash of imagination became reality. The door was opened, her mother was there with her arms wide, her father in the background. There was joy on their faces, a warm welcome home for their surviving child.

"We're disgraced, you realize that? Absolutely disgraced."

Her mother was crying. Her father, his dead pipe pointed at her like a weapon, kept moving in small circles around the room. She had been home for twenty-four hours before the opportunity came to tell them. At first she had been tempted to say nothing. Their eagerness to look after her made it more difficult. Jack's death had aged them. Her mother's grief had turned inward, gnawing at her energy and enthusiasm for life. Her hair had gone gray before Angela sailed overseas.

She had slept late, exhausted by the long journey. The tiny child was making its own demands upon her. Her father had morning office hours. He joined them for lunch, as he had always done. There were no concessions to shortages and rationing. The dining room table was polished and laid, and the daily help, who'd been there since Angela was a toddler, did the washing up afterward.

"My goodness, you've put on weight, Angela. That dress is quite tight. I suppose it was all that starchy Italian food."

The dress wouldn't fasten properly. None of her skirts fitted comfortably either.

"Mummy. Daddy," Angela said. "I've got something to tell you. It's not the food, I'm afraid. I'm getting fat because I'm going to have a baby."

Her mother was pouring tea. There was no coffee to be had. She stopped, the pot suspended, and slowly a red flush crept up her face.

Her father spoke first. "I hope that's a joke. Even if it is in bad taste."

"No." Angela tried to keep her voice steady. "I wouldn't joke about a thing like that. I'm pregnant. That's why I've been sent home." She looked at their stricken faces and had managed to say, "I'm so sorry. So sorry to burden you with this," when her mother burst into tears and her father lost his temper.

"Disgraced," he cried. "Thrown out of the Red Cross and sent home. Angela, how could you have done such a thing?" He didn't wait for an answer, or an explanation. "Didn't you think how we'd feel? What about your mother? Hasn't she gone through enough after Jack's death, without you letting us down?"

"Don't. Hush, don't," her mother pleaded. "It's no good going on like this. Calm down, darling. Don't upset yourself." Then to her daughter, she said, "He's not been at all well lately. He shouldn't get worked up."

"I don't want to upset either of you," Angela said. "I didn't know you hadn't been well, Daddy. I shouldn't have said anything. I wish to God I hadn't. I wish I hadn't come home at all."

She got up and stumbled out of the room. There was no key in her bedroom door. She wanted to lock them out, to weep her disappointment and hurt away without either of them having second thoughts and coming up to talk to her.

She put her hands on her stomach and clenched them defensively. "Poor little thing. Nobody wants you. I won't stay. I won't have you born here if they feel like that. . . ."

And of course her mother came and knocked after a little while and sat on the bed and tried to make amends.

"Daddy didn't mean that. He was just upset. We've talked it over, and naturally we'll do what we can for you. You must understand, my dear, it's quite a shock for us."

"I know it is." Angela felt so weary. She looked at her mother for a moment and said the unthinkable. "Weren't you in love, Mummy? Can't you remember how you felt?"

"Of course I was," she protested. "But I waited till I was married."

"I *am* married," Angela said. She got up and began aimlessly to comb her hair.

"What do you mean? You never said anything about being married!"

"It won't count here," she said. "But he wanted it. He minded a lot about the baby. So he got a priest in Sicily to marry us. He's American. He wanted me to go to the States, to his family."

Her mother said, hesitantly, "Why didn't you?"

"I had a good reason," Angela said. "I didn't want to bring up the baby in that environment."

"Bring it up? You mean you're going to keep it?"

Angela put down the comb. She set it straight in line with her old silver hairbrushes and the little glass jars with silver lids.

"Don't tell me you'd want your grandchild to be adopted."

"It might be the best thing for you," was the answer. "But there's no need to talk about that now. Come downstairs; your father's very upset, Angela. It's become so dreadful, and we were so excited to have you home."

"All right, Mother. You go on, and I'll tidy myself up and come down. Just ask him not to shout at me, will you?"

"He won't," her mother promised. "He'll be calm. We've got to work out what we're going to say to people."

"That's not a marriage," Hugh Drummond muttered. "Some mumbo jumbo, without a certificate or any legal proof. He just made a fool of you, Angela."

There was no use trying to explain Steven's attitude. She remembered Major Thompson's contemptuous remark: "They don't mind murder, but they won't accept a bastard child." What would her father make of that?

"I've been thinking," Angela said. "I shouldn't have come home and just landed you with this. You're right, Daddy. It was bad enough losing Jack. I've got a little money in the bank; I can go to London and get a job and have the baby there. It'd be best, wouldn't it?"

"No, it would not!" he retorted. "Don't be silly, Angela. Of course you'll stay here; it's your home. You can have the child in the cottage hospital. So don't even think of doing anything else, please."

He was not a man given to displays of affection. Even the ritual kiss good night had been dropped before she became an adolescent. But he showed his irritation easily enough. His children were supposed to take his love for granted, but Angela never had. And now she couldn't see the remorse that had followed the sharp reproof.

Joy Drummond understood him. She said to her daughter, "Angela dear, your father and I love you, and we want to help you. We were just shocked and upset. You weren't very tactful, you know."

"It wasn't easy for me," Angela answered slowly. "I could have written, I could have told you on the phone. I thought that'd be cheating, and I owed it to you not to do that. Anyway, as you said, Mummy, we've got to have a story ready. What do you want me to say? I got married in Sicily, and my husband was killed at Salerno? People round here won't question that."

"You're determined to keep the child?"

"Yes. Absolutely determined."

"You may change your mind," her father suggested. "I've known it to happen."

"It won't happen to me."

"What name will you take?" her mother asked. "What was *his* name?"

"It doesn't matter. I don't want the baby to have an Italian name."

"You said he was American," Joy Drummond protested.

"Italian-American," Angela explained. "I'll think of an English surname."

It was hard for them, and she must make allowances. Their lives had run on in the same sedate routine for over thirty years. Trivia was their safeguard against sorrow. The loss of the daughter who'd died as a baby, the death of their only son. And now a grandchild without a father.

Her mother said, "My grandmother was a Gates; that's a nice name. What do you think, Hugh?"

"Too short," he said. "Like Smith or Brown. It's up to Angela anyway. . . . Well, surgery in half an hour. I could do with a cup of tea."

"I'll make it," Angela offered.

"No, no, you sit down. I won't be a minute. Mrs. P. made some biscuits."

Her mother hurried out. There was a long silence. Her father lit his pipe and puffed at it aggressively. Angela put a small log on the fire and poked it into a blaze.

"I want you to know one thing," she said. "I was really in love with him. I still am."

"After the way he treated you? After leaving you in this predicament?"

"He didn't; I left him. I told Mummy. He wanted me to go to America and wait for him with his family. I said no. I got myself sent home, and I shall never see or hear of him again. But it wasn't anything cheap, and I'm not ashamed of it. I just hope you won't be either."

"Shame doesn't come into it," he said. "Damn! Tobacco's so wretched these days, can't get my pipe to draw properly. Why did you leave him, if he wanted to do the decent thing? I don't understand."

"I can't tell you," Angela decided. *I can't risk you turning against the baby if you know about Steven. You couldn't come to terms with it, any more than I could.* "There was a very good reason, but that's all I can say. I've got to make a new life for myself and the baby and try to put it all behind me. But it's not going to be easy."

"It certainly isn't," he agreed. "Especially if you meet someone and want to get married. But that's a long way off. I think it'd be better if my partner looks after you and does the delivery. Jim Hulbert's a good chap and knows his stuff. I was never that keen on obstetrics anyway. You'd better have a checkup in a couple of days and get things on course. Ah!" He got up as his wife came back into the room. "Joy, give me that tray—it's quite heavy."

Joy Drummond managed one of her bright smiles. "Angela, tea and a biscuit? Better make it two now." Her eyes were red-rimmed, as if she had been crying.

"Thanks, Mummy. One biscuit'll do."

Her father went off to the surgery, and she helped prepare their dinner.

"You'll need a ration card and the extra orange juice and cod-liver oil for the baby," her mother rattled on. "It's awfully good the way mothers are looked after these days. Mrs. P.'s daughter is having a baby, and she was saying only the other day that she's better fed and healthier than Mrs. P. ever was."

It was all so odd, so unreal. Angela peeled potatoes and felt as if she were watching a play in which someone who looked like her was the protagonist. The housekeeper, Mrs. P., and her daughter; the free orange juice and vitamins provided by a thoughtful government; the child of a Mafia gangster nestling in her womb—all played a part. But it was the sudden memory of the burning sun of Sicily on their naked bodies the first time they made love that forced her back to reality.

"If you marry," her father had said, seeing the practical problems. There would never be another man after Steven Falconi.

She came up to her mother and put an arm around her. "Thank you," she said quietly. "And thanks to Daddy too."

"Oh, Angela," Joy murmured. "I'm sorry we took it badly at first. I do hope you'll forget about it. Now, will you make the gravy or shall I?"

"Whatever's the matter, dear?" Joy Drummond asked. "You look as white as a sheet."

The letter from Walter McKie had come with the morning post. Angela opened it while they were having breakfast. Her father had left on an early call, and they were drinking tea and eating toast with a thin scrape of butter and some of the precious jam ration.

"Angela, are you all right?"

Angela covered her face with her hands. For a moment she felt

[38]

everything around her fade. Her mother rose quickly and came to her.

"What is it? What's happened?"

"My best friend is dead." Angela held on to the flimsy airmail letter. "The hospital was bombed just after I left. She was killed, Mum. They were nearly all killed. Oh, Chrissie, Chrissie . . ." She wept.

"You mustn't do this," Joy admonished her. "You mustn't get upset. For the baby's sake."

"I can't believe it. I just wrote to tell her about the trip home and ask how things were. This is from her boyfriend. It was a freak, he says. A German bomber unloaded and then crashed into the mountains."

"What a terrible thing!"

"The place was full of wounded," she went on. "Nobody had a chance. Mum, I think I'm going to be sick."

Afterward, she lay on her bed and read the letter again. Steven Falconi had come back to Sicily to search for her. He had left, believing she was among the dead. Major Thompson had arranged a return flight to Naples for him the same day. No one had challenged Steven's assumption, so she had nothing to worry about, Walter said. Steven wouldn't be trying to trace her now.

Christine was dead; and the last glimmer of hope had died with her.

The boy was born on the eighteenth day of May. It was a short labor, and the midwife delivered him. There was no need to call Jim Hulbert. Her parents hurried over to the cottage hospital. Her mother brought flowers from the garden.

"Eight pounds," Hugh Drummond exclaimed. "He's a big chap."

"He's very dark," Joy Drummond reflected. "Lots of black hair."

"Italians *are* dark." Angela's father had a snap of irritation in his voice.

"Not all of them, Hugh," she protested. "Some are quite fair. Think of the old masters; they painted blond people. How are you feeling, Angela? It wasn't too bad, was it? He's a dear little boy."

"I'm fine," Angela said. "Just tired, Mum, that's all. It was quite quick for a first baby. He is lovely, isn't he?"

"Yes," her mother agreed. She touched the top of his head with her finger. Poor little thing. No father. People round about were saying what a tragedy for Angela, losing her husband like that, and wasn't she brave. But Joy wasn't sure how many really believed it. Angela had called herself Lawrence, after a distant Drummond connection. The child would be registered under that name. The birth certificate would show he was illegitimate, but there was nothing they could do about that. It could be kept locked away.

"Come on, Joy. We mustn't tire her. We'll be off now, Angela, and you go to sleep. I'll tell the nurse to come and take the baby. Nice little chap. Big, too," he remarked again.

"We'll pop back at teatime," her mother promised. "Or I will anyway, if your father's busy." She bent and kissed Angela's cheek.

She was alone then, in the little sunny room, with the flowers from the garden arranged in a vase on the windowsill. A beautiful sunny day, the eighteenth of May, 1944. She looked down at the child in the crook of her arm. Steven's son. He would never see him or know him.

The nurse came in and said, "Mrs. Lawrence! Tears? Now, now, not after such an easy time and that beautiful boy at the end of it. Here, let me take him. You go to sleep, and I'll bring him back at teatime."

Nineteen days later the invasion of Europe began. The end of the war seemed imminent by the time the child was christened in the village church. She named him Charles Steven Hugh. There was a party at the house afterward. It was a very nice party, and the Drummonds enjoyed it. They were especially pleased that Jim Hulbert was paying so much attention to Angela. He was a good man, too old for war service but steady as a rock. They didn't put it into words, but their hope was mutual. It would solve everything if something developed between Angela and Jim.

Lucca Falconi said to his wife, "Our boy has changed, Anna. I watched him at the party. He's not himself. I don't know him anymore."

Steven's mother said, "He talked to everyone; he did his best. It was a wonderful evening, all the family gathered together, all our friends, welcoming him home to us. He's a hero, Lucca, don't forget. He was grateful, I know he was."

"Grateful maybe, but not enjoying it. Not taking part—acting like a stranger. I haven't been able to get close to him since he came back. Piero says the same. He doesn't want to talk about the business; he doesn't want to talk about the future. He was brave, he got a medal and I'm proud of him. But the war's over. And our troubles are over too. Thanks to him. He won't talk about that either."

"He went through a bad time," Anna protested. She dreaded her husband's getting angry with either of their sons. The only time she stood against him was in their defense. He said angrily, "Has he told you about it? Has he talked to you when he puts up barriers to me, his father?"

"No, Lucca, no. I just feel it. I know my son. He's full of sorrow. Give him time to settle, to feel at home again."

"I haven't got time to give," Lucca Falconi answered. "The tax claim has been dropped; we're ready to go out and expand our business. And we need Steven. He's been out of the army three months. It's time he got his feet on the ground. I'll talk to him tomorrow."

"Don't be hard on him, Lucca," she pleaded.

"He's my son and I love him," he answered. "But he's a man and he knows his duty. Now go to sleep, Anna." He reached out and switched off the light. Steven's mother turned onto her side and began to say her rosary, as she had done every night since her son left for the army.

Lucca had been talking for almost an hour. He had spread out the books and the ledgers on the table, insisting that Steven go through them while he explained. And he could feel the resistance. He stopped in the middle of a sentence, then he spoke in dialect, as they all did in private.

"You're not paying me attention," he accused. He was so angry his sallow face was pale.

Steven didn't deny it. The battle had to come sooner or later. He knew what he was going to say. "I'm sorry, Papa. It doesn't mean anything to me anymore."

His father took in a deep breath. "I see. I see," he said. "You get a special job from the army. A way to help the family. No danger, no risks—"

"I did that job," Steven interrupted. "The Internal Revenue did a deal. They let us off the hook."

"And what did you do?" Lucca demanded. "You go and get a transfer. You get yourself into the fighting. The worst of the fighting around Rome! You act like the all-American hero, and you get a medal." He swore a blasphemous Sicilian oath. "You had no right to do that, Steven! You'll be the head of the family one day. You could have been killed, and for what?"

"For the same thing as the others who didn't get home," Steven said. "For the right to live a decent life. You told me you were proud

[41]

of the medal. You showed it off during the party. Now you accuse me. Papa, I fought because I wanted to; I had a good reason. And it taught me something."

Lucca waited; he was shrewd, and he sensed that bullying his son was the wrong tactic. He said quietly, "Tell me, what did it teach you? I want to know. I'll listen. You tell me."

"It made me sick of killing," Steven said slowly. "I killed Germans. It didn't make me feel better. I thought it would, but it didn't."

He wasn't looking at Lucca; he spoke almost to himself. "And I saw my own men die. I saw boys wounded, screaming for someone to shoot them to stop the agony. I saw brave men and cowards on both sides, and there were times when I didn't know which I was myself. They gave me the Distinguished Service Cross. I tried to feel I'd earned it. I want to be proud of it. If I go back to the old ways, I can't be proud."

Lucca came up and put an arm around his son's shoulders. There were tears in his eyes. "My son, I didn't know.... Forgive me. I didn't know what you'd been through. Of course you earned it. But you've got to put all this behind you. You've got to start your life and look to the future."

Steven said slowly, "I don't want the old life, Papa."

Lucca went on holding him. He was patient, he felt so much love for his son. *He's wounded,* he told himself. *Only it doesn't show.* "What life do you want?" he asked him. "You want to leave us? You want to leave the family?"

"No," Steven said. "I love you and Mama and Piero. You're all I've got now. It's the way we do business: I can't go back to it."

"You knew we had to be rough at times," his father reminded him. "I never asked you to do anything like that. That was Piero's side of the business. You were the clever one, the graduate, the son who could make music out of a balance sheet. And anyway, it's changed. Times are different now. We're respectable, legitimate."

He hugged Steven close. Wounds healed, even the invisible ones. Time was what was needed.

He said softly, "We don't need to break heads, Steven. We oil wheels." He rubbed his finger and thumb together. "It works better. So you don't need to worry. I need you, my son. It's been hard without you. I need you to take some of the burden off my shoulders. I'm not so young; I get tired these days."

"I could go into business," Steven said. "I could try banking."

Lucca kept control. "You could. You could go out into the world and do whatever you wanted. But it would break my heart. Do me a favor. Come into the office next week and put in a few hours, just to straighten out some problems for me. And I swear to you, it's respectable, legitimate." He looked at his son and pulled a wry grimace. "Well, almost legitimate," he said. "We may have to bend the rules a little. Sometimes. But no violence. No hurt to anyone. That's all in the past."

Steven said at last, "Let me think about it; give me a little time."

"All the time you need," his father promised. "Just an hour or so next week, that's all I ask."

He opened a bottle of wine with his son and they talked of Piero's coming marriage. She was a good girl, from a neighboring family. They'd known each other since childhood. "There'll be children," Lucca said. "Your mama will like that. And she'll steady Piero down. That's all he needs, a good wife and a family."

Later, Lucca had a stern word with his younger son. "Steven's coming into the office. I'll get him down to work. But no heavy talk from you, or anyone. If it's needed, do it, but don't bring him in on it. You understand me?"

And to his wife he was comforting. "Steven's suffered. More than we realized. I remembered that poor boy of Giovanni's. Still in the psychiatric hospital. I was hasty, Anna. You were right. He needs to feel the family around him. Help him forget. There's the wedding. . . . He'll meet some nice girls, get back into the old life. Just give him time. He'll settle down. Next thing, he'll find a wife. Maybe that's what he needs."

But it would be six long years before that part of his prediction came true.

On May 18, 1950, Steven Falconi got married. It was his little son Charlie's sixth birthday. Three thousand miles from the children's tea party in England, Steven drove his new wife away on their honeymoon and called out another woman's name as he took her virginity.

They had married in Palm Beach. First a full nuptial mass in the Church of Santa Margarita and then a huge reception at his uncle's house. She was a beautiful bride, with dark hair, brilliant black eyes and a voluptuous look about her. Clara Fabrizzi was the only daughter of Aldo Fabrizzi, who controlled the garment factories on the Lower East Side of Manhattan and had just acquired a string of hotels on the

Florida coast. A marriage of dynasties, the Fabrizzis uniting with the Falconis. Both families were pleased; other alliances would follow as a result. She was an heiress and a rich prize, even for a man as important as Steven Falconi. They looked good together, leading off the dancing that evening. He was tall and a war hero. The Falconis' business was flourishing, and money was filling the family's coffers and finding its way across the Atlantic to Switzerland.

Clara's dress had cost a fortune, and there was another fortune in diamonds around her neck, her father's gift. She was twenty-one, her virginity guaranteed by her family to the Falconis, and she was passionately in love with the man they wanted her to marry. The men exchanged crude jokes about the wedding night, and the women, some of them well past their first blush, wondered what it would be like to be bedded by Steven Falconi. None of them could claim to know, because he hadn't looked at any of his own women since he came back from the war.

There was music and dancing, and a lot of men got drunk, while others slipped away and talked business in little groups. The weather was hot and sunny as in the old country, and the ocean lapped blue at the edge of the private beach. Special caterers had come down from New York with the best Italian dishes and the finest Italian wine and French champagne. Two rooms in the mansion were given up to displaying the wedding presents. The ice-blue Cadillac with bulletproof glass and armor plating was Aldo Fabrizzi's wedding present to his son-in-law. It waited outside, festooned in white ribbons.

The fathers stood together, watching their children circle the open-air dance floor as the band played the "Wedding Waltz." Fabrizzi was small and stocky; in his youth he had been a boxer, and he still walked with the light spring of a man used to moving in the ring.

"They look good," he said to Lucca Falconi. "Your boy and my little girl. They'll have fine-looking children."

Lucca nodded. He was pleased, happy about the whole arrangement, happier still because his son had found a suitable wife and would settle down at last. The war had been bad for him in many ways. Still, he had come back and taken up his responsibilities in the end. A very good organizer and a real moneyman. He owed the first to the army and the second to his college education.

"He'll be a good husband," he assured Fabrizzi. "He doesn't run around with women. He doesn't gamble. You know my son—no vices."

"No vices," Aldo Fabrizzi agreed. "Except he likes to work all the time. But my Clara will teach him how to play. He's going to be a lucky man."

"Talking of luck, and talking of gambling," Falconi said, "what did you think about my proposal? You know, for opening a new casino in Nevada?"

"Musso runs the gambling there, you know that." Fabrizzi had a habit of pulling at his lower lip when he was thinking about business.

"Together," Lucca suggested, "we are bigger than Musso. Why the fuck should he have all the cake? Think about it. He's not so young, and that son of his is eyeballed on dope. He wouldn't give us trouble."

"I'll think about it." Fabrizzi nodded. "We'll talk tomorrow, maybe. I better dance with my wife."

Fabrizzi's plump little wife had only managed to give him the one daughter. If she knew about his passion for big-breasted blondes, she never said anything.

Falconi took some champagne. Pity he hadn't had a chance to try out the idea on Steven. Gambling was very big money and getting bigger. It was time to give Tony Musso a push and see what happened. He might just take a fall.

"I'm so happy," Clara whispered to Steven as they circled. "You love me, don't you, Steven?" She had beautiful eyes, and they were limpid with her love for him.

"You know I do," he answered, and drew her closer to him. She was everything a man could want. There was passion in her. It had smoldered during their courtship. Steven was the one who drew back. They would have children.

He had bought a magnificent brownstone on East Fifty-second Street. His father was building them a vacation house at Palm Beach as his wedding present. And together the two families would enlarge their business interests.

Clara was an educated girl—that was important to him. He couldn't have married a girl with no interest beyond her home and the bambinos. Clara liked going to concerts and the theater. She had an eye for modern art, which he couldn't understand, but if she wanted pictures, that was okay by him. He desired her. No man could help but want her, and he pressed her closer still until the waltz blended into one of Sinatra's popular romantic songs. There'd been no significant woman in his life since he came back from the war. Nothing had filled the void in his life, not even the devotion to business that occupied every moment of his days. The empty space was there inside him. He had tried to get himself killed in battle because the pain of losing Angela and his child was driving him mad. When he came home, he couldn't tell anyone what had happened. It was his private grief, a secret anguish he carried inside. He still dreamed of that dreadful dust-filled wasteland, with the smell of burning corpses in the air, and woke up sweating.

He held his new bride tight against him and believed that love for her would grow and fill the emptiness.

They had rented a house at Boca Raton for the first part of their honeymoon. The staff was handpicked. They were Falconi's people, and the house was guarded day and night. The family had enemies along that coast. Later, the couple would fly off to Europe, where the bodyguards weren't necessary. Clara had grown up with armed men watching her father and dogging her wherever she went. It was part of the lifestyle of a Mafia chief's family. It had made her feel important as a child.

That first night, they had dinner on the terrace, with the moon rising like a silver medal in the sky and the sound of the waves whispering against the shore. Steven raised his glass to her.

"*Carissima*. How hungry are you?"

"I'm hungry for you," she said. "And I've no shame about it. I don't want food, my darling. I want you to make love to me."

He didn't need to undress her, to teach her anything. She stripped off her clothes and stood white and naked before him. In the blaze of passion that engulfed him, she became another woman in his arms, another voice that cried out under him, and the name escaped him without his knowledge. "Angelina." The silk-sheeted bed felt like the dusty earth of Sicily, and the sun of long ago burned his back.

"Angelina." She froze as he lay beside her afterward. He stroked her breasts and murmured to her in Italian, but she couldn't move or answer. It had been painful, but she rejoiced when he hurt her because it fused them together. It was a fierce and primitive satisfaction, as much emotional as physical, when he spent himself inside her. And then she heard another name, uttered twice, at the moment of fulfillment.

Steven was asleep, one arm anchoring her to the bed. She lifted it and slid away. The salt taste of tears was in her mouth. She was naked and cold, with sweat drying on her body and a soreness from the ruptured hymen. There was a little blood, as proof of her purity. She should have been so proud of that. She pulled the unworn nightdress over her head and got back into bed. Unhappiness welled up in her, until she rolled away to the very edge and sobbed into the pillow.

When he woke in the morning and drew her toward him to make love again, she stiffened and drew back.

"I hurt you, *carissima*," he whispered. "Forgive me. It'll be better for you this time. Come here to me."

He tried to take the rigid body in his arms, to soothe and stroke her into responsiveness. She turned her pale face up to him. There were great dark circles under her eyes.

"Tell me about Angelina," she said. "You called her name last night. Tell me about her."

I owe it to her, Steven convinced himself. *I've hurt and humiliated her, and I've got to put it right between us. She's my wife now. I'll make her understand.*

He took her out onto the terrace in the early-morning sunshine and held her hand while he spoke of what had happened in Sicily seven years before. Clara listened, watching his face, judging every intonation in his voice. She saw the pain in his eyes as he relived the nightmare of the devastated hospital. When he spoke of finding the watch stained with her blood, he looked away.

"You married her," Clara said. "You married her in the Church."

"She was pregnant with my child," he repeated. "What else could I do?"

"Nobody told my father about this," she said. "That wasn't very honorable."

"Nobody knew," Steven protested. "You are the only person in the world I've told about it. They're dead, and it's over. I love you, Clara. I don't know how it happened last night, but you've got to forget it."

"You didn't have to marry her." She spoke quite coldly now. "She wasn't Sicilian. How did you know the child was yours? How many other men did she fuck besides you?"

The crudity astonished him. He felt a sudden flare of anger. "Don't ever use that kind of word again, Clara. And don't talk about her that way. I've told you, she's dead and you don't need to be jealous. Now get changed and we'll go for a swim."

"What did she look like?"

He felt the anger come again at her persistence. He wanted to hurt her for what she'd said about Angela and the child. "Not like you. Blond and blue-eyed. Very pretty."

He saw her flinch. *I love her,* he said to himself, *but she's got to learn not to go too far with me.* "I said we'd swim." He turned to go inside. "I told you to get changed."

Women didn't disobey their menfolk. If it wasn't a father, it was a brother and then a husband. She got up and followed him inside. They went down to the beach side by side. He didn't hold her hand or say anything. He dived in ahead of her.

Fiercely she argued with herself, trying to be calm. *I don't have to be jealous. She's dead, she and her child. But I heard her name cried out instead of mine, and I saw the look on his face when he talked about her. But I love him so much I'll have to submit.*

She followed him up to the house and into the bedroom, stripped off her bathing suit, and then threw herself on the bed. She lay there with her legs apart and her breasts swelling as she looked up at him.

"I'm your wife, Steven, and I love you so much I could die. Forgive me."

He made love very kindly and gently, trying to gain her forgiveness, but she clawed and bit like an animal, as if her ferocity could bind him to her and drive out the dead. And she said, gasping in his arms, "You'll forget her. I'll make you forget her. . . . I'll eat you alive till you can't think of anyone else."

Desire drained away from him. "Behave yourself," he commanded her, and she shrank back, wounded. "That's not what I want from you. I pay for that, Clara. I don't want it from my wife."

She spat a vile Sicilian insult at him, and he slapped her across the face. Two of the men patrolling the outside of the house heard their raised voices, looked at each other and shrugged. They were in shirt-sleeves and slacks, shoulder holsters unfastened to allow instance access to their guns if anyone approached. They heard the new Donna Falconi shrieking hysterically at her husband, and one of them sucked up his saliva and spat.

"I'd take my belt to that one if I was him. She needs the shit beaten out of her."

His companion grinned. "You ever see the Don lose his temper? Holy Jesus, he'll kill the little bitch. Come on, let's leave 'em to it. You take the south side of the house, I'll go around the east. Giorgio's keeping his eyes open out back."

[48]

They sailed for Europe on the *Queen Elizabeth*. They were reconciled because they had to be. The families were now bound by a far-reaching business alliance. There was too much at stake beyond their personal happiness, and they accepted this in their different ways.

Steven argued with himself that Clara was still very young and her parents had spoiled her rotten. But she loved him, and he knew he must come to terms with her jealousy. It would pass in time, as she matured and her self-confidence grew. He had asked too much of her too quickly. He chided himself for having underestimated the fiery Sicilian temperament.

When she cried and begged him to love her, he came very close to tenderness as well as sexual desire. They'd be happy, he insisted.

Clara suffered. It was a new experience for her, and she was driven mad from loving a husband she couldn't possess. She had led a charmed life, protected from the least disappointment or frustration. She was helpless in this situation, at the mercy of an unbridled temper and her passion. Suspicion tortured her, so that she watched him constantly. She tried to please him but was never sure she succeeded. She was beautiful, and the admiring looks of men aboard the liner told her that she could have anyone she chose. But the ghost of a dead woman mocked her in Steven's arms. And the ghost of a dead child. That at least she could send quickly to its grave. She knelt by her bed at night and prayed to the Virgin and the saints to make her pregnant.

She knew her father was delighted with the marriage. In calmer moments, she realized that he would dismiss a wartime love affair with a shrug and wonder what she was complaining about. He wouldn't be pleased if there was trouble. He expected a good marriage, grandchildren to gladden his old age, and all the benefits of a treaty with Lucca Falconi. She would have to win Steven, and the way to do it was to give him a son as quickly as she could.

Paris enchanted Clara. She visited every art gallery, and to please her, Steven bought several expensive modern paintings for their new home.

They also explored the world of fashion. Clara fell in love with Dior's designs, which suited her svelte body admirably. Steven felt proud to see heads turn when they entered a restaurant. And Clara shopped for him. There were lavish presents of ties and shirts from Charvet and a magnificent Boucheron platinum watch. She stood beside him, watching his reaction, demanding over and over if he liked this or that. She was a child at heart, he thought: extravagant, impulsive, and demanding too, but it was all part of being in love. No half measures were possible. The extremes of her nature were a surprise to him. The Sicilian courtship, albeit American style, had left them little time to get to know each other in any depth. When they had managed to be alone, every moment was taken up in hungry sexual exploration, which was quickly stopped before it went too far.

Underneath the facade of culture and education there lurked a primitive Sicilian woman, single-minded in her love, black-hearted in her hatred. And clever. She had a brain, and its keenness surprised him. The more he understood her, the less he dismissed her quick intelligence. But she was still the adoring bride, willing to be guided, erotically submissive to whatever he asked.

They were happy together in Paris; so happy she begged to stay an extra week. The week lengthened into a fortnight.

She said to him one day as they walked arm in arm up the Faubourg Saint-Honoré, "You love it here as much as I do, *caro,* don't you?"

"I guess I do," Steven agreed.

"Then why don't we buy an apartment here?" she said triumphantly. "I could use part of Papa's settlement. We could come in the spring maybe, when you weren't too busy. Why don't we, Steven?"

He stopped, taken by surprise. Her eyes were bright with excitement.

"I've even asked around," she admitted. "There's a lovely apartment for sale close by the Invalides. Couldn't we see it?"

Steven hesitated. This was a honeymoon. Time taken off from the important things in life. Their home was in the States. A place in Florida was realistic. An apartment halfway across the world was not. She saw the refusal coming, and the brightness changed to a sullen, tearful look full of reproach.

"Clara, sweetheart, it's a crazy idea. We'd never spend any time in it. How could we? We're going to have a place in Palm Beach. We'll have kids—we won't want to leave them behind."

Kids. She bit her lip. That very morning, she'd learned she wasn't pregnant yet. The idea of a romantic rendezvous in Paris was some kind of compensation for that disappointment. Every year, she had imagined, they could slip away and have a secret honeymoon in the place where they had started to be really happy.

"We could just look at it," she said. "What's the harm? We're not doing anything else this afternoon."

"If you look at it, you'll like it," he answered. "And we'll have an argument."

"If we don't like it," she countered, "there won't be an argument. Steven darling, it was just a silly idea, I guess, but it sounded like fun. I was going to surprise you. See it this afternoon and buy it for us. Maybe I should have done it."

"Maybe you shouldn't have," he countered. "I don't like surprises, sweetheart. If you're bored, we'll go see the place. But not to buy it or anything."

It was a mistake to have indulged her, and as soon as the concierge let them in, Steven knew it. There was a magnificent reception room, over thirty feet long, with a fine Louis XVI marble fireplace and a brilliant Beauvais tapestry running the length of one wall. They could buy it with the apartment, the agent explained, because it was too big for the owners' new house. Long windows looked out over the Seine. Clara opened one and stepped onto the tiny balcony. She avoided Steven's eyes; her instincts warned her not to pressure him. The room, in all its elegance and beauty, would speak for itself.

The dining room was long and narrow, its walls hung in crimson silk. The parquet flooring made their footsteps echo. The bedroom was small, without a view and painted a cold French gray. The bathroom, compared to their American one, was primitive but could be modernized. The bedroom needed only clever decorating and a handsome bed. Ideas chased through her mind but stopped at her tongue. He wouldn't agree. She knew he wouldn't. He would see all the practical disadvantages and simply say no. It was her money, but he would still feel he had a husband's right to dictate how she spent it. She walked back through the rich dining room and into the great salon, her full mouth set tightly.

She said sweetly, looking up at him. "I know we can't have it, *caro,* but isn't it lovely?"

"It's one hell of a room," he said, looking around once more. "It's got everything, if only we didn't live three thousand miles away." Then he thanked the agent, who understood that this was not going to be a sale. "You won't have trouble selling this."

She slipped her hand through his arm as they walked out onto the street. For a moment she turned and looked back at the building. The facade was white stone, built in the handsome classical style of the Second Empire, when Napoleon's nephew, the last emperor, remodeled Paris to his grand design.

"Well, never mind," she said. "It was fun seeing it."

He was surprised that she gave in so easily and grateful because she continued to be pleasant for the rest of the day, which was unusual when she didn't get her way.

Everything went wrong in Monte Carlo, where the scene was set for a romantic climax to the honeymoon before they were to fly back to New York via London.

They had a suite booked in the Hôtel de Paris, overlooking the harbor. Big flower arrangements and champagne in an ice bucket awaited them with the manager's compliments. The weather was perfect; the sea sparkled like a big blue diamond, and the yachts rode at their moorings in arrogant splendor. There was a gala night at the casino, to which they had been invited, thanks to a friend with influence who owed the Fabrizzis a favor. He had secured the coveted entrée to the social event of the season.

Clara was exquisitely dressed in a cream silk Dior evening dress. It flattered her pale skin, which she never exposed to the damaging rays of sunshine, and the long, silky black hair that swung down to her shoulders. She wore her father's diamonds around her neck and Lucca Falconi's diamonds in her ears. She entered the casino on the arm of her tall husband and registered the looks of admiration. There was a flush of happiness and pride in her cheeks, partly owing to the secret she was keeping from Steven. The Paris apartment was hers. She had concluded the deal before they flew down to Nice.

The manager and his assistant saw them enter. They were men of impeccable manners and suave appearance, with sharp eyes and cash-register memories.

"That's the one," the assistant murmured.

For a moment the manager's automatic smile came loose. "How did they get in here, Pierre?"

He whispered a local name. "He wanted an invitation for a friend's daughter and her husband. On their honeymoon, he said. He vouched for them personally. I said, Pass the names through to my secretary, and she'll see they get an invitation."

"If His Highness gets to hear of this, you're fired," the manager muttered, bowing his head in greeting to a distinguished gambling client. "The mob's never set foot in here till tonight. I want him watched. I want someone on his tail when he's eating or gambling or taking a piss.

He's come here for something. I want to know who he talks to, who seems to know him. And see that name's struck off the list."

"Falconi?" the assistant said under his breath. "I've already done that."

"I mean the bastard that got him in here," the manager said, moving forward to kiss an English duchess's hand.

There was a performance by a troupe from the Ballet Russe, which nearly sent Steven to sleep after a magnificent seven-course dinner, enhanced by the finest wines and vintage champagne. Afterward the guests found their way to the gambling tables, and that's when Steven came to life. He quickly noted every detail of the doyen of casinos, filing them away for future reference: the rich decor, the air of exclusivity, the impeccable dress and bearing of every member of the staff, all in full evening dress.

The gala was graced by the prince himself and a large party. Clara stared with open curiosity, and for a moment the prince stared back, trying to place this new beauty. Steven was not beguiled by princes, but he was intrigued by the source from which so much royal revenue was drawn. The air smelled of money, cigar smoke and expensive scent; of out-of-season flowers that bloomed from every stately vase in every available space; and of the indefinable odor of human excitement as the tables began to fill up.

He passed through the roulette salon. Every kind of gambling was in progress, from simple blackjack to the heavy silence of the baccarat room, where fortunes were lost and a few made. Class! The word screamed at him. That was the keynote of the whole place. Discreet, opulent, challenging the clientele to prove they had the money and the nerve to play there.

It was the greatest contrast to the casinos in Nevada, which were noisy and garish, staffed by hoods in tight tuxedos, with holsters bulging under their arms. Whores draped themselves around the bars and gambling tables, getting a percentage if their customers drank and bet more than they meant to, before they were taken upstairs to be fleeced.

Even the biggest and smartest casinos run by the Musso family in Las Vegas were second-rate compared to this. True, the croupiers here had the same feral look in the eye, the same slick movements, and doubtless the invisible button near the knee to alter the draw of the cards or the balance of the wheel. But that was all they had in common. Class, he said to himself. Here losing money was a privilege. He moved a little closer to the baccarat table. A blond woman wearing enough rubies and diamonds to pay off the national debt was playing with demonic concentration. Greed distorted her otherwise beautiful face. She was winning, the counters piling up at her elbow. After each hand, she pushed a handful into the slit in the table for the croupier.

"Merci, Altesse," he said each time, and made a little bow.

Someone close to Steven murmured to him in English, "You wouldn't think the Germans lost the war, to look at her, would you?"

"She's German?" Steven said.

The man was in his middle thirties, with a beaky English face and a slight drawl. "Princess Beatrix von Arentz," he answered. He had been told to follow the American, and in his view, the best way to watch someone in a place like this was to talk to him. It wasn't the conventional method, but then he'd never done anything conventional in his life. Except gamble away his own inheritance.

"Stinking rich husband," he volunteered. "Amazing how they pull themselves up by the boot straps, isn't it? I think he made it out of scrap." He had a rather high-pitched laugh, which he muffled with his hand. "Plenty of that around in Hunland after the war. She's crazy. She comes here every night and never moves from that table till they close. *She's* the princess, by the way. God knows what sewer the husband crawled out of. He usually goes home by now and leaves her to it."

"She's winning," Steven remarked. "She's winning an awful lot of money."

"Not as much as she's lost," the Englishman remarked. "Casinos are like bookmakers, don't you think? They always end up with a profit. Do you play?"

"No," Steven answered.

"The beautiful lady?"

Clara was close beside him, motionless and silent. The Englishman said, "I'm Ralph Maxton. I do the PR here."

"My wife," Steven responded. "She doesn't play either. I'm Steven Falconi. Glad to know you."

There was a sudden burst of applause. The princess had won on a huge wager. Now she looked beautiful in a lean, Nordic way, all bone structure and pale-blue eyes. She gave a brilliant smile.

Clara said to him in Italian, "Take me home."

He looked around in surprise. "Why? You said you were enjoying it. What's the matter?"

She whispered furiously, "You've been staring at that blonde long enough. I'm going."

He said to the Englishman, "Excuse me," and followed her. She moved very quickly, pushing her way to the cloakroom.

He was waiting when she came out with her wrap. "Just a minute, Clara. Just wait a minute. You've had your fun, but I'm not ready to go yet. This is business, you understand."

"What do you want to do, try and pick her up after I've gone?"

Their voices were low, but it was obvious they were having a row. Steven saw one of the staff moving toward them with a determined expression on his face that said more clearly than any words, "We don't allow unpleasantness here."

"Okay," he said. "We go back to the hotel. And by Christ almighty, Clara, you're going to get this straightened out!"

It was an unpleasant ride. He was livid with anger, and any other woman would have backed away. But Clara didn't. As soon as they entered their suite, she tore off her necklace and then the earrings and threw them wildly across the room.

"You stood there staring at that bitch," she shouted. "Looking at her, looking at her tits. I saw you! Blond, like that other whore!"

He didn't slap her. He didn't trust himself. He looked at the screaming Fury a few feet away from him, accusing him of an imagined lust.

The happy days and passionate nights spent in Paris suddenly vanished. The bitter, violent row at the start of their honeymoon in Boca Raton was not an isolated incident. He'd struck her then because she'd lashed his dead wife and child with her jealous tongue and cursed him like a washerwoman. If he touched her now as she called him a liar and ranted about betrayal, he might lose his temper. He dared not do that. He was so angry and disgusted that it wouldn't be safe. He turned and walked out of the bedroom, slamming the door.

She followed, dragging it open. "Where are you going?" she demanded. "Back to the casino? Back to find her?"

He calmed himself. He unclenched his hands and made his voice quite even.

"I'm not your father. You've got us muddled up. I'm going out, and I'll see you when I come back. If I come back."

He heard something smash as he closed the door and walked down the hall to the elevator. He went to the bar. "Bourbon on the rocks," he ordered. "You have Camels here?"

The barman said smoothly, "We have all brands, monsieur."

"Two packs," Steven said.

[55]

"Very good, monsieur. I'll bring them to your table."

The bar was quite full. He wasn't interested in the people. He needed to sit somewhere alone and put down that drink as fast as possible. What the hell am I going to do with her? he asked himself. The bourbon lit a fire in his stomach, but it didn't help him find an answer. He had thought he was in love with her; he wasn't. The second bourbon induced a mood of bitter honesty.

He had blinded himself with sexual desire and the advantages of combining forces with the Fabrizzi family. He'd married the girl for the right reasons, except that they were wrong for both of them.

And with her female instinct she divined the truth. No matter how he indulged her, or made love to her, she didn't hold his heart. A life of hell yawned at their feet unless something could be done. He hated her brand of violent temper; in a few years she would be a shrew. He hated the jealousy that exploded into insults and accusations without allowing a word of explanation. It was like living with two people— the charming, lively companion and passionate bedmate changed into a spitting Fury, foul-mouthed as any slut. There was a simple remedy available, and he knew his own father and his younger brother would recommend it. Teach her a lesson once and for all. If it laid her up for a few days, so much the better. A man has to be the master. Her father would understand that. He wouldn't let it happen more than once, but he would see the need and look the other way.

But I can't do it. Steven Falconi downed the last of his third bourbon. *If I'd never gone to college, if I'd never known Angela, I might have used my fists on my wife.* He didn't mean to think of Angela, but slowly she materialized, as if she were flesh and blood. The third drink was having its effect.

He could see her so clearly, hear the distinctive English voice and the shy smile. He had fallen in love with her as he would never fall in love with Clara. But she was Clara's best protection. He couldn't hurt her because he had known Angela. The irony of it made him smile for a moment. How Clara would burn if she knew that. She'd rather suffer his violence than be indebted to the dead woman he had loved.

"Excuse me, do you have a light?"

He glanced up at the woman standing by his table. *Jesus,* he thought, *they have them in here too.* She was very attractive, elegantly dressed. He didn't stand up. He flashed his lighter for her, and she bent down to the flame.

"Thank you," she said. "I must have lost mine. Are you staying here?"

"Yes. Would you like a drink with me?" He was appraising her openly. Good figure, nice breasts, expensive scent. He thought of Clara, and the revenge appealed to him.

"Thank you. I'm very bored. I hate being alone. I'd like a glass of champagne."

She would order that, of course. She spoke very good English, and he liked the French accent. He wondered what the price tag would be.

"I'm staying here too," she volunteered. "I come for a month every summer. It's such a comfortable hotel."

She smiled at the waiter who came to take the order. He seemed deferential.

"Good evening, madame."

"Good evening, Jacques."

"Champagne for the lady," the formula slipped out before Steven could stop himself. "And a bourbon on the rocks for me." He could screw as well when he was drunk as sober.

She said, "My name is Pauline Duvalier. When my husband was alive, we spent longer here. He liked to gamble. It bores me."

"Like being alone?" he asked her.

She extinguished the cigarette, half smoked. He noticed a square-cut emerald on her left hand. A very big price tag, by the looks of that.

"You haven't told me your name," she reminded him.

She had calculating eyes, but there was humor in them. He wondered what she found amusing.

"Steven Falconi."

"That could be Monégasque," she remarked. "There's a lot of Italian blood in the people here."

"How's the champagne?" he asked. He swallowed hard on the bourbon. He was feeling like it. Anger was a form of arousal, and he was very angry with everything. Most of all with fate and with himself.

"It's nice. Are you alone here?"

They didn't usually ask that. What the hell business was it of hers anyway.

"No. My wife's upstairs. You're an attractive lady, you know that?"

"I should hope so," she said, and she laughed. "You're an attractive man. Very attractive. I've been watching you getting drunk and thought what a pity. What a waste. Would you like to come up to my suite? I

[57]

don't want any more champagne, and I think you've had enough to drink."

He got up from the table. He was quite steady. "Suite?"

"Suite," she repeated. "I have the same one every year. Perhaps I should make something a little clearer to you. I am inviting you because I want to. If I see a man I want, I don't wait for him to ask me. Shall we go?"

"Sure, why not?" he said, and followed her to the elevator.

It was a better suite than his. Inside the door, she turned to him and smiled.

"I'm not a *poule de luxe*." She mocked him gently. "You don't have to pay me, except in kind, Monsieur Falconi. I like to be undressed. Shall we go through to the bedroom?"

She woke him before five o'clock. "In half an hour the hotel cleaners come on duty. If you go now, you won't meet anyone."

He sat up, stretching wearily. It had been a long night, and she had tested him to the limit of his stamina. She smiled down at him in a friendly way. She wore a silk dressing gown and was smoking one of his Camel cigarettes.

"I enjoyed myself," she said. "I hope you did too."

He got out of bed and took the cigarette from her, drawing on it deeply. The taste of her was in his mouth and on the end of the cigarette.

"How often do you do this?" he asked.

"Not too often," she answered. "Your clothes are over there on the sofa. When I see a man I like. How long are you staying here?"

"Another four days."

"We could meet again," she suggested. "Perhaps you'll have another row with your wife."

"How the hell did you know that?" he demanded.

She shrugged. "A woman alone has to be careful. I asked about you before I introduced myself. There's only one reason a man on his honeymoon sits by himself and gets drunk. What are you going to say to her?"

Steven finished dressing. "That's my business."

She shrugged again. "Of course. I shouldn't have asked. You know my suite number. If I don't hear from you, I wish you bon voyage, and perhaps one day if you come back to Monte Carlo . . ." She opened the door for him and held out her hand. "Goodbye, Monsieur Falconi."

They hadn't once used each other's first names.

"Goodbye, Madame Duvalier."

They shook hands. She closed the door immediately and, throwing the dressing gown on the floor, slipped back into bed and fell asleep.

Clara heard him come in. The long hours of that night had passed without the mercy of sleep for her. Broken shards of china lay on the floor. They splintered as he walked on them. She couldn't weep anymore, or rouse herself to anger. *I'm broken,* she said to herself. *He's broken me. If he comes back I'll kiss his feet, I'll tear my hair and grovel, if he'll only come back and forgive me.*

She ran to him, tripping over her nightgown in her eagerness. She threw her arms around him, and her tears welled up again, pouring down her face as she clung. She smelled the other woman's scent and gave a cry of anguish.

"Where have you been? All night long I've waited."

The scent was in her nostrils. She almost gagged on it. Joy. Perhaps the most expensive perfume in the world.

"Sit down, Clara," he said. "Stop crying and working yourself up. I want you to listen to me. Listen very carefully." He held her away from him, forcing her to sit on the bed.

"You went with another woman. I can tell."

"You're right, I did. And every time you do what you did last night, I shall find myself someone else. Maybe for one night, maybe for longer. I never looked at any blonde in the casino. My mind was on business. Family business, Clara. I was calculating how much she must have lost that they were letting her win so much. My father and yours think it's a business we should get into.

"All you could think of was that I wanted to screw her. So you made a big scene and we had to leave before I was ready. You screamed at me like some whore off the street. So I'm telling you: You want me faithful, you want me to be a good husband? Then you never do that again. You never speak of my wife Angela. I said my wife. Close your mouth, Clara. Don't say anything."

"Why don't you hit me?" she demanded. "You're killing me instead."

"Because it wouldn't stop you," he answered. "I know you by now. You wouldn't care so much as you'll care about this. There's a woman in the hotel. I can see her anytime I want. It's up to you. Now I'm going to take a shower. Think about it. And clear up that mess outside before the breakfast gets here."

* * *

She was sitting up in bed when he came back. She'd brushed her hair and rubbed a little color into her lips. She'd collected the broken china and cut herself, so there was a handkerchief with a little stain on it wound around her hand and tied at the wrist. She held out her arms. "I've been punished enough. Forgive me."

He made himself embrace her. He pitied her and hated himself, but his heart was cold and his spirit weary. He wondered if the pendulum would swing upward again.

She closed her eyes and stayed quiet. "A woman in the hotel." Not a whore. Whores don't use Joy at fifty dollars an ounce. She'd find her. She made herself that promise as she leaned her head against him and they seemed to be at peace.

She did her best to make amends. At her suggestion, they returned to the casino that night. The German princess was at the baccarat table again, gambling with increasing recklessness. She was losing.

"Hello." It was Ralph Maxton again. Word had come through to the manager's office that Falconi was back. He bought them champagne and tried his charm on the new bride. She was extremely beautiful, if you liked the type. He saw the single-minded concentration on her husband and thought it must be rather a bore to be adored to that extent. Falconi was easy to talk to. He asked a few questions, which Maxton parried, and finally he went to another table, where the stakes were lower, and politely lost a sum of money. It was a gesture, and in spite of himself, Maxton applauded it. He had style, this Italian gangster. Unlike the ones he'd met in Nevada while he was ruining himself. He was surprised when Mrs. Falconi suddenly spoke to him. Falconi was still at the table, taking the shoe this time.

"Are you married, Mr. Maxton?"

He laughed. "Oh, Lord, no. Not in this job. No wife would put up with it."

"But a lot of women come here on their own," she remarked. "They like gambling, I suppose."

"Yes, they do. Women get the bug as badly as men. Some of them are widows or divorced. They come and play roulette and enjoy some company."

"And I suppose they pick up men?" The question was posed with an innocent stare that didn't deceive him for a minute.

"Not in this casino, Mrs. Falconi."

She shrugged and turned away from him. She couldn't stop thinking about the woman in the hotel, the woman who wore Joy.

She wondered how long Steven would stay tonight. She wished this irritating Englishman would go away and pester someone else. She wanted to be alone with Steven, to reassure herself that all was well between them. *Tomorrow I'll go to the head porter,* she thought. *I wonder how much money it will take.*

The head porter couldn't help her. He pretended not to see the roll of currency she took out of her handbag. It was more than his job was worth to take the slightest risk. He made as much in a day's tips as the lady was offering.

"I'm so sorry; I can't help you, madame," he said. "Perhaps the reception desk could assist you."

The receptionist declined to look at the register and tell her of any women guests who were alone. Clara was pressed for time. She had dressed hurriedly and come down ahead of Steven to make her inquiries. Back home, she'd have got what she wanted. She swore under her breath. He'd picked her up in the cocktail lounge, most likely. The smell of bourbon was as strong as that hated scent when he'd come back in the morning. She went to the bar. There were several couples having a drink before lunch. And two women alone. One she didn't even look at. She was gray-haired, absorbed in a novel. The other one? Clara stared at her, and some primeval instinct assured her that she need look no further. She passed close by. The woman was sipping a Campari. The scent of Joy stung Clara's nostrils. She was amazed at her own cunning as she approached the young barman.

"Isn't that lady a famous actress?" she whispered. "My husband said he met her last night."

"No, madame." The boy shook his head. "That's Madame Duvalier. She's a regular guest here. Comes every year. Maybe she said that to play a joke on Monsieur Falconi?"

"Maybe." Clara gave a savage smile. She turned and looked once more. Sophisticated, very chic, no longer young. Clara went outside to find Steven.

They chartered a boat and sailed around the coast. There was a picnic and a lot of wine. She felt sleepy and sensual in the heat and wanted him to make love to her in the cabin. It seemed better to her than ever. She felt she had reached him again and that surely, please Virgin mother and all the saints, she would conceive this time.

Afterward, they dived off the boat and swam in a sea as clear and cold as sapphires.

"What are you thinking about, *caro?*" she asked him as they dried in the sun on the foredeck. She reached out to take his hand, but he didn't notice. Hers lay outstretched toward him, until slowly the fingers curled up.

"Business," he answered, his eyes closing against the glare of the sun. "I think we should look into casinos back home."

"That's Musso's territory," she said dully.

"There's room," Steven answered. He wasn't used to discussing things like this with a woman, and he changed the subject. Only men talked about business. "I'm going for another swim," he said, and dived off without waiting for her.

That night Clara put in a call to her father in New York.

The line was crackly. "How's my little girl?" he kept asking.

She cried into the telephone.

"What's the matter, sweetheart? What's wrong? Aren't you happy? Come on, tell Papa."

"I will," she promised. "Oh, Papa, I miss you and Mama. I've been so happy, but something's gone wrong. There's a woman. She's making a play for Steven. Papa, what can I do?"

There was silence for a moment. She thought they had been cut off. Then her father's voice came back on the line.

"You leave this to me, *cara mia*. Just tell me the name of this dame and where she can be found."

Clara did so. She said, "Thank you, Papa. Thank you," and cried again. Then she hung up.

They flew to London. It was a typical English summer, chilly and overcast. Clara was cold and bored. Even the art galleries and museums were dull by comparison with the glories of Paris. She hadn't mentioned the apartment in Paris to Steven. There'd be a right time and place, but it hadn't come. She went to the Italian church in Clerkenwell on a private pilgrimage and prayed for a child.

"Don't worry about it," Steven told her. "It'll happen. In God's good time, as my mother would say."

"It's not what she'll say to me," Clara protested. "I want a honeymoon baby. They're always lucky children."

She nestled into his side and murmured, "I'll be glad to go home. I want to move into our own house."

[62]

Steven said yes, he would like that too, and went on thinking of the Musso family and their stranglehold on the gambling in Nevada. The honeymoon was over. It was time for Clara to become a wife and hopefully a mother very soon. And for him to get back to business and the men's world.

The man had been watching Pauline Duvalier for three days. First in the hotel bar, then in the restaurant; now her luggage was coming down and her car waited at the entrance. He had never even met her eye, and she didn't notice him because he was middle-aged and bald. She drove herself in a prewar Lagonda. He envied her the car, as he followed it up the winding Moyenne Corniche, carved out of the face of the mountain way above the coast. He saw her turn into the gates of a villa.

Big, expensive place; must have wonderful views. It was to look like a robbery. He drove past and then managed to make a turn higher up. Coming down again, he eased the car just inside the gates. There were tall pine trees, providing shade and privacy. He couldn't see the house once he was under them, and that meant he couldn't be seen. It had to be a daylight job. The gates would be closed at night, and a car's headlights would be seen for miles from up there. He got out and slipped his hand into his trousers pocket. He was stocky and powerful underneath a layer of fat. Though past his prime by fifteen years, he was still a strong man. He was good with women and the elderly.

There'd be servants about the place. His watch said eleven-thirty. Not time for lunch yet. He crept on the soles of his feet, keeping in the shadows under the trees.

It was a big villa indeed, with a large open terrace and doors leading into various rooms. He was close against the wall when he saw her. She came out onto the terrace. She was smoking a cigarette, and she'd changed into slacks and a shirt. Robbery with violence. She stood there for some minutes, thinking of something, frowning.

In the old days he had collected from the brothelkeepers in Marseilles. When he was young, they gave him a choice of the girls along with the protection money. Then he moved to Nice after a bit of trouble when someone had died after a beating—a greedy ponce who didn't want to pay up. There was plenty of work in Nice. Shopkeepers, restaurants, brothels—they all paid dues, and he was one of the debt collectors. He had a wife and three children. They lived in an apartment on the seafront. He was well paid. He did odd evenings at the casino as a bouncer.

The woman still didn't move. Then just when he thought he might have to come up behind her on the terrace, which he didn't fancy, she swung around and went inside. He pulled the stocking over his head and followed her. He carried no weapon. She didn't see him or hear him. He rabbit-punched her, and she fell without a sound. Locking the door, he heaved her up from the floor and onto the bed. She didn't feel anything because she never recovered consciousness. When he had finished, he turned out the drawers, threw a few things on the floor and put a gold necklace, two rings, and a gold lighter in his pocket. He slipped out and got back to his car. He was sitting at a traffic light in Beaulieu when Pauline Duvalier's maid came to call her for lunch.

The doctors at the American Hospital in Nice told reporters that they doubted the unfortunate woman would survive her injuries. Every bone in her face had been smashed, and she was certain to lose the vision in her left eye. It made headlines in the national press.

3

 "It's very sweet of you, Jim," Angela said gently. "But I don't want to get married again."

They were sitting by the fire, and he had taken her hand and, for the third time in the past year, asked her to think it over.

"You don't have to hurry about it," he said. "You've got the boy's future to think of, and he really needs a father. I'm very fond of him, and he's fond of me. All I want is to make you happy, Angela."

He was the soul of kindness and honesty. By now her father had retired with a bad heart, and Jim Hulbert had taken over the practice with a younger partner, who was married and had a baby. Jim wasn't a bloodless man either. Most women could have been very happy with him in spite of the age difference.

Yes, Angela thought, I could have settled down here and been a good doctor's wife, spent my life in the village where I was born and raised my children as I was raised. If I hadn't met Steven Falconi. If he didn't look at me out of my son's eyes.

"I know, Jim," she said. "But it's no use pretending I'll change my mind; I won't. I know all the arguments against it, but I know I can bring up Charlie myself. In fact, I asked you over tonight because I've got something to tell you."

He looked downcast. It hurt her to refuse him, to dash his hopes. But it would be less than honest to stay on and let those hopes survive.

"You're leaving here," he said.

"Yes, I am. How did you know?"

"Your mother mentioned something."

Mrs. Drummond had been her usual tactless self, too anxious to mince words. "You'd better do something, Jim," she'd said, "before she goes off and gets this job she's so set on. Go and ask her again, won't you? Make her change her mind." Her parents wanted the marriage. It secured the practice, gave Angela a home and a husband they liked and trusted. And most of all, it provided a stable background for the boy.

They loved Charlie in their own way, but his foreign looks distressed them. "There's not a drop of Drummond blood in him," Angela's father had complained to his wife, and then added guiltily, "But he's a fine little chap all the same."

"I've applied for a job with a firm in London," Angela told Jim. "They want a personnel officer. It sounds interesting, and the money's not too bad. I went for an interview, and they've accepted me. My nursing training helped."

He thought, *Not only that. Don't you realize what an attractive, intelligent woman you are?* "What about Charlie?" he asked.

"I had an argument with my father about that," Angela admitted. "I thought of taking him to London and sending him to school there."

Jim Hulbert frowned. "Wouldn't that be an awful upheaval? He's only got a few more weeks till the holidays, and then he's off to prep school."

"That's exactly what my father said. He said I was being selfish even to suggest moving him. He hit the roof when I mentioned keeping him at day school until he was thirteen. 'All boys need to get away at eight'—that's what he said. 'You can't keep him tied to your apron strings.' It does seem very early to go to boarding school; but my brother went at seven. He loved it. So in the end I said we'd keep to the plan. And my father's taken out a policy to pay for his education right up till he's eighteen. I talked to Charlie about it and explained. He said, 'I'd love to be with you, Mum, but I'd hate London.' That made up my mind for me. I shall miss him dreadfully, but he's better off here in his own home with Mum and Dad till he goes away in September. I'll be back every weekend. So in two weeks I'm moving to London."

He said nothing for a moment. He rose, took out his pipe, filled it and tapped down the tobacco. Lighting and drawing it took some time.

"All right, my dear," he said. "Maybe you know what's best. I love you, and I always will. If you change your mind and get fed up with London, I'll be here. We've had some very happy times together. Kiss me goodbye, will you?"

"Of course I will," she said. "I don't know what I would have done without you, Jim. You've been a darling to both of us. Thank you for everything." She stood up and walked into his arms.

"Good luck anyway," he said. "I'll be off now. We could have dinner together before you go."

"I'd love to," Angela said.

When he had gone, she poked at the fire and poured herself a glass of wine before going to bed. It was sad, but also a relief. She didn't want to marry him or anyone else. She had to change her life, had to stop relying on her son for happiness. The idea of a job had appealed to her more and more as her son grew older and more independent. And she dared to hope that at some point she would find contentment.

I've got a lot of energy, she decided. *And it's eating away inside me instead of being put to use. I'm bored too, to be honest. I'm not ready for a life bounded by the village and its activities. If I had a man to love, if it was possible with Jim, yes, but not otherwise. I'm going to see what the outside world has to offer before it's too late.*

She stood, set the guard in front of the fire and locked up. Her parents had gone to bed long before. She opened the door of her son's bedroom and looked inside. He was asleep, sprawled in the manner of small boys halfway across the bed, with the pillow crumpled under him. Gently Angela pulled it away and settled him properly.

He murmured, and she bent down to kiss him. For a moment his arms locked around her neck.

"Mum?" It was a sleepy whisper.

"Yes, darling. Go to sleep. Good night."

"Night." He had drifted away immediately.

She watched him, half lit from the open door.

I wonder where he is, she thought. *I wonder what he'd think of you. He's probably forgotten all about us. Men don't mourn. Only fools of women like me do that.* She closed the door firmly and went to her own room.

❦

She found a flat, a top-floor walk-up, in Chelsea. It was meanly furnished, but it was the most she could afford. In the evenings she found herself looking at the pictures of Charlie that lined her bedroom wall. She hoped he wasn't too lonely staying with his grandparents. She almost gave up and went home during the first month.

Her job at the medical supplies firm in Wigmore Street was interesting. She liked people and was popular with her co-workers. But London was cold and unwelcoming. Her neighbors in the converted house muttered good morning and hurried by; every evening she came back to the empty flat. In desperation, she began going to the local cinema alone, or taking long walks along the Embankment.

The weekends at Haywards Heath were overshadowed by the journey back on Sunday evening and the wrench of leaving Charlie behind. He had his father's deep black eyes, and they filled with tears when she kissed him goodbye. Joy Drummond didn't make it any easier.

"You've got thin," she declared, examining Angela on her second visit home. "And you look so tired. I bet you're not eating properly."

"Mother, I'm fine. I have a very good lunch, and I cook for myself in the evenings."

Joy ignored her signal to stop and went on relentlessly. "Cook for yourself? Good Lord, haven't you made any friends? Don't tell me you sit there night after night on your own!" She sighed and said, "I don't know why you want to do this, dear. I really don't. We all miss you, especially Charlie—don't you, darling? Why on earth don't you drop the idea and come home?"

Angela kept her temper. Her mother meant well; that was the trouble. *I can't get angry and tell her to please shut up, but any minute she's going to have Charlie in tears.*

She said in a too loud voice, "I love my job and I'm very happy. Now Charlie and I are going for a walk before lunch. Come on, darling."

Mrs. Drummond looked after them and sighed again. She had a habit of talking out loud when she was alone. "What a fool of a girl," she said. "Turning down someone like Jim, who's so fond of her ... going off to London to live by herself. Don't tell me she likes it. She looks perfectly miserable."

She was still expressing these thoughts aloud when she went inside to see if her husband wanted anything. He was leading a very quiet life since his heart attack. He had mellowed. He missed his daughter and worried about her, but unlike his wife, he never put his feelings into more than a very few words.

"How does Angela seem?" he asked.

"Who knows? She's gone off for a walk with Charlie. Do her good after that awful London air. I can't breathe when I go up there."

"You haven't been to London for three years," he remarked.

"I couldn't breathe then," she retorted. "I wish she'd be sensible. She's so obstinate, that's the trouble."

"Takes after me," Hugh Drummond suggested. "I think she's done the right thing. If she's not going to marry Jim, she's got to make a new life for herself. We won't last forever. Leave her alone, Joy. Let her work it out for herself."

"Oh, I will, I will. I was just talking, that's all. It'll be worse when Charlie goes away to school this fall."

"It'll be better," her husband countered. "Now what's for lunch?"

It had been a long and busy day. Angela was tired. A niggling headache was just beginning. It was almost time to go home, but a long solitary evening in the impersonal flat had never seemed less appealing. She told herself not to be childish and finished filing her papers. An early night wouldn't do her any harm. The trouble was, there were so many early nights. Then the door to her office opened. She looked up. It was a girl named Judy from the accounting department. They'd had morning coffee together once or twice. She was popular and breezy, and there was a jauntiness about her that brought Christine suddenly to Angela's mind.

"You finished, Angela?"

"Yes, nearly. I've just got to put this lot away."

"We're going round the corner to the pub. Why don't you come along?"

Angela hesitated. They were all younger than she was.

"Come on," she urged. "There's a crowd of us going."

"I'd love to," Angela said. "I won't be a minute."

She didn't even notice that her headache had gone. The pub was smoky, full of noise and people, and cheery. She had a gin and tonic and found herself saying how difficult it was to make friends in London.

Judy, sinking her second gin and orange, agreed heartily.

"Oh, you can drop dead in London and nobody'll even notice. I come from a small town on the south coast, and I nearly died for the first few months up here. But you've got to get out and help yourself. That's what I found. No good waiting for the neighbors to knock on your door, because they won't. Knock on theirs first and say, Hey, here I am, come in and have a drink or something. That's what you have to do."

Angela was enjoying herself. People drifted in and out, and most seemed to know each other. She discovered that it was a regular hangout for the younger staff in the office.

[69]

"We call ourselves the PPCs," one young man told her, balancing a pint of beer in one hand and waving a cigarette about with the other. He was pleasantly tight, and so, Angela realized, was she.

"PPC? What's that?"

"Professional pub crawlers! We crawl from this pub to the next pub till we can't crawl any further."

She thought it was the funniest thing she'd heard in years.

It was a great meeting place, that pub. There was an easy comradeship about pub life in London that she would never have found in the country. Friendships were struck up and continued beyond the confines of what was known as the Medics Arms. Nobody even knew its proper name. There were no barriers of class or age. The Harley Street specialist stood elbow-to-elbow with the antique dealers and shop assistants and Angela's tipsy friend who worked in the surgical appliances department. She was asked out to dinner, to the theater. She took Judy's advice and gave parties in her tiny flat.

An earnest young radiologist with a practice in Welbeck Street started taking her out regularly. Once he knew she was a doctor's daughter, he began to talk of marriage.

There were other, less happy memories of those early years in London.

Charlie, coming back from his first half term at Melville Hall and saying, "Mum, can I have a picture of you and Dad? The other boys have pictures."

And the sad lie she'd told him. "You can have one of me, darling. But I haven't any pictures of your father. He was killed so soon, you see."

Her mother dying unexpectedly from cancer, so quickly and with such little warning that Angela couldn't believe it had happened. Her father, looking very old indeed after the funeral, refusing to let her give up her job and look after him.

"Don't be a damn fool, Angela. Things are going well for you. You're happy up there. I've had a good run for my money, and I'm all right. Old Mrs. P. can look after me, and you pop down when you can. I'll miss your mother, though," and he had devastated Angela by bursting into tears.

Happy memories, sad memories, and always the joy of her son to enrich what was good and compensate for what was not. He was thirteen and just going to public school, very tall, better-looking than his father, with something of the Drummonds in him after all. He had become the light of his grandfather's life. There were photographs on the mantel of Charlie playing in the school first eleven, Charlie in the rugger team as a winger, even disguised in a fencing mask, posing with another little boy for the Melville Hall magazine. Hugh Drummond turned up at every Sports Day, prize-giving and school concert. *What a lot he's given to Charlie,* Angela thought. *And what a lot Charlie's given to him. My son has the father he needed, and Dad's got a son to make up for the one he lost in the war.*

The Wigmore Street job had led to better things. Having taken a secretarial course and gained a diploma, she became the assistant to the medical director of a large private health insurance company.

She'd heard about the vacancy from a friend, one of many she had now. If she spent an evening alone, it was from choice. The attic flat in Chelsea was replaced by a smart apartment hotel in Sloane Avenue, with a restaurant and maid service. It provided total privacy for a woman living alone if she wanted it. And sometimes she did. She had many men friends but only two lovers in the five years since she'd come to London. She had not been in love with either of them. There was no commitment beyond a mutual attraction and compatibility. When marriage was mentioned, Angela was firm. She wasn't interested. Charlie didn't need a stepfather just as he started adolescence. It sounded reasonable. The truth was something else. She faced that truth sometimes in the loneliest hour of the night, when the clock by her bedside pointed to four and she knew sleep wouldn't come. It didn't happen often, but when it did, she admitted that her love for Steven Falconi had not died. It would one day; it must. But not yet. Perhaps never, because her son was his living reminder.

Money was not a problem. Her salary was generous, and surprisingly, her mother had left her everything. It wasn't riches, but it provided an income and a little capital when she needed it. "To my beloved Daughter, Angela Frances Lawrence," the will had read.

Hugh Drummond's explanation had been typically down-to-earth. "Of course she left everything to you. I don't need anything; I'm quite all right. We talked about it, and she said you were the one who'd benefit most. And the boy, of course. Quite right."

She wore her mother's engagement ring, a little sapphire with two diamonds on either side, and the Sicilian wedding ring she'd worn around her neck at the Palermo hospital. Falconi's ring. She was Falconi's wife so long as she wore that ring. And Charlie had a dead hero for a father.

Her son was fifteen when she decided to change her job and take him away for a holiday. Her relationship with her boss had reached an impasse. She didn't want to start an affair with him, and the only solution was to leave. It was the end of August, and they were together at Haywards Heath in the old house, with her father and a decrepit Mrs. P. going through the same routine they had followed for forty years.

"When do you start your new job?" he asked her.

They were sitting out in the garden, her father underneath a big, colored garden umbrella that hadn't been used often enough to fade. It was hot that year, and the doctor didn't like the sun. Charlie was lying on his back, holding a book in the air.

"End of September," she replied. "Charlie, you can't read like that. Why don't you sit on a chair?"

"Don't nag, Mum," was the response. "I like reading lying down. Don't I, Grandpa?"

"Used to like it myself," Hugh Drummond agreed. "Pity you had to leave that job," he said to Angela. "I suppose it's a good thing to move on."

"I think so." She wouldn't have dreamed of telling him the real reason. "It'll be interesting, and I'll travel. That's what really appealed to me, even if it is less money."

"Never thought you'd be a businesswoman," her father said.

"I'm not," she insisted. "I just smooth the edges for the businessman. I'm a good organizer. I enjoy it."

The job was a complete break from her last position. She was to be the secretary and personal assistant to the head of a small but dynamic advertising firm. And no personal problem likely there. Her boss was David Wickham, the senior partner. He was not interested in women; he lived with his associate. David had the flair and the older man the money. Angela thought they were both cultivated, pleasant and amusing. "Working for us," Wickham had told her, "won't be easy, Mrs. Lawrence, but I promise you it will be fun."

She looked down at her son, still obstinately reading with the book high above his head, and smiled. He was going through a lanky stage, and the first round of serious exams was approaching next term.

She said suddenly, "Charlie, I've been thinking. I could do with a holiday. Somewhere abroad. What do you think? Shall we go away somewhere?"

He rolled over and sat up, bright with expectation. "What a super idea! Where shall we go?"

"How about France? Lots of sunshine." Seeing his face, she said, "Wouldn't you like that? Or would you be bored?"

"Oh, I wouldn't be bored, Mum. I'll go to France if you want to."

"That's not the point," Angela said. "Look, darling, it's a holiday for both of us. Where would *you* like to go? Come on—you say."

He hesitated for a moment. "Well, I'd really like to go to America. I know it'd cost too much money, but Jordan went there when his sister got married. They went to New York, and he said it was the most *super* place. He never stopped going on about it. I suppose we couldn't go there, could we? Just for a week?"

"New York," she heard her father say. "What on earth do you want to go there for? All those frightful bloody skyscrapers? What's wrong with France? You'd get lots of swimming and tennis."

"It's the skyscrapers I want to see," his grandson insisted. "The Empire State, Rockefeller Center. Jordan climbed right up into the Statue of Liberty's head!"

"Charlie darling," Angela said, "would you really like to go there?"

"Oh, Mum, could we? You mean it? A week'd be fine, if we could manage it."

"I think we could afford more than a week," she told him. "On one condition."

"Anything," he promised. "Just name it!"

"You don't read upside down from now on. And when we get back, you work really hard at school."

"Don't you worry. I'll get distinctions in every subject! New York. I can't believe it. Wait till I ring up Jordan and tell him!"

"Not on my phone you don't!" Hugh Drummond called after him as he rushed into the house. "They jabber on for hours, these young people. No idea of the cost. . . . Can you afford this, Angela? I can help out a bit if need be. Always thought America was damned expensive. He was jumping up and down, wasn't he? Very excited."

"Yes, he was," Angela agreed. "Don't worry, Dad. I've got some extra money. Mum's dividends have been very good lately. Charlie deserves a real treat. He's had such good reports every term. He'll love New York. We'll go."

Thanks to David Wickham, they'd been lent a small apartment on East Seventieth Street. Two bedrooms, a living room and two bathrooms. And the luxury of television. Wickham had provided them with a list of restaurants that were good but not expensive and some suggestions for sightseeing. Her new employer had asked her to contact two clients, whose offices were on Park Avenue. She could call them after a few days.

Charlie loved everything. He loved American food, American soft drinks, hamburgers and ice cream. They went to the Frick Collection, which Charlie enthused about just to please Angela, and to the Statue of Liberty. They walked up into the dizzying height of the great head and looked out onto the panorama of the Hudson River. In Central Park, they joined the stream of foot traffic down myriad paths and took a ride in a horse-drawn carriage. They strolled down Broadway at night, marveling at the lights, and went to see the latest hit movie. The variety in restaurants was staggering. They ate German and Chinese, Indian and Japanese. And the days sped into each other until one morning Angela realized that it was time she paid David Wickham back for all his kindness.

The first client gave her an appointment in his office at eleven o'clock and then invited her out to dinner. He was a very important manufacturer of luxury leather goods, with stores in seven major cities. He was also friendly and, in true American style, eager to show her the best restaurant in the city. She accepted and left Charlie in the apartment for the evening, with a supply of Coke and hamburgers, in front of the television.

"I've got a headache," Clara Falconi stated. "I've had a headache for three days. Not that you give a damn, of course."

Steven didn't even turn around. He knew all about Clara's headaches. He'd said to her once, driven beyond patience by her complaints about her health, his family, and their life together, "You've got a headache, but I've got you. And Jesus, that's some headache, I can tell you!"

It had led to one of their worst rows. He stayed away for a week, while she calmed down and went to see yet another specialist. There were no children after nine years, and no explanation either. She didn't conceive, and Steven broke every male taboo by going for tests himself, although he knew they were a farce. He'd already got one woman pregnant. His tests showed a high fertility count. At least it gave him a respite from Clara, who was always accusing Angela of deceiving him. More than anything, he wanted to stop her taunting him with that.

She dismissed the idea of adoption with scorn. He didn't press it. He didn't want someone else's child.

"Ever since Sunday," Clara said, "I've had this goddamned pain in my head. You know I hate those lunches with your father and mother and your brother and his bitch of a wife sneering at me. They push those children up my nose every chance they get! I won't go again. I've made up my mind."

He turned and said, "My father likes to have the family for Sundays. And when he asks us, Clara, we go. Like we go to your family. I don't hear you griping about that."

"They understand," she retorted. "They're *my* family. Don't you think Papa's disappointed? Don't you think he'd like grandchildren?"

"After nine years, he's forgotten." Steven was brutal. Aldo Fabrizzi was no friend to him. Clara had seen to that. But he went to the Fabrizzi house anyway for the family gatherings, and Clara was not going to disrespect his parents by refusing to accompany him.

"Well, I'm not coming tonight," she countered. "My head's bursting. You can entertain your senator on your own."

"Okay." He didn't argue, though the senator would be bringing his wife. He was a valuable contact. There was talk of a federal investigation into gambling, an open hearing before a Senate committee. That had really alarmed Steven, and he needed the senator's news and views.

It had taken five years of pressure to divest the old warrior Musso of his monopoly. His son had died of a heroin overdose. Fabrizzi had arranged for someone to give him a lethal fix. But Musso gathered his men and held fast. He wanted no partners, and he loosed a little well-aimed violence at the Falconi and Fabrizzi families himself. Some minor characters had died.

The Falconis and Fabrizzis were so well guarded that it was impossible to target them. They bought up property as close to the Musso casinos as they could. He was constantly surveyed by enemies, and several times fires broke out in the gambling halls. People began to drift away. Musso's take was dropping. He was old, his son was dead. Not long afterward, he had a mild heart attack. Suddenly the fight was over. There was a meeting, at which Steven was present, and the truce was arranged. The deal cut Musso in for a good percentage of his own profits, and control passed directly to the Falconis, with the Fabrizzis as equal financial partners. Steven was given the management of that side of the business. And he had built it up steadily over the last four years into a huge investment, branching out into hotels and restaurants and resorts, with the gambling as a lure. It was Steven's idea, too, to entice Hollywood stars down to entertain the clients. A veil of respectability was drawn over the uglier side of the organization. It became a kind of show biz spectacle.

And he had remembered Monte Carlo. Class was all-important to attract the big-time spenders. The smoky rooms full of housewives risking their few dollars on a crooked wheel were offset by the plush salons and tuxedoed attendants paying court to the superrich.

Steven was a big shot now: respected, admired and feared. When he talked, even the older men listened. He had proved himself by using his brains. There were plenty of others to supply the brawn. Lucca Falconi was right to be proud of his eldest son. Of course he was proud of his younger boy, Piero, too, with his clutch of handsome children. But Piero wasn't clever like Steven; he was tough, and he made his father think of the old days, when a man had to think fast and act faster to stay alive. But the old days were gone. Now they were in a business just like any other.

Steven finished dressing. Clara watched him bitterly. She wondered whether he would call up some other woman and take her along. There were always other women. Like her empty womb, her jealousy obsessed her.

No, she decided. The senator took bribes from the families, but he was careful of his reputation. Steven wouldn't antagonize him by taking out one of his whores instead of his wife. She hoped her absence would embarrass him. She hoped one day she could hurt him as he had hurt her. He picked up his wallet, buttoned his jacket and went to the door.

"Steven"—her voice commanded his attention—"don't wake me when you come in."

"Take a sleeping pill," he said, and went out.

He had a driver and a man sitting in the front seat keeping watch. The car was plated and the windows were bulletproof glass.

"Les A," he told them, as his bodyguard ushered him into the back seat. He leaned against the leather cushion, searching for a cigarette.

She wouldn't come with him. Okay, she wanted to be persuaded, cajoled. She wanted to do her duty as a wife and make out it was some kind of favor. To hell with her. He said it to himself, lighting the cigarette, seeing the traffic weaving in and out. There'd been a murder attempt on him eighteen months before, as he rode along like this, alone in the back seat. A car had pulled up alongside at an intersection, and suddenly the window was rolled down and a gun was pointing at him. The glass shattered but held. His driver didn't take a chance. He shot the lights and sped to safety. Nobody knew who was responsible. He and Clara had been going through a particularly bad time in their marriage when it happened. They lived a life of hell together, and there couldn't be a divorce. Not while Aldo Fabrizzi was alive. When he died, Steven would file against her outside New York City, and she could do her goddamnedest after that. His father hated her; all the Falconis hated her now. Not just because she was childless, but for the bile on her tongue and the arrogant way she behaved.

He dismissed her from his mind. He had business to attend to. Maybe it would be a pleasant evening. He liked the food at Les Ambassadeurs. His taste had changed over the years, and the mammoth Italian meals his relatives and compatriots enjoyed didn't appeal to him much. Clara wouldn't eat more than a mouthful of pasta. She said it ruined her figure. She was very conscious of her looks and spent lavishly on clothes and furs and treatments. She was beautiful as a mature woman, but he couldn't bear to sleep with her anymore.

The senator and his blond wife were waiting at the bar. Steven kissed the woman's hand gallantly; she thought he was very attractive. Dangerous too. She liked that. The men ordered Scotch on the rocks, she chose a brandy sour, and they moved to a cocktail table. Steven had been making small talk, apologizing for Clara's absence, when he happened to look straight at the door and saw Angela walk in ahead of an older man. The lights were flattering, not too bright, and the atmosphere a little hazy with tobacco. But he saw her. She even hesitated for a few seconds, so that he had time to stare at her and make sure he wasn't going crazy.

"Mr. Falconi?" the senator's wife inquired. He didn't answer. He didn't hear her speak. He sat and stared at a dead woman who had come to life and was smiling, walking toward a table not twenty yards away.

"Mr. Falconi, do you have a light? I've left my lighter at home."

It was the second time she'd asked. He felt for the gold Dunhill and clicked it for her.

"I'm sorry," he managed to say. "I've just seen an old friend. Excuse me."

He didn't go up to her. He went to the barman. "There's a man and a woman over there. Do you know them?"

"I know him. Mr. Forrest. He comes here often. I don't know the lady."

"Are they booked for dinner?"

"I guess so. He asked for the menu."

"What the hell's he doing?" the senator murmured to his wife.

"I don't know. He's talking to the barman, not an old friend."

"They're funny guys," her husband said. "I'm sorry, honey; I'm going to have to talk a few things over with him. It won't take long. I thought his wife would've been here."

"That's okay." She smiled at him. "I don't mind. Just so long as you throw me a word now and then."

Steven leaned closer to the barman. He had money in his hand. Quite a few folded bills were visible.

"Get Louis," he said. "Tell him to call the lady to the phone when they're at dinner. And give me the nod before he does it. You got that clear?"

"No phone to the table?" the man inquired.

"No. Out in the booth."

"You know her name? Who's calling her?"

"Try Drummond," Steven said. "Don't say who's calling. There's fifty here. Twenty-five for you, the same for Louis. No mistakes."

"No mistakes, Mr. Falconi."

He went back to his guests and said, "Shall we go to our table? I've reserved in the back room."

As they went out, he glanced behind him. She was sitting with her back to him. He could see the shining blond hair and the set of her neck on her shoulders. It wasn't an illusion. It couldn't be. He'd heard everyone has a double somewhere in the world, but he didn't believe it. Even with her back to him, he knew it was Angela. How could she have left him so heartlessly? His rage was growing. He went through the motions of ordering dinner and studying the wine list, while he watched and waited for her to come back into the restaurant. He had to see her once more in a clear light, making allowances for sixteen years.

She was different, of course. The girl of twenty was in her thirties now, older and sophisticated. She wore a black dress, very simple, and had the same sun-colored hair he used to thread through his fingers. She had the same kind look in her eyes. But it was the slight smile, the one he had imagined on her lips so often at the height of his frantic grieving, that engulfed him in anger. He had to keep his hands out of sight, because they shook with the force of it. *She wasn't dead.* She'd cheated him. She'd let him believe she and their unborn baby had been destroyed by a bomb.

The senator was talking about the federal investigation. "You know what it is when these sons of bitches get their teeth into a thing like this. However straight your operation is, they're going to start screaming corruption and racketeering."

"I know," Steven heard his own voice answering and was surprised at how normal it sounded. "That's why it's so important for us to know what line they're going to take, so we have a chance to put our case. We'll have the best legal advice, but we don't want to get caught up in an investigation, be subpoenaed. My father's not so young, and he's got a weak heart." The lies tripped off his tongue, while anger twisted his insides into knots.

It was she. He couldn't be mistaken. Looking at her in the adjacent room, he recognized every movement, every gesture. "Try Drummond," he had said. It was the last chance to prove that the woman wasn't Angela. If she was some incredible look-alike, she wouldn't respond to the name. The message would be meaningless.

He watched as Louis went to the table and murmured to the blond woman. The senator stopped in the middle of a sentence. Falconi was paying no attention. He was staring at a couple across the restaurant. The woman was on her feet, her partner rising only to be waved back.

Steven saw the anxious expression on her face as she hurried out. He had wept tears for her, believing her dead. She was alive, and he had been betrayed.

He said to the senator, "Excuse me. I'll be right back." He followed her out to the telephone booth in the foyer and was just behind her as she pulled the door open. She had lifted the receiver when he thrust himself in with her, pulling the door closed, sealing them inside. The booth was soundproof, so if she screamed, no one would hear her. It was light enough to see her face, for her to see him. He crushed her against the wall and caught her arm, locking it behind her. The telephone receiver swung on its cord, knocking against them.

He thought she said, "Steven. Steven," but didn't hear his name, only the voice he knew so well.

He leaned against her, hard, hurting her, and whispered, "Angelina?" He felt her body forced against his, remembered too well its contours. "Angelina," he said again. "So many years . . . where have you been?"

[79]

"Steven? It's you, Steven?"

"It's me," he told her.

"Let go of my arm," she said, her voice trembling. "You're hurting me."

"We're walking out of here," he said. "We're going somewhere we can talk about old times. I have a gun. You try and get away from me and I'll kill you. You understand me, Angelina?"

"You don't need to threaten me," she said. "I understand. I'll come with you."

He smiled down at her. "Sure you will," he said. He drew her out of the booth. He gripped her by the elbow, so tightly that his fingers sank into the soft skin. "We get your coat. You send a message to the boyfriend, and you make it sound good."

At the checkroom, he said, "Send a message to Senator Fuller. Say I've been called away suddenly." He dug into his pocket and scattered change. "And the lady's leaving too. Aren't you, honey?"

"Yes," Angela said. She spoke to the attendant. "I'm with Mr. Forrest. Tell him my boy's not feeling well and I've had to go home."

"You have a coat?" the girl asked her.

"It's a cape. It's over there. Here's my ticket——"

"Never mind the ticket," Steven interrupted. He took the cape and threw it over his arm. He said to the doorman, "Call up my car, will you, Stanley?"

He was holding Angela so tightly she couldn't have pulled away. He hurried her out onto the pavement and thrust her into the back of the car as it pulled up, his bodyguard shielding him before he slammed the door and jumped into the front. The car sped away.

He leaned forward and spoke to the driver. "The apartment," he said, and then closed the glass partition.

"Where are we going?" Angela asked. He wasn't holding her now. She had drawn away from him, into the corner. There was a red mark on her arm that would turn into a bruise.

"To a place I take my whores," he answered. "I pay the honest ones. What sort of a whore runs out on her husband—never sends a word, a letter, anything? Tell me, what sort of a *woman* does that?"

She saw the hatred in his face and turned away. "My God," she said. "What's happened to you?"

"Go ahead and pray," he mocked her. "You'll need to, Angelina."

"I'm not afraid of you," she said. "So you needn't threaten me."

When the car stopped, he spoke to the driver in Italian, telling him to wait, and then he turned to Angela. "We're going up to my apartment. There's a man behind us. So don't try anything."

She didn't answer. She walked into the lobby and into the elevator. On the fourth floor they got out. Steven's bodyguard unlocked the door and went ahead of them.

"Okay, Don Stefano," he announced, and stood aside for them.

"In here," Steven directed.

She found herself in a large duplex, with sprawling white sofas and mirrors. She saw herself and him reflected everywhere she looked. He faced her, rocking slightly on the balls of his feet, his hands clenched into fists.

Suddenly he reached out and caught her left hand. "You married again? You married some other bastard? What happened to my child?"

"I'm not married," she said. "That's my mother's ring and the wedding ring you gave me."

"You got rid of my child?" he asked her, and his voice was very quiet. "You went home and got rid of it?"

She looked at him, and suddenly he saw contempt and an anger to match his own. "If you think that, you can go to hell. I had a son, Steven. I even called him after you."

He said slowly, "Now tell me why you ran out on me."

"Because I found out what you were. I didn't want my child brought up to be like you. And how right I was! You're vicious and cruel, Steven. I couldn't see it then, but I can see it now. You threatened to kill me, and I believe you meant it. You're everything they said you were!"

"Who said?" he demanded. He took a step toward her. "Who said? What are you talking about?"

She turned away from him. "They sent for me," she said. "They showed me a dossier. They told me what you were really doing in Sicily. I'd never even heard of the Mafia, but I didn't need to. It was all there: your family, the people you wanted me to go and live with—murder, crime, every vice in the book. I tried to deny it. I tried to defend you. But it wasn't any use. I couldn't live with you. I couldn't have my child brought up with people like you. So I got myself dismissed and I went home."

"Why?" he questioned. "Why did they tell you?"

"You asked for a passage for me," she reminded him. "After I read the file, they asked me if I still wanted to go."

"And you said no," he countered. "So they got themselves off the hook. By showing you all that crap."

"Wasn't it true?" she challenged him. "Isn't it true now?"

He didn't answer. He sat down heavily, staring up at her.

"I went back to Sicily when I heard about the hospital. I searched for you. I was going crazy. They were still digging bodies out. Nobody knew who or how many were still buried there. I was trying to find you. I saw the watch I gave you, all smashed up. Blood on it. They said it was found on one of the bodies."

"I gave it to Christine," she said. "She was killed."

He didn't seem to hear. "I thought you were dead," he went on. "You and the baby. I tell you, I went crazy. You talk about what I did in Sicily. I'll tell you what I did after I got back to Naples. I went into a regular unit. I wanted to fight. I wanted to kill the bastards who had killed you."

There was silence then. The mirrored images were still. At last he spoke to her.

"Will you have a drink? You look like you could use one."

"No. I'd like to leave."

"Of course. Sure. Would you mind if I had a Scotch? It won't take long." He poured himself a drink. His hand was shaking. He had behaved like a savage, threatening her, using his strength to hurt her. "You're vicious and cruel." They were her words, and they were no less than he deserved. He came over to her and held out the glass. "Take a little," he said. "We used to share our wine, remember?"

"It was a long time ago," Angela answered. "Things have changed."

"You haven't," he said. "I knew you as soon as you came in that door. For sixteen years I thought you were dead, Angela, and then you walked in that door and I thought I'd gone crazy. Do you have any idea what it felt like to see you alive and know I'd screwed up my whole life?"

She took the glass from him. She sipped the whiskey. "It must have been a shock. It was a shock for me too. But it's sixteen years. You've made your life, Steven; I've made mine. And I really want to go now."

He said, "Can you forgive me? Can you forgive me for treating you like I did? Can you try and understand a little?"

"There's nothing to forgive," Angela told him. She handed him the glass, and for a second their fingers touched. "I shouldn't have said those things to you. You frightened me, Steven."

"I know," he said. "I know. I wish I could make it up to you. Sixteen years. It's a long time. Won't you give me a few minutes?"

He's suffered, she thought suddenly. *It's in his face and his eyes. He's not been happy.* "All right," she said.

"And you'll forgive me? You'll try to forget how I acted?"

"I'll try," she promised. "If you'll forgive me for hurting you all those years ago."

"Tell me about the boy."

"He's fifteen now. He's at school in England. He's doing very well."

"What did you tell him?"

"I said you were killed just after we got married. I changed my name to Lawrence and said I was a widow."

"You could have found someone," he forced himself to say. "You didn't have to do it alone."

"I didn't want anyone," she answered. "I had my parents. We lived with them till he was eight. I didn't want to marry again, although there was a man who asked me. But I didn't love him."

"I guess it wasn't easy, bringing the boy up without a father."

"He made it easy. He was a lovely little boy, and he's growing up into a fine young man. I'm very proud of him, Steven. I think you would be too."

There was no anger, no menace left in him.

She said, "I'd better be going now."

He came over and held out his hand to help her up. She hesitated and then took it.

"Do you have to go?" he asked her.

"Yes. It's getting late."

"Will I ever get to see my son?" He was still holding her hand.

"You must be married," she said. "You must have other children."

"I'm married," he agreed. "We have no children. We never will have. It's a marriage made in hell. Angela? Don't leave me. Please don't leave me."

"I've got to," she answered, but she didn't really want to. The closer he came, the more appealing were his low voice and penetrating eyes. "If you want to see him," she said, "he's here. I brought him with me. He'll still be up."

She drew back from him. Another moment and something might have happened that must never happen between them now.

He draped the cape over her shoulders. "What does he look like?"

[83]

"You," she answered. "You'll see for yourself."

In the elevator, he said to her, "Why didn't you wait for me? Why didn't you trust me, Angela? I'd have changed my life."

"Would you, Steven? Honestly?"

"I don't know," he admitted. "I did almost leave the family anyway, when I came back. I lost my taste for the work. But I'd never have let you go so easily. Jesus, I could have sent money at least."

"Without coming to find us and bring us back?"

"The first thing I'd have done," he said. "How well you got to know me, even in such a short time."

He handed her into the car. She gave the address of the apartment. Suspicion flared in him for a moment. "How come you're not in a hotel? Who owns this place?"

"A client of the company I'm going to work for," she explained. "It's very small, but it's much nicer for Charlie. And it's saved me a lot of money."

Satisfied, he relaxed. When they arrived, he told the driver to wait.

Angela opened the front door. "It's two floors up," she said, and went ahead of him.

He stopped her on the first landing. "Who do you say I am?"

"Mr. Falconi, who gave me a lift home from the dinner."

At the apartment door, she pressed the buzzer. The door opened, and Charlie stood there. "Hello, Mum. You're back early. Have a nice time?"

They were inside, and Steven Falconi could see his son clearly. Tall, dark, open-faced. A Falconi through and through, from the black hair to the olive skin and the deep black eyes.

He heard Angela say, "We did finish early. This is my son, Charlie. Mr. Falconi kindly gave me a lift home."

The boy held out his hand. "How do you do, sir."

Steven shook it. "Glad to know you, Charlie."

The boy had a strong, confident grip. *It's like looking in a mirror,* Steven thought. *Doesn't he see it too?*

"Do stay and have a drink, won't you?" Angela invited. For a moment their eyes met.

"I'd like that," he answered.

"Scotch? I have some wine if you'd rather."

"Scotch," he answered. "Water and ice. Thank you."

"I'll get it," Angela said, and went out, leaving him alone with his son. He found it difficult to speak.

Young Charlie said politely, "Do you live in New York, sir?"

"Part of the time. Mostly I'm in Florida."

"New York's such an exciting place," the boy said enthusiastically. "I've had such a super time. What's Florida like?"

"Very different. It's hot and sunny. There's good deep-sea fishing and waterskiing."

"Sounds terrific. I'd love to go there one day."

"Maybe you will," Steven said. "You're in school in England?"

"Yes. I go to Highfields. It's a super school. I've got my first lot of exams next term." He pulled a wry face. "I've promised Mum I'll do well."

"I guess you will," his father said. She'd brought up a fine boy, he thought. The quaint English manners, calling him "sir." His young nephews were spoiled and truculent.

Angela's son said suddenly, "Actually I'm half American. My father was in the American army. He was killed fighting in Italy. Just after Mum married him. Maybe that's why I like New York so much."

"Maybe," Steven Falconi agreed. "I'm sorry about your father."

"Mum told me all about him. He was jolly brave. Rotten luck for her, though."

"Here's your mother," Steven said, and got up. He took the whiskey from Angela. "I've been hearing about Charlie's school," he said.

"And I've been telling him about my father," the boy interrupted. "Where was the place he was killed, Mum?"

"Salerno," Angela answered. She didn't look near Steven Falconi. "A lot of Americans were killed in that battle."

She thought, *Anyone who saw them together would know there's a blood relationship. They're so alike it's uncanny.*

She said to her son, "Darling, I have some business to talk over with Mr. Falconi. Would you pop off to bed now?"

"Okay, Mum. Good night, sir."

They shook hands again. Steven watched him pat his mother affectionately on the shoulder, too grown up to kiss her in front of a stranger. He closed the door, and they were alone.

"You've done well, Angelina," he said slowly. "He's a great boy."

"I'm glad you think so."

"I want to do something for him. For both of you."

She shook her head. "Not money, Steven. We don't need it. I've got a good job, and my mother left me some capital. Charlie's school

[85]

is paid for till he's eighteen. My father did that. It's good of you and I'll always be grateful, but we don't need anything."

"Because of where it comes from? Is that it?"

"I didn't want to say so. I don't want to hurt you."

"You're not hurting me. You could be hurting the boy. What's he going to do when he leaves school? What about college? He's intelligent. Who's going to pay for that?"

"I will, if necessary," she answered.

He got up and paced the small room. "I can settle money on him," he said. "You can't stop me."

"No, I can't. You can make him rich, Steven, and ruin his life. He'd ask questions. He'd find out that I'd lied to him; he'd find out what you did to make that money."

"You deny him to me," he accused her. "He's my only son. And I married you, Angela. You're my wife, remember?"

"You have a wife," she said. "I'm sorry if you're not happy, but I shouldn't have brought you here. I shouldn't have let you meet him." She got up and went to the apartment door.

He came close to her and said, "You feel nothing for me?"

"I love my son," she answered. "I've made a life for him, and he's happy. I can't let myself feel anything for you, Steven, because of what it would do to him. Now please. Please go."

She opened the door and stood aside.

"I don't believe you," Steven Falconi said quietly. He reached out and put a heavy hand on her shoulder.

She said quickly, "No, Steven, don't. . . ."

"I won't, not with our son in there. I'll go now, Angela, but I'll be back."

Later, she went to the boy's bedroom and opened the door. He was asleep. Suddenly she rememberd doing the same thing the night she refused Jim Hulbert, just before leaving for London and a new life. She had done the right thing then, instead of taking the easy way out. She must do the right thing now. For her son, not for herself.

"You feel nothing for me?" His question haunted her that long night without sleep, and she dared not face the answer. Fear, anger, pity . . . a whisper of desire inside her when he touched her. Were those the sum of her feelings? Or was her love still there, a bar to other men, a weapon turned against herself. *We have to get away,* she kept repeating, *we have to, before he comes again. And he will. I know him. I saw it in his eyes. He won't let Charlie go. He won't let me go. And God knows whether I'd be strong enough next time.*

"Mum, why do we have to go early?"

"Charlie, I've already told you. I spoke to David Wickham, and he wants me to start next week. I'm sorry, but we've got to go back. I know you're enjoying it, but it can't be helped."

"But when did you speak to him?" he questioned. "You didn't say anything about it last night."

"I didn't have time. Now stop arguing, will you, please? I'll make it up to you another time. You don't think I want to go home, do you?"

He saw her blinking away tears. He muttered something very scatological about Mr. David Wickham, which would have surprised Angela had she heard it, and went in to pack.

She phoned for tickets on the afternoon flight to London. They cost a lot more than the originals, but there were no cheap seats. She telephoned the second client Wickham had asked her to see, made the same excuse she had made to Forrest, who had to be telephoned too. Her son was ill and she was flying him home. Mr. Forrest, who was extremely annoyed at having been left in the middle of dinner, wasn't sympathetic.

She thought, *He'll put in a bad word for me with the agency,* and then shrugged it off. It couldn't be helped. She wished there'd been an earlier flight.

"I'll be back," Steven had said. As she packed and tidied up the apartment, she dreaded hearing the bell, finding him standing there, forbidding her to go. But the hours passed, and nothing happened.

"I'll go down to the deli and get something for us to eat," she said.

"I'll go," her son offered.

"No, you stay here. I'll get some hamburgers. And don't answer the telephone."

"Why not?" he asked.

"Because I say so!"

She hurried out, and he grimaced. He'd never seen her in such a bad mood and so close to crying as well. He said something even nastier about Mr. Wickham and settled down sullenly to watch the wonderful American television for the last time. When the bell buzzed, he pressed the catch release and then opened the apartment door.

"Hello," Steven Falconi said. "Is your mother here?"

"Er, no. She's gone down to get some lunch. Down to the deli. We're going back to England, worst luck!"

"Mind if I come in and wait?"

"No, no, please come in. I'll turn the TV off."

"Don't mind me," Steven said. "Go ahead and watch."

The buzzer sounded again. "I'll get that," Steven said. He opened the door to Angela and said, "Let me take that," and lifted the package out of her arms. He turned to the boy. "If you were to take a short walk, Charlie, I might be able to persuade your mother to stay on in New York and finish your vacation. Would you do that?"

"No," Angela started to say, but the boy bounded up in excitement.

"Could you? Oh, that'd be super. See you later, Mum," and with a quick grin at Steven, he dashed out of the flat.

Falconi glanced at the packed suitcases and said, "I guessed right. I guessed you'd fly out today. I know you pretty well. Before you start giving me an argument, will you listen to me first?"

"You won't stop me leaving," she protested. "You can't stop me."

"I know that," he admitted. "Oh, I thought about it, Angela. I thought about taking you and my son to Florida and keeping you there till you'd changed your mind. But it wouldn't work with you. Don't look at me like that. Sometimes I think like a Sicilian, that's all. It wasn't serious. This is America. You're not allowed to kidnap your wife and son. Will you sit down a minute? I won't make a big speech, I promise you."

"All right, if you promise to go before he comes back."

"I promise," he said, "if you say so. But let's get this straight first."

"Get what straight?"

"This," he said, and took her in his arms. She didn't resist. He was much too strong. She tried to hold out mentally. He murmured to her in Italian, kissing her mouth, her eyes, her throat. Just as he had on the Sicilian hillside all those years ago. The same words, and the same rush of passionate feeling. He let her go and said softly to her, "*Cara mia,* remember? I love you. I said it then and I say it now. You can't lie to me now, can you? You feel it too."

"I feel it," she said desperately. "But it's no good. You can take me to bed, but it won't change my mind. It'll just make it harder for both of us."

"If there were no boy, would you say that?"

"No," Angela admitted. "No, I wouldn't. I still love you, Steven. I don't know if I could shut my eyes to what you are, but I could try. But not with him. Never."

"Tears," he said, touching her cheek with his fingertip. "It's time I made you happy, Angelina. Come stay close to me while I tell you something. In my family I'm the figures man. I add up all the sums and make the policy decisions. It won't make any difference to you, but I don't carry a gun. That was a crazy lie the other night.

"I've been doing some calculating for myself. I have money, respect; my father's proud of me. I'm Don Stefano to a whole lot of people. I'm a big man. I've got bodyguards who'd die for me, a hundred guys who'd do whatever I told them. I'll be the boss when my father dies.

"But I have no home life, no happiness, no children. I go to whores for comfort. If I give it all up, will you come away with me? We'll start a new life—you and me and the boy."

"You couldn't," she said. "You couldn't do it."

"I can do it. I will do it. If you promise me we'll be together, I'll go into business for myself. Legitimate business. Nothing to do with the families. I've thought it through. We'll leave the States. We'll live in Europe. I have to talk to my father first, but he loves me. When he knows about Charlie, he'll help. I have a younger brother. He can take over. I swear this to you, Angela. On my honor. You know what that means to a Sicilian?"

"I know," she said. "If you swear like that, I know you mean it."

"Will you swear too?" he asked her. "Swear we'll be together?"

She laid her hand against his cheek. It was an old gesture of tenderness between them.

"If you will do that for us, then I swear."

"We'll be happy," he promised. "I'll never give my son reason to be ashamed of me. And one day maybe he can learn the truth. Maybe he'll be proud of a live father in the end." He took her hand and held it. "You'll stay in New York till I've made arrangements? It'll take a little time."

"I'll stay," she promised. "But what about my job?"

"No job," he countered. "That's all over. I take care of you from now on."

She said, "What about your wife?"

"She's not my wife. The marriage is null. She has no rights over me. I can walk out tomorrow. Kiss me, Angelina."

They kissed lingeringly and gently, and then she rested in his arms. Suddenly she felt a shadow come over her happiness. "What about her family? Aren't they part of it too?"

"Sure—her father's boss of the Fabrizzis. That won't matter. It'll be fixed between her people and mine. At a price, but it'll be fixed. Forget about it. There's the buzzer, my darling. He's back."

Angela paused by the door. "What do we tell him?"

"The truth," he answered. "You're staying on because I've made you a better offer. . . . Hi, there, Charlie, had a good walk?"

"Yes, thank you." He glanced quickly at Falconi. There was an empathy between them already. "Was it long enough? Are we staying?"

"I managed to persuade her. You're not going back home just yet. And I'm taking us all out this evening to celebrate."

"There's a new woman," Clara said to herself. She was in the Elizabeth Arden salon, having a facial. She looked at the reflection in the glass. The mask covering her face had set hard; her eyes stared back at her, circled in white like a clown's. She didn't need the expensive treatments. Her skin was soft and smooth as cream. A girl squatted on a stool beside her, manicuring her nails.

"A new woman," the inner dialogue insisted. "He's out most nights. . . . It's not just screwing. I know him, the bastard. It's different with this one. He's happy. He was singing this morning. I heard him." She rounded furiously on the manicurist. "Watch what you're doing—that hurt!"

"I'm sorry, madame. Can you hold your hand still, please?"

Other men desired her, Clara knew. Men who detected that she was a woman in her own right, not just the soft little breeding cows they had chosen. But she didn't want any of them. She wanted the husband who slept with her only to conceive a child. Since the last specialist's report, he hadn't come near her. Not for months. She abased herself, pleaded, offered herself without shame, but he maintained an icy indifference. At least he suffered. That helped. But now he was singing the old songs under his breath, not even seeing her, brushing her aside when she demanded his attention.

"I can't stand it," she went on, the mummy image staring at her in the glass. "I've got to find out. I can do something about it then."

The beautician appeared behind her. "I guess we're ready now, Mrs. Falconi. Gloria, have you finished Mrs. Falconi's manicure?"

"I've just painted on the final coat," the girl answered. She glanced up at her client. Clara spread her hands, examining the newly painted nails. Steven's big diamond solitaire flashed on her finger under the light. The hands were white, pampered, with scarlet claws, as if they had been dipped in fresh blood.

"I got rid of the first one," the silent voice exulted. "The one in Monte Carlo. That bitch Lita Montini stopped sniffing around after Papa had a word with her father. He sent her back home to her cousins in Linsano for a whole year. I'll find this one, whoever she is."

"Gloria's done a good job," the beautician said, smiling. "But of course you've got beautiful hands, Mrs. Falconi. Now shall we steam off that cleansing mask?"

An hour later, Clara stepped out of the handsome building on Fifth Avenue. The doorman, uniformed in the distinctive Arden livery, summoned her car. She was going to a charity lunch at the Waldorf.

As soon as she got home, she would call the firm of private detectives who had worked for her before. They had reported on Steven whenever she felt threatened. Nobody knew about this, not even her father. He wouldn't have approved. He liked such things to stay within the family. Clara didn't want the list of professional women who tripped in and out of the duplex on the East Side coming in front of her father. She kept that humiliation to herself. She had come to terms with the whores; they were paid, and they never lasted long. She didn't fear them, and she was able to control her jealousy. Women outside that category were a different matter. Apart from Lita Montini, who had dared flaunt herself to Steven, there were no true rivals. Until that night ten days earlier, when he had gone to dinner at Les A without her: that was when she began to notice the change in him. The detectives could start from there.

"I'm going to my father tomorrow," Steven said. "My brother will be there too."

"They'll try to persuade you," Angela said. "They'll try to talk you out of it."

"Sure they will," he agreed. He reached across the table and held her hand. "But my mind's made up. When they know that, when I explain everything, they'll come around to the idea. I know them. They love me. My mother will help; she hates Clara. Don't worry, sweetheart; it'll all work out."

"I do worry," she said. "I worry about you, I worry about Charlie. It's all happened to us so quickly. . . . Sometimes I'm horribly afraid."

"I know you are," he said. "I feel it. But you mustn't be. I know what I'm doing. I know what I want, and that's you and my boy, and nothing is going to stop me. . . . Shouldn't we be getting back?"

Angela had to smile. "Darling, he's not a baby. He's quite all right in the flat for one evening. He's had such a wonderful time. He never stops talking about you."

"We get along," he answered. "I never knew it could be this much fun, having a proper family."

They'd gone to the theater to see the latest Broadway musical; circled Manhattan island by boat; shopped at Macy's, where Angela had to stop Steven from buying the excited Charlie everything he admired in the sports department. They drove out of town to eat; he never took them to Little Italy, although his son wanted to go there. His friend Jordan had raved about the food there.

Steven and Angela found time to be alone together. Tonight he had chosen a charming restaurant up in Connecticut. It was small and intimate. He never suggested that they go to the duplex. They made love in the little borrowed flat while their son was at the movies or wandering through Central Park. And Steven made plans, plans for their new life together, while Angela listened and forced herself to believe it would really happen.

She didn't doubt him; he meant to do exactly what he said: to break with his family, his background and his old life, and start afresh far away from it all. She loved him for that single-mindedness as much as she loved the total commitment of their physical desire for each other. And the gentleness that accompanied it, the tenderness to her and the overprotective attitude toward his son. As they lay together in the brief times they were alone, he promised her that he would make up for it all: for the long years of coping on her own, of holidays spent working so that young Charlie could have a trip now and then.

Angela let him paint the extravagant pictures because she knew how much pleasure it gave him. A fine house, lots of help; France appealed to him, wouldn't she like to live in France, in the south— sunshine and lots of things for the boy to do when he came home on holiday. A honeymoon, to make up for the one they never had. "So many things I want to give you, my darling," he would whisper. "To spoil you and reward you for making me so happy. I'm going to make a pet of you. You're going to have everything you've ever wanted." And he didn't listen when she protested that she only wanted to live happily with him.

"After I've talked to my father," he said, "we could have a weekend together. Maybe go down to Washington, the three of us. I could show Charlie the Capitol, the White House. . . . It's a great city. We'd have a wonderful time. Shall we do that, Angelina? Would you like that?"

"I'd love it," she said.

"Then it's fixed," he announced. He turned her hand upside down and pressed the palm against his mouth. "Did I ever tell you how much I love you?"

"Once or twice," she teased.

"You'll never leave me, will you?"

"I couldn't," she said. "You know that."

"I know," he said. "I just need you to say it, before tomorrow. Now I'll get the check and we'll drive home. I want to see him before he goes to bed. We can tell him about Washington."

Lucca Falconi still lived on the Lower East Side. It was a fortress—a four-story building with a garden surrounded on three sides by a high wall, and with more Falconis in the houses opposite and on either side. Lucca and his wife had brought up their sons there; they were fond of the house and the neighborhood.

During the trial of strength with the Musso family, Piero had persuaded his mother to move their living quarters to the back of the house for safety. The windows on the ground floor facing the street were bulletproof and covered with grilles. The garden was a pleasant, shady place with a table and chairs, so they could all eat outside; umbrellas kept off the hot summer sun. The Sunday lunches Clara hated so much were often held in the garden during fine weather.

Lucca enjoyed being out of doors. He liked the security of his high wall and the peace of his garden. He did a lot of business out there instead of in the stuffy rooms inside the house. His wife, Anna, was always buying things they didn't need: tables, overstuffed chairs, oil paintings of the old country. He used to joke about it. "There's a whole industry turning out genuine fakes of views from Palermo just for you," he liked to say to her. She missed Sicily even after so many years, and she spoke poor English. One reason for giving Steven a good education was that Lucca didn't want him to grow up like the sons of other families: ignorant boys who knew how to use their fists but nothing else. His son had brains.

Piero had had trouble just getting through high school. Not much brains there but a good heart. He was a loyal son, with a lot of his grandfather in him. Lucca Falconi was content with his wife and his sons and his grandchildren. If he had a worm in his belly, it was that barren bitch Steven had married. He blamed himself for that. It was a bad marriage—no children, no comfort for his son—but it had been good for business. He reminded his wife about this when she complained about her daughter-in-law, but he only did it to stop her tongue. In his heart, he was in full agreement with her.

They were together, he and his sons, Steven and Piero, sitting out in the warm autumn weather. Anna had brought a big flask of Chianti and some olives and salami for the men to pick at. They spoke in dialect, as their fathers had done before them.

"My son," Lucca said to Steven. "My son, what you tell me isn't possible. I'm not awake. I'm dreaming a bad dream."

"It's no dream, Papa," was the answer.

"A fuckin' nightmare," Piero muttered in English. He shook his head, as he'd done several times already.

"A wife and a son," Lucca repeated. "And you kept this secret from us? From me, from your mama. All these years, and you never spoke of it to us?"

"Forgive me," Steven said humbly. "It wasn't a secret. It was a grief. I kept it to myself. Such a grief, I wanted to get killed after it happened. I couldn't talk to anyone."

His father nodded. He remembered only too well his crazy son getting a decoration in the war, risking himself. He'd been angry with him, but proud too. He had the medal and the citation in a big frame in his sitting room. Now he understood the reason.

"You had no right," his father rebuked him. "You should have told us. We could have helped you."

"I know," Steven admitted. He would never argue with his father over a family matter. He respected him too much. "I was wrong. But I come to you now. You call it a bad dream; Papa, to me it's like a miracle. After all these years I find my wife and I find my son. He's a Falconi—he's you and grandfather and me, all in one. And clever too. He studies hard. His mother has brought him up to be a proper man, with pride in himself." He knew how much this description would please his father. "I'm happy for the first time. For the first time in sixteen years I'm a happy man. I want them with me."

"It's not possible in New York." Lucca dismissed it instantly. "It's not possible in Florida. We all know what Clara is. She'd go to that old fart hole, Aldo, and start screaming. Your boy wouldn't be safe. Nor would his mother. It's not possible," he repeated.

"You could set them up someplace else," Piero suggested. He was in full sympathy with his brother. He had loved and admired Steven all his life. He had a happy marriage himself, and he doted on his sons and baby daughter. "We've got a big country, for Christ's sake. You could put them in a fine house and visit with them. Once, maybe twice a week. It could be business. Clara wouldn't know the difference."

Steven poured more wine into his father's glass. Piero shook his head; he scooped up a fistful of olives and dropped them into his mouth. He spat out the stones with force and accuracy. His children loved watching him do it. "Papa's planting olive trees," the eldest would say, and they all laughed. His children were very spoiled. His wife was not allowed to hit them.

Steven said carefully, "It's not enough. That's why I've come to talk to you. To ask my family to help me. I'd like Mama to be here too. Can I call her?"

"I'll call her," his father said. He had a wary look that Steven knew well. He was expecting to hear something that he wouldn't like. "Anna! Anna! Come on out here!"

Steven's mother came quickly. She looked at her sons in surprise. This was supposed to be men's talk. Business. Women had no place in it except to serve the men.

Her husband said, "Sit down, Anna. Stefano has some news for you. He wants to tell you something."

Steven got up and pulled out for her one of the chairs. He bent down and kissed her on the cheek. She smelled of his childhood: warm, spicy herbs and the violet scent she loved to wear.

"It's all right, Mama," he said. "It's good news. Don't worry."

He didn't get the chance to explain anything, because suddenly his father spoke up and told her everything in an angry voice that forbade her to be sympathetic.

"He married an English girl in the war. He married her in our church in Altodonte, so it's a valid marriage. She was carrying a child. He did the honorable thing. I would have supported him and taken her into the family. But he thought she was killed and the child with

[95]

her, so he said nothing. He came home to us all and said nothing."

Steven's mother had given a little cry of anguish. Lucca quelled it impatiently. "But it wasn't so. The girl was not killed after all. She is alive, with a son, and Stefano has found her, here in this city. Not two weeks ago. That's what he has already told me. Now he has some more to say that he wants you to hear. So tell us, Stefano. Why is Piero's suggestion not enough?"

Piero hastened to ease his mother's mind. It flustered her when her husband was angry. She had never got over her awe of him.

"I said he could make a home for them over here, but not in New York or Florida, where the families have interests. Someone would find out. Clara would call a vendetta on them. That's what I suggested, Mama." He glanced across at Steven. "But he says no. He says it's not enough."

"I want to be with them as my wife and son," Steven said. He didn't look directly at his father. "As Papa said, it was a true marriage. I married Clara in good faith, but it's not a marriage."

"No," his mother agreed in a low voice. "You're right. Thank God there were no children."

"I am going to leave Clara and live with Angela and my son as a proper family. I lost them once because of what happened in the war. I can't lose them again. I've come to ask for your blessing on what I'm going to do. You and Papa and Piero, my brother."

"What are you telling me?" his father interrupted. "What are you really saying, Stefano? You can't throw Clara out and bring in another wife and child, without the Fabrizzis declaring open war. Piero is right. It would be a vendetta, down to the last of us and the last of them. Aldo Fabrizzi would never forgive such dishonor to his daughter. So what are you really saying, my son? You're not so clever that I don't see through you."

Steven said, "You know better than I do, Papa. I can't live with my wife and son anywhere in this country. I have to leave the States. I have to leave the family. I'll tell Clara I'm leaving and going to live abroad. If you disown me as your son, then there will be no vendetta. My wife, Angela, and my son, Charlie, will be safe because no one will know they exist. There won't be a war between you and the Fabrizzis. If I am dead to you, to my own people, then Aldo Fabrizzi will accept that."

He saw tears spill onto his mother's cheek. She wiped them away with her apron, as her forebears had done in times of grief.

"You want to leave us," his father accused. "You want to be dead to us? No wife, no son, can mean that much to any man! I heard this sort of talk from you when you came back from the war. I won't listen to it a second time. No! No, Stefano, I won't give my blessing to such a thing. If you do it, you go with my curse!"

"Don't say that," Steven asked him. "Don't break my heart, Papa. Don't threaten me. You have Piero. He can run things for you as well as I can now. He has boys to follow on."

"Leave the family," his father went on, disregarding him. "Leave the Falconis and our old traditions? Our old ways? Live like a stranger among strangers, because of this woman and this boy? Ah, I won't curse you, my son, because you're out of your head! You've gone mad! But I curse them instead!" He got up, knocking his chair over, and stormed into the house.

Steven's mother said, "He won't change his mind. I know him. He won't change. You can't do this, you can't break his heart. He needs you, *caro*. He's getting old."

"He's strong like a lion," Steven answered. "And you know it, Mama. He could run the Falconis without Piero or me, if he had to. Don't cry anymore. Go in to him. He always needs you when he's upset. Calm him down. I'll talk to him again when he's calm."

She got up and went inside.

Piero lit a cigarette. He offered one to Steven.

"Ma's right," he said after a pause. "He won't give permission. He won't risk a fight with Aldo Fabrizzi, and if you leave that bitch, there'll be trouble for all of us. I've been thinking, Steven." He inhaled and blew out noisily into the warm air. He was a very physical man, who ate and drank loudly and moved roughly, knocking into things if they were in his way. He had a naturally violent temperament. "I've been thinking. There's a guy in Westchester. He runs a business. He has drivers who do contracts now and again—not piecemen: they specialize in cars. They'll guarantee to run anything off a fuckin' road and finish it off with fire. How about that for solving the problem? No Clara, no problem. I can arrange it."

He tipped up the Chianti bottle. It was empty. He looked inquiringly at Steven, his head a little to one side. "How about it?"

"No! No, Piero!" Steven put a hand on his brother's shoulder and pressed hard for emphasis. "No," he repeated. "You hear me? I mean it. Don't even *think* like that, you understand?"

"Okay. No need to break my neck. If you say so, that's it. It's more than she'd give you. Remember that time someone took a shot at you at the intersection? I wondered about that bitch as soon as I heard."

"Nobody touches Clara," Steven repeated. "We've never put contracts on our women. Just stop and think where that would end, for Christ's sake."

Our women. Piero couldn't argue with that. The syndicate murdered as many women as men, but the wives and daughters of the families were safe.

"Okay," he said. "Forget it. Pa's stopped shouting. Ma's getting to him. I'll go get another bottle. I'm thirsty. You?"

Steven said yes, for something to say. *He's my brother and we've loved each other since we were children. We're not alike and we've nothing in common outside of the family and the business. But we're fond of each other all the same. I've got to remember that and not remember that he offered to have his sister-in-law murdered.* He went into the house, brushing past Piero as he came out with more Chianti. There was silence inside. He went to his father's sitting room and knocked on the door. His mother came out, closing it behind her. She stood with her back to it. Her voice was very low.

"He won't see you," she said. "He says to go away and think about it. Come back when you've seen sense."

"I won't see sense, Mama."

"O merciful Madonna—what are we to do? Listen to him, Stefano. He loves you. You're his pride, you know that! Think about it. For my sake."

"I've never lied to you, have I?" he asked her. "No. Well, I won't lie now. I won't change my mind. He won't change his. I'll come again, Mama, just to say goodbye. I love you." He held her against him and comforted her, as so often she had done to him when he was a child. "One day I'll bring my son to see you," he whispered. "I promise you. Now go inside and give my father my respects and say I'll come again in a few days. No more than that, eh?"

"No more," she promised. "And I'll go on trying, *caro.* I'll go on pleading with him."

"Stop Piero from finishing the bottle out there," he told her gently. "You don't want him going home drunk. You know how mad it makes Lucia."

He let himself out the front door. His car was waiting. As always, he was ushered quickly into the back and driven off. He looked back to the house where he had grown up, and then he resolutely turned away.

He thought suddenly, *When this is done, I'll be able to walk places like other men.* But it didn't ease the pain of that parting with his father. Only time would do that.

They flew to Washington the next morning. The boy sat between them, full of enthusiasm, plying Steven with questions. Steven had bought a book on the history of the capital and pointed out the chapters he should read.

Angela and Charlie were booked into a small hotel in Georgetown; expensive and exclusive. Angela couldn't stop Steven from heaping every luxury upon them. He had booked himself into a downtown hotel as a precaution. The senator he had invited to Les Ambassadeurs was not his only contact in Washington.

Over dinner in the Georgetown hotel that night, Angela turned to them both. "Why don't you two go sightseeing? I'd love to do some shopping tomorrow morning. We could meet for lunch."

Steven understood. She wanted him to be alone with his son, to draw them closer together. The pretense that he was offering her a job couldn't go on once they left America.

"Well, if that's all right with you, sir." He turned eagerly to Steven.

"I guess so. We'll start with the Capitol and the Lincoln Memorial. If your mother would like, we can all see the White House in the afternoon."

"I'd love that," Angela said.

Charlie went up ahead of them. He wanted to watch television in his room. They sat in the lounge and drank coffee, and under the table Steven held her hand.

"Was it true about the shopping?"

"Well, partly true. I thought it would be nice for you to go off together."

"You won't let me buy you anything? Some new dresses, a coat for the winter?"

"A mink coat?" she teased him. "No, thank you, darling. Charlie's not that naive. We've got to do everything right till the time comes. Oh, I wish it were tomorrow—I wish we could get on a plane and fly straight home, the three of us. How long will it take, Steven?"

"Aren't you happy?" he asked. "Is it so hard to stay with me?"

"I'm uneasy," she confessed. "I keep thinking it's all so wonderful, being with you, seeing you and our son getting to know each other, and at the back of my mind there's this feeling that it won't last, that something will happen to stop it."

"I shouldn't have told you about my father," he admitted. "That's what's made you worry. You mustn't, Angela. You've got to trust me. I can hurry things up from now on. Another week—is that too long?"

"I'm sorry," she said. "Of course it isn't. But I'll have to stop putting David Wickham off. He must have time to look for someone else. I wish you'd let me take the job till we get settled."

"No job," he insisted. "I take care of you and my son. When we leave, you go home, put Charlie in school, and then join me wherever. You'll have plenty to do, sweetheart. Don't worry about that. It's late. Can I come up with you?"

He was playing with her hand, stroking her fingers, moving the rings to and fro.

"If you promise to go on doing that," she murmured, and got up.

Piero's wife, Lucia, was playing with the baby when the telephone rang. Her husband was lounging on the sofa with his feet up, reading the sports section of the newspaper.

"Answer it, honey," he mumbled.

She balanced the baby on her hip and went to pick up the receiver. She called out to him, "It's for you!"

"Shit," he exclaimed. "Who is it?"

"He didn't say. Just says he wants to speak with you."

"Okay, okay. I'm coming," Piero grumbled. He threw the papers on the floor, heaved himself up and took the telephone from her. He bent and smacked a kiss on the baby's cheek. She chuckled. "Yeah," he said into the phone. "It's Piero."

A voice said, "This is Louis from Les A. I've been trying to reach Don Stefano, but he's out of town."

Piero came alert. He waved Lucia and the baby away. "So?"

Louis's voice was low. "Some guy's been asking questions about him," he said. "He slipped the girl on the desk a twenty, and she told me."

"What sort of guy? What the fuck was he asking?"

"Who was with him when he came to dinner here. One specific

date; I remember your brother *was* here that night. This guy kept asking about a woman. He's an agency legman. I thought Don Stefano ought to know."

"Yeah," Piero said slowly. "Yeah, thanks. Did your girl tell him anything? Did she take the twenty?"

"Sure she did. Said she'd seen your brother, but there was no woman with him. So the guy goes to Eddie at the bar and tries the same line. Eddie takes a twenty and a phone number. He gives it to me. I guess you want it."

"I want it," Piero answered. He wrote down the number and stuffed the scrap of paper back in his pocket. "Thanks, Louis. We owe you. I'll tell my brother." He hung up and stood chewing on the pencil for a moment. A private detective asking about Steven and a woman. Only one person would pay for that. He took out the paper and dialed the number.

"Taylor Investigators," a woman's voice said in a bored tone.

Piero slammed down the phone. He swore under his breath, a long, fierce Sicilian obscenity. Clara was spying on Steven to find out about a woman. It didn't take much to figure out who that woman would turn out to be. Steven had called her Angela. Piero thought on his feet, and when he thought, he didn't waste time before he acted. Steven was out of town. If he was being followed and he was with the woman and his son, then Clara would be told.

He shouted out to Lucia. "Put the kids to bed, will you? Stay out of the way till I call, honey."

She came close to him. "What is it? Trouble?"

"Trouble for Steven," he said. "I got to deal with it. Move your sweet ass, sweetheart."

She made a provocative face at him and jerked her hips. "I'm moving it," she said. "You just take care, that's all."

It was all organized within an hour. Piero's trusted henchmen were summoned to the house and given their instructions. Three were to take care of the agency itself, and the others were allocated to the legman on the Falconi assignment.

Piero shouted for his wife when they had gone. He slapped her on the bottom. "You been keeping it warm for me?" he demanded. "The kids asleep?"

"They're asleep." She smiled at him. "You want to go to bed?"

"What the fuck's wrong with the floor?" he demanded, and heaved her up against him.

Much later, they were eating, when the first of the calls came in. Piero answered, swallowing down his food.

"Okay, okay," he said, nodding, wiping his hand across his mouth. His brand of vigorous lovemaking always made him hungry. "You tell Gino from me, he's done well. Tell his boys too. Sure. . . . Yeah."

Lucia didn't question him. She filled his glass with Chianti and ladled out more lasagna. Additional calls came. The guy who had been asking questions at Les A wouldn't be asking any more. He'd gone through a sixth-story window. All the way down. The agency staff had been worked over before the office was smashed with pickaxes and hammers till it looked like a toothpick factory. The records were piled up in the middle and burned, all but Steven Falconi's. His would be delivered to Piero that night.

After Lucia had gone to bed, he sat up, waiting for the dossier. He flipped through it quickly. He hated reading; it made him impatient. The terms. Written reports to the client. Client. He cursed out loud. Clara Falconi. As he had suspected, she was spying on her husband. He concentrated. Les A. No information there, but during the week subject tailed to an apartment on East Seventieth. Occupants a Mrs. Lawrence and her son. Subject seen with them at the theater, in restaurants, on a boat trip around Manhattan. Piero had begun to sweat. He looked at the last date. Two days before. The reports to Clara were scheduled weekly. This was the first. They had intercepted it just in time.

Piero threw down the folder. There'd be another tail on Steven, wherever he was. But no agency for the tail to report back to. Any professional would get that kind of message. He'd just fade away and count himself lucky. But Clara would pass on the job to someone else. A dead man, a case of arson, and a few people with the shit beaten out of them wouldn't worry Clara.

"He's nuts," Piero lamented aloud, thinking of his brother and wishing he dared go against him and break the unwritten rule of the family. It would have been simple. A perfect solution. He hated Clara so much he'd have run her off the road himself and enjoyed every minute of it. He imagined the car turning over and ending in a ball of orange flame. . . . But Steven had said no, and he had never disobeyed Steven in his life.

Piero wasn't greedy for more power or ambitious to be the Don when his father died. He had everything he wanted. The idea of full responsibility didn't appeal to him. He preferred to take orders from the top. He coped with situations like the agency easily enough. Administration at Steven's level would worry him. Dealing with senators, that kind of crap. He put the idea out of his mind. His father was there, the rock on which the Falconi family rested. Piero didn't have to think so far ahead. Just far enough to warn Steven. In the morning. He'd call first thing. After he'd seen the newspapers. He'd given them some headline, he grinned to himself. Like the old days, when he was a kid. And he was confident. Nobody would identify his men, nobody would talk. No one testified against the families and stayed alive. The police would recognize the Falconi signature too, but there was nothing they could prove. And there were officers on the family payroll who would make sure the incident wasn't pursued too closely.

He locked the dossier away and went up to join Lucia. On his way, he looked in on his sleeping sons, then opened the nursery door a crack to make sure baby Caterina was all right.

"It was a great trip," Charlie said to his mother. He'd picked up words like "great" from his father, and he said "okay" a lot, trying hard to sound American. "He's so nice, isn't he, Mum? Paying for everything like that—he must be jolly rich."

He glanced at her, uncertain how to say what was uppermost in his mind since the weekend. "What sort of job are you going to do for him? Is he in the same sort of business as Mr. Wickham?"

"No, darling. He's got a lot of interests in a lot of businesses. He wants me to be a liaison between them—a super personnel job, I think you'd call it. Lots of traveling." She decided to cross one bridge then and there. "In fact, we might have to live in France. It's not certain, but it is a possibility."

He frowned. "Mum, I wouldn't have to leave school, would I? I mean, I'd hate that."

"Oh, of course not. I wouldn't hear of anything like that! You'd just come over for holidays. It's not definite, Charlie, but it *is* likely. You wouldn't mind, would you?"

"No," he said after a pause. "Not if it's good for you. Wouldn't we live at home at all? What about Grandpa?"

"We'd spend time in both places," Angela assured him. "You could have your friends to stay in the summer. We'd be in the south, he said."

He brightened immediately. "Gosh, that'd be great!" He paused. "Do you like him, Mum? I think he's a bit keen on you."

[103]

"Yes, I like him very much. He may like me; I don't really know."

"Mum," he announced in triumph, "you're going red!"

She aimed a playful slap at him, which he dodged. He went off whistling to spend some of his pocket money at the corner drugstore two blocks away. He had made friends with one or two American teenagers, who were delighted by his clothes and accent.

Angela hurried into the bedroom. He was quite right, she realized, seeing herself in the glass. Her face was still a guilty scarlet.

She was meeting Steven for lunch downtown. He had called her that morning as usual.

"I want you to meet me," he had said. "Don't bring Charlie. There's a little place called the Garden, over on Forty-third. Take a cab, my darling, and be there by twelve-thirty. I've got something for you. No, I can't tell you what it is. I have to go now. Twelve-thirty, the Garden, Forty-third Street. I love you, *cara mia.*" Then he had hung up.

The air was turning colder. She had bought a ridiculous hat with a bright-colored feather in Washington when she was feeling particularly happy. She decided to wear it for him at lunch that day. He had a surprise for her. It must be a present. She couldn't go on refusing him. She felt excited and a little guilty. A cruising taxi picked her up on the corner. The driver noted the address. He was a talkative man, and he loved English passengers because they were too polite to tell him to shut up.

"How long you been here, lady?"

"Three weeks," she answered.

"You like our city?"

"I love it. I've had a wonderful time."

"It's a great place. If it wasn't for the crime. Jesus, you seen the morning papers?" He didn't wait for her to answer. "Right across the page. Some guy working for a detective agency gets thrown out of a window six floors up, and they take the agency apart. Three people in the hospital, half the building burned out."

"How terrible," Angela said, not really interested. "Who did it?"

"Mafia," he retorted, making a face in the driving mirror. "Three guys worked that place over, and nobody even gives a description! Nobody seen anything, nobody heard anything. Jesus," he said again, "you don't finger those guys. It's Mafia for sure. I guess that agency was on to something. So they wipe it out! It makes me ashamed, you know that, lady? It makes me ashamed what people like you think of this city when a thing like that can happen. And what do the cops do about it? I'll tell you. Nothing! And why? Because half of them are on the payroll, that's why."

Angela wasn't listening. Mafia. A man thrown to his death; people terrorized and beaten, too frightened to describe the brutes who had done it; a building almost destroyed by fire. "I make the policy decisions. . . . I don't carry a gun." She held fast to that, insisting that it removed him from the violence, the taint of murder even at a distance. His promise: she held faster still to that, because without it there was no possible choice but the one she had been forced to make all those years ago. *He's giving it up. He's breaking with his past, with his own people. We're going away where none of this can touch us.*

"Lady." The driver had pulled up and was reaching to open the door for her. "This is it. The Garden. That'll be two fifty."

Angela didn't know how much she gave him. She hurried under the little green awning and into the restaurant. Steven was waiting for her, sitting at a table facing the door. He took her coat and guided her into the banquette seat beside him. He looked strained and taut.

"That hat," he said. "I've never seen you in a hat before."

"I bought it last weekend," she said. "Steven, what's the matter? What's wrong?"

He signaled, and the waitress hurried over. "Two dry martinis," he said briefly, and then turned to Angela. "Nothing's wrong, sweetheart. I like the hat. It suits you. How's Charlie?"

"He's fine. He's having lunch at the drugstore. There *is* something the matter. Please tell me."

"You have to go back," he said, speaking low. "I've got tickets for a flight this evening."

She stared at him. "Go tonight? But why? You said a week."

"Something's come up," he explained. "I want you and my son to leave by tonight. It's all fixed. I've got the tickets right here."

"And I'm not to be told why?" she countered. "That's not good enough. I wanted to take up my job and wait for you. You said no. Now suddenly it's all changed. You've got to tell me why."

The menus were placed in front of them. The waitress began her set speech about the recommended dishes.

"Not now," Steven interrupted. "Not right now."

She went away with a sullen look.

Angela said, "I'm not going unless you tell me."

"I've been followed," he said. "My wife hired a detective. He was checking on me. It's not safe for you and Charlie anymore."

[105]

"Does she know about us?" Angela asked.

"Not yet. But she will. So you understand now, my darling. You must leave tonight."

He was surprised when she said, "Could I have another martini?" and drained her first one. He signaled the waitress to bring two more drinks.

"What would happen to Charlie and me if she did find out? You said there wouldn't be any danger. You said it could be fixed at a price. You're not telling me the truth, are you?"

"Don't say that," he countered. "I thought it would be like I said. I didn't know she suspected anything. One of the people they tried to question tipped off my brother. He warned me this morning."

The waitress brought their second martinis. She didn't mention the menu again.

"Aren't they still following you?" Angela asked him. The cocktail was so cold it burned her throat.

"No," Steven said. "My brother fixed it. But she'll hire someone else. Believe me, Angelina: I wouldn't send you and my boy away unless I knew I had to. Don't look at me like that. It's going to kill me to let you go without me."

"The agency," she managed to say. "The one that burned down, where the man was killed—the cabdriver said it was the Mafia. Does that have anything to do with this? Steven, if you lie to me now, I'll know it. I'll walk out of here and never see you again."

It was a long time before he answered. He didn't pretend; he considered the consequences and said at last, "I won't lie to you. If I lie now, it'll be the start of more lies. You won't trust me; I won't trust myself. If you leave me because I tell you the truth, then it wasn't going to work for us anyway." He paused. "It was the same agency my wife used. I told you, my brother got the tip-off. He didn't consult me, because he didn't know where I was. I'd have stopped him. I've stopped him before. I'd have found another way. But he couldn't take the chance. He did what he felt had to be done to save your life and Charlie's.

"He bought me the time to get you away before Clara could go to her father. It could have been a matter of days. Piero knew that. He knows the way these things work. She finds out about you, and all it takes is a telephone call. So he gave the order. Here are the tickets, Angela. I can't drive you to the airport. I can't see you again after you leave here, in case there's another tail on me. I can't even say goodbye to my son." After a moment he said, "Give me your hand, won't you? Don't turn away from me."

Their hands met and gripped. There were tears in his eyes. "You wanted the truth," he said. "You said something would happen. It did. I'll come to England. Will you be there for me?"

Angela reached up and took off the hat. The bright feather brushed against him. "I bought it because I was so happy," she said. "I loved the silly feather. I don't think I could eat anything. Do you mind?"

He shook his head. "You want me to get the check?"

"I was thinking," she went on. "While you were telling me about it, I was thinking. I knew already, as soon as I asked. Since we've been together again, I've known what loving you was going to mean. So why am I shocked, Steven? Why haven't I faced it before?"

"Because you couldn't," he said. "You told me. You couldn't face it for the boy."

"I couldn't face it for myself either." She stared ahead of her, as if looking into the future. "I can run away from you a second time. I know you won't try to stop me now. We've been too close for that. I can go back to my old life and tell Charlie the job with you has fallen through. He'll be disappointed; he said this morning, 'I think he's a bit keen on you, Mum.' He was teasing me, laughing about it. He'll forget about you. He hasn't learned to love you yet. But I have. I love you, Steven, and if you love me, you'll get on the plane tonight and come with us. If you do that, we have a chance. If you stay here, we'll never see each other again. Next time, it won't be your brother who does something like that. It'll be you. Now get the check, and I'll find a cab outside. Give me the tickets."

He stood up. He handed her an envelope. "And I got this for you," he said. It was a Tiffany box. Angela opened it. An emerald glowed on its cushion of white velvet. She closed the box and put it in his hand.

"Give it to me tonight," she said. "On the plane."

She didn't say goodbye or look back. She left him standing there.

4

"He won't see you," Steven's mother repeated. "He doesn't sleep, he doesn't eat. . . . His heart is breaking, Stefano, but you know his pride."

"I know it, Mama," he answered. "But there's no time for it now."

He put her aside gently and went to his father's room. She watched him apprehensively, mouthing a silent prayer. She had wept when he came and told her. He was her favorite, her lovely son who'd made them all so proud.

Steven didn't knock; he opened the door and walked in. Sitting in a chair, his father looked up, then started to his feet. Steven noticed how tired he looked.

"You come in here without knocking?" his father said. "Where's your respect?"

"Papa," he answered, "I'm a man, not a boy. I have respect for you, you know that. But I have love for my father, and I can't go without saying goodbye. Mama tried to stop me, so don't blame her."

"You haven't changed your mind?" his father demanded. "You're turning your back on your own people?"

"Not on my people," Steven countered. "Not on you or Mama or Piero. But on what Piero did last night. He's told you about it?"

"He's told me. He did right."

"He did it for me," Steven said. "But it's been done for business other times. That's why I'm leaving. There's no place for our kind of business in the life I want. I'm turning my back on that, not on you. Can't you understand? Can't you even try?"

"No!" Lucca Falconi exploded. "No, I don't understand! I give you a good education, send you to college, try to make something better than a hood out of you, and this is my reward: you get fancy all of a sudden." He struck his fist against the table. "I should have treated you and Piero the same," he said. "I made a difference between you. I was wrong. Piero is a good boy. I thank God for Piero now."

"Papa," Steven protested. "Don't say things like that. It isn't fair. I did my share; I did whatever you asked me! I helped make a lot of rackets into a multimillion-dollar business, bigger than you ever dreamed. How can you reproach me because I want some happiness in my life?"

"I'll tell you how." His father turned on him bitterly. "I remember when you came home from the army. I remember you in this very room, telling me you wanted to quit then. I made excuses. I said to myself, 'He's had a bad time, the war was rough.' I was so proud of you. . . . I loved you."

There were tears in his eyes. Suddenly he looked like a tremulous old man.

I can't, Steven thought in despair, *I can't do this to him. . . . In all my life, I've never seen my father cry.*

Lucca turned away from him; he rubbed his eyes with a hand-kerchief. "Your mother pleaded. I listened to her," he went on. "So I said to myself, 'Be patient. Give him time. He's your son, your eldest boy.' I took you so gently, Stefano. I let you take your own line. No violence, you said, and I said, Yes, yes . . . that's in the old days; we're legitimate now. I was soft with you, because I'd gone soft in my head!" Again, he struck the table with his fist.

"You talk about doing your share! Well, let me tell you—Piero did your share! Who dealt with Musso? Eh? Who set it up that he had to make peace? Your brother! He got his hands dirty, and he took the risks for *you*—while you sat in your big office keeping your nose clean and your eyes shut! You don't like what he did to the detective and the agency? You want white hands, my son? Then let the Fabrizzis kill your woman and your boy! That's the choice. If you can't live with the truth, then get out! Run, hide yourself. The family is no place for you. I wish you'd never been born." He sat down, glaring up at Steven.

Steven said slowly, "You lied to me, Papa, to keep me in the business. I knew it, but I didn't ever want to hear you say it. It doesn't matter now. I owe my brother, I know that. I owe you and Mama too. And I love you. Don't think it'll be easy for me to walk away from all of you. You're my family. But I've made my choice. I'm going tonight. I'll see Clara before I go; I'll make it easy for you with the Fabrizzis.

But I promise you this: If you ever need me, if things get tough here and you want me, I'll come back. I swear it."

Lucca stood up again. Steven walked toward his father.

Lucca glared at his son, daring him to defy him and come closer. But Steven refused to be stared down. Suddenly Lucca was locked in an embrace that he wasn't strong enough to break. He heard Steven say, "Goodbye, Papa. Remember. If you ever need me." And then Lucca's arms came up, and he held his son for a moment. He didn't speak. He didn't trust himself. Steven understood and left him.

He called Piero. The car took him uptown to the building they owned, which contained the offices of a half-dozen companies that controlled various enterprises. Steven's office was on the top floor. It was big and luxurious, as befitted his status.

His secretary was outside at her desk as usual. She smiled and said, "Good afternoon, Mr. Falconi." So far as she was concerned, it was a legitimate business, a trading corporation that paid big salaries and bonuses.

Steven opened the door to his private office with a special key. He went through his desk drawers. He had a file of private papers, a list of his stock holdings, government bonds, property interests. A fortune of over two million dollars. Some could be quickly liquidated, others would take time. He called his brokers, gave some brief instructions, and then hung up before they could argue. The rest could be left to Piero. Steven trusted his brother to do what was best for him and to keep the details secret.

He put some personal documents, including his will, into the shredder, then called his brother to say he was on his way down.

"You're crazy," Piero kept saying. "You're selling at the wrong time. You're losing good money, for Christ's sake! What's Pa going to say? Why the fuck do you have to go *tonight!* I fixed the agency; Clara's got nothing on you or the kid and his mother. Oh, yeah, she'll get herself another gumshoe, but so long as you've gotten them out, what can she do?"

"Nothing," Steven answered. "I'm not doing this because of Clara. I'm going now, Piero, before my life gets screwed up all over again. Wish me luck, won't you?"

"Ah, for Christ's sake," Piero protested. "You know I do. You know. If it's what you want, it's okay by me. Don't worry about the assets. I'll take the best advice and get the best I can for them. I'll get you a new passport and a driver's license—just tell me the name...."

"Lawrence. I'll tell you where to send them," Steven said. "I don't know just yet where I'll be. I'll square it with Clara. I told Papa I'd make it easy for him. And you've got to go along, Piero. So far as you and the family are concerned, I'm yellow shit. You understand that?"

"I guess so." His brother sounded uncertain. "It won't be easy. But you're goddamned right. We can't have a war."

"No war," Steven agreed. "But if Papa or you ever need me, just send word. I'll be back. Say goodbye to Lucia for me. Kiss the kids."

Piero hugged him, fighting back emotion. He could best express it by cursing at the fate that separated them. He was so unhappy that he wanted to go and hit somebody.

No war. No war with the Fabrizzis. So his father said, and his brother. He'd said it himself. But now he wouldn't have minded. He lit a cigarette; he struck the match so hard it broke. He picked up the burning end, not feeling the pain as the flame licked his fingers. Peace needn't be forever.

"Is it the new job?"

Angela said, "Yes, darling. But we have had a lot more time here than we expected, haven't we?"

"Yes, we have, Mum."

He'd been very good about it, puzzled by the dramatic change of plan, but he hadn't grumbled. He helped her pack, and together they tidied the little apartment. He stacked the luggage in the hall and looked around wistfully. "I'll never forget this place," he said. "It's been the best holiday ever. Is he coming to see us off?"

"Who?" Angela asked, knowing exactly whom he meant.

"Your boyfriend." He grinned. "Sorry, Mum, only a joke."

She didn't answer. She went into the bedroom and shut the door, saying, "I must see I haven't left anything behind. I'm always doing it."

She sat down on the bed where they had made love, talked of their plans for a new life: their small oasis. If she closed her eyes she could imagine him there with her, the feel of him close against her, the sound of his voice saying he loved her. *I've asked the impossible. He won't come. I know he won't.* She opened the door and shut it hard behind her, as if she were closing it on something tangible. But something else, something much more important, lay in that room. She had just shut the door on memories, on the exultation of their passion for each other, on the fantasy that they could extend it into the framework of an ordinary life. *He won't come,* the silent voice insisted. *You know it.*

"Charlie darling, we should be going soon. The traffic gets so snarled up at this time of the evening. Are you all ready?"

"Yes, Mum. Ready."

She saw his bright face and forced herself to smile. *You mustn't know, whatever happens. You mustn't know what we've both missed.*

It was a long, slow journey to the airport, inching through traffic, while everywhere the lights sprang up and New York lifted the veil on its evening face. The cabdriver didn't talk, unlike the one that morning, who had helped to wreck her happiness. She sat looking out of the window and saw nothing but a blur.

"Maria, where's Mrs. Falconi?"

The maid shrugged. "I don't know. She gone for lunch. She no say when she come back."

Maria was a widow. Her husband had been one of Don Lucca's humbler "soldiers," killed during the battle with Musso. Her reward was a free house and a well-paid job with the Don's eldest son. It kept her safe in the family. The family always looked after its own.

Steven went through to the big drawing room. Clara had gone overboard with some fag decorator five years before, and the place was cluttered with checks and stripes and tables thick with trivia, which drove Maria crazy when she tried to dust. It wasn't the kind of room where he could put his feet up, nor did he dare spill ash on the specially woven carpet. Their house wasn't a home.

He poured himself a Scotch and wondered where Clara was. Lunch was taking a long time. Lunch followed by one of her endless shopping sprees. His watch showed five o'clock. Angela's flight would leave at eight. He had to pack an overnight bag, get there and check in. His ticket would be waiting.

He settled down to wait, stilling his impatience. She'd be home soon. He'd told her he'd spent the weekend in Florida. Then he had hurried out of the apartment. He'd expedited arrangements with the efficiency of a veteran business traveler.

He'd made the decision and acted upon it. Making the decision had been the hardest part: to leave his family on such short notice;

to wind up his life in a few hours and set off into a world he didn't know. A strangers' world, without the protection and support of his own kind.

He was not a coward. He had faced death in the war and death as part of his life as a Falconi. It was a risk inherent in his heritage. It didn't trouble him. But after Angela had left him that afternoon, courage had been needed. The courage to cut loose from it all and make a new life with her and their son. He didn't hurry that choice. He stayed on in the little apartment, ordered food he didn't eat, and thought about the future. He thought of the look on her face, the despair and the confusion when she had said to him, "I've known what loving you was going to mean. So why am I shocked?" Business, he called it. It covered a broad spectrum. It made murder and extortion sound respectable. He went through the books and added up the millions. He sat in on the meetings where the policies were formulated. He didn't carry a gun. He didn't have to. There were men with guns all around him. They did the killing. Piero's men had responded to a personal call with clubs and hammers. They'd tossed a human being from a sixth-floor window, to smash like an egg on the street below.

So it was done to protect him. To protect Angela and his son. Piero would do the same to protect a business interest. As his father would. As he himself had done in the past. And Angela had known. For all her innocence of his way of life, she had seen through to the fundamental truth. "Next time, it won't be your brother. . . . It'll be you."

And suddenly the choice was clear. Not easy, but clear beyond doubt. Who could be sure, Steven asked himself, that without this ultimatum he mightn't have been persuaded to some compromise . . . kept some thread of attachment to his old allegiance. If he left that night, the thread would be cut forever. Only his pledge remained, and nothing would stop him from honoring that pledge if ever he was called upon. "If you ever need me . . . I'll come back." To his father, to his brother.

It left him with his honor. He smiled slightly. How strong the Sicilian blood was still—as strong as in his son, with his dark hair and Falconi eyes. One day he would take him to Sicily. The choice was made with that thought. He had paid for his food, slipped into his car and told the driver to go straight to his father's house. . . .

Lost in his thoughts, he didn't hear Clara open the door. He looked up suddenly and saw her standing there, a ribboned box on one arm.

She dropped the box on a sofa and slipped out of her mink stole. Sitting down across from him, she crossed her legs. He could feel the tension coming from her. The detective agency, of course. She couldn't say anything, but she knew. "Isn't it early for you?"

"Early for what?"

"To start drinking."

He looked hard at her over the glass. He drained the whiskey. "I need it," he said. "So will you."

She responded instinctively, as Piero's wife, Lucia, had done. "There's trouble? What's up?"

"Trouble for me," he told her. He saw a flash of satisfaction light her face and then vanish. "What would you say, Clara, if I told you I was quitting?"

"Quitting? You mean quitting me? Leaving me?" She jumped to her feet then.

"Quitting you, quitting the family." He said it calmly. "I've dealt myself out. And I've been dealt out. *Finito Benito.*"

She said, "You're crazy. I don't believe you. You can't quit the family, and you can't leave me! You're drunk!" She turned away impatiently. "I should have known better. Go sober up. Mario and Nina are coming over for dinner. Take a shower, do something!"

"Wait a minute," he said. He stood up. She was aware at once that her accusation wasn't true. "I saw my father today. I told him what I've told you. I want out. I said it. He didn't believe me either. Not for quite a while, Clara. He said I was crazy, too."

She was rooted, listening to him. Her pale face was as white as the blouse knotted at her throat.

"But I'm not crazy. I don't want to go on in the business. I don't want to live with you. I don't want to do anything I've been doing since I got back from the war. I should have made a new start then. I wanted to, I tried, but I let Papa talk me out of it. The war changed everything for me."

She interrupted him with a furious cry. "The war's been over since 1945! What the hell are you talking about?"

"You and my father," he said, "saying the same words. He cursed me, Clara, do you know that?"

"I can believe it," she said. "So would any father if a son talked to him like that!" Then with an effort she forced herself to be calm. She said, "Sit down, Steven. I'll get you a Scotch. You're not drunk. I shouldn't have said that."

"Get yourself one," he countered. "I have to pack."

She turned on him, frantic, as she realized he meant it. She barred his way to the door. "Pack? You're not going anywhere. You're not going to walk out on me, on all of us! Why? Why, Steven?" She caught his arm, her long nails sinking through the cloth, seeking his skin.

He wrenched away from her. "Because I hate myself," he said. "I hate what I am, Clara. That's what I told my father. I want clean hands. I want a new life. That's when he cursed me. He called my mother and Piero, and he cursed me in front of them. They didn't say a word. They didn't defend me."

"I'll curse you too," she shouted.

He pushed her aside. She followed him into their bedroom. He was putting clothes into an overnight bag. Blind with tears, she came and caught hold of him, and in spite of what the years had brought her, her love came rushing back.

"Take me with you," she begged. He hadn't known she could surprise him still. "I don't care. They can throw me out too. I'll go with you, Steven." She held on to him, weeping. She tore at her blouse, ripping the silk over her breasts in her anguish. "If I'd had a child this wouldn't have happened," she lamented. "We'd have been happy. Mother of Jesus, why did you do this to me?" She rocked to and fro, and he took time to sit beside her and try to ease her pain. His heart was empty, but he could still feel pity at that moment.

"No child would have made any difference," he said. "This is something in me, Clara. It's always been there. I told you, the war changed me. It changed a lot of people. I have to go away and work it out for myself."

He left her and closed the bag, snapping it shut. She looked at him, her perfect makeup streaked from her tears.

"They won't let you go," she said. "Your father and my father. You know what it means when they curse you and cast you out. You know what happens in the old country. It's no different here."

"I'll take my chances," Steven said quietly. "If they come, they come. Go home to your mother, Clara. She'll take care of you for tonight. My father will have spoken to your father by now."

He went out and closed the bedroom door behind him. He left the apartment quickly, hurried down the passage to the elevator. He had dismissed his car and bodyguard. They thought he was staying home for the evening. Outside, he set off down the street to find a taxi.

"He's left his clothes," Clara said. She had stopped crying.

Aldo Fabrizzi put his arm around her shoulders. "So you see, it was just a fight he had with that old slob Lucca. He'll be back, you'll see."

"No." She shook her head, refusing his comfort. "He meant it, Papa. He's gone. I told you, he's gone forever. He's quit the family; he's quit me."

Her mother tried to help. "An overnight bag means overnight. Maybe a day or two. Men get notions sometimes. He'll work it out."

Clara ignored her. She meant well, but she was stupid. Clara couldn't tolerate her stupidity at that moment. She needed her father's shrewdness.

"Why hasn't Lucca called you? He's cursed his own son and thrown him out. He has to tell you; he has to make it known to everyone."

"He hasn't called," her father stated. "That's a good sign. Now, Clara, sweetheart, calm yourself, eh? Go wash up and we'll have something to eat. You stay with us tonight. Mama's right: men get notions, they act like they're crazy, but then they see sense. Luisa, how about some dinner?"

His wife hurried away to the kitchen. She prepared the meals because Aldo liked her cooking and refused to have a cook in the house. His wife had fuck all else to do, he thought bitterly, with no grandchildren to take up her time.

Aldo looked tenderly at his daughter. He hated to see her desolate. He couldn't bear it when she cried when she was a little girl. It was worse now that she was a woman. How he hated that son of a bitch— he'd never made Clara happy, never given her children. There had been no joy in the last few years. Still, she loved him. If she was right and he had quarreled with his father and walked out, then a joint sentence would be passed on him. Clara would be free to find another, better man. He went out to the kitchen to talk it over with his wife.

"My daughter comes home saying she's been deserted, and what do I do about it? Nothing! What kind of a father am I, eh? I wait for that arsehole Falconi to give me the news that his goddamn son has fucked up, while she sits crying. . . ." He glared around him, as if Steven or his father were in view.

His wife said, "You think it's true, Aldo? You think he's really left her?"

"I don't know," he muttered. "I was just talking for her benefit out there, not because I believe it myself, for Christ's sake. I'm going to call Lucca. I'm going to tell him we have Clara here and I want to know what kind of crap we've been given!" He strode to the kitchen phone, where Clara couldn't hear him.

The telephone was answered by Piero. He didn't wait for Aldo to explode. He said, overriding him, "We have a family crisis. A crisis for your family too. My brother—" He managed to pause for emphasis, and his own emotion made it sound very real. "My brother has broken our father's heart. . . . My father can't talk to you, no. He's upset. He can't talk to anyone. . . . You say Clara is with you? . . . Yeah, I'm sure. My father wants a family conference. Tomorrow. He says will you come to the house. No women. Just us, the family. He says can you say nothing to anyone till tomorrow. . . . Okay. . . . Believe me, for what he's done I could cut his balls off. . . . Tomorrow early—ten o'clock." He forced himself to say, "Give love to Clara from Lucia and the kids," and then hung up.

Aldo Fabrizzi put the telephone back. His wife looked up at him. "It's true," he said. "He's screwed up on them too. We don't tell Clara tonight. Let her eat something and get some sleep. I see them tomorrow, and I'll know what to do. I'm going to twist their balls for this, Luisa. No son of a bitch shames Aldo Fabrizzi's daughter!"

He stopped himself from slamming the kitchen door. Wiping the rage off his face, he went back to Clara. "We'll eat soon," he said soothingly. "Let's take some wine together first, eh? And you smile for your Papa, will you?" He reached over and patted her hand. It felt cold.

"I'll try," she promised. "Maybe you're right. Maybe he just blew his top and he'll come back when he's cooled off."

"Maybe," her father agreed. "Now you drink this—put some color back in the cheeks. And don't worry. Leave everything to me."

The flight was called. Angela got up, with Charlie beside her. She had discreetly searched the terminal, watching the doors until the very last minute. But after hearing the boarding call, she lost hope. They joined the line of passengers and proceeded onto the aircraft. They were settled in their seats, hand luggage stowed away.

Charlie saw his mother's white face and said, "Don't worry, Mum. You're not scared of flying, are you?" She hadn't minded the trip out.

In fact, she'd been as excited about it as he was. He dug into his pocket. "Here you are—have a candy. I bought some specially. They're jolly good. And by the way . . ."

"Yes?" she said, willing herself to smile at him.

"It's been the most super holiday," he said. "Thanks for everything."

"I'm so glad, darling," Angela said. The candy bar was soft and sticky in its wrapper. "I'll keep it for later," she told him.

She opened the book she'd bought for the journey and tried to make sense of the first page. It could have been Chinese. There were tears stinging her eyes, blurring the print. She mustn't let her son see. She was reminded of another journey, so long ago, on the hospital ship with her unborn child, and the agony that tore at her heart. It was no less this time. She felt her son tugging at her sleeve.

"Mum! Mum, look! There's Mr. Falconi. Gosh, he's on our plane!"

He was astonished by his mother's behavior. The book fell on the floor and she was up in her seat, twisted around to look as Mr. Falconi came down the aisle toward her. And then pushing past Charlie, not even waiting till he got up.

And there was Mr. Falconi, blocking the aisle for the latecomers behind him, saying to his mother, as he held both her hands, "I thought I was going to miss it."

And his mother smiling and out of breath, as if something wonderful had happened, like winning the lottery or inheriting a fortune. "I thought . . . I thought you'd missed it too."

Then he was ushered away up to the front by the stewardess. Charlie bent down and picked up the book. His mother had trodden on it in her haste. Her high heel had scored right across the sickly-looking heroine on the front cover.

"I don't want that, darling," she said.

She was flushed and laughing at him, and he said, "Mum, did you know he was going to be on the same plane?"

"No, no, I didn't. But I was praying he would be!" And she linked her arm through his and squeezed it hard. "I'll tell you all about it," she said. "I promise."

The light came on, instructing passengers to put out all cigarettes and fasten their seat belts. The engines gained power, filling the cabin with a roar of thrusting energy as the plane began to taxi forward.

In a few minutes they were airborne, and the panorama of New

York glittered below them out of the cabin window. Charlie leaned across to stare out.

Then he sat back as the steep climb began. "You're keen on him too, aren't you, Mum?" he said.

"Yes, darling, I am. Is that all right with you?"

"It's great," he said, and grinned at her. "I like him a lot. If you don't want that candy bar, can I have it?"

Piero turned from the window, letting the lace curtain drift back into place. "They're here," he said to his father.

"How many?"

"Aldo and that kike lawyer of his. Two of his people beside the driver."

"Let them in," Lucca Falconi said. He went to his favorite chair and sat down. The garden wasn't an appropriate place for this meeting. He was in mourning for a lost son. The gloomy sitting room was just right. There was Chianti on the table. A big silver box of cigars. He looked like a man who had suffered a heavy blow. He looked like a man who was grieving. All this was true, but he must also look like a man who hated his own son, who had banished him from his life and forbidden his name to be spoken. Aldo Fabrizzi would not be easily fooled. He had brought his lawyer to talk terms for Clara. Lucca got up heavily, as if he had grown suddenly older, and shook hands with Fabrizzi.

"You know Joe Hyman? I brought him along to speak for my daughter." Fabrizzi's eyes were like arrow slits in a stone wall.

"Come in; take some wine. Piero, you pour, will you? Mr. Hyman, you'll have a glass?"

"Thank you, but I don't drink alcohol this early."

"It's not alcohol," Lucca said sharply. "It's wine." He turned away. He hated Jews. He hated Poles and the Irish too. He looked at Aldo Fabrizzi and said, "We have trouble, my friend." He spoke in the dialect. He wondered if Hyman understood. Probably, since he worked for Fabrizzi, he would know Italian. But not the dialect.

"You have trouble, and so does my daughter," Fabrizzi agreed. "Is he sick in his head?"

"I don't know," Lucca answered. "Better if he was. There are doctors, clinics, for that kind of trouble."

"Then why?" The question came out like spilled gravel. "Why has he left Clara and betrayed his family? Betrayed you and me both."

It was Piero who answered. They had rehearsed the scene together, and he came in on cue. "Because he's a yellow shit! Because ever since someone took a shot at him last year, he's been peeing in his pants."

He stopped as his father held up his hand. "You speak when I tell you, Piero. You have a big mouth. He's still your brother."

"He's no brother of mine," Piero insisted. "And no son of yours either!" He gulped down a glass of wine and glared at Aldo and the Jewish lawyer. Piero had a reputation for violence. He was believed, he could see that. He sat down. He'd played his part for the moment.

Lucca said, "Maybe Piero is right. He talked about enemies. He said to me here in this room, 'I've had enough of the business. I want out. I've had enough of the family.' I reminded him. I told him what he owed to me, to our traditions. To Clara. What kind of a life will you give her? I asked him, and he stands there and says, 'I'm going alone.'

"I ordered him, Aldo. I pleaded, I begged. I never thought I'd live to see such disrespect from my own son. I gave him everything. You know how much I loved him. He was my eldest boy. I did everything for him. And he spits in my face and says he doesn't want it. He doesn't want what I've made for him."

Aldo said nothing for a time. Then he shifted in his seat and said simply, "I feel for you, my friend. But you have a good boy left. Me, I have only my Clara, and her heart is breaking. It's a dishonor, you know that."

"I know it," Lucca agreed. "Those were my last words before I cursed him as his father. You've dishonored both families; that's what I said. You're a coward and a traitor. You've no balls, and you're not my son." A tear glinted in his eye, and he let it drop onto his cheek. "Ask what you want, Aldo. I'll pay the price of his dishonor to you and to Clara."

"Where has he gone?"

They had been waiting for that question. "He wouldn't say," Piero answered. "He wouldn't tell Papa. He knows what's coming to him. There ain't no pisshole where he can hide after this!"

Aldo said quietly, "You're looking for him?"

"The word has been passed," Lucca Falconi said. "He'll be found. I think he's gone West. But we'll hear. It'll take time, that's all. When we find him, I'll do what has to be done."

"You'll need a good man," Aldo said. He glanced at his lawyer. "He may have no balls now, but he had them plenty in the war. We take care of him together, Lucca. That way, our interests are safe. And Clara holds her head up again. You talked about a price."

"It's only what's due to her." Lucca nodded. "And to you. I will provide for Clara."

Aldo signified his satisfaction. He grunted. "You're a man of honor," he said. "But first we have to talk about the business. Who's taking over from *him*?" He wouldn't lower himself to mention Steven by name.

"Piero," Lucca answered. "And there's a cousin in Florida who's a good man with figures. They'll take care of everything together. I'm sending for the cousin. You will meet him; I know you'll think he's a good choice. Tino Spoletto, my uncle's sister's grandson. He's done good work in Florida."

"When does he get here?" Aldo asked. He had never heard of the Spolettos before now. An idea was being born as he spoke. A very small, unformed idea, but growing. If the Falconis were bringing in relatives that distant, then they weren't as strong on the administrative side as they made out. And Piero was a muscleman. Twenty years ago he'd have been running protection rackets from the street. He'd never have seen the inside of that plush uptown office.

Lucca was answering. "Two weeks. He has to move his wife and family; find a place to live."

He signaled to Piero, who refilled their glasses. The lawyer accepted a cigar. Nobody lit it for him.

Piero said in dialect, "With my father's permission, I'd like to ask something."

"Ask," Lucca commanded.

Piero bunched his fists and squared his shoulders. He summoned hatred. He thought of Clara and the Fabrizzis, who were forcing him to denounce and revile his brother.

"I want to be the one who puts out the contract. I want to do it and come to you, Don Aldo, and my father, and say, 'It's done. I've wiped out the dishonor to my family.' "

Lucca didn't hesitate. "I give permission, my son. I give the responsibility to you."

"I said we should do it together," Aldo Fabrizzi interposed. "It must be a joint contract."

Lucca paused. It was going as he had expected. He was proud of Piero. Piero was doing very well.

"Give Piero three months," he said slowly.

"A month," Aldo amended, knowing it would be nearly impossible to track down the miscreant in so short a time.

"A month," Falconi father and son agreed together. "We guarantee it."

They had caught him, and he accepted it. "One month, thirty days. After that we join you in the contract."

"Agreed," Lucca Falconi said.

"Maybe," Aldo suggested, as if it were of little consequence to the main issue, "you and me and Joe here should talk about some money for Clara?"

"The fucking house and half a million dollars!"

"We couldn't offer less." Lucca calmed his son. "You know that. You don't think I want to give them anything. You think I like giving money to that barren bitch?"

"It won't buy them off," Piero responded. "No matter what you give them, they'll want Steven's head on a fucking plate!" He got up and banged his hand flat on the table; the empty glasses jumped. "How're we going to do it, Papa? How're we going to fool them?"

The old man looked up at him. He looked sad and tired, and it grieved Piero to see his grief.

"I should be strong," Lucca muttered. "He's betrayed us all. I shouldn't protect him. I should be strong."

"You love him," Piero said. "I love him too. This isn't Sicily, Papa. I've got Lucia and the kids to go home to; he had nothing. You're being a strong man. I believe that."

"I can't forgive him," Lucca said. "I can't forgive what he's done."

"You don't have to," his son said. "But that's between us. Our family. We're not making a blood sacrifice for the Fabrizzis. So I ask you again. How do we fool them?"

"We give them someone else," Lucca Falconi said. "Before the month is up. You said you would fix it."

Piero nodded. "I'll fix it. Now, Papa, I'm going to call Mama. You look tired, you know that? And I'm going to tell her not to worry. She's been out there crying since those bastards came in here. And I'll call Lucia. You and Mama come over to our house for dinner tonight. See the kids before they go to bed. It'll cheer Mama up. And you too, maybe."

"You're a good son," was what Lucca said as Piero went out. *A good son with a brave heart, but it's going to take all we've got to keep Aldo Fabrizzi from cutting our throats now that your brother's gone.*

Clara rounded on her father. "I don't want him dead! I don't want that, you hear me? I want him back!"

Aldo pitied her. He hated to see her crying and tearing herself to pieces, but she couldn't move him. He said, as his people had done for centuries before him, "It's a matter of honor, Clara." There was no appeal from that sentence. She should know this; for all the education and the fancy ways she'd adopted, she was a Sicilian, and she knew as well as he did what had to be done. She couldn't move him. He said, "I'm sorry, my little girl, but that's the way it is. If the Falconis don't find him in thirty days, then we find him. Now dry your eyes; go help your mother."

Clara glared at him. As if she were a child: Stop weeping over the broken toy, *carissima,* and go help your mother in the kitchen.

"No!" she shouted at him. "I'm going home. I'm getting out of here." She brushed her mother aside when she tried to reason with her. Aldo stayed silent, reading a newspaper, while the women argued. She'd go, but she'd be back. Luisa didn't know how to handle her; she'd never been any good with Clara. He heard the front door slam. His wife came back into the sitting room. She sat down.

"She's crazy," she said. "I don't understand her. I don't understand how she could want a man who's done this to her."

"It doesn't matter what she wants," her husband said. He lowered the newspaper for a moment. "I've spoiled her, that's the truth of it. Whatever she wanted, I said yes. But not now. She'll learn to live with it."

Clara let herself into the house. The box with her new hats was still on the table in the sitting room, the ribbons untied. His empty glass was by the sofa. The emptiness, the silence, made her want to turn and run out into the street again. She walked into the bedroom. How long since he had come there to make love to her? Too long to bear remembering. Her frantic pleading mocked her. "Take me with you. . . . They can throw me out too." But he had rejected her. Not cruelly, but with kindness. The kindness of finality. She couldn't cry anymore.

Maybe her father was right. Maybe the old solution to misery and betrayal was the only way. In the old days, the women kissed the wounds of their dead and cried out for vendetta. That cry was answered until the last member of the offending family had been killed.

Perhaps when Steven was dead, she might begin to live her life, to be free of the jealousy that tortured her, free of the desire that had brought her groveling to him in the past. She kicked off her shoes and lay on the bed. How many nights she had lain there, waiting for him to come in, imagining the woman he was with.

Her eyes closed; she was near falling asleep from exhaustion. Then they opened suddenly, and she sat up. There had been a woman. The agency hadn't found her because someone had murdered the investigator and trashed the business. Steven had done it. Someone had alerted him that he was being watched. So the order was given, and that was the end of the agency. And then he walks out. He walks out on his whole life, just like that.

She reached for the telephone. "Papa?"

"I'm eating, Clara." He was angry with her.

She said, "Papa, forgive me. I was wrong. I'm sorry."

"It's forgotten," he said. "You want to come home?"

"No. I'll stay here overnight. But I want to tell you something. When they find Steven, I don't think he'll be alone. I just want you to know that."

She rang off before he could ask for explanations.

"Are you happy?" Angela asked him.

"You know I am." He looked down at her. "I miss the boy. He didn't want to go."

"I know he didn't, but you mustn't spoil him, darling. He adores you, that's the trouble. But he had to go home and get ready for school. I'll have to go too."

In London, Steven had gone ahead of them; he didn't want them to check in together. He explained to Charlie that he had business to attend to and he'd meet them at the Savoy Hotel that afternoon. Angela filled in the time for the boy with lunch and a movie.

Steven went directly to the hotel, where he registered under the name of Franks and booked Angela and their son into a separate suite. He wasn't known at the Savoy, and once installed in his own suite, he knew he must stay out of sight. He examined himself in the bathroom mirror and rubbed his fingers across the dark stubble that was already growing after the flight and no morning shave.

He had always been clean-shaven, dark and smooth-skinned. A beard would alter his appearance. A beard, a false passport, a driver's license under a new name, and a few touches of gray in his hair. Nature provided the best camouflage. It wouldn't take long.

He checked the time; it was morning in New York. Asking for an outside line, he dialed his brother's number.

"It's me," he said. "Just to say I've booked in at this number. . . . Yeah, everything's okay. Send the documents here, addressed to Franks."

Piero protested. "Why pick a kike name, for Christ's sake?" He was pathological about Jews.

Steven ignored it. "How's Mama?"

"Okay. She's upset; you know how she is. I'll tell her that we talked. You keep out of sight, you hear me? No risks. It's red hot here. The whole fucking neighborhood is talking about you walking out on Clara and the family."

Steven could imagine. "Don't worry," he reassured his brother. "I'm lying low. I need those documents. Hurry them up, can't you?"

"They'll be there," Piero promised.

Steven hung up. Then he called Angela and Charlie to ask them to his suite.

They were so happy, the three of them. Charlie thought his idea of growing a beard was a fun thing to do. He accepted that Steven couldn't go out until the scruffy growth had thickened and he looked respectable. The boy had only one week left before he had to go back to school, and Angela kept him busy with shopping and expeditions.

But she insisted on taking him back to school alone, leaving Steven behind.

"What am I going to do without you?" he persisted. "Why can't we go to your father's and then take Charlie back to school together? You can't hide me, Angelina."

"I don't want to hide you," she protested. "Darling, try to be patient. Give me a little time to think of something. I can't just turn up with you and say to my father, 'This is my husband. He wasn't killed after all. I told you a pack of lies.' And what's Charlie going to say?"

"All right." He turned away from her. "I won't argue. But I'm not staying here for long. I want my son, and I want you. That's why I'm here."

"I know," she pleaded. "I know, darling, but it's not so simple."

"It wasn't simple for me either," he said. "I've gotten so close to my boy, I feel I've known him all his life. We've done everything together, just like a family. Charlie accepted that. He's accepted me like a father. So you're going to have to square it, Angela. Because I won't wait around. Now I'm going out for a while."

She called out, "Steven darling, please. You can't!"

"I can," he said. "I don't look like myself anymore. To tell you the truth, I don't know who the hell I am."

He left the suite without saying when he would be back.

She cried a little, because she couldn't bear to be at odds with him. He'd been so generous, so loving. She sat by the window and looked out across the Embankment to the Thames. It was dusk, and the lights were springing up along the opposite bank, with a thin mist rising from the river. He'd given up everything to be with her and with his son. He'd left his family, friends, job. Of course he was feeling disoriented. And she was hesitating, thinking of petty things like local gossip and facing her father with an old lie that didn't matter anymore. Charlie would accept whatever they told him. She had seen him and his father grow so close in such a short time. The bond between them was instinctive.

When he came back hours later, she was waiting for him. He looked at her. He didn't smile.

"Where have you been?" she asked. "I was worried."

"I took a walk."

"Steven . . ." She came and put her arms around him. "You're right. I've been selfish and stupid. I'm so very sorry, darling. I telephoned my father while you were out. I said we'd be home tomorrow and I was bringing someone with me. Someone very special."

"You mean it?" He raised her face and looked into her eyes. "You really want it like that? I didn't mean to pressure you."

She managed to laugh at him. "Oh, yes you did," she said. "I've been sitting here feeling perfectly bloody for the past three hours. Are you happy now?"

"I'm happy," he said, and began to kiss her.

"Well," Dr. Drummond said. He'd said it three times. "Well, I don't know what to say."

He looked at his daughter and back to the man who sat beside her, holding her hand protectively. It was so confusing, such a shock, he couldn't quite take it in. My husband, she'd said. Charlie's real father. No, he wasn't killed. I told you a lie. And then the American interrupted, defending her.

"It wasn't her fault. She was right to do what she did. I wanted her to live in the States, bring up the child with my family. I scared her off. I asked too much of her. Now I want to make it up to her."

"I still don't understand it," the old man said. "It's all so very extraordinary. Of course, as soon as Angela said she was bringing someone home, I thought there was something in the wind, but I never expected this."

"Not even when you saw him and Charlie together?" Angela asked.

Her father looked surprised. "No. Why should I?" The beard had certainly disguised him. . . .

"They're very alike," his daughter pointed out.

He considered for a moment. "I suppose so. They're dark, you could say that. But I still don't see why you said he was dead." He returned to the lie that seemed so unnecessary and so vexing. "What a silly, irresponsible thing to do!"

Angela answered, "I *was* silly and irresponsible, Daddy."

"Didn't you mind?" he demanded of Steven.

"I don't mind now," he said. "It was like a miracle when we found each other in New York."

"Must have been," Hugh Drummond agreed. He cleared his throat and groped for his pipe, not knowing what to say next. They seemed happy enough. He was a fine-looking man; no wonder she hadn't wanted poor old Jim. He must have seemed like a stick-in-the-mud after this fellow.

"Does Charlie know?" he said suddenly. "It's going to be quite a shock for him, you must realize that. What's he going to think of you, Angela?"

"We're not saying anything yet," Steven answered. "He's going back to school. It's a busy time for him. He's got his studies to think about. There'll be time enough. But we wanted you to know the situation."

"I think that's very wise," he said. "If I were him, I wouldn't be pleased to find out I'd been told a lot of lies." He gave his daughter an accusing look. He was thinking of his grandson. What they did with their own lives was their business, but he wouldn't countenance their upsetting the boy. "God knows what your mother would have made of it all," he announced, and having stuffed his pipe, he began to puff hard as he held the match to the bowl. Angela was wearing a big green stone on her left hand. He didn't know what it was. He wasn't much on gemstones, and the thing was too large to be anything he would recognize.

"How are you going to live?" he asked Steven that night, while Charlie helped his mother wash up the dinner dishes. "Do you have a job over here?"

"Not yet," Steven answered. "But there's no need to worry. I've got assets."

"Depends," Hugh Drummond muttered. "Most shares bring in a pittance these days. As for government bonds . . . biggest damn swindle, if you ask me. We all bought them to be patriotic."

Steven was glad Angela wasn't there. He understood the old man's need to ask questions, but he had a need of his own to answer them. She would have been embarrassed.

"I'm worth over a million dollars in stocks and bonds, and I have property in the States worth more," he said.

"Good God!" Angela's father stared at him. "Good God. Have you really?"

"Really," Steven echoed him. "So like I said, you don't need to worry. I can take care of them."

"I should think so," was the answer. "Nice to know anyway. I've left this house and whatever I've got to my grandson. Angela's got a bit from her mother, but I wanted Charlie to have something behind him. He won't need it now, I suppose."

"He'll need it," Steven answered. "He'll be proud to have it because it came from you. He talks a lot about you."

"Does he?" The old man smiled with pleasure. "Does he indeed? I think the world of him. He's a fine chap in every way. Straight as a die. And clever too. He'll do well, make no mistake."

At the door of her single room, Angela held out her arms to him. "This is a nuisance, I know," she said. "But it can't be helped. It's only till Charlie goes back to school."

He held her close. "I can wait," he whispered. "So long as it's not too long. It wasn't as bad as you thought, was it?"

"No. I'd imagined all kinds of reactions from my father. He can be very difficult. He's mellowed a lot, and all he really cares about is Charlie. But he was good about it, and you were wonderful with him. Thank you, darling."

"I'm used to old people," he said. "We're brought up to respect them. It's important to us. Did you see our boy's face when we said we were both taking him back to school?"

"Yes." Angela nodded. "He was thrilled. When shall we tell him?"

"Tomorrow," Steven said. "I'll tell him. But I guess he knows already."

"I'm going down to get some groceries for your mother," Steven announced. "How about coming along?" As they walked back toward the house from the High Street, Steven said, "There's something I want to tell you."

The boy looked up at him. "About you and Mum?"

"We're going to get married, Charlie. Would you like that?"

"Gosh, I'll be thrilled skinny!" There was no flicker of doubt, no hesitation. His smile was a delighted grin. "I thought you might when you turned up on the plane. It's super news. Just super!"

"I want to make your mother very happy," Steven Falconi said. "And I want to be a father to you, Charlie, if you'll let me."

For a moment his son looked shy. There was a little color in his cheeks that was close to a blush. "It's felt a bit like that already," he said. "I hope you don't mind."

"I don't mind," Steven said. "It's what I want most of all."

If they hadn't been walking along a damp English country street with grocery bags in their arms, he'd have taken his son in his arms and embraced him.

They drove back to London from the school at Highfields. Steven had been introduced to everyone as "Mr. Falconi, my stepfather." The headmaster congratulated them and asked them in for a glass of sherry. It was a strange world to Steven, with a code of conduct that was so alien to him that he might have been among Martians. He sipped the bad sherry and answered the predictable questions about how he liked

England and where he came from in the United States. Only they called it America, with shortened vowels. He felt as if he was just as alien to them. He hoped the education was good and that the school was the best available. There were a lot of things he didn't know about, things he might want to change. He escaped from the headmaster's stifling sitting room as soon as he could make an excuse.

But Charlie was doing well. He was a credit to this old, rigid system. The formality, the distance between the pupils and the staff, which was so evident, had produced his son. He mustn't forget that. He must give himself time to adjust.

In the car on the way back, Angela said, "I know you thought they were stuffy, darling. But they run that school very well. And he's so happy there. You could see that."

"Sure he is," he said. "It's all so different from back home, that's all."

He squeezed her hand and smiled. He didn't say anything, but he had already made up his mind that he didn't want to live in England. When they arrived at the Savoy there was a message for him from Piero, the only one who knew where to find him. He checked the time. His brother would be home by now. It wouldn't be safe to make contact through the office. While Angela bathed and changed to go to the Grill for dinner, he put the call through.

Lucia answered. She said, "Wait, I'll get him." She was a good woman. Not even in front of her own children would she call him by his name.

Piero came on the line. "It's okay," he said. "Lucia's taken the kids upstairs. How are you?"

"I'm fine," Steven said. "Just fine. I've grown a beard. Even you wouldn't know me! How are Papa and Mama? How are things?"

"Okay, no problems. They came, had a meeting. We worked out the details. We paid your wife off."

"Don't call her that," Steven protested. "How much?"

"Too fuckin' much," Piero said. "Half a million smackers and the house. You should've let me take care of her when I offered. Now listen. You got something you can send me? Clara gave you a wedding ring, didn't she?"

It was still on his finger, on the right hand.

"Yes," he said. "It's engraved with the date. My initials and hers."

"Send it," Piero said. "Right away. You going to be at this number for a while?"

"A month, maybe more." He paused. "What are you going to do, Piero? What's my father going to do?"

"Fake an accident," Piero answered. "Send Fabrizzi the ring. That way he'll be convinced. Don't worry about it. Stay low and take good care, eh? How's the kid? He okay?"

For a moment Steven pictured the headmaster's sitting room, with its hard chairs, the walls covered with rows of boys posing for team photographs. Cricket. Football. The taste of sweet, cheap sherry.

"He's fine," he said. "We just left him at school. Kiss Mama, will you? Say to Papa . . . well, you know what to say."

"Send me that goddamned ring," Piero said, and hung up.

Angela came into the room. She wore the same slim black dress he had seen that night at Les Ambassadeurs. Her hair was loose and shining, the way he liked it.

"I'm ready, darling. How was your brother? Nothing wrong, is there?"

He came and took her hands. "Everything's okay. . . . You're beautiful, Angelina. Let's go to dinner. I've got plans I want to talk over with you."

They flew to Monte Carlo in November. The weather in London was cold and miserable, with days of drizzling rain. They stepped off the plane beneath blue skies and into pleasant, warm air. A hired car waited for them. He took Angela's arm and hurried her across the road and into it. Then he checked himself. There was no need to move quickly, to seek shelter. All that was in the past. But habits die hard. He still felt uncomfortable sitting in the middle of a public place without a wall at his back.

He had bought her a mink coat, which she carried over her arm. She didn't need it in the mild midwinter of the Côte d'Azur.

"It's so beautiful," she said, gazing out the window at the bright sea below them, the land falling away from the curve of the Moyenne Corniche. Palm trees and handsome villas, charming little fishing villages clinging to the edge of the ports. "Darling, I'd no idea it was like this. I thought it would be dry and dusty. Like Sicily."

"I thought you liked Sicily," he said.

"I liked you, not the place," she corrected. "This is green and pretty."

"It's a soft country for soft people," Steven told her. "Too much money. Too much of everything. Sicilians are hard because they've had to be."

"You're not hard," she said gently. "That's what I love about you."

"Not with you," he said.

"Not with Charlie either," she said. "You'll spoil him to death if I let you."

"I'm disappointed they wouldn't let him come," he said. "For one weekend. It's no big deal, but they wouldn't let him."

"Of course they wouldn't." Angela shook her head. "He's only just gone back. How could they let him fly out here when everyone else was getting down to the term's work? Be reasonable, darling. I told you it was impossible, but you *would* ring up and ask."

"I hate that sonofabitch headmaster," Steven said. "Back home, they'd have let a boy go for a weekend with his parents. Don't let's talk about it, sweetheart. You're used to being pushed around by creeps like that. I'm not. I hope you like the place where we're staying. It's not fancy, but it's comfortable. We can drive across into Monte Carlo inside of twenty minutes."

"Are we going to the casino?"

He looked out the car window. They were descending onto the coast road now. The signposts said Villefranche. They were very near.

"No," he said. "Not the casino. I've been there. Someone would remember me. These guys have photographic memories. They never forget a face or a name."

Angela said, "How can you trust this man Maxton?"

"He's no friend to the families," Steven answered. "They busted him for everything he had in Nevada. That's why the casino down here employed him. They've always kept our people out. We'll talk. If he doesn't like my proposition, I'll think of something else."

"You could have started up in London," she reminded him. They had argued about that, but Steven was adamant. Too many links with the States.

She was thinking of Charlie at school in England while they lived in France. It had sounded so easy when she spoke to him about it in New York. Easy for him too. There were always holidays and half terms and the important things in a boy's life, like Sports Days and prize-giving.

She closed her mind to the misgivings. She had to think of Steven Falconi first—of his need for identity and purpose, and above all for safety.

Villefranche enchanted her. It was like a toy fishing port, with little boats lined up in the harbor, a few restaurants still open for local patronage. The season was long over, and except for themselves, the little hotel was empty. It was more of a guesthouse, with all services performed by the patron and his wife. Offering a tariff that was plainly a bribe, Steven had persuaded them to open specially.

They had dinner on the quay: good fish, rough wine from the nearby vineyards. She gathered the scraps and gave them to the starving cats that roamed outside. The other customers thought she must be American or English to waste good food on animals.

Steven apologized for the accommodations. "It's not for long. Just till I talk with Maxton. Then I've got a surprise for you, darling."

"I wish you wouldn't be so silly," Angela said. "I love it here. You forget, I'm not used to luxury and smart hotels. This is my idea of heaven, just the two of us and this dear little place.... What sort of surprise? I don't trust you, Steven."

"You're right." He laughed at her. "But I think you'll be pleased. I hope so. I love to see you looking happy."

"I'm very happy." She reached out and held his hand. "I love you so much. And it changes all the time. I'm so glad you got rid of that wedding ring. I hated you wearing it."

"Why didn't you say so? I don't know why I wore it. What do you want for a wedding present, Angelina?"

"Darling," she chided him. He was always buying her presents. The mink coat had been chosen without her and brought back to the Savoy as one of his many surprises. "I've got an engagement ring, my coat, all the clothes you've bought me. I don't want anything except the marriage certificate that makes it legal for Charlie. If it weren't for him and Daddy, I wouldn't care a damn. I'm married already."

"It'll be great having him here," Steven said. "And your father. He's quite a character."

"He likes you," she said. "It's funny. He was always so offhand with me and my brother when we were children. When I see him doting on Charlie and spoiling him, I can't believe it's the same person. It'll be strange, won't it, getting married in a registry office?"

"It's only for the piece of paper. But we'll make it special. You'll see."

The next day she left him behind and drove across to Monte Carlo. The man Ralph Maxton was coming to see him at the hotel. Without realizing it, Angela had accepted the Mafia principle that women had no part in business.

Monte Carlo. She'd seen movies featuring the casino, where Hollywood heroes broke the bank. She'd read about the gala evenings and the celebrities. Lady Docker had become a national figure to the British, starved of glamour by the war and the mean years of austerity after it. Millionaires were rare and enviable creatures; their wives, draped in diamonds and mink, were even more so. Monte Carlo was the dream setting for a fantasy world, presided over by a prince who had married a beautiful American film star.

It was beautiful; more beautiful than Angela had imagined, with its backdrop of blue, its cloud-wreathed mountains and the sugar-candy palace perched on a rock overlooking the sea.

She parked the car and walked. There were huge yachts, ocean-going by their size and tonnage, moored in the harbor, their pennants flapping in a stiff breeze. The shops were opulent, discreet, and they boasted the great names in French haute couture, the jewelers of world renown—Van Cleef & Arpels, Boucheron, Cartier. She passed the glittering windows, pausing now and then to admire without wanting to possess. When she reached the splendid wedding-cake facade of the casino itself, she was amazed to see that its doors were open and people were hurrying inside. Middle-aged Frenchwomen, most of them housewives with shopping baskets on their arms, were slipping in for a morning session in the Petit Salon, where the stakes were a few francs. And there were men too, ordinarily, even poorly dressed, driven by the same demon that possessed the rich who would come later in the day—greed and hope.

She had read somewhere that for some unfortunates, it was the thrill of losing that impelled them. She wished Steven had chosen another business, something that wasn't tainted by human weakness and venality. Impulse made her turn and go into a very large and expensive-looking hotel. There were no street cafés open where she was, and the harbor was a long walk down. She was tired and rather cold. It was a very handsome hotel, and a polite receptionist directed her to the cocktail bar. It was empty; she almost turned back. Then the barman smiled at her.

"Madame?"

She said, "Would it be possible to order some coffee?"

"Coffee is served in the lounge, madame," he said.

"Thank you." She didn't know where the lounge was. She felt

conspicuous and silly for having come in. Then there was a movement, and she saw that she wasn't alone after all. A woman was sitting at a table in a corner, playing patience. She had silvery hair under the soft overhead light. Angela sat down. The barman came to her table.

She said, "Gin and tonic," because it was the first thing she could think of. He brought it with a dish of olives and cheese straws. The bill was tucked underneath. The drink was iced and made her shiver. She drank half of it and decided to go. She put down a five-franc note and got up. She didn't want to wait for change. As she left the table, the woman packed away her playing cards and turned around to signal the barman. Angela saw her fully in the light and just managed not to catch her breath. It was a travesty of a face. The left eye was covered with a patch; the nose was spread unnaturally, and there was a deep indentation where the right cheekbone should have been. Obviously she had suffered a terrible accident and had undergone extensive plastic surgery.

Her good eye was dark and large, with a penetrating stare that raked Angela from head to foot. The woman raised her hand and snapped her fingers imperiously, diamonds flashing. The barman hurried over. He carried a bumper of champagne. Angela kept her head down, avoiding the poor woman. How terrible if people stared.

It was really quite sharp outside. She should have brought her coat. She walked very briskly down to where the car was parked and drove back faster than she meant to. Maxton would have gone by now. She wanted to get back to the warmth and coziness of their hotel, to find Steven waiting for her. She couldn't get the woman's broken face out of her mind.

"Mr. Lawrence?" Ralph Maxton was little changed. The nose seemed more prominent, the hair looked thinner at the temples, but otherwise he was the same. They shook hands briefly.

Steven said, "What can I get you? A drink? Some coffee?"

Maxton shook his head. "Nothing, thanks." He considered the tall, bearded American closely. The name Lawrence meant nothing to him. Only the desperate situation he was in had made him agree to the appointment with a stranger out of nowhere. Lawrence. A stranger and yet not quite . . . He leaned forward. "I have the feeling that we've met before," he said lightly. "And of course I'm curious to know how you heard about me."

"I approached the casino at Monte Carlo," Steven said coolly. "Someone had a forwarding address."

"A recommendation?" Maxton inquired. "From a mutual friend? I must admit I can't think whom we have in common among our acquaintances?" He ended the sentence as a question.

Steven had anticipated the situation, but decided to play it by ear. The pale eyes were very shrewd; he wasn't a man to ask that sort of question without expecting an answer.

"You have a good memory, Mr. Maxton," Steven said. "I came to the casino with some friends. A long time ago. But before we go any further, there're a few questions I want to ask you. Why did you leave the casino?"

"We had a disagreement," he said. "The management and I decided to part."

"What sort of disagreement?"

Maxton looked into the shrewd face opposite him and decided not to waste time telling lies.

"I started gambling," he said. "I hadn't turned a card or touched a chip in ten years, and then one day I gave a friend some money and told him to play the wheel for me. We got away with it a few times, and then they called me in and said I was sacked. I'd broken the sacred house rule. After ten years I was out. No compensation, nothing."

"Did you make money?"

Maxton gave the short, high-pitched laugh that Steven remembered.

"Good Lord, no. I always lost. It wasn't that. It was the principle. I saw their point, but I thought they might have been a little more generous than they were. I'd given them good service."

"I'm sure. So how long has it been?"

"A year." He reached into his pocket and took out a packet of Gitanes. Matches followed. He inhaled and sighed with pleasure.

The cheapest cigarettes and no lighter. It must have been a very long year, Steven judged.

As if Maxton had read his mind, he said, "I couldn't get work anywhere else, of course. Word gets around. I was blackballed. So I did this and that and hung around. I've got used to living here, and I've made some good friends. But . . ." He spread his hands in resignation. "Even their largess started to run out. Not that I blame them. So I was naturally intrigued to get your call."

He talked a lot, Steven noted, but it was a good cover. He was shrewd and intelligent. He wouldn't have lasted ten years with the casino if he hadn't been valuable to them. But for the one weakness.

"I thought I'd chance it." Steven decided to take the initiative. "I remembered meeting you when I came to Monte Carlo. You were doing PR, you said. I made a few inquiries before I called."

"The answers weren't *too* bad, I hope?"

"They told me what I needed to know about you. You were available. So I decided to talk to you about a proposition."

Ralph Maxton stubbed out his cigarette. The movement showed that the edge of his shirt sleeve was frayed.

"Mr. Lawrence," he said. "Before you tell me about this—er— proposition, there's something I must make clear to you. I inherited quite a sum of money when I was twenty-one. I also enjoyed gambling. I enjoyed it so much that it was becoming an embarrassment to my family. They suggested I go to America. My mother had connections in Boston, and there was some talk about banking and business. I didn't pay much attention to work, but I thought America would be fun. I had a pal I'd teamed up with in New York, a Canadian. Such a nice chap. We ended in Las Vegas. He got in so deep, I even went to the gentlemen concerned and actually pleaded with them to let him off. It wasn't a lot of money, actually—his last couple of thousand dollars. They were Italian-American gentlemen. I'd dropped twenty thousand English pounds at their grubby little tables, but they wouldn't even listen. My Canadian friend took a train to the coast one night and walked into the sea. Sorry," he said, producing the cigarettes again, "I'm being long-winded. But I don't and won't touch anything or anyone connected with people like them. Although I'm sure you're not!"

"You needn't trouble yourself on that score," Steven said firmly. "I have the same feeling about the gangster element as you do about your old employers. I want to open a casino here. I want to finance it and run it, but I need a front man, and I need someone who can hire the right staff and get it organized."

"It sounds extremely interesting. Not particularly easy, though. Between the principality, Nice and Cannes, they've got the big-time gambling tied up along the coast. With one exception." Maxton paused. The slightly mocking pose was cast off abruptly. "Antibes is a possibility. It's near Juan-les-Pins. There are fine hotels, lots of rich clients. Grand villas, but no casino. The girls and boys go into Cannes, which isn't that far away, or they come here. You might think about Antibes. Are you planning to build? That's millions, I warn you. And the French will make life as hellish as possible. They hate foreigners coming in."

"I'd thought of buying," Steven said. "If I could find suitable premises."

"Need to be pretty big," Maxton remarked. "And central. That cuts out the old-fashioned Edwardian monstrosities inland. You've got to site it where it can be seen every day. Have you looked yourself?"

"Not yet. As it turns out, I'm going on to Cannes from here with my wife. Day after tomorrow."

"Good opportunity for you to see what's on the market."

"Why don't you come over to Cannes and help me see what's available?"

"I'd be delighted. Does that mean I'm hired?"

"I guess so, if you're happy about it," Steven said. "Five hundred dollars to start. If we find something, we'll talk terms then. I pay in advance."

"I am glad to hear it. My friends'll be even gladder. I can pay some of them back. Thank you, Mr. Lawrence."

"Steven," he insisted. "After you've paid your friends back, get some new clothes. We'll be at the Carlton. Call me there." He stood up.

Maxton's attitude was cool. He was broke, but he showed neither servility nor respect. Steven had never met this type before. He supposed it was peculiar to the English. He didn't like it. But he needed the man. To start with. He held out his hand. It was the families' custom to confirm a deal by clasping hands. Maxton looked surprised for a moment. When he did shake hands, his grip was firm.

Steven said, "I'll make out the check. Or would cash be easier?"

"Cash would be *much* easier. Thank you so much." He took the money Steven proffered and walked to the door. "See you in Cannes," he said.

The acrid smell of Maxton's strong, cheap tobacco pervaded the room. Steven opened the window to clear it away. He wondered suddenly whether he would ever see the man again. A gambler, a sponger; he'd sunk low in the last year. Only that curious arrogance had been untouched by the vicissitudes he'd experienced. Hunger had apparently been one of them: his shabby suit hung on him like a sack. He might take the money and disappear. But Steven knew he wouldn't. Whatever he was, or had become, Ralph Maxton was a man who kept his word.

He'd booked the best suite in the Carlton at Cannes as a surprise for Angela. There was no casino at Antibes, Maxton had said. If he could find a building, get a foothold . . . Maxton knew people. Knowing the right sort of people had been his job in Monaco. Steven's mind was racing ahead, seeing possibilities, excitement rising as it used to when he was planning an expansion of the family interests. He thought of his father and his mother and his brother. He suffered a pang of homesickness, of loneliness for them all, that made him groan aloud. They had stood back-to-back with him when he'd asked. Never mind his father's anger. That was only just. They had been loyal to him. He only wished he could repay them. One day maybe. If this project took off and was a great success, they'd have reason to be proud of him again. To forgive his rejection of the only way of life they knew. To understand that there were other ways to gain respect and maintain honor.

When Angela returned, he took her in his arms and made love as if they had come together after a long separation. And in the evening they sat in the little restaurant that overlooked the sea. He told her briefly about Ralph Maxton.

"You'll see him in a day or two. I'm not saying any more, or it'll spoil my surprise. But it looks good, my darling. Everything's going right for us. We're going to have a wonderful life together. You and me and Charlie." He leaned across and kissed her. Outside the window, the hungry cats were waiting patiently.

"This is my wife, Angela," Steven said. "Ralph Maxton."

"How do you do?" He shook Angela's hand and gave a tiny bow. An English lady: very pretty, poised but rather shy. She gave him a charming smile.

"Have a seat," Steven said. "You'll have a drink, Ralph?"

"Thank you. That would be welcome."

They had entered the second-floor suite, overlooking the Croisette. "Come and meet my wife," was the invitation. Maxton recognized Angela's type as soon as she walked into the sitting room. What the hell, he said to himself while they were introduced, was she doing with someone like Lawrence?

"We've had a busy morning," Steven announced. "But I think we've found what we want, haven't we?"

"I think so," Maxton agreed. "Provided we can get the owner to sell it."

Angela smiled up at her husband. There was no doubt about her feelings for him. "That's wonderful news. But you mean it isn't on the market?"

"No," Steven answered. "It's empty, though. Ralph heard about it. We went through the agents and looked at some properties, but they weren't suitable. Not big enough. Or too far out from the center. This would be ideal if we can get it."

She said to Maxton, "How did you hear of it?"

He was quite an ugly man, with a hook nose and a long, thin face. But after a few minutes one didn't notice, because his manner was so engaging. He gave her his full attention.

"Through friends, Mrs. Lawrence. I've lived and worked in Monte Carlo for some years, and the Riviera's rather like a village. Everyone knows everyone else's business. This building belonged to a Russian aristocrat before the First War. He used to spend the winters here, and he had a French mistress at the time. It was designed on a very grand scale; more like a palace than a villa. When the Revolution came, the count got the chop, and the lady went on living there till she died. Then it was sold to a rich manufacturer, who used to let it, and during the war the Germans requisitioned it. They didn't know quite what to do with it, but it was used as office and storage space. Very little damage was done as a result. A speculator bought it after the war. It was said he meant to sell it as a hotel, but nothing came of it. Too expensive to convert and run, is my guess."

"It must be enormous," Angela said.

"It is," Steven said. She could see that he liked it and was excited. "Too big for anyone to live in, but it would be just right for us. And wait till you see the site!"

"Directly overlooking the sea," Maxton explained. "With about four acres of grounds. They're in a bad state, but they could be landscaped and made rather beautiful. The main coast road runs a hundred yards away from the entrance."

"It's ideal," Steven insisted. "It's perfect."

"When can I see it?" Angela asked.

"Anytime you like, Mrs. Lawrence. I managed to get hold of a key."

He hadn't fooled Steven. They went to the agencies and looked at everything unsuitable just to whet his appetite, and then Ralph had brought him to the great crumbling palace by the sea and produced a key from his pocket.

"A friend of mine knows the owner," he'd explained. "He's had the key for ages in case someone expressed interest, but nothing happened."

"Let's see inside," was all Steven had said.

Double commission. Real commission to the "friend," whoever he or she might be, and hidden commission to Maxton if he brought off the sale. It didn't matter. When the time came, he'd let Maxton know he knew. What was important was the potential of the place. They'd picked their way through the jungle of overgrown garden and into the vast, damp-smelling house, shuttered against vandalism. Steven didn't waste time. He didn't bother going up the stairs to the first floor; he only had to look at the sweep of them to imagine what an entrance they would make for the *salons privés* where the rich would go to lose their money.

He had said to Ralph Maxton, "I guess this is what I want. Let's go back to the hotel. My wife's expecting us."

Angela turned to Steven. "Darling, can we go and see it after lunch?"

"Of course. That suit you, Ralph?"

Maxton had nowhere else to go. "Suits me perfectly," he agreed. "What time shall I come back?"

Her response was generous. "Why don't you stay to lunch? Then we can all go together."

"Good idea," Steven added.

His hesitation would have escaped anyone less acute than Maxton. For a moment he was tempted. But it wouldn't be wise. He stood up. "You are kind," he said sincerely to Angela. "But I've arranged to meet someone. If I came back at, say, three o'clock, would that be all right?"

"Fine," Steven said. "We'll see you at three."

Angela got up too. "I'm sorry you can't stay. Next time, you must."

He gave his little bow and left them. He went down in the gilded elevator and out into the bright, crisp sunshine. Marvelous climate, even in November. He had a new suit, a decent shirt and a topcoat. He felt for the key in his pocket and rubbed it between thumb and forefinger like a talisman.

"Good old Great-uncle Oleg," he murmured. "What a laugh you'd have out of this." Then he made his way inward off the Croisette to a small café, where he ordered himself a cheap lunch. Lawrence would buy the place. He was the kind of man who made up his mind. There'd be no second thoughts. He was a man obviously used to making big decisions with a lot of money involved. Used to getting what he wanted.

Maxton drank very little; alcohol was not his weakness. You couldn't gamble unless you had a clear head. For ten years he'd kept clean, drinking no more than a glass or two of wine, maybe some champagne with clients when they were winning. When they lost, he paid for the drinks and encouraged them to try their luck again. What a shitty way to live. What a wonderful way to die, at the end of it all. During that lean and hungry year, he had thought about dying. Nobody would have given a damn if he'd followed his poor friend of long ago into the sea and let it take him to its peaceful depths. He had considered the idea, even tossed a coin in his despair, and been relieved to see the toss in favor of living.

His friends had been so good to him; two women had helped support him, and they had been the first to get some of his five hundred dollars back. One had said she loved him, and he believed her. But he didn't love her. He had never loved anyone, for he hated himself.

This was a second chance. He was as superstitious as the next gambler; he thought of fate as an entity, usually malignant, sometimes capriciously kind. Fate had brought him and Steven Lawrence together at the last moment to save him. He would work for Lawrence, build up a new casino, take his place among the rich and wasteful people of his world. Great-uncle Oleg, roistering with his French whore, would smile on him from the shadows. It was family legend that he had opened his trousers and pissed at the Bolshevik firing squad.

By three o'clock Maxton was sitting in the front of Lawrence's big, rented Cadillac and they were driving to the Palais Poliakoff. The first thing Lawrence had said was that they must change the name. Maxton agreed. But he would think of some way to resist it later.

"Well," Steven asked her. "What do you think, sweetheart? Do you like it?"

He wanted her to be enthusiastic; he wanted her to see the plaster freshly gilded, the rotten floors carpeted, the wrecked chandeliers sparkling and restored to their old glory. He held her hand and asked her to support him, and she did. Not because she could share his vision of the future, but because she loved him too much to cast a doubt. To Angela it was a huge, run-down white elephant that would cost millions.

But she held tightly to his hand and said, "You'll make it wonderful."

"And you'll help me?" he demanded. "You'll go every step of the way with me, Angelina? I'll need you. I'll need you to take care of the decorating, and the grounds—we'll make the grounds a feature. There's a terrace right on the sea. I'm going to rebuild that, have it lit at night."

Maxton had opened the shutters. They had walked up the great staircase and opened double doors onto a series of huge reception rooms with superb plasterwork ceilings and majestic marble fireplaces. The chill sunshine streamed in through cracked window glass, and Steven stood with Angela beside him, visualizing how it would look.

Ralph Maxton had withdrawn, leaving them alone. He could see that she was bewildered, even overwhelmed, and admired her for concealing it. It wasn't her world. He knew what kind of world she had lived in. A nice country house, a village, a respectable, professional father, Women's Institute mother. His own family owned villages like that in England. His mother had been president of this institute and that local charity until she died.

He had flown back for her funeral in the grim Derbyshire church where all his family were buried, and he hurried back to Monte Carlo the next morning. No one had been pleased to see him or sorry to see him go. He was an outcast. The epithet "black sheep" had actually been uttered by an ancient relative still using the vernacular of sixty years before. His father had been too preoccupied with his own grief to make any effort for a son who had caused his mother so much shame and anguish. Ralph felt they would all have preferred that he not come at all. He had fled to his place of exile, where the sun shone and he was accepted by his peers.

No, this place wouldn't be easy for Angela Lawrence to encompass. This was dross and tinsel, in spite of its grandeur. No real values for her in Steven Lawrence's dream. Maxton reproved himself. He mustn't be morbid or sentimental. He went back downstairs to wait for them. When they came down the staircase and into the entrance hall, he walked up to them, smiling, and said, "Impressive, isn't it? Did you think so, Mrs. Lawrence?"

"Oh, yes. It's certainly impressive. My husband wants me to have it decorated. I'm going to need a lot of help."

"We've been jumping the gun," Steven interposed. "It's not bought yet. It's not even priced. Come on, darling, we'll go back. Ralph, we'll take you back, and the car can drop you off at your hotel. It's up to you now to get the details. We mustn't run ahead of the deal before it's made."

He whispered to Angela as they went outside and Maxton locked up. "I don't want him to think I'll buy at any crazy price," he said. "I'll get it, but at my figure."

"But he's working for you, isn't he?" she asked.

"He's working for himself, and for the owner, and then for me. Don't worry, I know these guys. They take a cut out of everything. That's okay, so long as it's not too big. Now, my darling, when we get back, why don't we call Charlie, tell him all about it?"

"Yes, of course we can," she said. The school didn't encourage parents to call unless there was an emergency, but she didn't want to dampen his spirits. "But I don't think it'll mean much to him," she said. "He has no idea what a casino even looks like."

"He will," he insisted. "He'll get the idea when I've talked to him. It'll be his place one day."

5

He was a humble man, a man of no importance in the family hierarchy. But he'd had his hand in the till. There was no excuse, because he was doing well enough out of his delicatessen, and the amount he paid in dues was the same for everyone with his profit margin. He'd been greedy and dishonest, salting away part of his takings. And he'd been found out.

Piero Falconi liked to keep tabs on everything that happened, no matter how trivial. The conviction and punishment of a humble man who had turned thief was part of his responsibility. He decided to look at the condemned man. He'd been called from his shop and held in a warehouse. His wife was told he'd been sent out of town on family business. She didn't protest. She hoped he wouldn't be away long, because she had to manage the shop on her own.

He didn't see Piero. He didn't see anyone, because he was blindfolded. He had stood trial in that warehouse and argued with tears, pleading for his life. He told lies, hoping to be believed. He wasn't. He was taken away without knowing what his sentence would be.

Piero looked at the man. He was about the right age, though different in build and nearly bald. But he'd do. Piero nodded at the two men who guarded him. The man was slumped in a chair, abandoned to fear and despair, without enough hope to move. One of the guards silently moved up behind him and slipped the garrote over his head, pulling it tight. It took him a while to die, writhing and choking. Then at last his executioner released the cord, and the body fell forward onto the floor.

Piero said, "Load him up and get him out of here. Take him to Freddiano's place. He'll set it up like an accident." He walked out.

Freddiano was a truck driver. He had the body rolled up in packing paper in the bottom of his truck, with a load of cases piled on top of it. He drove through the night and the following day, stopping to eat at diners and snatch sleep in his cab. He arrived in a small town on the southeastern seaboard when it was just getting dark. He was tired and hungry. He stopped at a gas station with a small snack bar. While he was inside eating, the owner's two sons removed the body and loaded it into the trunk of a secondhand Ford. In that and a pickup they drove out of town and parked on an isolated road. There wasn't a house in sight and no car had passed while they waited. They took the dead man out of the trunk. He wasn't stiff to handle anymore. They put him behind the wheel of the Ford. The older of the two sons of the garage owner noticed something.

He said, "Jesus!"

His brother looked where he was looking. The corpse had lost a finger on its right hand. They poured gasoline on the front seats, drenching the figure slumped over the wheel. They trickled gas along the ground away from the parked car; the engine was left running. They lit a twist of paper and tossed it onto the oily snake creeping across the road. Then both men took off at full speed for the safety of the pickup. They dropped flat behind it. There was a roar, a bright sunburst of flame and then an explosion as the Ford's tank ignited. When they stood up to look, there was nothing left but a red-and-orange ball surrounded by a river of flames.

Back at the garage, they found the truck driver drinking coffee and reading the sports page of the newspaper. He paid the bill and left. Nobody said anything.

The local police poked around among the blackened ruins of the car and found what was left of the dead man. The local newspaper carried a report of the accident, and the coroner issued a certificate of accidental death. The victim was identified by his brother. Strangely, a finger was missing. The name was given as S. C. Falconi, a resident of New York State. It meant nothing to the people of the coastal town where the accident occurred.

Three days after the inquest, copies of the newspaper report and the death certificate, wrapped around a small cigar box, were delivered to Aldo Fabrizzi by special messenger. He read the clipping, studied the certificate and, last of all, opened the little box. Inside was the real proof from the Falconis that the debt of honor had been paid.

He filed the death certificate. He was a practical man. Clara would need it when she remarried someday. He kept the wedding ring and threw the rest away. He looked at the ring and was satisfied. Clara had bought it herself, ordered the inscription. He had been irritated because she insisted on buying it at Tiffany's instead of using a local jeweler. The initials, the date, were as he had seen them. He indulged in a quiet moment of satisfaction. Vengeance was sweet indeed. Then he went to find Clara. "He's paid for what he did to you. You can be proud again."

He hadn't expected her to react as she did. She looked at the ring and then collapsed, screaming in hysteria. It shocked and terrified him. For a few moments he thought she had gone out of her mind. They got a doctor, who sedated her and ordered a nurse to stay with her. Aldo's wife, Luisa, raved and accused him of driving their daughter mad with grief.

At first Aldo was distraught. He had relied upon Clara's healthy hatred to sustain her. Instead he realized the intensity of her love. But he was tough, even with the child he loved. She would calm down. She would accept in her heart what she had agreed to in her head. He waited, and after a few days he went in to see her. She looked ill, with deep black pits under her eyes.

He took her hand and held it. "*Cara mia,* it's time you got up. You have to live your life and start again."

"Tell me something, Papa."

"Yes, *carissima?*"

"Was he alone?"

"Yes. He was alone. There was no one with him."

She turned her head away. He squeezed her hand. He felt a response.

"I thought there was a woman."

Aldo and his wife had thought so too, after their long discussions. He said, "It seems there wasn't. But it doesn't matter. What's done is done. He shamed you and me and his own family. He's paid the price. But you're the one I'm thinking of—you should be glad, Clara. You should be glad you're free and justice has been done." He spoke tenderly yet firmly to her in the Italian they always used when they were alone.

"If there was no woman, then I can live with it," she said.

He nodded. He understood his daughter. He bent down and kissed

her cheek. Now she would get better. He went out of the room to tell
his wife.

"It's your brother," Angela called out.

Steven was in the hall with his son, decorating the Christmas tree.
Hugh Drummond was fiddling with the string of colored lights. Snow
had fallen outside. It was going to be a proper Christmas. Parcels
wrapped in bright paper were stacked under the tree. They'd been back
from France only ten days.

Steven handed her the box of glittering plastic balls. "You take
over, darling." He went into the sitting room and closed the door.
"Piero?"

He listened for a few moments. His brother spoke in dialect. "Fabrizzi bought the accident story. Your ring clinched it. The old bastard
came to see Papa and embraced him and said he shared his sorrow."
He spoke in English. "Yeah, in those words. I could've kicked his balls
in. Clara had to have the doctor. No, she's okay now. Grieving, he said.
Like fuck, I said to Lucia. So no worries, Steven. You're in the clear.
And us too. How's everything going? You got the place in France tied
up yet?"

"I signed the contract a week ago. Never tangle with a French
lawyer; I nearly went crazy. But it's fixed, and all I have to do is pay
on completion. I wish you could see it, Piero. It's going to be one hell
of a casino when I've finished."

"Maybe one day I'll bring Lucia and the kids on a trip to Europe. . . . We might stop in."

"I'd like that," Steven said. "The family's well?"

"They're fine. Mama's got a cold. You know how she is in the
winter. I told Papa I'd be speaking to you. He sent messages."

Steven didn't ask what they were. He knew his father. He wouldn't
forgive his defection. Piero was trying to make it easy.

"Send them love from me," he said. "You're staying home for
Christmas?"

"No, we're going down to Florida. Mama needs some sun. What
about you?"

"We'll stay with Angela's father. She's well, and the boy's great.
He keeps growing taller, Piero. I wish you could see him too."

"Like I said, brother. One day maybe."

"A Merry Christmas," Steven wished him. "And thanks for what you've done for me. If you hadn't stood by me, I couldn't have made the choice."

"So long as it's what you want," Piero answered.

"It's what I want," Steven told him. "I miss the family like hell. But I wouldn't change anything. I'll keep in touch."

He rang off. It was settled. The Fabrizzis believed he was dead. There'd be no war between his father and them. Clara would find another man, get married. The book of his old life was closed for good.

It was a strange feeling of finality. He didn't go back to the hall and the Christmas tree. He threw some logs on the fire. It was a cold house by his standards. He had no experience of an English Christmas. It would be very different from the noisy, crowded gathering back home.

"Steven?"

He looked up and saw his son standing there.

"Aren't you coming back? We've nearly finished."

"I'm coming," he said. His heart lifted again. He put an arm around the boy's shoulders. "When I'm married to your mother," he said, "I'd like you to do something."

"What?" The young mirror image smiled up at him. He was shorter than Steven by only a few inches.

"Call me Father."

"Do I have to wait till you and Mum are married?"

"Not if you don't want," Steven answered.

"All right then, Dad. Let's go and do the lights before Grandpa blows a fuse again."

They were married in London. It was a registry office, and Steven had filled it with flowers. The registrar said he was sure other couples would enjoy them afterward. Hugh Drummond and Charlie were there, and so was David Wickham. Angela had insisted on inviting him. He'd been so understanding when she had let him down. Steven didn't like pansies, and he was cool when they were introduced. Wickham had given them an expensive wedding present: a cut-crystal decanter and six cognac snifters. Angela was delighted, and Steven was annoyed. He didn't mind Angela's inviting the doctor who'd been in love with her. He was the kind of rival Steven tolerated easily—solid, older, as romantic as a brick wall.

She looked very beautiful and very happy. She'd chosen yellow, a bright spring color for a dismal January day. She carried a little posy of yellow and white flowers and wore a hat with a brief silk veil. He suddenly remembered the hat with the feather she'd worn at that lunch in New York. The day that had changed his life. He tried to forget the pain his decisions had since caused and concentrate only on the happiness that Angela now made possible for him. He held her hand, and together they went through the ceremony, thanking the registrar afterward.

David Wickham congratulated them and then kissed Angela lightly on the cheek. "Lots of happiness, my dear," he said. "Such a jolly wedding service. I *hate* churches ... so gloomy."

Steven could have kicked him.

Then their son was embracing them and Angela's father was patting him on the back and they were out and on their way to a wedding lunch. They had chosen the Savoy again, where Steven had booked a private room. It was, as Wickham kept on saying, a very jolly lunch, with lots of champagne and splendid food, even a wedding cake with two tiny figures on top.

It was their son who surprised them all by getting up and proposing the toast. His face was rather flushed from champagne and excitement. "Here's to Mum and my new father," he said loudly.

"Long life and happiness," Hugh Drummond prompted him.

He repeated it, raising his glass to them both. "Long life and happiness, Mum and Dad."

Angela's eyes filled for a moment. She said, "Thank you, darling," and everyone rose to their feet and drank to her and Steven. She had never imagined she could be so happy.

Ralph Maxton had a merry Christmas. Lawrence had finally agreed to the price. One million francs. Maxton had taken two percent commission on the deposit. He decided to celebrate. He booked himself into the Hôtel de Paris—one of the cheaper rooms admittedly, but then the hotel was full. He was persona non grata at the casino, but he didn't care. He was glad to be back in his old haunt and visibly prospering. He asked one of his women friends to join him. Not the one who had shown settling-down symptoms when she lent him money. His companion was as footloose as he was, a woman who depended upon lovers and gambling and so far had done very well with both. She claimed to be Lebanese and traded on her exotic looks. Ralph thought French with a dash of Moroccan was more likely. She had a delightful sense of fun and a flamboyant attitude he found amusing. Sometimes, when she splashed champagne over herself and invited him to try the vintage, shrieking with laughter as they lay on the bed, he imagined his father's reaction.

For Christmas, Ralph bought her an expensive Hermès bag. She accepted it, pouted because it wasn't jewelry, and then whispered mischievously that she had something for him too. They were sitting in the crowded cocktail bar, and even Maxton was a little drunk.

"What?" he demanded. "What's my present then?"

She slid her hand under the table. "Me." She giggled. "And you know what that normally costs." They both laughed immoderately at the joke. "Thank God that old fart Bernard is back with his wife," she went on. She took a cigarette out of a gold Boucheron case and handed Ralph the matching lighter. He held it steady with some difficulty.

Bernard was old, and a fart. Maxton knew him and thought it a fair description. Madeleine fleeced him mercilessly when he came to Monte Carlo. He couldn't keep away from the baccarat table or from her. He said she made him feel a young man again. Ralph believed that too.

"Ah, Ralphie, my darling, what a pity you're not really rich. Then I could move in with you."

"How do you know I'm not?" he asked her.

"Because you'd have a suite, my darling, not that little fart hole on the top floor! You know the only thing I can't stand about this hotel?" She didn't wait for him to answer. "That!" She pointed to the woman with her back to them, sitting with a bottle of champagne on ice, playing patience. "Every time I see her, my stomach turns. Why does she show herself, Ralphie? Why doesn't she hide? I would, if I looked like that."

"She lives here," he told her. "She's lived here for years. It's a strange story. She used to come here with her husband, twenty years ago. He was very, very rich. Rumor said he'd played the black market for the Germans during the occupation. Anyway, he died and she used to come here during the season alone. She was a damned good-looking woman. I often saw her about. She'd pick up the odd man now and then, but she didn't go in for waiters or bellboys. Her name's Pauline Duvalier. She lived in a villa up by Beaulieu. She was robbed one day and beaten till they nearly killed her. That's all they could do, apparently, to mend her face."

"What a horror!" Madeleine exclaimed. "I feel quite a *frisson*. Let's have some more champagne."

Maxton continued: "She sold the villa and came here. She has a permanent suite, and she never leaves the hotel. She's become a sort of landmark, one of the Monte Carlo legends."

"If I owned this place I wouldn't keep her," Madeleine declared. "It must put people off. I'd tell her to go."

Maxton allowed himself a cynical smile. For all her charm and gaiety, she was a heartless creature. He patted her hand and said, "When God made you, darling, he missed out on only one ingredient."

She demanded to know what she lacked.

"Nothing," he retracted. He felt sober suddenly, and he didn't want to. "Here's our champagne. Drink up, darling, and then you can give me your present."

It wasn't all pleasure and self-indulgence. Maxton made contacts among the casino employees. Knowing that their movements and associates were checked by the casino detectives, he rang up his old boss and asked to meet him. On neutral ground, of course.

They had a drink together. The older man had heard Maxton was back and in funds. "You seem to be doing well," he remarked.

"I am. No thanks to you. I couldn't get a job anywhere along the coast."

The other shrugged. "Well, Ralph, you knew the rules. You can't blame us."

"Oh, no hard feelings. I know you people play quite rough when anyone oversteps the mark. That's why I've asked you here. I want to put my cards on the table. If you'll pardon the metaphor."

No smile. No lightness of touch. No education either. Stop treating these people as if they'd gone to Winchester like you, he chided himself. Little arrogant touches like that had made him secret enemies in the past.

"I'm here because I've been asked to open and manage a new casino."

"The one in Antibes?" They had heard about it as soon as the first approach to the lawyers had been made. They heard everything concerned with gambling on the coast.

"The one in Antibes," he confirmed.

"And who's the buyer? We were told it was a consortium from West Germany."

"I can't divulge that," Maxton said. "It's confidential. And for all my faults, Maurice, I never gave away anything to anyone. Which is probably why I've got the job. No, the reason I'm here is to try and recruit some staff."

He saw the angry flash in the man's eyes.

"You've come poaching from us?"

"I've made inquiries, that's all. I wanted you to know. I don't like being underhanded. You have the best men. If anyone wants a change, I'm prepared to see him."

"You shouldn't do this," Maurice said. He was pushing back his chair.

Maxton raised a hand to stop him. "Be realistic. You're the best. There's nothing to touch Monte Carlo anywhere in the world. If anyone working in the casino wants to leave, then they're not good enough for you anyway. I'll only get what you'd have to sack in the end for one reason or another."

After a pause, Maurice sat down again. "You're a shrewd man, Ralph. You have brains. It's a pity. You could have risen high if you'd stayed with us."

"Thanks. It's a nice compliment. But we both know I'd gone as high as I was ever going to get. I'd still be doing exactly the same if I were here today. No one who isn't Monégasque or French gets a chance at the top. At least I've got an opportunity to manage something this time."

"And you think it'll succeed? Against us, against Nice and Cannes?"

"I think so. Not that you need to worry. But the others might."

Maurice stood up. He told the waiter to charge the casino for their drinks. He held out his hand, and Ralph Maxton shook it formally. There was no friendship, no human warmth, but a business understanding.

"It was good that we discussed this," the older man said. "I shall tell the directors they needn't worry about the staff. You're quite right. Only the second-rate would want to leave us to work for anyone else. I wish you luck." He didn't, but Ralph thanked him.

By the middle of February he had lined up a small but competent staff, including one of the best croupiers. He didn't offer them bigger wages. As Steven had instructed, he offered them shares in their own enterprise. Each man would have a stake in the casino. And a personal stake in keeping out the con men and the professional cheats.

He cabled Steven in England, asking him to come down. He got an answer the next day. "Deal completed. Kindly arrange suitable rented accommodation for my wife and self. Arriving Saturday next week."

Though Maxton wondered why they didn't go to a hotel, he rang up all the best agents and got a list of flats and villas available. But first he telephoned his contact in Monaco to ask when his final commission would be paid on the sale of the Palais Poliakoff. The man, a postwar speculator, was living close to the Italian border. Perhaps he would cross it without honoring his debt. He had been short of money and living on credit, with few assets but the crumbling palace itself. Maxton needn't have concerned himself. The draft was paid promptly into his bank. When Maxton inquired after the owner, he was told that he had taken a long holiday.

"Someone suggested it was Cosa Nostra buying the property. He didn't wait around."

So that was why he'd paid up so promptly. A German consortium; the Mafia from Naples. Let them all speculate. What did it matter? All they'd ever discover was the name Steven Lawrence. They could make what they wanted of that.

"I hope you like it," Ralph Maxton said. He had met them at the Nice airport. Steven had hurried down the steps and across the tarmac, Angela on his arm. They passed through customs very quickly in spite of the amount of luggage that came with them. Ralph was well known to the police, the immigration and customs officers. He had smoothed many paths for clients in the old days. He gave Steven a brief report as they drove along the coast road.

"Buildings," Steven remarked, looking at the construction under way in Nice. "Nothing but new blocks going up. We're in for a boom."

"It looks like it," Maxton agreed. He glanced into his mirror. Angela was sitting in the back. She looked pale and hadn't said much.

"We had a bad flight," Steven had explained at the airport. "My wife didn't like it, did you, sweetheart? Quite a bumpy ride."

"I've engaged a maid and a cook for you," Ralph told her. "The villa's ready. Shall we go there first?"

Steven answered. "I'll stop off at Antibes. I want to see how the builders are getting on. You take Angela to the villa and come back for me. You could put your feet up, darling."

"I'm all right now," she insisted, and smiled at him. She didn't look it. "It was really awful. I thought we were going to crash."

They turned in at the gates, and Steven jumped out of the car. The palace was shrouded in tarpaulins, and scaffolding was going up outside.

"Give me a couple of hours," he called to Maxton. Then he was taking the steps two at a time and vanishing through the entrance into the building.

"It's chaos in there," Ralph remarked. "We're only about fifteen minutes away. I hope you like the villa," he said again. "I think you will. It was the best one available."

It wasn't a big villa. He'd had Angela in mind more than her husband when he was viewing those on the list. She wouldn't want a vulgar, overpowering place. This was charming and intimate. Comfortably furnished in French Provincial style, it had a beautiful garden. The Parisian owner wanted to let it for a year. It was up in the hills, with plenty of shade against the scorching summer sun.

He didn't know how long they intended to stay or how often they would come. But the Palais Poliakoff would take at least a year to repair and furnish. He could imagine Angela being happy at the villa. He'd rented it.

He brought her inside, and the maid appeared. She was a thin-faced woman in a blue smock. Angela shook hands with her.

"I'm Janine," she announced. "Welcome, madame. My mother is in the kitchen. Shall I tell her to prepare something for you?"

"Some coffee, please," Angela said.

"I've ordered lunch," Ralph explained. "They're a good couple and they won't fight, as two strangers might. Here." He helped her off with her coat. "Let me take that. Now, do you want to have a quick look around and then do as your husband suggested—put your feet up, have your coffee?"

"I want to look around first," Angela said. "This is so pretty, Mr. Maxton. I know I'm going to love it. You've been so kind, arranging everything."

"It's what I'm paid for," he remarked lightly. "But it's been a pleasure. This is the drawing room. The dining room adjoins. It's not too big, but you'll have plenty of space. Some of the places around here are so vast they can be rather gloomy."

She looked less pale already, exclaiming with enthusiasm over the reception rooms. And then, with her disarming candor, she said, "This is the prettiest bedroom I've ever seen. And look at the view over the garden!" She opened French windows and stepped out on a balcony.

"It'll be quite cool," he explained. "If you're here in the summer."

"Oh, we will be," she said. "I don't think Steven wants to go back till he's seen things taking shape. Let's go down and find our coffee, shall we?"

The cook came in with a tray. She was plump and cheerful, as a cook should be.

Angela sat down and said, "I feel at home already. Steven will love it here."

"You're feeling better, aren't you, Mrs. Lawrence," he said. "You looked really rough when you arrived. It must have been very stormy."

"It was terrifying," she admitted. "We were thrown all over the place. Steven didn't mind; he kept telling me not to be frightened, but I couldn't help it. I'm afraid I made rather a fuss. I'm not used to flying."

"Personally," Ralph Maxton admitted, "I loathe it. I like trains and cars and ships. My mother used to say that if God meant us to fly he'd have given us wings. It was one of the few things she said I heartily agreed with!"

He laughed his high-pitched laugh, and she thought suddenly, *That's the only thing I don't like about you. That cold laugh.*

"Does your mother come down here?"

"No, Mrs. Lawrence. She's dead, I'm afraid. She wasn't the sort of person who came to the Riviera. She and my father liked to stay put."

"Please," she said. "Call me Angela, won't you?"

"You're very kind. Are you sure Mr. Lawrence won't mind?"

"Good Lord, no. He's the most informal person."

"Well, if you say so, Angela it is."

"More coffee?" she asked him. "Do you go home often?"

"I never go home at all," he said. "The last time was for my mother's funeral."

"Oh! Where is your home?"

"Derbyshire. In the bleakest, coldest corner of it, to be exact. And where do you come from?"

"Haywards Heath," Angela said. "My father is a doctor. He's retired now. We've always lived in the village. He still does. I do hope he'll come out here and stay with us. He's rather a stick-in-the-mud too, like your parents."

Maxton smiled politely at the idea. He couldn't imagine any resemblance between a country GP and his awe-inspiring father.

"My son's coming out for Easter," she said.

He was adept at hiding his surprise at most things. But he was taken unawares. "I didn't know you had any children."

"I was married before," she said. "During the war. He's sixteen now."

"Oh, I see. You must have married very young."

"I did." Angela finished the coffee. "You're not married, are you, Ralph?"

"No, no, no, not me. Nobody'd put up with me on a permanent basis. Good Lord, look at the time. I'd better go and pick up your husband."

"And this time," Angela insisted, "you stay for lunch."

When he had gone, she went upstairs. The maid had unpacked most of her suitcases already. She wandered through the guest rooms, inspecting the place that would be her home for how long? She didn't know. It had a restful atmosphere. She had imagined some awful Gothic monstrosity with turrets and phony battlements; she'd seen a number of them dotted along the coast behind their ornamental gates, many of them slightly rusted, relics of a vanished age. This was a charming house, where she and Steven could be happy.

She was downstairs and, on impulse, asked if there was anything special in the wine cellar. She had been cowardly and silly on the flight, and she wanted to make it up to Steven. Yes, she was told. The maid, Janine, reeled off a list of spirits, wines and liqueurs. Champagne, of course. Would Madame like that before lunch? Mr. Maxton had told her to put some on ice in case. Mr. Maxton had thought of everything.

When Steven came in, he hurried to her and hugged her. "Angelina, you must come down with me after lunch and see it. There's been so much done already."

She saw Ralph Maxton in the background. He could blend so that you hardly noticed him. Or not, if he chose to make his presence felt. He wasn't looking at either of them, and yet she knew he was.

Lunch was relaxed; excellent food and some choice wines. Maxton set out to be amusing; he had a sharp tongue, but the joke was often at his own expense. Angela liked him for that. When he started telling anecdotes about the casino they forgot the time. He was a gifted storyteller with a light touch. He had Steven's whole attention.

He's enjoying himself, Angela thought, playacting, holding the stage. He's not really at ease with Steven, and this is his chance to get a little closer to him.

Like a true actor, Maxton knew when to bow out, leaving his

audience wanting more. "I am sorry," he said. "I've bored the two of you to tears with all these old stories. I must be on my way."

"I've enjoyed it," Steven said. "You must tell us some more."

"Oh, I will, if you give me any encouragement. Some of the early stuff is fascinating. Before the Great War, when the Russians used to come for the winter season."

"Like Count Poliakoff?" Angela asked him.

"Yes, there are some amazing stories about him. Anyway, thank you for lunch. I'll call in tomorrow morning, Steven, and we'll go through the estimates and progress reports if that suits you."

"Nine o'clock," Steven suggested.

"Nine o'clock it shall be." And with a little bow to Angela, Maxton left them.

"He's a strange man," she said that night. "I can't quite make him out."

"Don't you like him, darling?" Steven frowned. "I thought you got along well."

"Oh, of course we do. He's very nice, very amusing too. It's just that he's different. He spoke about his home and his family in such an odd way. How much do you know about him?"

"Everything," Steven said. They were sitting in front of the fire, holding hands. He was a very physical man, always touching her, claiming her. They hadn't gone back to the building. He said she looked tired and he'd been selfish to suggest it. Tomorrow they could spend a lot of time there. "I know everything about him," he continued. "I had him checked out before I made any contact. You're right, sweetheart, he is an odd guy. His father's some English lord. Ralph started gambling in the clubs and private gaming parties in London. He got mixed up with some crooks, who fleeced him, so he was sent to the States. They should have known better. He borrowed a lot of money and lost it. He was in hock so deep he took his mother's jewelry and tried to sell it. The family paid him off. I guess they wrote him off in the end. So he got a job with the casino, and he stayed clear of the tables for ten years."

"But why did they employ him? Why did you?"

"Because with his background, he knew everybody. He knew how to handle his own kind. He puts on a very good front. You've seen it. People fall for that sort of thing. And being a cheat himself, he's good at spotting cheats. He did a wonderful PR job for them in Monte Carlo. He's sharp as a tack, darling, and that's what I need. He's got class. I like that. And he knows all the press. They'll write us up when the time comes. This Count Poliakoff who built our place was some relation. He doesn't know I know that. I just wanted to make sure he didn't have a stake in selling it. He didn't. Just the commission."

"I hope you can trust him," she said. "I feel rather uneasy about him now. Why shouldn't he try and cheat you in some way?"

Steven smiled down at her. "Because this job is his last chance. He'll never get a better opportunity. I've given him responsibility. I think I can trust him. So don't you worry. It'll work out fine for all of us. Now why don't we go up and try out our new bed?"

Upstairs, undressing her, he said, "Why don't we have another child?"

"If we go on like this, we'll have a dozen," she protested.

He stroked her full breasts, molding them between his hands. "A girl next time," he said, kissing them.

The curtains were open, and his body was silver in the light of a big cold moon. She drew him down and opened to him. "You're the sort that only has boys."

It was taking shape. Even Angela could see the skeleton of the palace fleshing out. Every day she went with Steven, picking her way among the building materials, watching the plasterers and bricklayers moving from room to room, with carpenters repairing damaged paneling and doors. The marvelous ceilings were cleaned off and regilded, and the scaffolding was coming down from the facade.

Time passed quickly because there was so much to do. Maxton was everywhere, directing the work, closeted for hours with Steven, poring over plans and costs. Angela was designing color schemes. She'd turned one of the guest rooms into an office, pinning up samples and patterns. She traveled to Lyons to look at specially woven silks and velvets, and together she and Steven scoured antique shops along the coast: he didn't want modern reproductions in the grand salon. It was Maxton who persuaded him to invest in eighteenth-century Aubusson tapestries instead of pictures. Bad pictures wouldn't do, and genuine period works of art would cost a fortune. Tapestries were not fashionable and therefore cheaper. Maxton also had an eye for good furniture.

"How do you know so much about it?" Angela asked him once as he rejected a handsome black lacquer commode as a nineteenth-century copy of a Régence piece.

"Oh, we had a few nice things at home," he said. "I suppose you get an idea when something's right. My mother was always banging on about it. Bored me stiff."

"You must tell me about her one day," Angela suggested.

He looked at her and smiled. "Not much to tell. She was quite sweet when you got to know her. Not that I and my brothers and sisters ever did till we were nearly grown up. We had full-time nannies."

"How many brothers and sisters?"

"Two brothers, three sisters. All well married and respectable. Not a bit like me. Come and look at this. This is rather nice."

He wouldn't talk about himself. Every attempt to draw him out was waved aside with a flip remark or a self-deprecating joke. He wouldn't let Angela come close, and yet she knew he liked her, as much as he disliked her husband. She couldn't explain why she sensed this, because the two men worked in harmony and were friendly on a superficial level.

Maxton was invited to dinner once a week. It was always on a Friday, at the end of a working week. And as he once said of someone else, he sang for his supper. He fed them scandals, named names, conjured up the great courtesans of the past and their rich protectors, and in the spring, when the coast began to come to life, he started introducing them to selected people.

He had an extraordinary memory for names and faces and could pinpoint the background and origin of anyone they met.

"You've got to start off on the right foot here," he said. "We must make a campaign plan. It's called social climbing." He laughed in his mirthless way. "The French are terrible snobs. And one never really gets to know them; not that you care. You want a good smart guest list to get our opening off the ground and some minor royals and film stars, and I'll have a go at getting Nettie Orbach to grace us with her presence. She always draws the press."

"Who's Nettie Orbach?" Steven asked.

"Wasn't she a child bride or something?" Angela said.

"Quite right. Married some Bolivian at sixteen and went off with a few million smackers after a couple of years and hooked some Kraut prince with more millions. There've been five husbands in all, and she's on the prowl for number six. She eats gossip columnists for breakfast.

And they just can't get enough of her. I'll see what I can do. Nettie does owe me a favor. More than one."

"What sort of favor?"

"Nothing to worry about," he told Steven. "She was in Monte a couple of years ago, and one of the paparazzi got hold of some photographs she didn't want published. I bought the negatives for her."

Angela went back to England to collect Charlie and her father. They were coming out to spend Easter at the villa.

Hugh Drummond was reluctant to make the trip. He made excuses about leaving the house and the garden. Mrs. P. thought she was keeping an eye on him, but it was really the other way around. She was quite forgetful, he said, and might easily go off, leaving the gas on. Angela didn't take any notice. He wasn't a man you could bully, and she'd never known how to cajole him. She relied on Charlie to do that. And of course he came because his grandson urged him, and because he wouldn't see him otherwise during the holidays.

To Angela's surprise, Ralph Maxton had offered to fly back to England to bring her family out.

"But you hate flying," she protested. "You said you did."

"Not quite as much as you do," he answered. "I'd be only too happy if it would help."

"Wasn't that kind of him," she said to Steven afterward. "I said no, of course. I've got to get used to small planes if we're going to live here for long periods. But I was very touched."

"Yes, it was thoughtful. But he's paid to be thoughtful. He's paid to do whatever is needed. And very well paid, don't forget. So you don't have to be so grateful, or I'll get jealous," he said teasingly.

She looked at him and laughed. "Oh, I wouldn't worry about Ralph, if I were you."

It was a glorious spring. The villa gardens bloomed luxuriously, and Angela watched her son and his father play tennis and go riding in the hills together as the sunny days followed one another until the holiday was nearly over.

Her father preferred the garden and a book to the long walks she had associated with his spare time. He looked thinner, and she asked him if he was really as well as he maintained.

"Perfectly well." He sounded irritable. "Don't know what you're fussing about. When will they get back, do you know?"

He missed the boy, and she could see that he was somewhat put out by Charlie's infatuation with his stepfather.

"They've gone down to look at the palace again. You *will* come and look round before we go back, won't you? I know Steven would like it."

"Yes, all right. Not that it's going to mean anything to me. Must be costing a mint, by the way he was talking. Hope he knows what he's doing."

"Oh, he knows," she said. "One thing I've learned about Steven. He's got a head for business."

"And you're happy," he surprised her by saying. "You seem to be."

"Daddy, you've no idea how happy I am with him. It just gets better and better. I wish you'd stay on here for a bit. Why don't you?"

"I've got to get home." He shook his head. "The place'd go to pot if I wasn't there. That lazy old bugger John doesn't even weed the border at the front if I'm not after him. It's lovely here, and it's been very nice. Very nice indeed. But I'll be glad to sleep in my own bed. Ah, isn't that the car? They must be back." He heaved himself up and went in search of his grandson.

Angela picked up his book, marked the page and placed it on his chair. Not so long ago she would have been hurt. But not now. She could be tolerant of the selfishness and insensitivity of old age because Steven's love was proof of her own worth. He had given her confidence in herself. She knew that her father loved her in his own way and within his capacity. He didn't have to show it, because Steven's love was enough. He's given me so much, she thought. Thank God I've given him Charlie. It helps to make it even. Then she got up and hurried out to find them.

"It's amazing, Mum," her son said. "It's huge, isn't it? And so swish. Will I be able to have my friends over and take them along?"

"As soon as it opens," his father promised. "You're coming to the opening, Charlie. You'll be there with your mother and me."

"Have you fixed a date yet, Dad? When will it be ready?"

Steven had an arm around his son. He hugged him. "August," he said. "At the height of the season. It'll be a gala evening, and I'm going to show them that anything the other casinos do, I can do better!"

"I bet you will," Charlie declared. "I can't wait. Isn't it exciting, Grandpa? You haven't seen it yet!"

"No. But you tell me when, Steven, and I'd like to—er—have a look at what's going on. Is that chap Maxton coming round this evening? He plays a damned good game of piquet."

It was odd how well her father got on with Ralph Maxton. They played old-fashioned games that Angela had barely heard of, and Ralph managed to let the doctor win. Steven thought it was amusing and rather spoiled the picture by telling her that Ralph had been a notorious cardsharp in his early years.

"When he wanted money he played bridge. If he wasn't winning, he palmed the cards. But he's being kind to your father, and that's good."

Hugh Drummond was impressed by him. "He's a gentleman," he said to Angela. "It makes all the difference. I know that place in Derbyshire. I went there one year when your mother and I were on a walking tour. Magnificent house. They're the old aristocracy. He's a very charming chap. Very charming."

It made her smile to realize that her father was a snob.

"You know, Ralph," Hugh Drummond said to him one evening, "I've really enjoyed my time out here. I didn't want to come at all."

They'd finished their piquet, and the doctor was lighting a pipe before bedtime. Steven, Angela and Charlie had gone for a late swim.

"I'm glad you did," Maxton said. "And the weather does make a difference. I always found the rain so depressing at home."

"Never noticed it," Hugh said. "Don't like it too hot myself. Funny, that's just what Steven said when he stayed with us at home. He didn't like the English weather. I suppose most Americans feel like that. I was rather annoyed, to be honest."

He leaned a little toward Maxton. He felt mellow and in the mood to confide. It was a rare impulse for him, and a sign of age, as he reminded himself. Old men turned into chatterboxes if they weren't careful. But it was pleasant to speak one's mind now and again.

"I wasn't all that struck by him at first," he said. He puffed happily away on his pipe.

"Oh?" Maxton was careful; curious, but cautious not to say anything critical of his employer that might be repeated. "Why not?"

"Too foreign," Hugh Drummond said. "Not just American, but rather sort of . . . Italian. I suppose it was because of the name I thought of him like that. After he changed it to Lawrence, it was easier. Silly how a detail can make so much difference."

"I suppose so," Maxton answered. Changed his name. So he wasn't Steven Lawrence. He smiled easily at the old man. *Careful now. It's none of your business if he calls himself something else. You've got a long nose, Ralph, as your old bitch of a nanny used to say, twisting the end of it to make you cry. So don't go sticking it into other people's business.*

"Lawrence is a good old-fashioned name," he said after a pause. "Was it difficult to pronounce—his real name, I mean? I had a Polish friend who called herself Browning because nobody could get their tongue around the Polish. Can be a nuisance for a businessman."

"Yes, I bet it can," Hugh Drummond agreed. "It wasn't a real tongue twister: Fal-something-or-other; can't quite remember, because I hardly ever heard it. But I must say, he's made Angela very happy. And he loves my grandson; that means a lot to me. One more hand, Ralph, before I take myself off to bed?"

"Why not?" Ralph agreed. "I expect you'll beat me again."

When the doctor had gone up to his room, Ralph let himself out and drove down to his flat on the coast. Lawrence wasn't Lawrence. Odd. Then he firmly dismissed his curiosity. *Nothing to do with you. If he wanted you to know, he'd have told you. Stay in line, Maxton. Stay snug in this extremely agreeable gravy train and mind your own business.*

The time came for packing up and going home, and Steven came with them. They spent a few days in the house at Haywards Heath. It was cool and it rained.

Steven said, "Darling, I'm missing the sun. Let's go home."

She realized that she was missing it too. Missing the villa, which seemed less than ever like a rented house; missing the excitement of helping him create the new casino.

"I'll tell Daddy. He won't mind, now that Charlie's gone back to school."

"It would make sense if he moved over with us," Steven said. "I think you worry about him, don't you?"

"A little bit. He's got very old suddenly. But he wouldn't dream of it. He's a very self-contained man, very independent. He wouldn't be happy out of his own environment. But thank you for offering." She reached up and gave him a kiss. "I do love you," she said, and then hurried out to find her father.

The maid, Maria, watched Clara. She was frightened of her mistress. She had such bad moods, when she lost her temper and shouted for no apparent reason. She was always finding fault. She prowled around the house like a caged tigress—restless, bored, unhappy. No husband and no children, Maria thought sourly. All her beauty treatments couldn't soften that face. And she couldn't find herself another man yet. It wouldn't be proper. Maria missed Steven Falconi. He was a real Don, like his father. A good man, kind to his own people. A man you respected. She wondered if she could go and see Don Lucca and ask if she could get a job with someone else.

Clara was restless. She wasn't sleeping well either, but she wouldn't take pills. She knew too many women who'd started on that path and slipped into tranquilizers and dependence. She would cope on her own. The maid got on her nerves. She was always shuffling about, pretending to work. She was a sly old bitch, and Clara didn't trust her. She was one of Falconi's people. Clara toyed with the idea of sacking her. It gave her pleasure to imagine it. But she did nothing.

It was getting hot and humid in New York. Her parents were moving to Key West for the summer. She didn't want to go with them. She didn't know what she wanted to do or how to occupy herself. Her father had already mentioned the need to marry again.

"I don't want another man," she declared, and for the moment he accepted that. But only for the moment. In a few months, when there wasn't a pretense of mourning, he'd start pressing her. She felt dead sexually. Cold in body and in spirit, as if she, and not Steven, had died. He'd paid the price of his betrayal. They'd killed him, as she'd warned him they would. She wished in her desolation that she had been with him in that car.

She had a hair appointment and lunch afterward at the Plaza with two women friends. They weren't Italians. They didn't belong to her world, and she had nothing in common with them except money and a liking for clothes and plush restaurants. She didn't feel like going. The day stretched ahead in emptiness. Dinner with her parents, TV in their family room, and usually an invitation to stay the night. She dreaded going back to her lonely house.

Clara wanted to scream. She had been looking at a fashion magazine without taking any of it in, flipping the pages impatiently. She threw it aside and got up. She was thinner than ever, taut inside her black dress. No appetite still, living on her nerves. Maybe she couldn't face dinner at home that night, with her mother's sidelong glances at Aldo, as if to say, What she needs is a good husband to take care of her, maybe some children this time. She'd go to a movie instead. . . . But they'd be hurt. She couldn't cancel on them. She went into the bedroom to get ready. The hairdresser and the lunch would kill her enemy Time for a few hours.

She retouched her makeup, drawing darker lines around her eyes to emphasize their size. They were huge and black as sloes in the thin face. She painted her mouth scarlet and opened the dressing table drawer to choose some earrings. There was a smart new fashion jeweler whose costume pieces were as pricey as the real thing. Kenneth Lane earrings and a matching brooch. They looked good. But the earrings pinched, and swearing, she pulled them off.

There was the little box. She'd put it in the drawer, right at the back where she couldn't see it, but it had worked its way forward and was under her eye. Her fingers touched it, a small square leather box with gold tooling around the edges. Inside was Steven's ring, which she'd made her father give her. *Open it,* temptation urged her. *Touch it, indulge your pain.* She took it out. The proof of his death. The pledge given by the Falconis that the debt to her was paid in full. It lay cold in her palm. She remembered the wedding service, when she had exchanged it for the one still on her finger. The fierce joy and expectation welling up in her as she circled the room in his arms, dancing the "Wedding Waltz." She shut her eyes. It was an agony she couldn't resist reliving: his beautiful hands grasping her waist, sensitive and erotic. They had always roused her when she looked at them, imagining their touch. They'd struck her too, and even that became a memory she savored. Once she'd slipped the ring off his finger and locked it over the one he'd given her. It was a symbol of her passion, her need to possess him completely and be herself possessed.

She did the same thing now. She slid the ring on her finger, over her own wedding band. It hung loose. So loose that if she bent her hand it fell off, clattering onto the dressing table. She stared at it. She tried again. Again it fell off.

Clara held it in one hand, turning it to see the inscription. It was visible, a little worn but still quite clear. "S. & C." and the date in figures, "5/18/50." It was the ring she had given Steven. The ring he had been wearing on the day he walked out of that bedroom and left her. But it was three sizes bigger. She went through the ritual again, with the same result.

She held it up and stared at it again. No man with hands like Steven's could have worn it. She clutched it tightly, and her reflection in the mirror contorted suddenly until the face was hardly recognizable.

She stood up, knocking over the stool. She kicked it aside. She shouted a blasphemous Sicilian oath.

"Porca Madonna!"

Maria heard it and cowered. She hid herself in the kitchen. She heard the bedroom door slam on its hinges and then the front door, hurting her ears. An hour later she answered the telephone. The hairdresser was calling to ask if Mrs. Falconi had forgotten her appointment.

The ladies at the Plaza waited half an hour, then decided she wasn't coming and started lunch.

"Clara, Clara, you can't disturb your Papa. It's business."

Her mother pleaded, wringing her hands. She had never seen her daughter like this. She was used to temper and outbursts, but not this deadly rage.

"This is business, believe me. Now do you call him, or do I?"

Clara swung away from her. She was trembling. She couldn't unclench her hands from the handbag that held the box with the gold ring inside.

Her mother was arguing again. She was such a fool, such a stupid fat doormat of a woman. Savage thoughts chased through Clara's brain, cruel, unthinkable criticisms that yesterday she would have suppressed with shame. *No wonder Papa goes for big tits and blondes.*

She shouted suddenly, "Shut up! Shut up and listen to me! Give me the number."

"He'll be angry," her mother said. "He's with Gino over at the warehouse. There's a meeting today."

Clara didn't listen. She knew the number of the warehouse where her father summoned his henchmen. She knew the big upstairs room above the containers and storage, where they sat around a table. It would be smoky, and smell of wine and garlic and human sweat. She knew, because she'd been there once. Aldo had given her a fur coat for her eighteenth birthday. He'd laid minks and silver foxes out on the table upstairs in the warehouse and told her to pick what she wanted. She chose the most expensive, and he had laughed and put it on her himself. She had it in a closet somewhere. A pastel-blue mink, which was not fashionable anymore.

She dialed the number, and a man answered.

"I want to speak with Don Aldo."

"He's busy." The tone was rude.

Clara spat back, "It's his daughter. You tell him it's urgent."

"Okay."

It seemed a long time while she waited. Then her father said sharply, "Clara? What the hell do you want?"

She said in a calm voice, "If there's any of Lucca Falconi's people with you, don't say anything. They've cheated us, Papa. Steven's alive." Then she hung up.

She turned to her mother. "That'll bring him home," she said.

"Yes, yes, it's been altered, all right."

The jeweler put down his loupe. He had been an associate of the Fabrizzis for many years, a second-generation Russian Jew who ran a pawnbroking business on the West Side and fenced stolen goods for a few big clients. Aldo trusted him.

"Made bigger?" Clara demanded.

He nodded. "By two sizes at least. It's well done. They haven't spoiled the inscription." He checked again, with the loupe to his eye. "You wouldn't see it without this, Don Aldo. It's a good job," he said again. He handed it back.

Aldo weighed it in his hand for a moment. "Thanks, Leo. I just wanted to be sure, that's all."

"They used eighteen karat, even, to keep the color of the gold the same," Leo added. "I guess it was altered for someone else to wear."

"I guess it was," Aldo said. "Thanks. The family's well?"

He never neglected the formalities. It was expected of him to inquire about the Rabinoviches' welfare and to spend a minute or two while Leo answered.

The woman was fuming with impatience. The old Jew was surprised to see the Don with a brunette, however striking. He brought his blondes along to buy them jewelry. Not too expensive, but nice pieces. Leo always gave him a special price.

He said, "Julia's had some troubles. She has pain in the hip, but as I tell her, we're not so young anymore. But the boys are well and the grandchildren. They make life good for us."

"Give Julia my best," Aldo said formally. "And keep well."

They got into the big limousine, Aldo's bodyguard in the front seat, and sat in silence as the car sped home. He took his daughter's hand and held it. It was a fierce grip that sealed a pact between them.

"They gave us a dummy," he said. "They set us up, Clara. They cut the finger off some guy and changed the ring to fit. They won't get away with it. I promise you."

"I know they won't," she answered. "I want him found, Papa."

He turned and looked at her. She was all he cared about, his only child. He'd watched her suffer, tear herself to pieces over Steven Falconi. He thought suddenly, *She's clever, my girl. She's got a brain. She saw through it.* He was proud of her.

"We'll find him," he said. "But we settle with all the bastards now. We wipe them out."

"Yes," Clara said. "And we take over everything that's theirs."

He noticed that she had said "we." It didn't sound as presumptuous as it might have. As they drew up before the entrance to his house, he said gently to Clara, "You were tough on Mama. I don't blame you, but you will make it right."

"I'll make it right," she promised. And as soon as her mother came out to the hallway to meet them, Clara put her arms around her and said, "Forgive me, Mama. I didn't mean it. You're the best mother in the world."

She looked at Aldo, who nodded in satisfaction. He liked peace in the family. He sat down and let his women wait upon him. He took wine, a man at ease in his own home. And he planned the systematic murder of the Falconis, down to the last surviving male.

Tino Spoletto hadn't wanted to leave his home in Florida and come to New York. His wife had complained bitterly about uprooting the children from their schools and selling their nice house. They had a good business. They owned a chain of restaurants and bars, with illegal betting on the side. Tino didn't need to employ accountants. He was too good with figures himself. He carried everything in his head, and he was never out by a cent.

Not once had he been in trouble, even as a boy. He was the quiet one in the Spoletto family, always doing well at school. His wife, Nina, was happy with him, contented with their life and devoted to her three children. They were part of the family, but on the fringe. Little was asked of them except a favor now and again, which paid for their protection in their businesses. No one reneged on a debt to the Spolettos. No one in the local police department raided the back rooms where the bets were being taken.

[169]

When the call had come, Tino knew he must obey. It was an honor to be asked by Don Lucca himself to fill a place left vacant by his eldest son. An opportunity not to be refused. They'd sold their house, found a good parochial school for the girls and a high school for their boy. Nina wanted a house in a neighborhood where she'd make friends. They bought one in Little Italy. Her mother lived with them. She'd never learned to speak English, and at least now she could go to the nearby shops and find a few old women to gossip with.

And after all the months of settling in, they were happy. The Don and his family had taken them to their hearts. They were invited for the family Sundays, and the children played with Piero's children. Nina and Lucia Falconi went shopping and talked women's talk together. Tino hadn't moved into Steven's office. That was taken by Piero, now designated as the Don's successor. Nobody mentioned Steven. Tino didn't ask questions. There was disgrace and dishonor involved. It wasn't his business as a distant relative to inquire about details.

He was doing a very good job. Don Lucca was pleased with him, and Piero slapped him on the back and invited him out to Minoletti's for a good dinner and to talk business. Tino had respect for Piero, who would be the top man one day. He wanted to please Piero and was devoted to the old Don. He had been good to them, generous over the new house, fond with their children. The Don was a family man inside the family. Now when they came to the house on Sundays, he greeted Tino with a kiss.

It was a nice summer day, and they were in the walled garden. A big table with a white cloth was set out under the trees, and the women were busy in the kitchen while the men sat around in their shirtsleeves and talked over the Chianti.

Tino said, "I got a letter from a cousin yesterday, Don Lucca. She mentioned the Fabrizzis are having a big get-together at their place in Key West."

Piero said sharply, "How the fuck does she know?"

They hadn't heard anything about it. Courtesy between them indicated at least a mention, if not an invitation.

"She's in the catering business. Her husband and his brother specialize in wedding parties, anniversaries, that kind of stuff. They didn't get the Fabrizzis' order, but they know someone in the business who did. Eighty people, she said, and all the families too."

Don Lucca said slowly, "What sort of party?"

"She didn't say."

"I'd like to know who's invited," Lucca Falconi said. "And the reason." He didn't show his anger. They were partners and tied by marriage. Clara was a Falconi by name at least. Aldo Fabrizzi had said nothing about a big party.

Piero looked at his cousin Tino. He was sharp-eyed and long-eared. He'd picked up that item on the Fabrizzis and their "party." Piero could smell disloyalty in a man. And loyalty too. Tino was playing watchdog in his quiet way. Piero liked him for that. From the first day, he had made his feeling about the Fabrizzis clear to his cousin.

"I don't trust that old bastard Aldo. I don't trust any of them. So keep your eyes open, Tino. We won't always be partners with that load of shit."

"Maybe it's because it's so far away," Tino suggested. "Maybe they thought we wouldn't get to know about it." He picked up the bottle and refilled the Don's glass.

Piero banged the table. "You think it's a family council?" he demanded. "You think they're getting the heads of their people together to agree on something and not telling us?"

"It could be," Tino said.

Lucca Falconi leaned toward them. "This cousin of yours—can she get someone into the caterer's? Someone who can use their eyes and ears and let us know what they pick up?"

Tino looked abashed. "I did that already, Don Lucca. I hoped you'd think it's okay. I just had a hunch something was up."

"You're a good boy," Lucca said quietly. "You use your head. I like that. Good. You've done well."

He saw his wife and daughter-in-law and Tino's wife come out, carrying dishes of salad and cheeses, and said, "We say nothing about this to the women. My wife's not been too well; she mustn't worry, the doctor said. It's been a hard year for her. A hard year for us all."

"Leave it to me," Tino Spoletto said. "I'll find out what's going on. My cousin knows she'll be rewarded."

It was a noisy lunch, with everyone talking, Piero's children demanding their grandparents' attention and Tino's older family well behaved. The women were smiling and contented, and the Don presided over them all, blessed with three generations around his table. And the cousin who was becoming more and more like a son to him. If there was danger, the Don would be forewarned.

[171]

* * *

It was a matter of honor, the old men said. The grayheads spoke in solemn language, using the distinctive phraseology of their ancient culture. The younger men responded with the language of the ghetto and the back alley. "We blow their asses off!"

The party was on the beach. There was a big buffet, which went on all day; the children and their mothers, the girlfriends and sisters, were sunbathing, swimming, or playing in the sand. Their laughing and calling drifted into the room with the shutters drawn against the bright August sunshine.

Aldo Fabrizzi had spoken, and they had sat there in a heavy silence until he finished. Not even the young men so much as snapped a lighter while he talked. He called on them one by one, the heads of the eight affiliated groups within the Fabrizzi family. Eight powerful men, controlling little empires and armies of other men. They all owed their loyalty to Aldo Fabrizzi. He was their Don. In the old country, their grandfathers had paid tribute to such men. Gifts of the best wine, cheese, livestock; the proceeds of robberies and extortion. And risked their lives and the lives of their sons when the Don asked it.

But with the asking, there was always a promise. A rich reward for loyalty. Don Aldo had spoken about the reward and seen their excitement flash like the summer lightning on the Keys.

"I estimate their businesses are worth fifty million dollars, maybe more," he said. "The garment trade pays dues to them; they've got a stake in the construction companies that operate in downtown New York. They own casinos in Nevada and hotels along the East Coast, besides the cathouses and the dope. There's good money in them. If we get rid of Lucca Falconi, we move in and take over."

"We get rid of them all," someone said. "That punk Piero and the little creep Spoletto."

"Piero's no punk," someone pointed out. "He's rough; don't underestimate him."

"Yeah. So are we," the other man boasted.

"There are cousins and relatives spread all over," an older man remarked. "What about them, Don Aldo? We can't leave them to make trouble later."

"The blood relatives all go," he said. "The small people, the little soldiers . . ." He shrugged. "They follow a new capo, that's all. It always happens. They have to live; their families have to eat."

He paused. They were watching him, faces upturned as he stood at the head of the long table.

"I ask for your loyalty," he said.

There was no dissenting voice. "It's given, Don Aldo," they said, each in turn.

Then came the questions: How's it to be done? How long before we make our move? Do you plan to hit them all at the same time?

One of the capos spoke, expressing caution. "It won't be easy to get them to expose themselves. Falconi has played this trick himself. Remember how he took care of the Ryans?" The Ryans had been twenty-five years ago, Irish interlopers, hustling on Falconi territory.

"They'll come," Aldo promised. "They think they've gotten away with cheating me. They'll come. The three of them. Falconi, his son Piero and the blood cousin Spoletto. They'll come to a wedding."

There was a murmur. Aldo looked around. His smile was brief and frightening, like a wicked grimace.

"It's time my daughter, Clara, got married again," he said. "They'll come to the wedding. And we will all be there, with alibis. I think my Clara will like that."

Clara was bored. She had nothing in common with the other women at the party, and they didn't feel comfortable with her. They gossiped about the domestic details of their lives, their children, the schools, the trivia of married life that Clara couldn't share. She was alien to them in her status as a childless widow whose man had died in dishonor. She was aloof. She dressed too smartly, held herself proudly, showed a disdain for men that shocked them.

She drifted away to a table by the beach and ordered champagne. The dead-white dress she wore had a daring side slit that showed her long legs, bare and brown. There were gold sandals on her feet. Her dark hair was pulled back and dressed high, showing a graceful neck set off by big gold earrings. It was a simple, provocative look, achieved at great expense. The man watching her thought she looked like a swan.

He was lounging at the outdoor buffet table, sampling the food, joking with some young cronies. He watched the beautiful, sleek woman drinking champagne on her own, chain-smoking cigarettes. He was intrigued. She was Don Fabrizzi's daughter, the widow, whose Falconi husband had disappeared. When he stared at a woman she felt it and always looked back at him. This one didn't. That intrigued him too, and challenged him. He paid less and less attention to the talk of the younger men around him, boasting of prowess on the streets, prowess with girls. The men of importance were in the house with Don Aldo.

He was related to one of the Fabrizzi capos' wives. He visited with them regularly, although he didn't work for them. He had grown up in a separate district, far over on the West Side where the Guglielmo brothers ruled and he joined up with them when he left school. He flexed his broad shoulders and ran a hand over his thick curly hair. He slung his jacket casually over his shoulder and moved off toward the woman seated at the table.

Clara saw him coming. Clara had seen him watching her and taken pleasure in ignoring him. He was big and handsome and common-looking; very sure of himself. The sniggering clique of young men were elbowing each other and waiting to see what happened.

He came up to the table. She might be the Don's daughter, but so what? His technique always worked.

"Hi there, baby. Mind if I join you? You're too beautiful to be sittin' there all alone."

Clara looked him up and down. She *was* bored, and she had drunk a lot more champagne than she'd meant to.

"The bottle's empty," she said. "Get me a fresh one." She opened her bag and studied herself in a gold compact.

He smiled down at her. "I'll get it if you offer me a drink, baby."

She said, "Why don't you go get it and see what happens."

"Sure." He turned and clicked his fingers. "Tony!" he called out, and one of the youths at the buffet table started forward obediently. "Get a bottle for the lady. And bring a glass for me."

He pulled a chair out and sat opposite her. He smiled. He had magnificent white teeth.

Snapping her bag shut, she glared at him. "Who the hell do you think you are? When I want company I'll say so!"

"You look great when you're mad," he remarked. "I'll bet you scare the shit out of every guy who comes along. Only I don't scare easy. Not when it comes to a beautiful baby like you." He leaned a little toward her. She smelled a strong aftershave or hair tonic. Musky, vulgar. Like the man himself.

"Don't call me baby," she said. "Keep that crap for the waitresses. Why don't you go and pester them?"

"Here's the champagne," he said. "Thanks, Tony." He opened the bottle with a flourish. He poured her a full glass and helped himself. "This is good stuff. But then the Don does everything in style."

"Watch your mouth," Clara warned him. "He's my father."

He opened his eyes wide, mocking her. "You don't say? That makes you someone special, eh?"

Clara drank the champagne, emptying the glass.

"You'll get fried," he said. "Go easy on that stuff. Aren't you having fun? I'm Bruno Salviatti. I always have fun."

She jeered, "It must be wonderful to be you."

He didn't take offense. It seemed nothing offended him. He sat there looking good-humored and self-confident, and she didn't know whether to get up and get rid of him, or to go on sitting there, letting him play his cheap little game till she got tired of it.

"You're a beautiful dame," he said. "Why don't you try smiling?"

Clara did, and then she said, "Why don't you fuck off?"

He laughed. He reached over and grasped her bare arm. He had big, strong hands with fine black hair on the backs of them.

"Why don't I fuck you?"

They went walking, leaving the party in the distance. She was a little unsteady, a little light-headed. *I'm not dead, just because he's left me—I can still feel, still want a man. I've been a corpse for so long, waiting for a husband who didn't want me, lying in bed as if it was my coffin. If this big bull wants to hump me, why the hell don't I let him?*

"Loosen up," he kept saying to her, stroking her bottom, pinching the spare flesh of her buttocks between thumb and finger. He held her steady as they made their way toward the back of the big house, through a grove of palm trees in front of the summerhouse. Soon Clara was directing him, eager to find a secluded spot. She liked the feeling of being in command. The champagne had suddenly made everything easy. She felt like it; she was going to have it.

She knew where they could go. The summerhouse was empty now, though it had been occupied recently; there were dirty glasses and an empty wine bottle inside on the coffee table.

She said to him, "Salviatti, lock the door and close the blinds," and she pulled the dress over her head. She stood naked except for a flimsy G-string pantie. He hooked his fingers in each lace strap and ripped them off her.

"Okay," she said. "You say you're good. Now prove it!"

"It was their wedding anniversary," Tino said. Piero scowled at him. "They had a big cake, and the old people led the dancing. Thirty-eight years married. That was the reason for the party."

Piero said, "You checked this?"

Tino nodded. "I made some inquiries, I got a copy of the marriage certificate. It all checked out."

"So it was on the level?"

"Maybe, maybe not. Why Key West instead of some accessible place?"

"They got a fucking house down there, that's why." Piero was angry with Tino Spoletto's persistent suspicion that something was wrong. "They had a wedding anniversary, with a cake and dancing and the rest of the shit—so what are you eating your arse about?"

"It's a small house for so many people," Tino said. "They had to use the hotel and some guesthouses. I'm just mentioning it, that's all."

Piero lost his temper. He didn't want Tino to be right. He didn't want trouble with the Fabrizzis. He was consolidating his position, feeling his way without the shrewd guidance of Steven. He wanted a couple of years before he had to move against Aldo. He liked Tino and he trusted him. But he was angry at him for stirring it up.

He shouted, "For Christ's sake, you got nothing to go on! Okay, so they celebrated their fucking wedding and they didn't say anything to us about it. They haven't asked us other years, so what the hell does that prove?"

Tino shrugged his shoulders. He knew his cousin in that mood. Piero was uneasy, that was the reason for his outburst of temper. He was unlikely to listen to anything till he calmed down. But Tino gave it one more try.

"Thirty-eight years isn't special," he said quietly. "It's no big deal. Forty years is ruby. That's special; that everyone celebrates. I think we should be careful, that's all I'm saying."

"Okay, okay, okay." Piero's voice was loud. "Okay, we'll be careful. Now I've got fucking work to do."

At noon he pushed his chair back, picked up his jacket and went down one floor to Tino's office. He'd been rough on his cousin. He was sorry. And there was a creeping doubt in his mind that wouldn't be sworn and blustered away. He opened the door and called out.

"Hey, Tino? I'm going for some lunch. You want to come?"

They went down in the elevator together. Piero flung an arm around his cousin.

"For Christ's sake. I shot off my mouth. Forget it, will you? You're right. We'll watch it. No chances."

"You leave this to Anna and me," Luisa Fabrizzi said. "Go and sit with your papa. He wants to talk to you."

"If you don't mind," Clara said.

She hated helping with the dishes. Her mother always did it, and the girls in the family were expected to help her. Clara was not domesticated and resented being relegated to the kitchen. A young cousin was staying with them. She was a nice, simple Italian girl, who'd be in her element at the sink.

Clara went back to join her father. She wondered what he wanted to talk about; not marriage again. Not after she'd told him plainly that she would never tie herself to another man. Her mother had been in tears. He had been angry. She had stormed out and gone home, only to call them within the hour and apologize. She never let a quarrel last. She needed them too much, especially her father. Luisa spoiled her and fussed over her. It was nice to be pampered, having special food cooked for her, a bed always ready in case she felt like staying.

But her relationship with Aldo had changed and deepened over the last year. She was more than just his little girl, to be petted and protected. Subtly, she felt, he had accorded her a status that was unusual between father and daughter. He asked her opinion about people in his business. He talked things over with her, which was extraordinary. He explained some of their investments, coaching her on the financial side of their interests in the garment trade.

"You should learn to read a ledger," he'd said one day. "You should understand money and how to make it work for you."

Clara had never bothered with such things. Her father had managed whatever money he had settled on her, and then it was Steven's responsibility. She spent it; she didn't concern herself with managing her own investments. She wouldn't have known how. But now she was beginning to. Aldo had taught her a lot, and she was a quick and intuitive pupil.

He was sitting in his usual chair, coat off, collar unbuttoned, soft slippers on his feet. He looked up and said, "Come and sit down, Clara."

She lit a cigarette; she had started smoking heavily. "What is it? Mama said you wanted to talk to me. Is something wrong?"

"No, no. Nothing's wrong, Clara. Give me the ashtray." He had a thin black cigar, which was his indulgence after a good meal. He drew on it and tapped off the ash. He said, "You know how old I am?"

"Seventy-three. That's not old."

"It's old enough," he countered. "I've been thinking. What happens to everything when I go? I've no son, no close relation of my own blood to take over from me. Only you, Clara. Only you."

"It's not my fault. I know you wanted a boy."

"It wasn't God's will," he answered. "When you married, I thought that was the answer. I thought you'd have children, there'd be a grandson."

Tears came into her eyes. She said bitterly, "Don't reproach me. I tried, and you know it. If it wasn't God's will for you, it wasn't for me either."

"It doesn't matter," Aldo said. "I could have had a stupid son. Instead I have a clever daughter. Very clever. I've been watching you, Clara, seeing how you learned things, how you think. You know something? You think like a man when it comes to business."

"I think like you've taught me," she retorted. The tears had gone. There was a little color in her pale face.

He smiled at her. "Yes, but you think for yourself mostly. That's what I like best about you. And what you don't know you're not too proud to ask. You've always been a determined girl. And you've got as much guts as any man."

He paused. "I want you to run the business when the time comes," he said. "You can do it. You can look after what I've made and maybe make it bigger."

She got up and came to him. She knelt by his chair and lifted his hand and kissed it. She held it against her cheek.

"Oh, Papa. Do you really mean it? How could I do it? There's never been a woman at the head of one of the families."

"That's not the question," he said. "Look at me, Clara. Tell me the truth. Can you do it? Can you be a son to me as well as my daughter?"

"I can," she answered. "I know I can."

He nodded. He stroked her sleek black hair for a moment. "I think so too. But there's one problem. You've just said it yourself. The only way the family and the other families will accept a woman is if she has a husband. You've got to marry, Clara. A man will save their

[178]

pride. They'll take orders from him even though they know the orders come from you. There's no way around that."

She got up slowly. He looked up at her. She knew that expression only too well. No argument, no backtracking. He had made a condition that must be accepted unconditionally.

"A man will take over from me," she said after a pause. "He'll want to be the boss."

Aldo grunted, puffing on the cigar. "Not if we choose the right one."

She turned quickly. "You've chosen somebody for me?"

"It must be your choice," he said. "It must be a man who pleases you."

"You think you've seen one?" She was sarcastic.

"How about Bruno Salviatti," he said. "I heard the two of you paired off at our party. In fact," he added, seeing a blush creep into her face, "you went off alone for quite a while."

Clara stood her ground. "He made a play for me. He had his hand up my skirt, and I let him. I didn't think anyone would notice. It meant nothing to me. He's pretty-looking, and I'd had too much champagne. There are hundreds like him, hanging around the trattorias and waiting for *la bella fortuna* to smile on them."

Aldo was amused by his daughter's embarrassment. She'd picked up Salviatti and used him as he used his big-breasted blondes. She'd been alone for a long time. He knew her blood was as hot as his; she was no virgin. She didn't have to be chaste, only discreet.

He said, "If he pleased you, he'd be a good choice. He'd count his blessings and do what he was told. And he's fine-looking. A lot of women would envy you."

She didn't answer immediately. Bruno Salviatti: broad chest, small waist, thick curly black hair and big dark eyes. He'd count his blessings, just as Aldo said. Good clothes, money, a chance to swagger as the macho man married to the Don's daughter. He'd brought her to a rapid and violent sexual climax and been ready for more. She'd pushed him off and dismissed him.

She thought for those few moments, and Aldo didn't interrupt. She would never love a man like Bruno. She would never suffer on his account, because she would always despise him. The roles would be reversed. She would be the dominant partner. If it wasn't Bruno Salviatti, it would have to be someone like him. And she would end up as the power behind the Fabrizzi family.

Aldo was offering her everything he would have offered a son. There were millions of dollars in securities abroad, property investments, and the huge income from the rackets. And her father was right. She would need someone like Bruno to front for her. The families would never accept a woman. No man could take orders from her without losing face. Otherwise, when Aldo died the Fabrizzi empire would be divided piecemeal among the other families. She had come to know and admire her father's subtlety, the ruthlessness of his dealings. He had shown her a new and exciting world. A man's world, closed to women. If she did what he asked, it would be her world. The nursery and the kitchen were not for her. They never had been, once her marriage to Steven failed. Bruno Salviatti. It wasn't much to ask in exchange for what was offered. He'd warm her bed and do what he was told.

"I'll see him again, Papa," she said. "If I like him, then why not?"

He got up and came over to her. He placed both hands on her shoulders. She was still far too thin.

"I want you to be happy," he said. "You're all I have in the world."

"You're all *I* have," she said. "You and Mama. I want to work with you now. I won't think about afterwards. That's going to break my heart. We'll be together. We'll do it together."

He embraced her. It was a moment of deep emotion for both of them.

He spoke very quietly to her. "I didn't invite the Falconis to our anniversary. I must make it up to them, *cara mia*. I must invite them to your wedding. I'll make you a present of them. Lucca, Piero and the cousin Spoletto. How would you like that?"

They gazed into each other's eyes.

"I'd like it," she said. "But I want *him*. I want to see him dead."

"You will," he promised. "Only have patience. Wherever he's hiding, when he hears what's happened to his family, he'll come back."

She shook her head. "So we can kill him? Not Steven. He'll come to strike back, and we won't even know till it happens."

Aldo said gently, "I said you were clever, Clara, but you've still a few things to learn from your old father. It won't be *us* he'll come looking for."

"Then who?" she asked him.

He gave his brief, cruel smile. "Trust me," was all he said. "Now go and call your mother and Anna. It's time for that quiz show she likes on TV."

A month later Lucca Falconi got a call from Aldo Fabrizzi. They exchanged inquiries about each other's health and the well-being of their families, and referred in passing to the state of their business.

"I want to have a meeting with you," Aldo said. "Just you and me. It's a matter for the old men." He gave his throaty laugh.

"You want to come here?" Lucca suggested. "You'd be very welcome."

"No, no. Let's make it a dinner. How about La Scala?"

Lucca sounded pleased. "The food's good. Not as good as Minoletti's, but good."

Minoletti's was the Falconis' favorite restaurant. They owned part of it, and it was run by a family with close connections. For years, whenever Lucca wanted to eat out or take the family, he had gone there. It had always been like a fortress for the Falconis, especially during the war with Musso.

"You prefer Minoletti's, we can go there." Aldo said. He sounded disappointed. It was his invitation, after all.

"We eat in La Scala," Lucca answered. "I look forward to it. And this is business between us, or family?"

"It's family," Aldo said. "But what's to stop us talking business too? We meet at around seven-thirty Tuesday?"

"I look forward to it," Lucca said. He put the phone down. "What the hell," he muttered. "What the hell does that bastard want?"

La Scala was a big, fashionable Italian restaurant famous for its Neapolitan cooking. It was very pricey. Certainly Fabrizzi wanted something if he was prepared to spend that kind of money on a meal.

Lucca took two bodyguards with him. Aldo had two of his men. The two Dons sat at a table chosen because it faced into the middle of the main restaurant. The adjoining tables were allotted to the men protecting them. It was a natural precaution, which they took for granted. Both had enemies among the non-Mafia gangster groups. The Irish in particular had never made a formal peace with Lucca Falconi after the massacre of the five Ryans. Nothing was proved and no charges could be brought, for lack of evidence, but everybody knew.

As the Dons embraced and kissed each other on both cheeks, each thought the other had got older. Their henchmen watched, pretending to be friendly. The manager came to take their order. There were a lot of snapping fingers and hurrying waiters around them. They were important men. Respected members of the Italian-American community. Businessmen, who wore well-cut suits, custom-made shirts and shoes, and flowers in their lapels—a carnation for Fabrizzi, a rose for Falconi. Big contributors to charity. Men of many favors.

"My friend," Aldo said, "I'm not here to talk about the past. The past is the past, eh? It only brings pain to you and pain to all of us. I want to talk about the future."

"When you're our age," Lucca amended, "there's not too much future left. So we make the most of it. I believe in that. So what kind of future are we going to talk about? Yours or mine?"

"Clara's," Aldo answered.

"Ah." Lucca nodded. "I know how she grieved. I was so sorry she had been sick. But you say she's better now."

"She's better. She's a strong girl. But there were times when her mother and me were very worried. Very worried."

"I can believe that," Lucca said. "So what about Clara's future?" Money? he wondered. Is that what he's after? She's not getting any more.

"She's been a widow for a year," Aldo went on. "It's time she had a husband. I think I've found the right man for her. And she likes him. You know Clara: she wouldn't take anyone she didn't like."

"No," Lucca agreed. "She wouldn't. As you said, my friend, she's a strong girl. A girl with a mind of her own. Who is this man?"

Aldo pulled his napkin out of his collar. He turned aside politely and belched. "He's not one of our family. He's one of the Guglielmos' young men."

Lucca removed his napkin. The waiters were bringing them coffee. He asked for Strega. Aldo refused anything more to drink.

"Why a man from the Guglielmos? They're not friends to any of us."

"No, but why not make them friends? When your son married my daughter, there were advantages for both of us. Clara needed new blood. She met this man in Key West. We had some people down, and he was brought along. She liked him. They got along well. It's the first time I saw my daughter smile in a whole year. It brought tears to my eyes."

"I have no daughters," Lucca said, "but I know how a father feels."

"We talked it over, Clara and me and her mother. I said, You like him, go ahead. See more of each other. Make up your mind, and I'll make up my mind. I checked on him. He's a good boy. His name's

Bruno Salviatti. He worked his way up from soldier to capo in the Guglielmos' organization. He's a proper man. You'll like him, Lucca. And that's important to Clara. She said to me, 'Papa, I want Lucca's blessing.' She said those words. She feels like a daughter to you, you know that?"

"And I love her like a father," Lucca said solemnly. "She's suffered. We've suffered, you and I, Aldo. But we won't talk about the past. Tell Clara I wish her happiness. Her happiness makes me happy. Tell her that."

"I will," Aldo Fabrizzi said. "You'll come to the wedding? We're fixing it for January. Here in New York. They're young, and you know what hot blood is. They don't want to wait." He grinned.

Lucca chuckled. He raised his glass of Strega. "Here's health and happiness and sons to them," he said.

Aldo called for the bill, and side by side, surrounded by their bodyguards, they made their way through the restaurant, stopping once or twice to accept greetings from other diners. Outside, the big, sleek cars, armor-plated under gleaming paintwork, glided up to receive them. They drove off side by side and then, at the first intersection, swung apart and went their separate ways.

6

The casino was finished. The last decorator had left, the last curtainmaker had settled the drapes and swags of silk and velvet, the last piece of furniture was in place. They were a month late. The opening was now scheduled for September. Steven and Angela toured the rooms. He wanted to share his triumph with her first. He brought her there at night, to see it illuminated in its glory, as the rich and famous would see it.

The baccarat tables were in place in the *salon privé,* where only the richest were admitted. There were roulette wheels and tables for blackjack in the outer rooms, where the stakes were more modest. He held Angela's hand as they made their tour, and at one of the roulette tables, Steven paused and spun the wheel, throwing the little ball. It rattled into a red socket.

"Seven," he said. "My lucky number, darling. And so much of it is due to you. You've made it beautiful for me." He took her in his arms. "I want you to be part of this. I want you to be excited by what we've done together. You are, aren't you?"

"You know I am," Angela told him. "It's wonderful, Steven. I'm very proud of you."

"We'll have a good life," he said. "We'll make lots of money and we'll have a fine business to hand on to our boy. I'm not going to stop at this, darling. This is just the beginning. I'm going to build a hotel next. I'm going to invest in property. There's so much scope here on the coast. So I won't be just a gambler. You'd like that, wouldn't you?"

"Yes," she admitted. "I would. I worry about one thing."

"Tell me," he said gently. "Tell me what it is."

"Ralph's stories about people killing themselves because they'd gambled everything away. You won't let that happen, will you?"

"I don't believe half of what he tells us," he said. "He likes to make an impression. It's part of his job. What about the people who've made fortunes and walked off?"

"That doesn't happen very often," she answered.

"Thank God for that," he teased her. Then he said seriously, "But if it would make you happy, we'll have a policy. If it's known someone's getting in too deep, we'll close down the game. How would that be?"

"Oh, darling, will you really do that? I would be so much happier. And so would you."

He said softly, "I guess I would. I'll set it up."

It was a perfect night for a gala opening. The weather was hot, with a light sea breeze, the sky a backdrop of black velvet, diamond-studded with stars. The casino was bathed in light; even the gardens were illuminated.

Steven was there early, supervising the last details. Maxton had spent the day on the premises. He changed into evening dress upstairs in his private office. He was excited, and amused by that excitement. For years he had felt immune to strong emotions. Only the visceral thrill of gambling ever affected him, sending adrenaline pumping, making his hands tremble. But tonight was special.

It had come together very quickly at the end, as such projects tend to do, after delays and frustrations that made the opening date recede into improbability. Then it was ready! Everything was done, down to the last flower arrangement. The staff had lined up and passed inspection, and the croupiers and dealers were in their places, immaculate in evening dress.

Maxton had ordered champagne to be brought up to his handsome office, with its elegant desk and comfortable leather chairs and a cocktail cabinet for entertaining. He popped the cork and poured a full glass, then he raised it in a private toast.

"To you, Great-uncle Oleg. Wherever you are, you old devil. You'd have enjoyed tonight."

He had persuaded Steven not to change the name. And Angela had been his ally. Casino Poliakoff had a dignified, romantic sound. And it was good publicity. To whet public curiosity, Maxton had circulated stories, true and invented, about the origins of the splendid house built by a crazy czarist aristocrat for his French mistress. As a final touch, he had suggested that a portrait of the count be placed in the entrance hall.

"But there isn't one," Steven objected.

"I think I can get hold of a photograph. Then all we have to do is get someone to copy it in oils."

And to Angela he said later, "I didn't say anything to Steven, but the old boy was a sort of ancestor. His sister married my grandfather."

"He knows," she said. "Have you got a photograph?"

"Yes," he said. "I have. I actually brought an old album back with me last time I went to England. It had pictures of my mother I rather liked, and it seemed a pity to take them out, so I made off with the whole thing. There's a splendid snap of Oleg in uniform. I think we could commission a rather handsome portrait from it. . . . I didn't know Steven knew there was a connection," he added casually.

Angela said, "Steven knows everything about you, Ralph. Don't ever try to hide anything from him, will you? He wouldn't like it."

"I wouldn't be able to, it seems. Fair enough."

He hadn't been pleased, she could see that. He left her rather quickly. When she saw him two days later he was his charming, easygoing self.

They'd brought the boy over to attend the opening. Ralph thought it a ridiculous thing to do. Charlie was a nice fellow, in Ralph's view, but in danger of being ruined by his parents. Steven was the most indulgent stepfather, worse than Angela, who at least tried to insist that he not skip school and that he take his exams seriously. Steven's obsession with another man's son was very odd. He didn't seem the type to lavish paternal love on a stepson. Maxton resented the relationship. It upset his theories on fathers' attitudes to their sons. But he was intelligent enough to suspect that his own bleak family background was the reason.

It was laughable, but whenever he saw Steven and Charlie going off together, he felt a jealous pang. Steven was teaching the boy to play golf. He was not a interested in sports, but he had taken up tennis and riding and now golf, so as to be a companion to Charlie when he stayed with them. And then there were Charlie's friends. They flew in at Steven's expense and were put up at the villa. A boat with a skipper was chartered to take them sailing; every facility from waterskiing to scuba diving was paid for and organized. Again, Maxton recognized that he was jealous. He envied Charlie Lawrence his good looks, his self-confidence. He envied him the kind of love and attention that had never come Ralph's way.

And he watched Angela with her son; it gave him a new perspective on the role a mother plays in a boy's upbringing. She was gentle and affectionate, firm when it was in Charlie's interest, but above all, she was a friend to whom her son could turn if he felt in need of comfort or advice.

He marveled at her kindness, not only to those close to her but to him, the stranger who'd come into her life whether she wanted him or not. No woman had ever been kind to Ralph. He'd been made to feel he was a changeling by his family.

That was what his old nanny used to say when he'd been naughty. "I don't know where you came from, you're such a bad boy! A real little changeling you are."

He felt cold with hatred when he remembered her. He was always being punished. His bottom would sting from angry beatings with a hairbrush. There were six children under her care, but he was always judged the culprit, even when he wasn't guilty. "Up to bed with you— no supper. That'll teach you." There was no appeal against her tyranny. His mother was a remote figure who drifted in and out of her children's lives at set times, and her embraces were brief and never encouraged intimacy. Nanny ruled the nursery kingdom. She cuddled his brothers and sisters, settling them in her big lap and tickling them, or rocking them to and fro, but it seemed to Ralph that she hated him. He lived in fear, and those who wanted to stay in Nanny's good graces showed him no favor.

"I've spoken to her ladyship. *You're* not going to the panto-mime!"—the Christmas treat before he went back to preparatory school. He was seven, and the pantomime was Dick Whittington. He'd been looking forward to it all through the holidays. Now his mother had sided with the enemy and confirmed her sentence.

He watched from the window as the others set off by car, and he cried as if his heart would burst. There was no kindness in women. Even the nursery maid tattled on him to curry favor.

No kindness and no pity. They punished you when you were a child, and when you grew up, you knew what to expect from them. So you used them for pleasure, but you reserved your love for yourself. He was twelve when his tormentor died; a governess took her place with the smaller children, but it made no difference to Ralph.

He was growing up fast, a clever, ugly youth with a wild streak in him. No one understood him or tried to win his confidence. He seemed to have a natural penchant for trouble and no interest in the solid pursuits of horse, gun and rod. In fact, he hated hunting—a crime in his father's view. But he loved racing and even as a schoolboy had been caught making book on the derby and threatened with expulsion. He had shamed them all. He'd heard someone say once when he was still in his teens and in disgrace for some misdeed he'd since forgotten, "It's the Russian blood, I suppose—totally unreliable." He thought it was an aunt, talking to his father, but he couldn't be sure.

Steven was displaying a degree of nervousness about the opening that surprised Maxton. He was even more surprised at the new house rule that Steven had introduced. Clients were not allowed to gamble in excess of their known means. Experienced staff could quickly tell when a man or woman had begun to gamble out of desperation. They were instructed, on pain of dismissal, to close the game. Maxton had mentioned that such a ruling was unheard of in any gambling establishment.

Steven had dismissed the objection. "That's the way Angela wants it. She got upset by all the suicide stories you told her. I promised, and that's the way it's going to be."

He hadn't struck Maxton as a man likely to be swayed by his wife's moral scruples, but Ralph was wrong about that too.

The love of a good woman, Ralph Maxton mocked to himself, but it was self-mockery. And envy was deep there too. Lawrence didn't deserve her. He couldn't think of anyone who did. "I warm my cold heart at your hearth." He enjoyed poetry, and that line from a Renaissance verse often came to mind when he was with Angela.

He'd been ill with flu the month before, when preparations were most hectic, and she herself was working long hours on the decorations and the final touches in the public rooms at the palace. No one had ever bothered with Ralph when he was sick. The ladies who'd lent him money had received favors in return, not least a buoyant cheerfulness. When he was hungry and broke, he'd sung for his supper. Illness and depression were endured alone.

But Angela amazed him. And embarrassed him. She came to his flat with food and old-fashioned remedies for coughs and colds that made him wince with memories of his childhood. And he felt a strange sense of weakness as he let her arrange his removal to the villa. "You can't lie here all on your own with a temperature like that. No arguments. You're coming home, where I can keep an eye on you." He'd tried to laugh it off, but he was wrapped up and hustled out of the apartment, on his way up to her villa at Valbonne to be nursed.

It had quite unnerved him. He wasn't falling in love with her, he insisted, just because she was kind and made a fuss over him.

He had never been in love with any woman. Madeleine, the avaricious little *poule de luxe* who'd shared his Christmas bounty at the Hôtel de Paris, was his soulmate, his choice of female company. He felt safe with her.

No, he was not going to open his cold heart to Angela Lawrence. Perish the thought. As if to strengthen that resolve, he had included Madeleine and her aging protector in the guest list for the gala opening. He finished a second glass of champagne before going downstairs.

Steven was waiting in the main hall. He looked at his watch. Charlie was escorting his mother. He saw Maxton and said, "They're late. Five minutes late."

"The traffic's heavy," Maxton reassured him. He gave a quick glance at his own watch, a handsome gold Rolex. A present to himself. His old one had been pawned during the lean years.

"I see headlights." He came away from the glass doors opening out onto the portico entrance. "They're here," he said.

The doors were swung open by two liveried doormen, and Angela walked through them with her son.

"You look beautiful," Steven said. He took both her hands. "Doesn't your mother look beautiful?" he asked Charlie, and then, without waiting for an answer, he said, "And you look great, son. A white tuxedo—very smart."

"Mum chose it," Charlie explained. "Gosh, doesn't everything look terrific! Look at the flowers and all the lights."

Steven ushered them to the stairs. "We have fifteen minutes before the first guests arrive. Champagne's on ice upstairs. Come on. Let's drink to success tonight!"

Maxton watched them go. It was a very wide stair, so Steven was able to walk up between his wife and the boy, an arm around each. Maxton turned away.

He had engaged a fashionable string quartet to play during the reception. They were placed discreetly in the hall, with orders to provide light popular music for the first hour and a half.

Maxton checked his watch again. The gendarmes were on duty to direct the traffic, and a crowd of sightseers stood on either side of the entrance. Red carpeting ran across the courtyard and up the flight of marble steps, protected by a long red awning in case it rained. He had dressed the doormen and waiters in red and gold livery, with powdered wigs. Yes, he had agreed when Angela protested, it was very vulgar. But the clients would love it. He wondered how much his efforts had been appreciated by that smug bastard. Then he quickly shrugged aside the silly self-pity. Just because he hadn't been invited to join the family gathering upstairs . . .

He sent a flunky out to see if the cars were approaching. The big fish would arrive late. Only the arrivistes would be on time. He smiled at his own witticism. It made him feel better. He could tell Madeleine. She would appreciate it. He hoped she would bring her rich, ridiculous lover early rather than fashionably late. He wanted someone to share the evening with him. The flunky reappeared.

"There are cars approaching, Monsieur Maxton."

"Right. Go upstairs and tell Monsieur Lawrence."

Charlie was just proposing a toast. Angela remembered he had done the same on their wedding day. She was so proud of him, and he was so proud of Steven.

"Here's good luck tonight, Dad. Good luck, good fortune and lots of lovely money!" They all laughed and drank with him.

Steven said, "Thanks, Charlie. To *la bella fortuna*—and to you, my darling, who's done so much to make it come to pass." He took Angela's hand and kissed it.

Charlie grinned at them. "Mum's blushing," he said. Then, glancing out the window: "Gosh, I can see masses of cars."

The flunky knocked, and Steven said, "It's time we went downstairs. You ready, Angelina? And you too, Charlie. I want you with us."

The main hall was soon full; the buffet and champagne bars set up in the ground-floor reception rooms were crowded with people. The music was drowned out by the sustained chattering of four hundred people circulating around the food and drink, greeting each other, vying for the house photographers to take their pictures. Steven had given up shaking hands, trying to hear names; Maxton presented the important guests as they arrived, and he was close at hand when the prize guest arrived on the arm of a big, handsome man.

Maxton moved forward, taking a hand that glittered with diamond rings and kissing it. "Nettie, my sweet. How absolutely fabulous you look! Come and let me introduce you."

Angela saw the woman approaching. She was more than beautiful. There were so many beautiful women, exquisitely dressed and bejeweled, that she had lost count. But this one was exceptional. She was tiny, and yet she created space around her. She was always center stage. Dark hair with a single streak of blond from her left temple, a perfect face with huge blue eyes, and a pink, pouting mouth that opened in a charming smile as she came up to Steven.

"May I present Monsieur Lawrence. And Madame Lawrence? Her Highness Princess Orbach."

She lingered for a moment, letting her hand stay in Steven's. Her neck and bosom were hung with sapphires and diamonds, and huge earrings danced and flashed as she moved her head. Then she paused by Angela. "Madame." She inclined her head and kept the charming smile, but the blue eyes were filmed with indifference. She passed on, and her escort, who had an unpronounceable name, kissed Angela's hand, muttered, *"Enchanté,"* and hurried after his princess. After that, everything threatened to be anticlimax.

"Well," Maxton murmured. "At least she turned up. That's something."

"But she accepted," Angela said. "I saw her name on the list."

"That doesn't mean a thing," he corrected. "She says yes to anything that looks amusing, but she's quite likely not to come at the last minute. Now let's see how long she stays. That's going to be important. What did you think of the Hungarian hunk?" He laughed mirthlessly.

Angela had always hated his laugh. It cackled without a note of kindly humor in its high pitch. It was cruel, she thought suddenly, as if he laughed only at misfortune or at someone's expense.

"I don't know," she said. "He didn't exactly stop to make conversation."

"He daren't," Maxton said. "She calls the tune. She has the money. He thinks she's going to marry him, poor sod, but she won't. She'll suck him dry and then suddenly tell her friends he's such a bore, darling, I simply couldn't stand another *moment....*" He mimicked her mercilessly. "And that's the sentence of death among the so-called smart set down here."

Angela didn't smile. She said, "What an awful woman she must be. I'm going to find Charlie."

"He's through there." Maxton indicated the supper room. "Let me get you something to eat," he said quietly. "You're quite right. She is absolutely ghastly, but I've lived among those sorts of people so long I've got used to them. Thank God you haven't."

"I hope I never will," Angela said.

At eleven-thirty the gaming rooms were opened. Maxton had left Angela in Charlie's care after supper and hurried after a very pretty girl who signaled him from the doorway.

"I can't eat another thing, Mum," her son said. "Can I get something else for you? There's a super pudding called a Bombe Surprise. Have a bit of that?"

"No, thank you, darling. Are you enjoying yourself?"

"Yes, I'm having a super time. Who's Ralph gone off with? Jolly pretty, isn't she?" He watched Madeleine admiringly. She had an overweight man in tow and was introducing him to Maxton.

"No pudding for me," Angela said. "Let's go and find Steven. I haven't seen him for ages."

It was silly to feel ill at ease. Silly to be lonely among such a throng of people, some of whom she knew and had come up to her, all smiles and congratulations. Ralph had taken care of her. Charlie was solicitous in his concern that she share his enjoyment of the "super" food and drink, but she realized that he, too, was out of his element.

"Come on," she said.

He caught her arm, "Look, he's over there. I'll get him."

"No, don't. He's talking to people; we'll go and join them."

Madeleine was laughing. She pinched her protector's plump cheek and made a charming little grimace at him.

"Now, Bernard, my sweet, you know you're dying to go upstairs and win some money for me. You go on, and I'll come and bring you luck. One glass of champagne and then I'll join you, eh?"

Her fingers had left a little red mark on his sallow skin. He glanced at the ugly man, with his hooked nose and narrow features, and decided he could safely leave Madeleine with him for a little while. He was itching to play, and she was encouraging him. She always encouraged him to do what he liked, whatever form it took. And she had such an adorable laugh, like a naughty little girl. A vicious child, he called her, vicious and wicked and irresistible, like the gambling demon that devoured him equally. He left her with the ugly Englishman.

"Oh, *Dieu merci,*" she breathed when he had gone. "He's so *boring,* Ralphie . . . and such a dirty old devil. You know what he wanted me to do to him before we came here?"

"No," Maxton said firmly. "And you're not going to tell me. To me you're just a sweet little innocent. Now let's sink some champagne, shall we?"

She hooked her arm through his and pressed against him. "Okay," she said. "Then we go up and I get some chips from him and we have a bit of fun, eh?"

They settled into a sofa upholstered into an alcove. Madeleine made him laugh; she cheered his spirits and encouraged him to show the snide and cynical side that had upset Angela. He felt at home with Madeleine. They were part of the same worthless, superficial world. He poured and drank, never becoming drunk, just blurring the edges of sensitivity.

"Is that your boss?" Madeleine's strong little fingers gripped his wrist. "I saw him shaking hands with people in the hall."

"Yes. Didn't you meet him?"

"No." She lifted one silky shoulder in disgust. "My old fart wouldn't queue up—you know what he's like. My God, Ralphie, isn't he attractive?"

"If you say so," Maxton answered.

Steven was talking to a couple whom Maxton had invited to the villa. The man had made a lot of money out of property on the coast. Angela was busy with the wife; she'd feel more comfortable with the pleasant French matron than with the glittering Nettie Orbach and her kind. Maxton realized he was being nasty about Angela because she had rebuked him. He had never been able to accept criticism—a major failing. His father used to thunder at him, "Never in the wrong, are you, my boy? Well, God help you, you'll find out one day."

Madeleine was staring at Steven. Maxton knew that look: the narrowed eyes, the full, greedy mouth parting to show the tip of a libidinous tongue.

"You can forget him," he mocked her. "That's his wife, the blonde in the white dress."

"So what?" she demanded. "She's not anything special. His son's so good-looking too. Why don't I meet him, then?"

"He's seventeen, darling," Maxton jeered. "And it's his stepson anyway." He tipped the last of the champagne into his glass.

Madeleine turned to him, her eyes wide open now. "Don't be silly! Stepson, my foot! They're the image of each other. They *must* be father and son."

He'd never noticed it before. He took a long look at them, a proper look for the first time. She was right. Absolutely right. The same hair and eyes; very similar features; gestures and expressions that mirrored each other. You say stepson and nobody bothers to take a second look.

"You're bloody clever, aren't you?" he murmured. "Sharp eyes, haven't we, sweetheart? You're bloody right. The boy must be his."

She smiled and squeezed his wrist again. "Have they been telling Ralphie lies? And Ralphie swallowed them? Ooh, that's not like you, darling. You can spot a lie coming before it gets around the corner."

"That's because it's usually my lie," he countered. "I tell lies to people, and they tell them back to me. Let's go and see what your fat friend is up to, shall we? Maybe he'll give you a few francs to play with."

She got up, linking arms with him, and walked with the provocative hip swing that made men stare after her. He was cross, she realized. Poor Ralphie; the con man had actually been conned. She giggled. How very funny. He really was cross; she could tell by the set of his thin lips.

They went upstairs to the *salon privé*. Her friend was at the baccarat table. He had been losing, and he looked up, scowling, when she touched him.

"Where have you been? You said one drink," he complained.

"I'm so sorry, my sweet, but I'm here now, and don't you worry. I'll change your luck."

She did, and Maxton stood beside her as the cards came out of the shoe and he began to bet and to win. An hour later she demanded, and was given, ten thousand francs. She went off with Ralph to play roulette. She was lucky that night. Her excitement grew as her chips piled up.

He wondered whether she banked her money. The looks and the body wouldn't last forever, if he was right about the Moroccan blood.

"I'd stop now, if I were you," he said.

She looked up at him. There was a bright flush on her cheeks. "Why?" She lowered her voice to a whisper. "You mean the wheel's fixed?"

"Nothing like that," he answered. "We play on the law of averages here. We don't run any crooked games. The law of averages says you're going to start losing. But it's up to you, darling."

"I always do what you tell me," she declared. "I always think a man knows best." She gave him a huge wink, gathered her winnings and left the table. "I'd better go back to Bernard," she said. "I shan't tell him I won. Then if he's lucky he'll give me a present. When will I see you, Ralphie?"

"When's he going home?"

She changed the chips for cash, folding the notes into a tight little wad that fitted into her evening bag. It was a large bag, not a smart little *pochette. I bet she banks every penny,* he thought. *Good for her.*

"I'll let you know," she promised. She reached up and kissed him lightly on the cheek. "You're such fun, darling," she said. "I love our afternoons together. I'll telephone you." Then she slipped away, the bag with the money pressed close under her arm.

"My darling," Steven said. "If you're tired, why not go home? It's been a long evening. I'll call the car, and Charlie can go with you. Has he enjoyed himself?"

"Yes, he's loved every minute. But he's a bit young for it. I wouldn't let him gamble. He was very disappointed."

"I'll talk to him," Steven said. "You wait there, and I'll send him along to you. You were right. I'm going to tell him so."

He had to look for Charlie. He wasn't in the supper room, where breakfast was being served. He'd slipped away, sulking perhaps, and left his mother. No excuses, Steven insisted. He must learn. He must learn to take care of her and to respect me. I love him enough to be angry, even tonight.

Charlie was upstairs in the smaller salon, watching the roulette. He started when Steven came up behind him.

"Oh, hello, Dad. Dad, I wanted to cash some money and have a try on the wheel, but they won't give me any chips. Can't you say something? It's pretty stupid."

"The cashiers are doing what I told them," Steven said quietly. "You are not to gamble. Come with me, Charlie."

He unlocked his office, switched on a battery of lights and said, "Close the door. I want to show you something."

Charlie followed him. He felt embarrassed, even uneasy. Steven had never been angry with him before. He slouched, wondering whether he dared put up an argument. He shouldn't have left his mother. He was sorry he'd done that, but she'd made him feel like a child, when he wanted to feel grown up.

Steven flicked a wall switch, and the paneling slid back. "Come here, Charlie," he said. "Look at this." It was a closed-circuit television screen. It showed the *salon privé*. Steven flicked another switch, and the camera moved into close-up on one of the tables. There was no sound, just a picture. He changed it, from one salon to another, the roulette wheels, the card tables, zooming into focus, the faces enlarged until they filled the screen.

Charlie said, "Gosh, I've never seen anything like it. It's fantastic. You can watch everything that's going on."

"Yes. I can watch the games and the players and my own staff. I can see if anyone cheats or seems to be cheating. I can sit here and see people losing fortunes, making fools of themselves, getting drunk. I can see greed and cunning and people risking money because they want people to look at them."

Charlie said, "You make it sound awful. I thought it looked like good fun."

Steven said quietly, "That"—and he pointed to the overall view on the screen of the big gambling room beneath them—"that isn't fun. That is business. My business, and one day yours too. I don't gamble, and you *never* gamble, you hear me? You leave that to the suckers. Business isn't fun, Charlie. That's something I've got to teach you. It's not like anything else. It has different rules. If you want to succeed, if you want respect, you have to play by those rules. If you run a casino, you don't play around with the profits. That's number one. If anybody had given you chips or let you play at a table tonight, he'd have been fired. And number two, when I say take care of your mother, I mean it. You understand me?"

"Yes. I'm sorry."

"Now she's waiting downstairs. The car's on its way, and you'll take her home. And you'll apologize to her."

"I will," Charlie said. He had blushed red at Steven's tone. "I only went for a few minutes," he said. "I only wanted to join in, like everybody else."

"You're not everybody else," was the answer. "That's something else you'll have to learn. Now go on down and find your mother."

He switched off the screen. The panel slid into place. He sat down at his desk, searching for a cigarette. He had been hard on the boy. But it had to be done. He could have the world, but he must play by the rules. He was a kid still, Steven admitted. His life had been turned upside down by Steven's advent—money, travel, glamour, and anything he wanted. It hadn't turned his head, but it might in the end. The boy's pride was hurt. His feelings too, because of the way he had been judged and admonished.

Steven stubbed out his cigarette. He'd been sitting there longer than he realized. He was unhappy that he wouldn't see his son before midday. He locked up and went downstairs. The supper room was nearly empty, the bars not quite, but most of the midnight crush had disappeared. It was four in the morning.

He went upstairs on a tour of the rooms. Maxton was watching a game at the baccarat table. The hard core were still there. They'd be there till the casino closed. Steven went up to him.

"How's it going?"

"Fine. Two of the high rollers are fighting it out over there."

Steven was surprised to hear him use a crap-game term. "How high?"

"Half a million francs. Don't you want to watch? They hate each other's guts when they play, but outside they're the best of friends."

"Who are they?" Steven could see two men, competing in cold fury with the bank.

"French. Stinking rich. One's electronics, the other one's got steel and shipping interests. This is their idea of relaxation. It's a good omen they've stayed on. And so did Nettie Orbach. She didn't leave till after two. That means we've arrived!" He looked tired, his thin face sunken around the eyes and mouth. A very little drunk, Steven decided. Just a touch over the edge. Maxton smiled and said, "Congratulations. I think you've made the grade tonight, Steven."

"If it's true, then we've all made it. You especially. Thanks."

Maxton made him a little ironic bow. More than a touch over the edge. "Thank *you!* This time last year I had paper in my shoes."

Steven said, "Close down in twenty minutes. I'm going home."

Angela had let him sleep. He stood on the balcony in his dressing gown and stretched in the warm sunshine. Rich garden scents drifted up to him, and he saw her moving among the shrubbery. She must have been up for several hours. She loved gardening. She would grow things in the desert if she were set down there. Steven smiled, watching her. He loved her more than he'd thought possible. He loved her directness, and the honesty she had brought into his life, and the odd streak of obstinacy that nothing could move. He loved her for her gentleness of heart and her kindness.

Standing with the sun on his face, he thought of Sicily, and suddenly he longed for the red earth and rugged hillsides, for the hot skies and sun-bleached buildings. It was his homeland, the place of his birth. He wanted to go back to the spot where he and Angela had poured wine into the dust and made love for the first time. And he wanted to take his son and show him where the other half of him belonged.

He called down to her. "Angelina!"

She looked up and waved. "Morning, darling. Do you want breakfast?"

"I'm coming down. Order some coffee for me."

"I let you sleep on," she said as they sat together on the terrace. "It was such a long day. I woke up very early, I was still so excited about it all. It did go well, didn't it, darling?"

"According to Ralph, it was a great success. And he would know. I thought so too. You get a feel for atmosphere. You'll get a crowd wherever there's free food and drink and people to stare at. It's the electricity in the air that tells you. And the big gamblers came and stayed till the end." He smiled, holding her hand. "I want to go down and check the figures. I want to see what our profit's likely to be."

"When do you think we'll break even?" Angela asked.

"We won't begin to break even for a year," he said. "The winter is a slack time. But I can calculate pretty accurately what the revenue's likely to be. When we've recovered our expenses for the gala, we begin to recoup the initial outlay. Before you know it, we'll be rich!"

She said, "Charlie's gone out for a walk. He was awfully sorry he annoyed you. Don't be cross with him today, will you, darling?"

"Don't be silly. Last night was last night. Let's take a walk through the garden, shall we?"

"Why can't we talk here? I'll only bore you to death showing you the plants. You don't know a weed from a wisteria!"

"And I don't want to know," he agreed. "The garden's yours. I leave it all to you. I want to walk with you because I can't even kiss my own wife without that old bat Janine spying on me. Come on."

"You know she's a treasure," Angela teased.

"She's a snoop," he retorted, pulling her to her feet. "She needs to get a man of her own."

Janine was a domestic marvel. She cleaned and scrubbed and kept everything in spotless order. But she was incurably nosy. There were times when it got on Steven's nerves.

Out of sight of the house, shielded by trees and a great bank of flowering crimson oleanders, Steven took Angela in his arms. "I missed you when I woke up this morning," he said.

"I missed you," Angela answered, and drew his head down to kiss him on the mouth. It was a long kiss, and they stood pressed close together afterward.

"I was thinking how much I loved you," he said. "I saw you down in the garden and I thought, *I love her more and more every day.*"

"I love you like that too," she said. "In the beginning I used to worry. I used to think about what I'd made you give up."

"Like what?" He stroked her hair.

"Your family. Your whole way of life. I don't mean the bad parts, but your home and your friends. I was so frightened you'd regret it. I didn't see how I could make up for all that, even with Charlie."

"Then will you believe me if I tell you something? And never speak like that again? You promise me?" He was serious. The warm desire had gone out of him.

"All right, tell me," Angela said.

"I am happier than I've been in the whole of my life. I miss my family, yes. I love them. I love my father and my mother and Piero and my nephews and niece. I'm a Sicilian. We have very deep family ties, you know that. I'd give anything to bring you and Charlie and them all together. But as for the rest of it, you listen to me. Listen good, as we say. I don't miss the States. I lived there. I grew up there, but it's not my home. I didn't have any friends outside of the business. And I don't miss that. I don't miss traveling with bodyguards, riding in a bulletproof car, looking up and down the street every time I came out the door. I don't miss living off crime, Angela. I have a hunch I'll die in my bed as an old man, and I like the idea. I have a home, a wife and a son, and I love my life. And I have a business that doesn't have blood on the balance sheet. So will you look at me and promise to put all that stuff out of your head?"

"Oh, darling," she said. "I really will, from now on. So let's go for our walk, shall we?"

"I was thinking," he said. "We deserve a short holiday. I want to take Charlie to Sicily. We could spend a long weekend touring around." He slipped his arm around her waist. "Maybe go back up the hillside where we went the first day."

"He's due back at school," Angela said. "We promised he'd go back at the end of the week. Couldn't we go in the Christmas holidays?"

"Don't you remember how cold it gets in the winter? No, darling. I meant now, while the weather's good. It's the best time of year. Just a couple of days won't hurt. I'll show you Etna at night. That's really something to see. Say yes, sweetheart."

"If you want to that much, then we'll go," she said.

"No wonder I'm so crazy about you," Steven murmured. "And I'll call the school and make it right with them. They want a contribution to the new swimming pool, don't they?"

As they walked back to the villa, Angela said, "What are we going to tell Charlie? Why Sicily?"

"Because I was born there. It's my home. One day, when he knows I'm his father, he'll have something to remember. Let's see if he's back from that walk."

It began as a whisper, passed behind the hand in bars and trattorias, in the kitchens and living rooms in Little Italy. A whisper among the small people, the common soldiers in the mighty Mafia command: Don Aldo Fabrizzi talks business with his daughter. It had started with the cousin, Anna, who told her father that the Don shut himself up with Clara and discussed topics forbidden to women, while her mother and Anna worked in the kitchen. She hated Clara, who was cold and superior toward her. She liked Luisa Fabrizzi.

Her father sucked his teeth and didn't believe her. But he spoke about it, and like a tiny ripple on still water, the rumors began to swell into a tide. Roy Guglielmo and his brother, Victor, came to hear of it. They were incredulous. But they were curious too. They sent for the bridegroom-to-be, and over a hearty dinner with lots of wine, they congratulated him on his good fortune and asked about the bride. A clever girl, they'd heard. Her papa's favorite. He had himself a good thing going. Bruno was flattered and expansive. He boasted to the men who had been his bosses since he was a runner on the streets.

He laid her good and often, and she ate out of his hand. Sure, she had the Don's ear over most things. Which was good, he said defensively. Good for him, when he was the husband. Then he'd be the one to see the books.

She sees the books, the accounts, the *figures?* Victor asked him.

Wine made Bruno truculent. He'd resented being shut out, or sent away because Clara had to talk to her father. When he was married to her, he assured them, she'd learn a woman's place. They all laughed and made coarse jokes, and he staggered home feeling good about himself.

The Guglielmos were independent operatives, chiefs of a small but effective family. They ran the brothels and exacted protection money from every small business in their district. They had strong affiliations with the Licianos in Chicago.

Roy said to Victor after Bruno had left, "It looks like it's true. Holy shit! She goes through the books!"

Victor didn't answer in a hurry. He was a big, slow-moving man, but he wasn't slow-witted. "It figures," he said at last. "After a guy like Falconi, why pick an arsehole for a son-in-law? You think Fabrizzi's going to put Bruno in Falconi's place when he dies? Nah! He's got other ideas, Roy. Bruno's the frontman."

"It can't happen," Roy declared. "It's crazy. Fabrizzi's crazy if he thinks he can put a woman in a man's place."

Victor said, "It could break up the families. We have it fixed right for all of us. For Christ's sake. Mobs from Chicago, Detroit, you name it! They get word of this, and they'll come up here, moving in. We'll have a war for the Fabrizzi territory. The Irish, the kikes, the Krauts. The whole fucking lot will be grabbing a piece for themselves. We got to stop it."

His brother nodded. He paid the bill. "We'll need help. Fabrizzi's too big for us. But I'll lay you a straight two to one his people don't know what he's doing. Not the top men."

"Then maybe somebody should tell them," Victor suggested.

The meetings were very discreet. An oath of silence was taken at each one. Only five of the eight heads of the Fabrizzi family were willing to talk to Roy and Victor, but those five were important men, powerful and respected only second to Don Aldo himself. They listened to the Guglielmos and said nothing of the plan to wipe out Lucca Falconi and his people. That oath of silence was as sacred as the one they had taken when they agreed to meet with Roy and Victor. It was agreed in principle that something had to be done if the implications were true. Those who knew Bruno Salviatti were easier to convince. He might be a stud for the daughter, but he was no heir to Aldo.

It was suggested, and agreed, that a spy should be introduced into the Don's household. Someone who could check on the stories about weekly conferences between Clara and her father. One of his most trusted friends and henchmen from the early days offered to handle it. He was anxious to prove to them, he said, that the rumors were no more than silly gossip. He would ask Don Aldo to house a young relative for a few weeks. As head of the family, the Don would not refuse a plea for help.

"How much longer is she going to stay here?" Clara demanded.

Her mother was placatory. "Only a week or so. She's a good girl, she helps me, just like Anna did. She doesn't get in your way."

Luisa eyed Clara apprehensively. She was more difficult than ever these days. She had a handsome man, a wedding to look forward to, a new life; but she didn't seem to care.

She and Aldo talked privately together, and even at the family table they were apart from the women. She watched her daughter and wondered at the change in her. She showed little respect or regard for Bruno. His swaggering didn't deceive the older woman. She might not have Clara's sophistication, but she knew men, and she could tell he was ill at ease. And resentful. It wouldn't be a happy marriage unless Clara changed her attitude.

But she didn't dare say anything. She was glad to have someone like Gina staying with them. Of course, Aldo agreed to give her a home until the family problems had died down. He was a good man, and he knew his duty to his people. The girl's father was in prison. She had run away from her mother's boyfriend to save her virtue. If she was living under Don Aldo's protection, the mother and her man wouldn't dare try to force her back home. And by the time she did leave, her father's relatives would have sorted out the problem.

Gina was quiet and shy. Luisa was kindhearted and maternal by nature. She couldn't mother Clara, and there were no small children to occupy her. She was happy to take care of someone in trouble. She was happy to be needed. Clara didn't think of anyone but herself anymore.

Clara lit a cigarette. She resented having another girl living in her parents' flat. She had accepted the hard-luck story with little sympathy. If her father had to offer protection, she couldn't argue. But she didn't share her mother's opinion of the girl. Clara thought she was sly and far less the wronged innocent than she pretended. Clara positively disliked her and made it plain. Why couldn't some other relative have taken her in, she demanded when the original two weeks stretched out to a month, with no sign of her leaving.

"Only your father is powerful enough to keep her safe," Luisa explained. "The mother is living with a bad man, very bad. A man of violence."

Clara didn't care. She didn't feel easy with Gina on the other side of the door, but she couldn't explain that feeling to her father.

She had Bruno stay in her house when she wanted him. She took a cruel pleasure in their sexual relationship. He tried so hard to dominate her in the only way he knew and she was able to resist him so easily. The convulsions of the body never inspired a spark of tender feeling in her. Lust, but not passion. She indulged her lust, but passion was what she had felt for Steven. To Clara passion meant love, with its vulnerability and pain. She never thought of Bruno Salviatti in any context except bed. He was coarse and ill-educated, vain and stupid. She disregarded his good qualities because she wasn't interested enough to notice them. He was loyal, generous in his way, sentimental about children. He was brave. Roy and Victor Guglielmo weren't too worried about brains, but they could vouch for Salviatti's courage. Clara didn't think of him at all, and if she gave him expensive clothes, it was because his lack of style annoyed her.

Aldo was content. Bruno was full of respect for him. He seemed to treat Clara well. Luisa approved of him. She had never felt comfortable with Steven Falconi. And father and daughter were deeply involved in a business scheme, which had been Clara's inspiration.

She had drawn on her own experience in employing private detectives to spy on Steven. Why not start their own agency and enlarge it to a chain across the state? It could provide the material and the front for a blackmailing operation that could be limitless. Politicians, public figures, movie stars—she listed the money-making potential. It was a long-term project, possibly five years, and the parent agency had to be controlled at arm's length. The higher the fees, she insisted, remembering how she herself had been fleeced, the richer, the more vulnerable, the clients. Aldo was gratified, and intrigued. She was a smart girl, with smart ideas. He saw even further than she did in terms of the power such an organization would give the man who actually controlled it. He told Clara to find a suitable office, and then they would start by registering the agency.

Clara was engrossed in business. He had come to depend upon her as a sounding board for his own ideas. He consulted her on everything from a small discrepancy in the quarterly "take" to the abilities of someone he thought of promoting.

Within the year, she had become his closest confidante and adviser. And inevitably they grew a little careless. The door wasn't always closed, the telephone conversations were sometimes unguarded, and once Gina came into the living room while they were both double-checking some accounts.

Six weeks after her arrival, Gina's relative called to collect her. Aldo welcomed his old friend, and the old friend kissed him on both cheeks and presented him with a case of fine cognac and a humidor of Havana cigars. A piece of elaborate Victorian glassware was his gift to Luisa Fabrizzi. Gina could go home. Her mother had got rid of her boyfriend; the man would not trouble either of them again. They were forever in Don Aldo's debt.

Aldo felt gratified. He liked to confer favors, to be admired as a patriarch.

Clara said acidly, "They should have given *me* something. She's been getting on my nerves long enough." Then she forgot about Gina.

She had found a small detective agency in Newark, New Jersey, that seemed suitable. It was owned by two partners, former New York City policemen, one retired after a shooting, the other seeking more income to support a growing family. Both were men of reputation, with clean licenses. And not much money. The business had been established only two years, and Clara discovered that the family man had a mortgage on his house that was causing problems.

She drove down to Newark. It was a long day, but an interesting one. Posing as a prospective client, she managed to see and judge both partners in the firm, the Ace Detective Agency. How corny can you get, she wondered as she shook hands with the ex-cop who'd stopped three bullets in his stomach during a holdup. He had a lean, wary look about him, which she didn't like. He was still very much a cop, still missing life in the precinct. The man with the kids and the wife and the mortgage was in his late thirties. He was more what Clara had in mind. He was fit-looking, sharp-eyed. He was there with the lighter and the ashtray before she'd finished taking out a cigarette. He stared at the case a little too long. It was gold and expensive. He smelled a rich client. His partner smelled a rat.

She talked about her husband, reeling off the standard tale of suspected adultery, and noticed which one of them was bored and which was making his interest very apparent. She wasn't disappointed. She left without making a firm commitment, but promised to telephone when she'd decided to do something about it.

The married man was named O'Halloran. The other had an Italian name, and that had alerted her from the start. When Italians became cops they pushed harder against their own than against the Irish or the Jews. He'd have to go. If it worked as she planned, he'd be bought out. And O'Halloran would find himself with a new partner. A woman, whose only requirement would be access to his files, and whose contribution would be unlimited supplies of money and a brand-new office in midtown Manhattan.

She drove home. Bruno was coming for her. Clara never cooked, and eating at home with him bored her anyway. She'd made reservations at a new Chinese restaurant on Forty-seventh Street. She showered and changed, her mind busy with the details of her day. The weather was turning bitterly cold. She chose a dress of dark-red velvet that clung to her like a second skin.

Pouring a glass of bourbon, she settled down to wait for Bruno. He was never late. He came at eight o'clock exactly, sleek and trim as a boxer in a new pinstripe she'd bought him, with a heavy camel-hair coat draped across his shoulders. He was strikingly handsome, she thought calmly, and she let him fondle her and kiss her mouth open. When he started easing her skirt up, she pushed his hand away.

"Ah, baby," he protested. "What's the hurry?"

"I'm hungry. And this dress cost three hundred dollars," she snapped at him. "Stop pawing me. Come on, let's go."

He moved to the tray of bottles. She didn't see the look on his face, and she wouldn't have cared anyway. "I'd like a Scotch," he said.

"You can have one at Chow's. We'll miss the table."

She went into her room and swept back, wrapped in a long hooded wild-mink coat. He was drinking from a full glass. Clara glared at him.

"I said we'll be late," she said, her voice raised.

Bruno didn't move. "When we're married, I'll eat at home. I'll have my Scotch and my food on the table when I want it."

It wasn't much of a challenge to her. He often made gestures of independence, and she knew exactly how to cope with them. She drew the coat back, rested one hand on a jutting hip and said, "When we're married, big man, I'll be your little homebody wife. But right now, I'm going to dinner. You want to stay here, feel free."

He caught up with her outside the front door.

That night, when Clara was asleep beside him, Bruno Salviatti lay wide awake. He didn't like Chinese food. It left him feeling empty. He had been bored and sleepy through the evening because inside he was very angry and he couldn't let it show. He'd made love because she wanted it and she knew how to rouse him till he forgot about everything else. But afterward it tasted sour in the mouth. He felt like a circus animal, performing new tricks every time. At first he had been fascinated, challenged by her, lured by the prospects of such a marriage, but now he lay naked, hip to thigh with her, and thought how much he hated her already. She had bitten deep into his self-esteem. He found that hardest to bear. She diminished him as a man. Other women had bought him clothes and presents, but he'd accepted them as his due. He liked women to look up to him, and in return he could be generous, he could be good to women. This woman used and despised him.

He'd been ready to marry even before he met her, ready to raise a family. He was doing well, he had a reputation. Roy Guglielmo had given him a district. Then he saw her at that anniversary party and set out to make her. He wanted to show off before the young *ragazzi*.

It had looked like such a great chance to rise in the world, to marry the daughter of a don without sons or grandsons to follow him. It didn't seem so now. When he woke in the morning, Clara was still asleep. He didn't wake her. The maid was in the kitchen. She made him coffee and eggs. He thought, looking at her shuffling around him, *This will be my life. My life at home.* He banged out of the house without finishing his breakfast or looking in on Clara to say goodbye.

Ex-Detective Sergeant Mike O'Halloran was coming up on forty. He'd put his savings into the agency with his friend Pacellino, and for the first year his wife had been happy. Happy that he was not in danger, that he was home at regular hours and able to spend time with his children. She looked ten years younger, and their marriage picked up. It picked up so well that before they realized it she was pregnant.

That made four children, on top of the mortgage on the new house. After that it started to go downhill. Small debts became bigger; the agency had some lean months in the first year, and the doctor's bills for his wife and the baby were a worry. He was sorry she'd persuaded him to leave the force. She nagged, and he started losing his temper.

They got some good jobs, but the work wasn't consistent. A lot of it was small stuff, short on expenses. Routine surveillance for divorce; court appearances, which took time.

Pacellino was a bachelor. He had a small rented apartment and a girlfriend who worked in real estate. O'Halloran bore the real burden. When two days went by and the rich bitch from New York didn't phone in, he became depressed. She'd looked like real money. Then she called him personally and invited him to lunch. O'Halloran couldn't believe his luck. He even agreed to her request to keep the meeting private. Just between themselves. She had a proposition to put to him.

He didn't say anything to Pacellino. He just took off at lunchtime and went to the hotel she'd suggested. She was in the restaurant when he got there, a glass of bourbon on the table. He apologized if he'd kept her waiting. She had a cool look about her. She pulled her sleeve back to check her watch, and then she smiled at him and asked him to sit down. He had a gut feeling as he did so that this had nothing to do with a cheating husband.

His mind was a long way off his investigation that afternoon. He sat outside an apartment building, watching a client's wife go in to spend time with her boyfriend, and he thought about the offer the woman had made. She wanted a detective agency all her own, but she didn't want the connection made public. She had emphasized the necessity of complete secrecy, and there was just a hint of threat in the way she repeated it. She was a beautiful, sexy dame, O'Halloran admitted, but he'd just as soon put his hand into the tigers' cage at the zoo as try and feel her up. When she mentioned the investment, he managed to keep his face straight. If the business prospered, she added, they would expand to other major cities.

"I can see quite a network in a few years, if things work out," she had said, and he'd nodded eagerly.

It was all wrong, and he knew it. His instincts were flashing warnings like neon lights, but he had gone on sitting there; she had made it sound so reasonable. The agency would move to New York, where she had an appropriate office in mind. He would recruit a reliable staff. His police connections would surely help there. He'd agreed that they would. The agency must have a broad perspective, offering a comprehensive service to clients, and it must be prepared to accept business from corporations.

At one point O'Halloran had been constrained to interrupt. "Lady, I did twenty years on the beat and made detective sergeant, but what I don't know about corporations you could put in a book!"

"You don't have to know about them," was the answer. "That'll be my responsibility. You'll just do what's needed, when it's needed. Okay?"

"Okay," he'd said, and from that moment, he had shut down the switch on the warning lights. He needed money; he was being offered the chance to be rich for doing the same sort of thing he was doing now for peanuts. He could afford good schools for the kids, nice clothes for his wife, a new car. He had leaned toward her and said, "So long as it's legal, it sounds like one hell of a good deal to me."

As he sat slumped down in the car seat, listlessly watching yet another marital two-timer sneaking out after an afternoon in the sack, he remembered her smile. It was a strange sort of smile, almost friendly for a moment. He had given her something she wanted, and she was pleased with him. He had laid the foundation for their partnership with a lie, and she answered it with a lie of her own.

"It will always be legal," she'd said. "I promise you that. Do we have a deal, Mr. O'Halloran?"

"We have a deal," he'd said.

She had got up and solemnly shaken hands with him. He insisted on paying for their drinks. She thanked him. She had magnificent black eyes. He was a bought man, and he knew it by the way she looked at him. He had a twinge about his old partner, Pacellino, and the holes in his gut.

"You're sure you wouldn't want Tony in on this?"

"I'm sure," she had answered. "I'll get the new office set up, and you get out from under him. Call me when you're ready to move. And make it soon."

He had her card in his pocket. Mrs. Clara Falconi, and a ritzy-sounding address on the East Side.

Nothing the time the errant wife emerged, he drove back to the office. His partner was out. He looked around him. The agency was small, untidy, run on a shoestring. He paused for a moment, tempted to call someone in New York and ask him to run a check on the lady. He even reached for the telephone. But he never picked it up. He didn't want an answer. He didn't want to know for sure what he suspected.

He typed his report for the afternoon's work and went home. He made a big fuss over his wife and kids and told them he'd had an offer to run a new agency in New York.

Steven was right about Sicily in the month of September. It was perfect. The fierce August heat had given way to a lovely constant temperature, with a light breeze that came up in the evenings.

They started in Messina, then drove up the winding roads and over the mountains to the coast. Steven showed them Greek ruins and Roman amphitheaters, abandoned for two thousand years to the ravages of sun and weather. They wandered through hillside villages where the streets were too narrow even to admit the painted carts that trundled behind the sad donkeys. They saw the grand fortress houses of the ancient aristocracy, mostly abandoned in favor of life in the agreeable confines of Palermo or on the Italian mainland. Little by little, Steven taught his son about Sicily, and the word Mafia crept in unchallenged.

Charlie listened, infected by Steven's passionate interest in the strange, barren country with such a violent history. It helped a lot that Steven was such a good storyteller. He made boring ruins and crumbling buildings come to life, and Charlie responded by asking questions and wanting to know more.

It was a pilgrimage full of memories for Angela. They crowded in upon her as they traveled toward Palermo. When they reached the city, she took Charlie to the site where the hospital had stood. A four-story hotel was built on it.

"I was a nurse here," she said. "My best friend, Christine, was killed when the hospital was bombed. There's nothing left of it now."

Charlie linked his arm through hers. "Don't be upset, Mum. It was a long time ago. Why don't we go and see the place where you married my father? You told me it was up in the hills near here?"

He didn't see the quick glance she exchanged with Steven or his nod of agreement.

She smiled at him, "Why not? It was in a little village called Altodonte. Do you think you could find it, darling?"

"I'm sure I could," Steven said. "I'd like to see it too."

Little had changed. True to his promise to the priest, Steven had arranged immunity for the village and its people. They paid no Mafia dues and suffered no Mafia murders. It was sleepy and sunlit. The paint on the houses was faded and peeling, the geraniums still bloomed in fierce profusion, the wash fluttered between the houses like flags of poverty above the dark little streets. The church was smaller than Angela remembered it, the inside even darker.

Her son said, "It must have been a funny wedding, Mum. It's jolly gloomy in here."

They walked up the aisle toward the gilded, painted altar, passing saints dressed in real clothes, faded flower offerings withering at their feet. The red eye of the sacristy lamp burned above them.

"It was a wonderful wedding," Angela said, and reached covertly for Steven's hand.

The door of the sacristy opened. It was a young priest, and he came hurrying toward them, buttoning his cassock.

He bowed to the tall bearded man, to the woman and the boy. He spoke no English.

Steven took some large bills out of his wallet. He handed them to the priest. "Give this to the families that need it most," he said in Italian. "And keep some for your church and yourself, Father."

"Dad must have given him a big present," Charlie whispered as they came out. "Did you see his face, Mum? He couldn't believe it."

"It's the custom," she explained. "And you know how generous he is." And then, because she knew how much it meant to Steven, she said, "Now we'll go and see where Steven's ancestors used to live."

Charlie stared at her. "You mean they were here too? The same place where you and my father got married?"

"Yes, isn't it a coincidence, darling? ... Steven, I was just telling Charlie that your ancestors came from this village. Would you know where the house was? It would be nice to see it, wouldn't it, Charlie?"

"It's not much," Steven said. He put his arm around Angela, pressed her close in silent thanks. "They were poor people, poor peasants. I think I know where it was."

Charlie asked him, "Will it still be there?"

"Nothing changes in Sicily," Steven answered. "It'll be there."

And it was, just as Angela remembered it from so many years ago. The door and shutters were freshly painted a bright green, and a young woman nursing a baby sat on the doorstep, her bare feet in the dust. She looked up at them suspiciously as they passed and briefly paused. The baby suckled greedily, and she gave it her attention when the strangers moved on.

Steven said to his son, "Not what you expected? I told you, they were dirt poor. That's why they emigrated to America."

Charlie said, "I don't blame them. Still, they must have done jolly well over there. Look at you, Dad!"

"Yes," Steven said. "They did well, Charlie. All they needed was the opportunity. But I'm proud of my ancestry. They were poor, but they were men of respect in this village. Now let's see if there's anywhere we can get something to drink and eat. You hungry, sweetheart?"

"Yes, and thirsty," Angela said. "It was good of you to help the priest, darling."

"It was expected," Steven said.

They had the best suite in the Palazzo Palermo hotel. Charlie had gone to his room to read after a rich Sicilian dinner and a lot of the heavy local wine.

Angela had laughed when she saw the bed in their room. It was an antique and quite narrow by current standards, but it made up in splendor for the lack of space. It was dressed in crimson silk, with gold cherubs supporting the drapery from the ceiling. More gold cherubs disported at the foot of the bed, and a red-and-gold confection topped with a ducal crown and coat of arms towered above the pilllows.

It was the bridal suite, the manager informed them. Furnished from the sale of the last duchess of Finciula's estate. The dressing table was a crimson-and-gilt extravagance, miniature cherubs supported an elaborate mirror above the silk flounces, and the chairs were carved and gilded thrones with matching footstools.

"It's unbelievable," Angela exclaimed. "It's amazing! Did people really live in rooms like this?"

"The Finciulas were poor," Steven told her. "They had big estates but no money. This stuff was sold for pennies, I expect. I can't wait to see you sitting up in that bed!" And they both laughed at the idea.

It was indeed a narrow bed, and their bodies were so close that it was well into the night before they finished making love and drifted off to sleep. In the morning, with the sun streaming through the drawn curtains and the shutters fastened back, Angela woke him.

"Last night was the best ever," she whispered.

"It was the bed," he teased her. "All the old dukes and duchesses must have been sick with envy, watching us."

"What are you talking about? You talk such nonsense, darling." She drew back, teasing him, holding him at bay as he strained to kiss her.

"It's not nonsense. If you make love in someone else's bed, they come back from the dead to watch you. All Sicilians know that. That's why they only put foreigners in here." He pulled her down on top of him. "And there's another superstition. When you do it like this, you make daughters. I want a daughter."

Charlie flew back from Italy.

"It's been a wonderful trip," he told Steven. "Really super. I'd love to come again."

Steven embraced him. Angela could see the pleasure in his face.

"You will. We'll have a proper holiday on the island. Now work hard, or I'll get in trouble with your mother for keeping you out of school."

Arm in arm, they watched the aircraft take off.

"He did enjoy it, didn't he? Maybe he felt some tie with the place."

Angela hadn't noticed anything beyond a schoolboy's enthusiasm, but she knew how much Steven wanted to think it was more.

"I wouldn't be surprised. You have such strong roots; but you brought it all to life for him, darling. You made it real. He got quite upset about the way the landlords treated their tenants. He actually said to me the Mafia were the only protection those poor people had. He'd always thought they were a lot of gangsters in America."

"And what did you say to that?" he questioned.

"I said what you said. It started out well and went wrong."

"It sure did," he said. "My grandfather killed tax collectors. Now we *are* the tax collectors. Come on, darling. I'm looking forward to going home. I must call Maxton and tell him to have a car at Nice to meet us."

"Why don't you spend Christmas here?" Ralph Maxton asked.

Angela shook her head. "My father's not well enough to fly out. He's insisting on staying at home, so we've got to go over and be with him."

It was a slight deterioration of his heart condition, nothing serious, Jim Hulbert had reassured her. But long journeys and upheavals were not sensible at his age. Especially during bad weather. Steven had agreed to a second Christmas at Haywards Heath, though Angela knew he wanted to stay in France.

The villa belonged to them now. He had persuaded the owner to sell it by offering twice its market value. So Angela could change the furniture and redecorate, but she found little to alter. She liked the previous owner's taste, and it seemed as if the task of transforming the casino had exhausted her inventive powers. She bought some pictures from a gallery in Cannes that specialized in good French contemporary art, changed the curtains in the dining room and decided to leave anything else till the spring.

A gala evening was planned for the middle of October, after which Maxton recommended that they close down till spring. When the casino was profitable, they could afford to stay open during the quiet winter months, but not yet. He and Steven had decided on a benefit performance as their curtain call for the season.

It was Maxton's idea to contact Renata Soldi's agent. She was the most promising young opera singer since Maria Callas.

"She'll come because she's poaching on Callas's territory. And the glitterati'll come to give Callas a poke in the eye. She's made a lot of enemies. Renata Soldi can't hold a candle to La Callas, but that's not the point. She'll pull the crowds. We'll sell out for the charity and pick up some of the big gamblers who can't afford not to be seen at this sort of thing. And we'll shut up shop with a bang!"

As always, Angela wished he would tone down the ruthless cynicism. It spoiled the excitement of the evening. She was looking forward to hearing Soldi sing. She didn't want to connect a great artist with malice and infighting toward another great artist and to see her audience as little more than spectators at a social blood sport.

Ralph Maxton saw her reaction and tried to put it right by changing the subject and talking about something agreeable. Like Christmas.

"It'll be fun having Christmas in England," he said. "You had snow last year, didn't you? It was just cold and rather wet here."

They were having their weekly dinner together, and Steven had left them at the table to finish their coffee while he made some calls. Angela knew he always telephoned New York around this time of day, so she kept Maxton on in the dining room.

"Where will you go?" she asked him.

He shrugged. "It depends. I was hoping to spend it with a friend, but she's got elderly relative trouble at the moment, so I don't suppose it'll come off. Is there more coffee there, Angela? . . . Thanks."

Madeleine was doubtful about sneaking off with him for Christmas. Her lover was demanding that she stay near him in Lyons so he could escape his family's clutches and visit her. As Madeleine explained, she was squeezing him for a really big present this year, and she didn't think she'd get it if she didn't stay close. She told Ralph how annoyed she was and pulled pretty faces, calling the old man a string of dirty names, but Ralph understood. She couldn't pass up a valuable piece of jewelry, or a block of shares, just to screw and laugh with him over the holiday.

He'd planned to spend Christmas in a new hotel at Val d'Isère. He was a good skier, and Madeleine was more athletic than she looked. They'd have had fun. He hated Christmas; it was so depressing, with its insistence upon family gatherings and children. He'd have to go up there alone. He was sure to find someone congenial. He had a lot of money to throw around on a pretty girl.

He heard Angela say, "What will you do, Ralph, if your plans fall through?"

He smiled in his twisted way, mocking himself. "Make new ones. I'm very adaptable. And be a dear and don't suggest I go home, because I want to see the family about as much as they want to see me."

"I wasn't going to suggest it," she said. "I was going to ask you if you'd like to come over and have Christmas with all of us."

To her surprise, he turned slightly red. "How very kind. Were you really?"

"Why not? If you can't or won't go to your own home, why not come to mine? Charlie'd love it, so would my father, and Steven and I would be delighted. Just so long as you don't have glamorous expectations. It's a very modest village house, but we'll have a happy Christmas, I can promise you. I love all the trimmings, the tree and the presents and going to midnight service. . . . Why don't you say yes? If your friend solves her problem with the relative, then we won't mind a bit if you cancel. How's that?"

"That's the nicest bit of blackmail I can think of," he said. "Hadn't you better mention it to Steven? He may not want the hired help eating his Christmas turkey."

"Shut up and don't be silly. He's very fond of you. We both are."

He was so adept at hiding his feelings that she noticed nothing except that hint of color. It was funny; she couldn't imagine Maxton being embarrassed by anything.

He leaned a little toward her across the table. She looked very pretty and soft in the subdued light, and however hard he tried, he couldn't find anything but gentleness in her eyes. He reached out and took her hand. He did it in an exaggerated way, robbing the gesture of serious intent. He raised her hand to his lips and, for the merest second, touched them.

"My fair benefactress," he declaimed. "Thanks to you, I shan't spend a lonely Christmas, sobbing into my pillow! Tell me, why are you such a very nice person?"

"Why do you make a joke of everything?" she countered. "I'm not particularly nice. I can be very nasty when I like, so just be careful!"

"That I doubt," he said. "Hadn't we better join Steven? Otherwise he'll come storming in and fire me for kissing your hand."

"You're an idiot." She laughed at him. "Come on. Let Janine clear the table. . . . You know, Steven says she gets on his nerves—she's always hovering round us. He even suggested I get rid of her."

"You'd lose the mother, and she's a marvelous cook, as we've just confirmed. And the next one could be a thief as well as a spy. All French servants spy on their employers; the Italians steal from them. I could have a word with her if you like . . . ?"

"No, don't bother. I'll probably lose my temper if I catch her outside the door and do it myself. As you say, Ralph, I don't want to lose both of them. That fish soufflé was delicious, wasn't it?"

"Exquisite," he said. He opened the door and stood aside to let her pass. "But I bet your Christmas turkey will be better."

"Darling, you don't mind, do you? It seemed awful for him to spend Christmas all alone."

"Of course I don't mind. Christmas is no time to be alone," Steven said. "If it makes you happy to have him come over, that's fine by me."

"Thank you, darling. I think it's a kindness. He's so bitter about life, but deep down there's a lot of niceness in him. He's so lonely, it's sad."

Steven smiled. "You find good points in everyone, sweetheart, that's your trouble. But don't become too sorry for him, or I'll get jealous."

"I can imagine," Angela teased in turn. "He's quite a charmer, so you better watch out."

They ended by hugging each other and laughing.

The gala was a sellout. Angela sat entranced by the strength and purity of the young opera star's voice. She had never heard Maria Callas sing in the flesh; she had to take Maxton's word for it that Renata Soldi was not in the same class.

It was a glittering evening, with the women dressed and bejeweled like peacocks, and afterward, when the concert was over and the supper room cleared away, she went upstairs and watched the closed-circuit TV with Steven. He was in a buoyant mood, pointing out the big gamblers on the screen. A number of them were women, including a famous Hollywood star.

Angela was tired after the long evening, and the song recital had been a powerful experience that left her feeling drained. The next morning they would close down the casino for the winter. The staff went on half pay—except for the croupiers and dealers, who kept their full salaries—but were free to seek employment elsewhere till the spring reopening. And the move to England for the Christmas holidays was drawing near. Charlie had phoned and written. He was in good spirits and assured them that he had been working hard.

She was sitting with Steven one chilly November evening, a wood fire burning in the fireplace and a sense of utter peace and happiness in her heart, when the telephone rang. It was New York.

Steven said, "It's my brother. I'll take it in the study, darling."

It was a long conversation. Angela almost fell asleep in the warm room.

"Angela." She roused with a start. She often drifted off in the evenings these days.

"Steven? What's the matter. Is something wrong?" She was instantly alert at the sight of him.

He dropped down beside her. "Clara's getting married again," he said.

"But isn't that good news?" she questioned.

"My family thinks so," he said. "But I'm not sure. I'm not sure at all."

"But why not?"

"The way Piero spoke, this guy sounds like some cheap punk who's good with the girls. He works for two brothers over on the West Side."

"Perhaps that's what she wants," Angela suggested. "Someone the opposite of you."

Steven was frowning, hardly hearing what she said. Clara—intelligent, educated, with a taste for music and the arts. He remembered her touring the galleries and museums when they were in Paris on their honeymoon. Clara marrying a good-looking, low-class muscleman from the Guglielmo mob? And Aldo letting her do it? Take such a step down?

Perhaps Angela was right. Perhaps the only way Clara could come to terms with her jealous sexuality was to go slumming. But he didn't believe it.

He said, "Why don't you go up to bed, darling? I won't be long. I just want to think it through."

"All right. I nearly dropped off while you were on the phone. Don't worry, it must be a good thing. She'll make a new life for herself. Wake me if you're worried. Promise?"

"I promise," he said, and kissed her.

Piero had been jubilant. He'd made coarse comments and laughed. "He's probably got a dick like an elephant's trunk," he said. "I hear she's never off her back. Now maybe Tino will stop worrying."

"Worrying about what?" Steven had asked him. Piero was dismissive.

"Tino worries. The Fabrizzis threw some goddamned party for all their people down in Key West in August, and Tino thought it was some kind of cover-up for a meeting. We weren't supposed to know." Steven suddenly felt a chill of warning. "You never told me," he said. "What kind of meeting?"

"Nothing." Piero dismissed it. "Some fucking wedding anniversary. That's when Clara shacked up with this Salviatti stud. Now they're getting married; Aldo's going to invite the world. He even called on Papa to discuss it. Clara wanted his blessing. You know how she loved all of us?" He chuckled at the idea.

"I know," Steven said. "She hated Papa's guts. And yours."

"They're playing it right," Piero insisted.

Steven asked him, "When is this wedding?"

"January. At Saint Mary and the Angels. We're all invited. Papa, Mama, me, Lucia, Tino and his family, the cousins from Florida, Uncle Giorgio." He'd ended by saying, "The heat's off you, Steven. And with a punk like that as a son-in-law, Aldo won't give us any trouble."

Something wasn't right. The pieces didn't fit. Piero's scenario was lacking one element. The only reason Clara Fabrizzi would marry a small-time Mafia hood was if she'd got pregnant in August, and the wedding was too late for that. So there must be another motive. A front for a secret meeting of the Fabrizzi associates? Tino suspected as much. And Tino was shrewd. A big wedding, Piero had said. With everyone invited. Steven was pouring himself a whiskey when he repeated aloud, "Everyone invited." Everyone from the Falconi family. Uncle Giorgio, the cousins. All gathered together in one place.

Steven slammed the glass down so hard that the bottom cracked. He didn't notice. He was reaching for the phone, to break all the rules and call his father. Piero wouldn't see it. Only Lucca, subtle as a snake himself, would listen to his son's hunch and accept his warning.

His mother was crying into the telephone. "Oh, my son, my boy. It's so good to hear your voice. How are you?"

"I'm fine, Mama. Just fine. So good to hear you too. You've had my messages from Piero?" He found himself swallowing hard at the sound of his mother choking back tears.

"Yes, yes. He tells me when he calls. I think of you all the time. I pray for you."

"I know you do, Mama, and I think of you and Papa and the family. I miss you all so much." Piero had told him she'd been unwell with a chest cold again. "How are you feeling, Mama? You taking care of yourself? You catch too many colds."

"I'm better; don't worry about me. Piero makes too much of everything. Lucia moved in to look after me and take care of your father."

"I have to talk with him," Steven said. "Get him to come to the phone; tell him it's important. I *must* talk with him."

"I'll try, Stefano, I'll try. Hold on."

It seemed a long wait to Steven. He knew his father's pride. He could imagine Lucca looking up at his wife, without pity for her tears. "No," he might be saying. "I have no son to talk with. There's nothing he has to say I want to hear. You want to talk with him, you talk."

Through the telephone receiver, Steven heard a door bang. "He won't speak to you," his mother said. "I can't persuade him. I'm so sorry, Stefano."

Steven swore in helpless anger. Then he said gently, "Mama, Mama, don't upset yourself. Don't cry. I understand how he feels. Listen to me. Just tell him this. Make sure he listens. Tell him not to go to Clara's wedding. Tell Piero not to go. It's a trap they've set for all of you. Tell him, Mama. Make him hear you."

She promised, and he hung up. He balled his fist and rammed it into his palm in frustration. He'd call Piero back right away, deliver the same message, hope he'd take it seriously. But Piero was an optimist. He didn't see around corners. He'd talked so jauntily about finally getting Clara off their backs, making crude jokes. He wouldn't want to hear that it was a ruse.

But Steven had to try. Piero was not receptive, as he'd feared.

Steven had been absent from the scene too long. Piero's awe of him was tempered with a growing self-confidence in his own abilities. Spoletto was the watchdog, and he had finally agreed that there was nothing suspicious. And Tino, Piero insisted, was *always* looking under the bed, for Christ's sake.

"You're getting jumpy down there. Back home we just get on with business and lead a quiet life. Clara's got herself a big hunk, that's all there is to it. Relax, brother, relax." He ended the conversation with a cheerful laugh.

In the morning Steven told Angela. He was restless, unable to stay in bed beside her. He paced up and down while he talked.

"I know it," he insisted. "I know it in here!" He struck his chest. "It's phony—the whole thing's a setup. Clara wouldn't marry a slob, and Aldo wouldn't let her. All that crap about wanting my father's blessing. Did I tell you about that? She hated my papa's guts, and at the end he hated hers. So they tell a pack of lies, they set a wedding date, and my family starts to sit back and look the other way. If only I could see Piero, talk to him face-to-face. He laughed at me last night, Angela. Can you believe that? What the hell am I to do?"

She got up and came to him. "Calm down," she said quietly. "That's the first thing. This wedding is weeks away. You don't have to do anything on the spur of the moment. You've got time, Steven. Your family's got time."

He pulled away from her. "No, they haven't," he said harshly. "I know the Fabrizzis. They'll fix alibis and get agreement among some of the other families for what they're going to do. They'll make it a matter of honor; they's how it's done. My father and brother and the rest of my family won't stand a snowball's chance in hell. And there's always a backup plan to an operation like this. If the situation changes, you make your hit earlier. I shouldn't have talked to Piero. I should have got on the plane and gone back when my father wouldn't talk to me."

Angela's color drained. "Steven, you can't! You can't go back. You'd be killed!"

"I swore an oath to my father; I swore it to my brother too. If there was trouble, I'd come back. Nothing can make me break that promise. Not even you, Angela."

She said, "What about your son? What about Charlie? What do you think it'll mean to him if something happens to you? And it's not just Charlie, either, now." She went back and sat on the bed.

[219]

He wasn't listening to her. He had become a stranger, a man caught up in a frightening, alien world.

"You go home to your father," he said. "Get ready for Christmas. Maxton can close up here. I'll join you there as soon as I can."

"No, Steven!"

He turned at the tone of her voice. "Angela, don't try to stop me. Please don't try to stop me. I have to do this."

She said, "You can't go back and risk your life. You've got another family to think about. I'm having a baby. I was keeping it as a surprise for Christmas."

She broke down and began to weep. He came and sat with her, taking her in his arms. She turned and clung to him.

"If you go you won't come back. You'll get drawn in. There'll be violence, killing—it'll be the end of everything for us."

"You should have told me," he said slowly. "You should have told me you were pregnant."

"I had it all planned. My Christmas present to you, Steven. You've said you wanted another child, and I wanted one too, to make you happy. Try to make your father see sense. Try once more, before you do something that could destroy everything for us. You gave up the old life. You had no right to promise anything that meant getting involved in it again."

He asked her, "What are you saying to me, Angela?"

She took a deep breath. "I'm saying this: I love you with all my heart, Steven. But you've got to find another way."

Maxton went shopping for Christmas presents. A present for the old father; he found a nice antique backgammon set. He could teach the doctor to play. He'd cut his gambling teeth on that particular game when he was in his teens. A tennis racket for Charlie from a smart sports shop in Monte Carlo. He'd actually bought it for himself in the summer and never used it. For Angela, what? What could he give that was personal enough and yet not too personal? The bibelots from Hermès—scarves, expensive gold-plated key rings and costly knick-knacks—were not Angela's style. In the end he chose silk-embroidered flowers in an oval frame. He wrapped it carefully. It was just possible that Steven might not be there when she opened it. His absence at Christmas had been hinted at, but not confirmed.

She had been crying on the morning they drove to the airport at Nice. She had a lot of luggage, he noticed. Steven drove them. He looked grim. In the departure lounge, Maxton pretended not to watch them say goodbye. His keen ears picked up their urgent whispers.

"Please, Steven, please change your mind! Don't go back!"

"I've got to go. We've been over and over it. It's the only way to make them listen. Oh, darling, I beg of you, try to understand."

"I know what will happen. I know it'll be the end for us. You've broken your promise to me. . . . I've got to go now. They've called our flight."

She literally pulled herself away from him and started off toward the gate. Falconi stood looking after his wife and then abruptly swung away and disappeared.

Maxton settled down in the seat beside her. He dug into his pocket. "From one coward to another," he murmured. "Have a drop of this before we take off." He held out a little silver flask of brandy. "It'll make you feel better." He had unscrewed a tiny cup from the top.

Angela took it from him. "I don't think anything will do that," she said, and drank it down.

The plane was taxiing onto the runway, the engines gathering power for the takeoff. She closed her eyes and then opened them, watching the ground speeding away from them outside the window.

"If you feel like clutching something . . . ," his voice said, and she gripped his hand as they lifted off with a thrust of the engines, the plane climbing steeply. "All over," he said. "Hang on if you want to, in case we get a few bumps through the clouds."

Angela said, "Thanks, Ralph. I'm all right now. It's just the takeoff I don't like."

"I don't like the bumps," he admitted.

"I think you're not frightened at all," she said. "You're just saying it to make me feel better."

They weren't holding hands anymore. The No Smoking and Fasten Seat Belts signs were switched off above their heads. People around them were relaxing, opening newspapers. There was a rattle as the drinks trolley started on its journey.

"You remember what you said when we took off?" Ralph Maxton reminded her. "If there's anything wrong and you think I could help, you will ask me, won't you, Angela?"

"Yes, Ralph, I will."

He didn't press her further. He ordered a drink for them. There were English newspapers on board. She tried to read. She felt sick with the baby inside her and heartsick at what lay ahead. Her father and Charlie had to be protected up to the last moment, the facade that Steven was on business kept going till the holiday was over. He hadn't changed his mind. She wouldn't change hers. She was sure it would end in disaster.

7

They met in the back of a corner trattoria in the area where the first immigrants to New York had settled.

They'd come from Sicily, from Naples, from Calabria, from the bitterly poor industrial towns in the north, and made their home in the rat-ridden tenements and tumbledown shacks of a sprawling slum. It was known as Little Italy. The little food shops were still there, selling pasta and salami and wine from the old homeland; the cafés and restaurants, the tenement blocks, the Catholic-run schools and the big churches built with poor people's money; the funeral parlors and the flower shops, the markets where the old women liked to congregate and bargain, talking their native dialect. It was the heartland of the Mafia and its Neapolitan offspring, Cosa Nostra. The trattoria was owned by one of the New York families; they ran the gambling and the drug factories and the whorehouses in part of the neighborhood. They were affiliated with the Fabrizzis, who were much bigger and more powerful. It was just before Christmas and snowing, with savage temperatures. The men came in their cars, wrapped to the ears in coats and scarves, hats pulled low against the wind that blasted around the corner. They went in one by one and were shown to the room at the back. They took their places at the single large table. When the door opened and closed and the last man was in place, the meeting was called to order by Joe Nimmi, an old friend and business associate of Aldo Fabrizzi.

The brothers Roy and Victor Guglielmo were among the group. Joe Nimmi was a powerful man, a senior Mafia capo, respected for his loyalty and wisdom. He spoke with due solemnity. Everyone was quiet. "You all know why we've come together," he said. "It's a sad day for me; maybe the saddest of my life. For forty years I've been a friend of Aldo Fabrizzi. We worked the streets together; we were like brothers. We fought side by side in those early days when the Irish tried taking over our territories. I've got the scars right here to prove it." He laid a hand on his chest. "Aldo's become a big man. We respected him. We owed him loyalty. But I tell you, he's been cheating on us." He looked around at them. "A few months ago he called us to a meeting. He says he wants to eliminate the Falconis to avenge his daughter's honor. But he lied. He had another reason. My niece Gina stayed in Aldo's house. I tell you the truth: I sent her there. I'd been hearing things I couldn't believe. Gina heard Aldo and his daughter talking business. Our business. She saw Clara reading the ledgers. Checking the figures. Aldo Fabrizzi wants the Falconis rubbed out. He wants the territories and their business to give to his daughter, Clara. He wants us working for her." He paused, and there was an angry murmur. He said to Victor Guglielmo, "Isn't this true?"

"It's true," Victor agreed. "They fixed the marriage so he could put the power in Clara's hands. Bruno's our boy. He admitted what was going on. We asked a few questions of our own. We found out she's running the protection for the garment business. There's a mouthpiece, but she's giving the orders."

Joe Nimmi took it up. "Men have ruled our society as they rule their families at home. No woman has ever been admitted. We are the Men of Respect." He gave the ancient Sicilian title in all its solemnity. "What he has done is a crime. A dishonor to us all. My friends, we swore an oath not long ago. It was a false oath. It doesn't bind me anymore. Are we to put a gun to Lucca Falconi's head, to kill so many of their family, so Clara can take us over?" There was a shout of "No" almost in one voice. He nodded. "What Aldo was planning would have meant war on the streets. We've had peace for many years. I say we keep that peace. We leave the Falconis alone. But I say Aldo Fabrizzi's life is forfeit. I call on you to vote."

He sat down. One by one, hands were raised. There were no abstentions. It was a solemn moment. Victor Guglielmo asked the only question: "What about Bruno Salviatti?"

Joe Nimmi shrugged. "We'll think about Bruno," he said. He cleared his throat. It had been a long, emotional speech. He asked for some water. Gradually the mood lightened. People started talking about family plans for Christmas. The meeting broke up, and they exchanged holiday greetings.

They left as they had come, one by one at intervals, speeding away in their cars, back to their homes or their offices. Joe Nimmi was the last to go. He stayed talking to the man and his wife who ran the trattoria; he shared a pot of coffee with them before going out into the cold. He gave them an envelope full of money and wished them a Merry Christmas. He pinched their plump little boy's cheek as he sat on his mother's knee.

"What a fine-looking boy," he said. He slipped a ten-dollar bill into the mother's hand. "Buy him something from me." He went outside into the street. It was nearly dark. A man in a Santa Claus costume was ringing a bell and collecting money for the poor.

"Mum, what's the matter?"

She was on her way out and Charlie was barring her way. "Nothing; nothing's the matter."

"You've been crying," he said, "I can tell. Why isn't Dad coming home? Come on, I'm not a baby. I want to know."

"I told you, it's business," Angela said. Charlie had grown amazingly since September. Grown and matured with the rapidity of his Sicilian blood. And he looked so like his father standing there. She had been a fool to think he wouldn't be aware.

"I don't believe it's business," Charlie announced. "The casino's shut down for the winter, Ralph was telling me. . . . You've had a row, haven't you? He hasn't even phoned to speak to me. . . ."

"Yes," she admitted. "We have had a row, Charlie. I didn't want him to miss Christmas. He may still change his mind. So don't worry about it, will you? Please?"

"Of course I'm worrying," he said angrily. "It's just not like you two—you never row about anything. Mum . . ." He hesitated and turned red. "He hasn't met someone else, has he?"

"Oh, darling, no. It's nothing like that! I can't really talk about it. And I'm going to be late. Grandpa's waiting in the car. I must go." She pushed past him.

If they went on discussing it, she might break down in tears. She had kept up a facade of cheerfulness, hoping to deceive her son. And hoping, in spite of everything, that Steven would call and say he'd changed his mind. She had noticed that Charlie was quite hostile to Ralph Maxton, and that disturbed her. Now she knew why. He resented any man but Steven near her.

[225]

"What kept you so long?" Hugh Drummond grumbled. "I won't have any time to get anything, at this rate."

She had found him very frail and inclined to be querulous. He wanted to get an extra present for his grandson and something for Maxton. He was always saying how much he liked Maxton. Ralph was very good with the old man; he listened patiently to his rambling stories of his early days in medicine, never once showing that he was bored. And the preparations for Christmas went ahead, with the question hanging over her that was becoming less of a question with every day that passed. Steven wouldn't go back on his promise. His responsibility to his family came before his love for her, their son and the baby she was carrying. There would be a hideous bloodletting in America, and inevitably he would become part of it.

She said, "I'm sorry, Daddy. Don't worry, we've got plenty of time before the shops close."

Charlie watched them drive away. He let the curtain fall back and stood staring down at the fire in the grate. He loved his stepfather. He wanted them all to be together, to celebrate this Christmas as they had the first one, just before his mother and Steven were married. He didn't want that beak-nosed bugger Maxton hanging around his mother either, making himself useful. The way he pandered to his grandpa turned Charlie's stomach. Charlie wasn't taken in. His grandfather's long stories about hospital life in the twenties couldn't possibly interest Maxton.

And now his stepfather was absent. A row about business, his mother had called it. A pretty serious row, to set them apart like this.

"Business my bloody foot," Charlie announced out loud. His best friend, Jordan, the instigator of his trip to New York, had flunked out halfway through his end-of-term exams and been sent home. His parents were getting a divorce. The news had shattered him. Charlie was shattered too. If it could happen to Jordan, then it could happen to him too. Unless he did something about it. He had learned that from Steven. You didn't sit on your hands and wait for fate to slap you down. You got up and threw the first punch. Steven had told him this when Charlie was having trouble with one of the senior prefects.

"Well, then," Charlie said, nerving himself, "I'll ring him. I'll tell him we'll have a rotten bloody Christmas if he doesn't come home."

Steven was packed. He was booked on the plane to Paris and then on to New York. He had called Piero and instead got Lucia, who panicked when he told her he was coming. "Just give Piero the message," he told her. "I'll contact him when I get there. And Papa's not to know." He'd hung up while she was still talking.

The villa was chill with impending desertion; the heat was turned low, and the windows were shuttered. Cat-footed Janine had driven him crazy, padding after him with sly little questions about when he was going to join Madame She'd probably seen his ticket lying on his desk. She was packed too, ready to move out with her mother till she was told to return. Realizing he was late, he looked around quickly to see if he'd forgotten anything.

There was a sad sense of finality. Angela had been gone for nearly a week, and he'd got as far as dialing the English number several times before he put the phone down. There was nothing to say that hadn't already been said. He didn't want to lie to his son; he didn't want to think about him and Angela and the baby she was carrying.

He was at the door, his coat already buttoned against the cold outside, when the telephone rang. He hesitated. Hope surged for a moment. It must be Angela. He went back and picked up the receiver.

"Look, Dad, whatever it is you've got to do, couldn't it wait? Poor Mum's miserable. We'll all miss you—it'll be awful. What sort of business is it?"

"Family business," Steven said. If only he'd gone a minute or two earlier; if only he hadn't stopped and answered. Charlie was turning a knife in his heart with every word. "My father has a problem. He needs me, Charlie."

"I didn't know you had a father," his son said. He sounded bewildered. "You've never mentioned him before. Dad, please, I know there's something wrong with you and Mum. She won't tell me, but I don't believe all this stuff about business. It's just an excuse! Jordan's parents are getting divorced. He's so upset he had to go home early. . . . Dad, there isn't something like that with you and Mum, is there? Dad? Are you there?"

After a pause Steven answered, "Yes, son, I'm here. Is your mother there? Let me speak to her."

"She's taken Grandpa to town. Why haven't you rung us up?"

"Charlie, I tried, but I couldn't get through. . . ." He let the excuse die away. He put one hand over the mouthpiece and swore in anguish.

There was a clock on his desk. If he didn't leave immediately he might miss his flight. He could still make it if he drove like fury and the traffic lights were on his side. He could still catch the plane from

Nice, change at Paris and be on his way to New York. His son was waiting on the line; he could tell him not to worry, not to think about Jordan and his parents and imagine that anything like that could happen to them.

He heard Charlie say, "Please come home for Christmas. Make it up with Mum."

Steven looked at the clock once more. Then he said, "I guess it can wait. Don't tell your mother we've talked. I'm coming. Don't you worry about a thing. I'm sorry to hear about Jordan."

"I didn't really think anything like that," his son protested.

"Sure you didn't," Steven said gently. "You keep this under your hat and we'll make it a surprise, okay?"

"Okay, Dad, super. See you!"

There was no doubt about the relief in Charlie's voice. Steven hung up. He opened the buttons on his overcoat one by one and sat down behind his desk. He picked up the clock and watched the hands move very slowly, till the last possible chance had gone. Then he reached for the phone and called the airlines to change his tickets and get a reservation for the next direct flight to London. As he was speaking, the door opened and Janine looked in.

"Monsieur . . . I thought you'd gone."

He said, "Not for another two hours. You take your mother and be on your way. I'll lock the doors when I leave." He turned his back, dismissing her. Reluctantly, she closed the door.

He sat on, waiting. The airline phoned back to confirm his change of travel plans. He had a seat on the seven o'clock plane.

"I didn't know you had a father. You've never mentioned him before." He covered his face with his hands. A life built on lies, on deceiving his own flesh and blood. A life in which his obligation to one family conflicted with his love for another.

Pride and guilt had made him risk everything that really mattered to him. He had stood against Angela because it was a reaction bred into him, one that he'd absorbed with the air he breathed since childhood. When the call came, the men went, leaving their women and children to weep.

But he, finally, hadn't been proof against his son. He remembered Angela's fierce reproaches during the unhappy days of argument and counterargument. They had wounded him, made him very angry.

"You think it's right to risk your life for your father and brother? They've chosen to live with violence and death! You owe them more than you owe that boy, who thinks the world of you? Then you're not fit to be his father...."

Bitter quarrels, tears, pleas on both sides. Pride and old traditions built an unbreachable wall between them.

He would have gone to New York anyway, if he hadn't heard the dread in Charlie's voice. "Jordan's parents are getting divorced. He's so upset..." The boy had sensed danger.

Steven thought suddenly, *That kind of gut reaction is a gift from God. It'll protect him always.* And then he realized he was thinking in the past, his own past, when he had to watch out for strangers, sit with his back to a wall in public places, consider every car pulling up beside him at traffic lights as a possible assassination threat. That bullet that had been fired at him in just such a situation was deflected only by toughened window glass. He could still hear the car screeching away. Not for his son. Not for Charles Steven Lawrence the life led by his father as a young man. He wouldn't need that sixth sense of danger. He said out loud, "Holy Jesus, what am I going to do if I haven't gone and Piero still won't listen?" and the phone rang again as if the oath had been a prayer and God had answered.

"Stefano?" It wasn't his brother. It was his cousin Tino Spoletto.

"Piero's out of town for the rest of the week," he explained. "Lucia didn't get a chance to tell you. She came to me, she was so worried. Can we talk for a while?"

The voice sounded thin, and the line crackled. Steven said, "Yes, we can talk. She told you my reason for making the trip?" There was a burst of double echo; the words "making the trip" were bouncing back. Then the line cleared. "She told me. Your mother was worried. I was worried too, but now I don't need to worry anymore."

"Why not? You mean Piero understands? Not two nights ago I spoke to him again and he said it was all crap. Those were his words to me. I knew I had to see him; there was no other way he'd open his eyes."

"They're open now," was the answer.

Steven said slowly, "What's happened? What's wrong, Tino?"

"Nothing, nothing. Piero went out to see to some business in Vegas. Your father and me went to a meeting last night. There were a lot of big men there. Men from the families. You were right—Aldo had a contract out on us. At the wedding, just like you said. But that was canceled at the meeting." He paused. "I can't say too much, you understand, but the families have decided against him. Your father gave his consent. There's nothing to worry about now. Me and Nina and the kids all send our best to you. Have a nice Christmas over there. And watch the papers. Around January twelfth. It'll be one helluva wedding party." The echo returned: "helluva wedding party."

Steven hung up. His instinct had been right. Clara's father had set up his family, with the wedding as a front. Now the same sentence had been passed on Aldo. He stood up slowly. He couldn't help imagining the scene. The marriage, the nuptial mass in Saint Mary and the Angels, the cortege of cars on their way to the reception. How would it be done? An ambush, a hidden sniper . . .

There was no vengefulness in his heart. He felt sickened.

Everyone was watching television when the sitting room door opened and Steven walked in.

He heard his son's cry of welcome, but it was Angela who sprang to her feet and ran to him. Hugh Drummond struggled to get up, smiling with pleasure, and Ralph Maxton kept still in the background. He had no place in this family reunion.

That night in their room, Steven told her what had happened. "Charlie called me. You mustn't mind, Angela. He did it for the best."

"Mind? Thank God he did. Oh, darling, when you opened that door and walked in, I couldn't believe it! And he was so happy tonight. So am I." They held each other close.

"I'd already decided," he went on. "I knew I couldn't do this to him and to you. Then I got the call from my cousin in New York. There's no danger to them now. I didn't need to go. But I'd made up my mind and told our boy before I knew that. I want you to understand that, sweetheart. You believe me?"

"You know I do," she answered. "You weren't right about this wedding?"

"I was right," he said slowly. "My father-in-law had it all figured out. The Falconi family were going to be wiped out."

"Oh, Steven, don't. It's like a nightmare."

"It'll be his nightmare now, not ours," he said. "And that's all we need to know. Forget it, my darling. It came near to us, but it won't ever touch us again. Forgive me, will you?"

She kissed him. "You came home to us," she said. "That's all I care about. We'll have a wonderful Christmas and pretend this never happened. The four of us." And she placed his hand on her gently swollen abdomen.

She slept deeply and peacefully in his arms that night.

They had a truly merry Christmas. The tree sparkled in the hallway; snow didn't fall, but the weather was cold and bright with sunshine—perfect for walking. Steven and Angela kept very close, drawing Charlie with them, realizing how near they'd come to being separated forever.

Maxton accepted his role of companion to the old doctor. He liked Drummond, and in spite of Charlie's jealous judgment, he didn't find him a bore. He was solid and accessible, so unlike Maxton's own father, a remote figure who would make an appearance at the big family Christmas dinner in the great hall in Derbyshire but who never really participated. Maxton imagined it sometimes, indulging in a little self-inflicted pain, then turning it to mockery. He had hated the formal gatherings at Christmas—the relatives summoned out of the woodwork, the ritual present-opening at three-thirty precisely, after they had all been forced to listen to the queen's speech.

He had hated the forced gaiety, which never included him because he was inevitably in disgrace about something: giving a vulgar comic book to an elderly aunt, forgetting to give someone else anything at all, making an ill-timed request for money to cover an overdraft. He never got it right, from the time when he was a little boy and he'd helped himself to too much champagne and thrown up in the middle of Christmas lunch. So he settled now for old Dr. Drummond and his stories and was grateful. Angela was happy again, happy that Steven was back, and their rift, whatever it was, had healed. She enthusiastically spread her happiness around. He remembered how his parents had despised the middle classes. The backbone of England, no doubt, but terribly dull and easily ridiculed. His family had a lot to learn from people like the Drummonds. He was glad to be with them, and yet he felt lonelier than he had for many years.

He had lost his private battle during that Christmas; he had fallen in love for the first time in his life. Analyzing it, he admitted that Angela had broken through the mistrust of women that had insulated him. Sexual attraction, a charming prettiness, these were easy to resist. But not her kindness. She was thoughtful and gentle in her dealings with other people. In all innocence she had pierced his tough defensive shell by treating him like someone who mattered, someone whom she cared about.

It had begun when he lay ill and alone, and she had taken him home to nurse. He had never known affection, and seeing it lavished only on others had fostered a deep sense of unworthiness.

Watching her with her family, and especially with Steven, Maxton experienced a degree of helpless longing that could only change to jealousy. And to fantasies in which her family disappeared and only he remained to claim her.

And then on Christmas morning, amid the debris of opened presents, Steven appeared with a bottle of champagne and, with his arm around Angela, announced that she was going to have a baby. The cork popped, glasses were filled, and they drank to the happy news.

"How splendid," the doctor kept saying. "What good news. Nice for you, Charlie, to have a brother or sister." He went around beaming, the champagne tipping over the edge of his glass.

Maxton watched the boy go up and embrace his mother and Steven. He didn't like Charlie. He saw more of his father in him than Angela. One day that English public school veneer would rub off. Finally he went up and congratulated them.

Angela said sweetly, "Thank you, Ralph dear. I'm so glad you're with us today. It's a real family celebration, isn't it, darling?"

And Steven looked down at her fondly and said yes, it was.

They had plans for New Year's Eve, and they were insisting that Maxton stay on. He couldn't come up with an excuse immediately but made a telephone call from the village to Madeleine, asking her to send a phony message.

The last thing he wanted was to stay and celebrate the new year with the inhabitants of those neat little houses round the village green. Nice, proper people, neighbors of the doctor and his late wife, people who'd known Angela all her life. He couldn't bear to be second best a moment longer.

Madeleine obliged. It was an ill-phrased telegram about a sick aunt who needed him, and he turned it very skillfully into a joke, reading it out to them.

"My friend thinks I need an alibi," he said, "just because she has to have one herself. You will forgive me, won't you, if I slip back ahead of the party? She is rather special, and it's been difficult for her to get away."

"Of course we don't mind," Angela said. "Are you going somewhere nice?"

"Our original plan," he said. "A little skiing, and a lot of après-ski!" His harsh, tuneless laugh rang out. He went to pack, to say his goodbyes, and to put space between him and all of them. If you're going, for God's sake hurry up and go. That was an old saying in his family. The departing guest was speeded off; those who lingered were not popular. Steven offered to drive him to Gatwick Airport, but he refused firmly.

"Jolly kind, but no, thanks. I'm not tearing you from the bosom of your family. I'll be back in Antibes in two weeks; I'll keep an eye on the villa and see what needs to be refurbished at the Poliakoff—you mentioned something about the cloakroom facilities." Back to business, back to the safe relationship.

"Okay, you do that. Sorry you have to leave us."

"Where will I contact you when I get back? Will you still be here?"

"No," Steven answered. "I'm taking Angela and Charlie away after the New Year. Somewhere in the sun. I'll let you know."

The doctor was sorry to see Maxton go; he cleared his throat and fiddled furiously with his pipe. Maxton understood that he couldn't say how much he'd miss his company. He shook hands and patted the old man on the shoulder. He had never dared such intimacy with his own father.

And then Angela came and kissed him on the cheek. He could feel the color sweeping up, betraying him. "Thank you for being so sweet to Daddy and to all of us," she said. "Happy New Year, Ralph."

"Thank you," he said. "It's been the best Christmas I've spent in a very long time. Happy New Year, Angela. Take care of yourself."

He sprang into the local taxi, waved to them and settled back. He had deluded himself with hope; now it was dashed forever. She belonged to Steven Lawrence, and she was pregnant with his child.

Back to the old life, Ralph, he said to himself as they drove away. He hummed a little tune. As a very small boy, he used to hum when he was unhappy. It gave him comfort.

The party was a success. Angela said so. Steven found it very dull. They were so low-key, these English people. They enjoyed themselves in whispers. He was charming and friendly to all of them and endured the inquisitive looks with patience.

Angela was in her element; Charlie too. Steven saw his son fitting in happily with boys and girls his own age, finding them fun. Steven thought them boring and stiff. He remembered the uninhibited, noisy parties back home, where the new year was welcomed in with shouts and music, everyone embracing and kissing, children of all ages romping around as midnight struck. He didn't say anything, but he couldn't wait to get to the sunshine of Morocco. And he had timed it deliberately. The twelfth of January, his cousin Spoletto had said.

On that day, he and Angela and their son would be thousands of miles away from newspapers and television. The Falconis were safe. That was all he needed to know. He wouldn't think about Clara and her father.

It was no concern of his.

Clara hated Christmas that year. She hated it because custom forced her family and the widowed mother and relatives of Bruno, her bridegroom, to spend part of it together. They gathered in Aldo's house for a big traditional dinner; they all exchanged gifts and drank toasts to the couple who were soon to be married.

Mrs. Salviatti was a fat, nervous woman, a gasbag who chattered on and on nervously till Clara could have screamed. She kept glancing at her son, saying to Clara, to Luisa, "Isn't he a handsome boy? Just like his father—and such a good son he's been. . . ." They were peasants, all of them, uncomfortable in tight suits, strangling in neckties, their women badly dressed; the children irritated her, running up and down without hindrance, indulged by doting parents, shrieking and getting in everyone's way. Clara hated them, and barely held on to her temper. Bruno, resigned now to his fate, was proprietary with her, forever pawing at her, until she snapped at him under her breath to leave her alone. He flattered her father, then preened in front of her. He'd given her a good ring; someone with an eye to the future had lent him the money. They all ate too much, and some of them drank too much too. One of the old Salviatti uncles fell asleep at the table. Aldo saw him, and his eye was cold. Someone got him up and took him to lie down. Several children cried from tiredness and overexcitement. There was much cooing and comforting. Clara felt as if she were in a waking nightmare.

The wedding presents had come flooding in. And a flood it was, from the humblest to the most important in the invited families. A lot of silver and crystal, for a second marriage. Wines by the case, linen and exquisitely embroidered cloths, ornaments, some of them garish, others fine antiques. Pictures with views of the old country. Clara couldn't stand nineteenth-century sentimentality, but Bruno liked the pictures and engravings best of all. She told him very early on that rubbish like that wasn't hanging in her house. Her wedding outfit had been ordered from Bergdorf Goodman. She chose it carefully, determined to look her best. What a contrast it would be to that other wedding, when she had gone to the altar in her virgin white, consumed with a young girl's passion for her bridegroom. She dwelt on her memories of that day: the marvelous singing in the church; the first sight of Steven waiting for her by the altar; the joy of their reception, everyone congratulating them, saying how beautiful she looked, how radiant with happiness; dancing the "Wedding Waltz" in his arms. There was no pain left in the memories now, or if there was, her hatred used it as a goad, urging her to the second marriage with a man she saw only as a means to an end—a life of power and independence, cleansed beforehand of all taint of feeling by an act of bloody retribution against her enemies.

And running through the fabric of that future life was a single scarlet thread. The agency she had created and controlled would find Steven Falconi. The search had already begun.

O'Halloran was a happy man. He liked his smart new office in midtown New York. He liked having two assistants to do the routine work, the boring grind that had been his lot for so long. He liked the battery of copiers and typewriters and recording machines; they signified money and success, like the gold-painted name on the frosted front door. Ace Detective Agency. She had kept the corny name. He liked the young secretary in the outer office; she called him Mr. O'Halloran and made him cups of coffee. Most of all he liked the money. His wife and children had moved to a new house and settled in. It was a decent house in the suburbs, with a garden and a new car in the garage. Finally, they were happy, and why shouldn't they be? He worked very hard and very successfully. He also worked hard because he was frightened.

His employer frightened him. Whenever she called him to come and see her, he could feel the presence of her father, as if he were on the other side of the door.

He had made a few discreet inquiries among his old contacts in the force. It was too late to turn back, so he felt free to find out a little more about his backers. All they had needed was the name Falconi. They immediately linked it with another, equally infamous, name: Fabrizzi. Aldo Fabrizzi had a daughter, who'd married a Falconi. Someone had fried him in a car, down on the coast. They were shit, those two families. O'Halloran had agreed. He said he was asking on account of a case he had on hand.

Then just you watch your step, his contacts had warned him. If it's tied in with the mob, don't touch it. The last private eye who went sniffing around ended up six floors down from his apartment window. They didn't leave much of his agency in one piece either.

O'Halloran promised to drop the case and tell his client to go look elsewhere. He went home to his new house and convinced himself that he was being too well paid to mind being scared. He just had to give that black-eyed bitch what she wanted. And what she wanted was dirt. Dirt of any kind. She'd put the first clients in his way herself. Divorce investigations; lousy stuff, as usual, but this time the quarries were rich, and their wives were out to screw them till the zeroes ran off the page. He did a very good job and they were satisfied. The fees were settled promptly. In his old business, he and Pacellino used to threaten to sue the clients, it was so hard getting the money. Word got around the moneyed circles that his was a very reliable agency. Other clients showed up, different from the women or their husbands or the small-time businessman trying to trace a bad debt. There were corporations who wanted a check run on prospective employees, on their rivals' employees, searching for scandal of a personal nature if they couldn't pin anything else on them. O'Halloran had spent his life among petty criminals; when he left the force and set up with his old partner, he found the sins of suburbia no less unsavory.

But the rich were something else. They knew how to root in the garbage and come up smelling sweet. And then, just before Christmas, she had sent for him unexpectedly. He had gone to the brownstone and was kept waiting. It looked like one of those places featured in women's magazines. When she came in, he got to his feet. She didn't apologize for keeping him so long. She didn't even ask him to sit down. She just walked up to him and held out an envelope.

"This is your Christmas present, Mike. I haven't time to gift-wrap it. And there's a personal favor I want you to do for me. You personally. The details are in that envelope. I'm getting married in January, so I won't be around till mid-February. But I want you to start in on this right away. And have a merry Christmas, won't you?"

"Thanks, Mrs. Falconi. And the same to you. Congratulations on the wedding. He's a lucky guy."

"I'll tell him," she said, "in case he doesn't know. See yourself out, will you?"

He opened the envelope in the car. There were ten thousand dollars and details of the favor she'd mentioned. He was to find her husband, Steven Falconi, who she believed was still alive. She believed he had faked his death and run off with another woman.

She emphasized a visit to one of the city's best-known restaurants, Les Ambassadeurs, giving a date over two years before. She suggested—he noted her tactful way of putting it—that he start with a list of all the diners that evening and go on from there. A previous investigation had come to nothing because the operative had inquired directly about Steven Falconi. He sure had; O'Halloran grimaced. And someone had made scrambled egg out of him. He was going to step very carefully. If this lady asked a personal favor, you didn't send your regrets. He had a feeling you would end up very sorry. No assistant could be trusted with this one. He sighed. When she said "personal," that's what she meant. He would have to take the case himself. He sat thinking about it when he got back to his office. So Falconi wasn't dead. The burned-out corpse belonged to someone else. Or so she thought. First thing was to check the details and the death certificate. He decided he'd better get on it right away, before she took time off from getting married and asked him what the hell he was doing about it. He banked the ten thousand in his personal account, and the next morning left New York for the town nearest the site of the accident. It was a real hick place, with a few scattered houses, a shabby supermarket and a gas station. The local police patrolled a wide area. He started with the back files of the county newspapers before he went anywhere near the police.

He noted that the dead man's brother had identified his remains. So if the lady was right, her in-laws were part of the cover-up. If she was right. He wasn't sure about that yet. Women could get obsessional about husbands, even a dame with ice in her veins, like "the lady." He called her that to himself and to his wife, whose initial curiosity he'd quelled with some glib lies, putting twenty years on Clara Falconi. She wanted an investment and some fun poking into other people's business. It might be kinky, but it sure as hell paid plenty. His wife didn't bother after that.

The local papers had made a big story out of the dead man in the burned-out car. A cigarette and a gasoline leak were blamed. It was all good clean provincial stuff. But to an experienced nose like Mike O'Halloran, something about it stank. Especially the low-key funeral—a cremation, for Christ's sake. Any mafioso worthy of the name was planted with full Catholic rites. Falconi's brother had made the arrangements. To them, it was the way you buried a dog. Unless you wanted to make sure nobody exhumed the corpse.

He wasn't surprised to find that the ashes had been scattered, and the funeral service confined to the immediate family. They killed each other like other people swatted flies, but they had their rituals about death. When a big man died, his assassins sent flowers and often wept at the graveside. It was part of the tradition of respect. Whoever got barbecued in that car, it wasn't the son and heir of Lucca Falconi. He didn't ask around anymore.

Whoever did it must have had contacts in the area. They might still be there. O'Halloran went back to New York and took his employer's advice.

He started his investigation with the dinner reservations at Les Ambassadeurs on the date Clara had given him.

He didn't try to bribe the maître d'. He didn't show a wad of dollar bills to the barman or the girl at the reservation desk. He went to see the manager and told him what he wanted. He had a story ready, and it sounded plausible. He gave the manager his card, and the manager was impressed by the office address. And by O'Halloran. He was well dressed, quiet-spoken. He had shed the provincial gumshoe image under Clara's brutal tutelage. She ordered his suits, she told him how to present himself to people like the suave and clever man who ran the smartest restaurant in New York.

"My clients," O'Halloran said, "want to stay anonymous. Until they can be sure of their case."

The manager understood that. He knew about clients and their need for anonymity. He said, "But surely the police are the right people to track them down?"

O'Halloran agreed. "Sure they are. But my clients don't want the publicity. They feel—and I have guaranteed it to them—that when the fraud is uncovered, the couple concerned will make full restitution rather than face criminal prosecution."

The manager thought that was a sensible solution.

"And they operate in hotels as well as restaurants?"

"They specialize in hotels," O'Halloran said. "They have worked their way through my client's chain of hotels and associated restaurants for the last three years. The sums of money have amounted to a big total. The last bill left unpaid was"—he consulted a nonexistent note in his briefcase—"three thousand eight hundred dollars. For a four-night stay." He cleared his throat. "They also filled a suitcase with ornaments, including some prints off the wall of the suite. It's become part of their trademark."

The manager said, "And the restaurants? They leave a signature there too?" He was personally interested now.

O'Halloran said, "The best vintage champagne, always a magnum. The guy always says they're celebrating. Then comes the caviar, the top of the à la carte list, and they disappear before you can put the check on the table."

"Well." The other man couldn't help looking satisfied. "We've had no such instance here, I assure you. So you're wasting your time coming to me."

"They came here to dinner," O'Halloran said. "They were here on September eleventh two years ago. We know because they left a receipted bill from your restaurant in the wastebasket the last time they booked into one of our hotels. It's our only chance to identify them. If you will let me have the names and what you know about them ... I understand that you keep records up to three years."

The manager nodded. "We do. We have a regular client list with credit ratings, and a list of casuals. I'll get it for you."

An hour later O'Halloran left the office. He had a number of names and a lot of information. Steven Falconi had dined there with the senator and his wife. Six other couples were of possible significance. The maître d', Louis, was instructed to give O'Halloran what help he needed, and Louis didn't disobey the manager. Two couples he knew only slightly; the men were business executives, and they came in from out of town with a client now and then. Of the remaining four, one was a regular client: Mr. Forrest, who ran a big leather goods retailing business. He'd brought a lady guest that night. The other couples were unknowns; they came in for dinner and were not seen again. O'Halloran said thanks, he'd been a great help, and drove himself back to the office. There'd been something evasive about Louis when he talked about Forrest.

Mike O'Halloran decided to pay the man a call.

Clara was trying on her wedding dress. It was a simple cream silk sheath dress with a fitted jacket trimmed in ranch mink on collar and cuffs. They'd made a hat to match, a plain pillbox in the same material.

Her mother was sitting in the bedroom of the brownstone, looking distressed. "You shouldn't do this," she was repeating. "It's unlucky. You know it's unlucky to wear it the day before!"

"Balls," Clara said briskly. "I've never believed in all that stuff." She took off the neat little hat and put it in its bed of tissue in the hatbox. Behind her, Luisa made the forked finger sign against the evil eye. Even when she was young, Clara had never listened to her mother. Now she wouldn't listen to anyone except her father. Luisa was a simple woman, but she understood simple things like jealousy. Bruno was jealous, and so was she. Father and daughter had shut them both out and didn't bother to be tactful about it. They paraded their intimacy, Clara especially, as if she gloried in her status of surrogate son. She was hard and coldhearted, Luisa thought bitterly. Clara was less of a woman because she was being given the respect from Aldo that belonged to a man.

It would end badly, Luisa felt certain. The marriage would fail like the first marriage. And Clara was defying every rooted superstition by parading herself in her wedding gown the day before she married.

There was a knock on the bedroom door. It was the new maid. Maria hadn't been able to stand up to Clara's tempers and moods, and her health began to suffer.

The new girl was made of stronger stuff. "Telephone, madame," she said, and closed the door.

"Who is it?" Clara shouted after her. "She's such a dummy," she snapped to her mother. "I've told her and told her to take a name." She lifted the extension by her bed. It was O'Halloran. She said, "Mama, this is business. Go find a magazine or something, will you? I won't be long."

She sat on the edge of the bed in her wedding suit and listened, while her long fingers beat a silent tattoo on her knee—a habit she had lately developed. Suddenly her fingers were still.

"I think I've found something," O'Halloran was saying. "Like I said, everyone checked out except this guy Forrest and the dame who was with him. I went to see him, and he was ready to talk about it—he was still sore at the way she'd behaved. She ran out on him in the middle of dinner, sent a message by the hatcheck girl that her son was sick. She called him later to apologize, but he wasn't buying. I got a lot of details about her out of him. She was English, representing some PR firm he used in London. So I figured I'd better talk to the hatcheck girl. She wasn't working for Les A anymore, but I found her. Now hang on to your hat, Mrs. Falconi. It took a little sweet-talking and a few dollars on the table, but she told me the woman left with your husband. She also said she looked like she didn't want to go, but he had ahold of her. The hatcheck girl was scared; she knew your husband, and she did what she was told. She remembered your husband sent a message to some senator he was with, and the dame said something about her boy being sick; she acted frightened. The girl said your husband would have scared anybody, the way he looked. He called her Angelina; she remembered that. . . . Mrs. Falconi?"

"I'm here," Clara said. "Angelina? Did you say that's what he called her?"

"Her name is Angela Lawrence; Forrest told me. He gave the address of the apartment she was staying at, so I went there. Two fags answered the door. I gave them a spiel about trying to trace a Mrs. Lawrence for a relative in the States, and they bought it. They liked to gab; you know the type. They'd lent the apartment to a Mrs. Lawrence and her son as a favor to the guy she worked for back in London. They spilled everything you could think of. Why don't I come over and see you? I've got a hell of a lot of stuff on this." She didn't answer. He backtracked in case he had gone too far. "Listen, it can wait if tonight's not convenient."

"It can't wait." She was breathing hard, with something choking in her voice. "You come on over. Give it half an hour. I'll see you then. And bring everything you've got with you. Don't make any other appointments." She put the receiver back on its cradle. She opened her free hand. The long painted nails had scored her palm, breaking the skin. Angela. She said it out loud. Angela. Angelina. The name he'd cried out as he made love to her on the first night of their honeymoon. Her mother had come back into the bedroom. She had one of Clara's fashion magazines rolled up under her arm. They weren't her kind of reading. "Clara? Clara, you all right?"

To her surprise, her daughter answered quietly, almost kindly. "Yes, Mama. I'm all right."

"You don't look it." Luisa's motherly instincts took over. "You look sick," she said anxiously.

She hurried to her daughter and slipped an arm around her. She was ashamed of her harsh judgment of the past few months. The girl was the color of a sheet. And in the deep black eyes there was a sheen of tears.

"Tell me," she said. "What is it? You nervous about tomorrow? Don't you want to marry Bruno? He's a good man, and he loves you, Clara. He'll make you happy." And she added something she had never dared say. "He'll be better for you than the other one. He didn't make you happy. You take care of Bruno. Be kind to him. He'll be good to you. I know it."

Slowly, Clara turned to her. She reached up and wiped a single tear from the corner of her eye. She said, "Don't worry about me, Mama. I know how to manage Bruno. Tomorrow's my big day, isn't it? It'll be a bigger wedding than the first one. People will talk about it for a long time. Now I'll call the car for you and you run back home. Tell Papa I'll be waiting for him right at eleven o'clock. I won't be late." She squeezed her mother around the waist and abruptly kissed her on the cheek.

Luisa flushed. It was the way Clara used to be: willful and spoiled, but she'd turn loving suddenly, and that made it all right. She said, "You sure you won't come home to us and spend the night? You want to be all alone here this evening?"

"I won't be alone, Mama," Clara stood up. She began unfastening the little buttons of the jacket. "There's a man coming over on business. We have a lot to talk about. And don't worry. I won't be late tomorrow."

Mike O'Halloran stared up at her. "Mrs. Falconi," he said. "She's dead. She's been dead for twenty years."

She had been walking up and down, up and down, pacing the floor like a prisoner in a cell. "It's the same one," she said. "Angela. Angelina. The same name. And she left New York on the same day my husband walked out on me!"

"There are thousands of Angelas," he said. "It's a common name. Why don't I get you a drink. I could sure use one," he added.

She made an impatient gesture. "She was at Les A that night. I'd had a row with Steven, and I didn't go. They met there, that's what happened. That's when it started."

O'Halloran poured himself a stiff Scotch.

"She had a son," Clara went on. "A boy of fifteen, sixteen—isn't that what the owner of the apartment told you? Well, that figures too. The woman was pregnant when my husband married her—"

"Listen, Mrs. Falconi," he protested. "This dame was killed—your husband told you. How could she be alive and in New York? It's all on account of the name." He swallowed hard on the Scotch. He couldn't stop her; she wouldn't listen to anything he said. She had made up her mind.

"Everything fits," Clara insisted. "How did he know she was dead? He never saw a body. He saw some goddamned watch he'd given her; it could have dropped off. She didn't die, Mike. She wasn't killed. She had the child and she met up with my husband that night at Les A. God knows what she told him. But he left me for her. He walked out on his family, they faked a death in that car to cover for him, and he's gone to be with her." She went and poured herself a drink, her hands shaking. The glass rattled against the bottle.

She came and sat down, facing him. She said in a low voice, "He wanted children. When I called her a whore, he hit me. We never had any kids." She clutched the drink in both hands, and suddenly it flew across the room, scattering the whiskey, crashing against the wall and splintering all over the carpet. O'Halloran had good nerves, but it made him jump.

He thought suddenly, *She's crazy. What the hell have you got yourself into?* He tried again. "You're speculating. You're crucifying yourself on a hunch, that's all it is. Okay, your husband ran out on you, and he's alive someplace. But you've no proof the first wife wasn't killed in that hospital. You've no proof that woman in the restaurant had anything to do with her."

She said, "I nearly had it. I set a detective on him; not for the first time. But this was different. He was so happy. He was singing. I knew this wasn't some hooker, like the others he screwed around with. But the detective never got further than that night at Les A. My husband took care of that. He had something to hide. And you've found it. Clever Mike." She scared him by bursting out laughing, and stopping as abruptly. "He married her," she said. Her eyes were black slits.

He said, "You told me. In Sicily."

"I want you to go there."

He swallowed Scotch the wrong way. "You what?" He coughed.

"I want you to go there. I want you to check up on the marriage, the bombing of the hospital. Then I want you to follow it up. Go to England. You know where this woman worked in London—didn't they tell you? Yes, they told you. Find her, Mike, and tell me when you do. Tell me if my husband, Steven Falconi, is living with her." She didn't laugh this time. She smiled, and it was as if she was in dreadful pain.

"You said I hadn't any proof it was the same woman. I don't need it. I know it here." She pressed one long hand against her heart. "I'm right. You'll find I'm right, and you'll come and tell me so."

"What about the agency?" He knew it was a hopeless try, but he took a chance.

"Fuck the agency," she said. "It can tick over. You've got enough people for that. This is the assignment I want you to work on. And don't worry, Mike. I know you. You like money, and there's plenty of it if you do this right. You can write your own expense account, and I won't even check it."

She watched him silently. He hesitated, argued with himself and made his choice. "Okay, if that's what you want."

"It's what I want," she said.

Mike O'Halloran got up. "And if this whole crazy business comes out that you're right—what happens next?"

Clara rose. She smoothed her hands down over her skirt, in search of creases that weren't there. "One time when we weren't getting along," she said quietly, "some years ago now, I put a scare into him. I had someone fire a shot at his car. I didn't mean to hit him, you understand. It was bulletproof, armor-plated. I just wanted to scare him into being nice to me. Next time, it'll be for real. You'd better go now. I have to get some sleep tonight. Tomorrow I'm getting married. See yourself out."

"Good night, Mrs. Falconi."

"Good night. And you get started right away."

He said, "Right away." He glanced at her as he left the room. She hadn't moved. Her hands were still smoothing her skirt. He closed the front door behind him. Sicily. England. He could write his own expense account, she'd said. On the way home he stopped off at a florist's and bought his wife fifty dollars' worth of flowers.

He hoped that would make it easier to tell her that he'd be away on a job for quite a while.

Steven had planned to fly to Paris and then directly to Morocco. But Angela wanted to spend a few days in Paris and show some of the sights to Charlie.

Charlie was less than enthusiastic, and so was Steven. Charlie didn't want to waste part of their precious holiday in the sun by going to museums and art galleries with his mother; and Steven was reminded of Clara. She was haunting his mind by day as well as by night these days.

Clara wouldn't be hurt; women weren't targets for high-level contracts on a Mafia boss. Aldo would die, and Clara's new husband, and perhaps even some Fabrizzi lieutenants who couldn't be trusted. Clara would see them being slaughtered. She would be spared, only to live with the memory of horror for the rest of her life. The thought of her plagued him, and it was worst of all in those few days in Paris. It seemed to Steven that they were following exactly in her footsteps, going to the Louvre, the Tuileries, the tomb of Napoleon at Les Invalides. Charlie was impressed by that, in spite of himself. He lingered by the great black marble mausoleum sunk deep in the heart of the monumental building and stared down. The solemn splendor of it caught his imagination. "I must say, Dad," he remarked at last, "it beats anything we've got in Westminster Abbey."

"Let's go," Angela urged. "It's overpowering. It's so dark."

"Death *is* dark," Steven said. "Such a huge tomb for such a small man!"

"He was a great man," Charlie protested. "Even though we beat him in the end. All right, Mum, we'll go; you're looking a bit green. But this is the best thing I've seen so far."

As they crossed the street, Steven looked up and almost halted in the path of the traffic. It was the Rue Constantine, and there on the opposite side was the classical facade of the beautiful apartment Clara had wanted to buy. The windows were shuttered. "A place we can come back to, just to remember how happy we've been." He could hear her saying it, feel the tug of her hand on his arm.

That evening, Angela said, "Aren't you feeling well, Steven? You seem so off color."

"I didn't want to stay here," he said. "I told you, I wanted to go on to Morocco. Clara and I spent part of our honeymoon in Paris. We've been to the same places, done the same things. It makes me think of her."

"I'm so sorry," Angela said. "You should have told me. I really wanted to let Charlie see it. All he really enjoyed was that awful tomb!"

Sitting on his lap, she slipped her arm around his waist. "Why are you thinking about the past now? Your family's safe, you told me. She'll be married soon. Why now, darling?"

He drew her close to him. "You've made me soft, you know that?

I don't feel the way I used to anymore." Aldo had planned to murder his father and his brother Piero; he deserved no pity. It never occurred to Angela that the executioners would be executed.

He reached up and kissed her. "Why don't we cut it short and go tomorrow? I'll telephone the Mamoulian and change our reservations. Charlie's had a bellyful of culture, and I've had a bellyful of Paris."

"I happen to have a bellyful too," she reminded him. "I felt some movement today. You were in such a funny mood I didn't tell you. Why don't you ring up now?"

He turned her around to face him and pressed his face close up against her. "If it's a girl," he said, "what are we going to call her?"

"If you go on doing that," Angela murmured, "it'll be a sex maniac, whatever its sex. Aren't you going to phone the hotel?"

"In a while," he said. "We can call from the bedroom."

On the way to the airport next day, he stopped off at a bookstore and bought his son a biography of Napoleon, translated into English.

"You look feverish," Aldo said. He touched Clara's forehead with the palm of his hand. There were two bright scarlet patches on her cheeks, but her skin was cold.

"I'm fine," she said. "Shouldn't we be going?"

"There's time," Aldo assured her. "And remember, when it happens, you've got to be surprised, eh? You think you could faint?"

"No," Clara answered. "But I'll try not to clap and cheer. I just hope you've got the best men."

"The best money can buy. Two top piecemen from the West Coast. They'll get them coming out of the church. And we'll be right there, with all our people. Clean-handed for all the world to see." He laughed, excited by his imagination. Hate had festered in him for a long time, and vengeance was only a matter of an hour or so away.

They'd betrayed his daughter; they'd humiliated and rejected his blood and tried to make a fool of him. The Falconis would pay for that in the only coinage acceptable. His hired assassins would gun them down as they left the wedding ceremony. Two superb marksmen, ex–army snipers who had gone into the contract business. They cost a fortune, but you paid for results. And the results were very final. He had enjoyed the planning of it. He had personally handed them photographs of Lucca and Piero and a snapshot of Tino Spoletto taken without his knowledge. They had studied them and nodded. They were men who didn't talk much. One of them said he wanted a closer look so they would be sure. Aldo gave them addresses and asked no more questions. He looked at his watch. Eleven-ten exactly. The wedding limousine was waiting outside, festooned with bunches of white ribbons.

Bruno Salviatti would be waiting for his bride in the church. Aldo had gone the night before with Luisa to make sure that everything was right. The church looked like a florist shop, with big arrangements of hothouse flowers, garlands stretching the length of the nave from pew to pew, and the altar itself massed with lilies and mimosa, the flower of Italy, specially flown in.

Luisa knew nothing of the plan. Women were never told about such things. She was delighted with the church, worried because Clara had defied superstition by trying on her wedding outfit the day before. . . . Aldo let her chatter on and smiled secretly. Clara had the nerve; he was proud of her coolness, the steel of her resolve. She had the heart of a man, he exulted. And maybe Salviatti would give her children. Then Aldo's cup would overrun with happiness.

"Let's go," he said. "Here, take your flowers, Clara. Are you happy. Are you happy with what your old Papa's fixed for you?"

She turned to him. "I'll be happy when I see those bastards dead at our feet," she said. "When it's all over, Papa, I've got something else to tell you."

He opened the front door and they went down to the limousine, shadowed by three bodyguards, as always. "Tell me now," he said.

"Not now," Clara answered. "Later. After the wedding."

"I know what you're thinking," her father said. The doors were closed, and the car moved away toward the Church of Saint Mary and the Angels. "You're thinking of Steven. Don't worry; he'll show up, and we'll be waiting." Clara glanced out the window for a moment.

The winter sun was shining. "I'm not waiting," she said.

Bruno was nervous. His wedding suit was tight, or so it seemed, and he was sweating in the warm church. The smell of flowers was overpowering. His cousin had the ring in his pocket. Clara for some mean motive had refused to give him a ring in exchange. Later he'd have one. All married men had a proper gold wedding ring. She was just being a bitch when she said no.

Once they were married, he promised himself, he'd make her behave herself. If she gave him the kind of lip she'd been handing out before the wedding, he'd take his belt and lather the skin off her. He rather liked the prospect. It made his sense of humiliation easier to bear. The organ played, and the congregation waited; people turned in their seats, watching as the pews filled up. He saw Don Lucca Falconi with his son and his sidekick Spoletto take their places high up in the church, places of honor, as in-laws of the bride. Lucca bowed to Clara's mother, who smiled and waved her hand to him. Bruno knew all about the first husband. He'd ratted on the family and on Clara, and they'd knocked him off. . . . Bruno didn't think about it much.

It was a hell of a marriage. Everybody said so. His friends and his family were all impressed. He was going to be a big man. Groomed for stardom, someone said. He liked the sound of that. Then the music changed to a triumphant peal, and they all stood. Clara and her father were walking toward them down the aisle.

"It's such a lovely place," Angela said. "And the weather is perfect." She reached out for his hand. They were sitting in the warm sunshine in the Hotel Mamoulian gardens. She felt relaxed and deeply content. This pregnancy was easy; very little sickness in the early weeks, and nothing now but a sense of expectation. Steven said she looked beautiful and teased her about a string of babies in the future.

Charlie was playing tennis with an American girl he'd met. She was flirtatious and pretty. He had already confided to Steven that he usually let her win.

The hotel was luxurious, the food exotic, and the service better than the best in Europe. Above all the sun shone, though it grew cold in the evening. There was nothing to do but wander through the lovely grounds or laze on the terrace. "I'm so glad we left Paris and came early," she said. "You were quite right."

"I hate Paris," he said. "I never want to go there again. I'm glad you like it here, darling. I'm glad you're happy." He held her hand tightly. "It makes everything right."

Angela said, "Why do you say that? Everything's perfect for us. I can't believe it sometimes. You and I and Charlie and a new baby coming. And just when it seemed as if our luck was running out, your family was safe after all. I prayed you'd come back to us. And you did."

He didn't answer. He went on holding her hand, seeing her smile at him. Let her believe in her prayers. Let her go on being happy and seeing the world through a prism of honesty and innocence.

As they sat there in the Moroccan sunshine, Aldo Fabrizzi was still alive. Clara had not awakened to go to her wedding. He didn't want to work out the time variable. He didn't want to look down at his watch and say to himself, "Now. It must be happening now." He had put an ocean between himself and his family and the act of cold-blooded murder. By the time they went back to France and Charlie flew home to school, it would be stale news. Angela need never know.

"Why don't we go and watch the tennis match?" Angela suggested. "Charlie's got a real crush on her; it's so funny."

"He's growing up," Steven said. "At eighteen I had a lot of girl-friends. He'll be a man soon. Let's go and watch them."

He helped her out of the chair. She didn't need help, but it was an excuse to touch her, hold her close to him for a moment.

"Come on, darling." She led him by the hand toward the sound of balls thudding and shrill cries of excitement. Charlie's laughter could be heard in the background.

The girl's parents were on a tour of Europe with their daughter. Their name was Thorpe; they lived in Westchester and were eager for companionship. The daughter was their only child and the center of their world. He was a senior executive with an oil company; he found Angela charming but reserved judgment on the husband. Lawrence was less than outgoing, he confided to his wife. And owning a casino was not his idea of a respectable business. Still, the son was a good kid. Nice manners, and Sharon liked him. It was so important that Sharon have a good time on this trip. She'd taken a lot of persuading to come with them. But she was an easy teenager. No problems. They encouraged Charlie but gave up on Steven and Angela after one dinner date. He couldn't have explained why a fellow American should make him feel so uneasy.

Steven was on his way down to the cocktail bar before dinner that evening, when he met his son rushing up to change.

"Dad?" They paused on the stairs. "You going to the bar?"

"I feel like a drink. Get dressed and join me. Your mother's coming later. Had a good day?"

"Great," Charlie said. "Mr. Thorpe's got the most fantastic radio. He tunes in to the States every day for the news broadcasts. He was just telling me about some gangland massacre at a wedding. It sounded terrible!"

Steven stood very still. His son looked excited. "Mr. Thorpe said it was like Saint Valentine's Day. I didn't know what he meant."

"Never mind," Steven said. "That happened a long time ago. I don't want you talking about this in front of your mother. She hates that kind of thing. It makes her feel bad. So you forget it."

"Yes, yes, I won't say anything." Charlie looked bewildered. "I'll go up and change. Shall I see if Mum's ready?"

"You do that," Steven answered. He still hadn't moved to continue downstairs. "And remember what I've told you. It's bad for a pregnant woman to hear about people getting killed."

He saw his son sprint up to the landing, and then he walked down to the cocktail bar. The Thorpes were sitting there. He went over. He didn't smile at them. He said, "Charlie's been telling me about the news from the States you got on your radio. My wife'll be joining me in a minute. I'd be glad if you don't tell her any horror stories." He went and sat at a table and left them looking at each other. After a few minutes, Thorpe whispered to his wife, and they both got up and left.

By the time Angela came down, Steven had put down two large bourbons on the rocks, and there was a bottle of champagne on ice waiting for her and for Charlie.

Clara made her wedding vows. She heard Bruno saying his and felt him slip the ring on her finger. She did everything she had done when she married Steven, but it was as if she moved in a dream. She had been cool, pitiless, in anticipation of the bloody revenge to be exacted by her father. Now, as she stood at the altar with Bruno beside her, she began to tremble. She had never seen death at close quarters. It had been so easy to contemplate because it wasn't real to her. Superstition flickered like a warning light inside her as she faced the altar. She had been brought up by Luisa to say her prayers, been educated by nuns, gone through the whole Catholic ritual of the Sacraments. To her, as to Aldo, it had been a matter of form once she grew up. Now, in the presence of God himself, she panicked. It shouldn't be done here. It belonged in the dark, down some alleyway, not in the shadow of the church. Fear rushed over her, and she turned, searching for her father. He was back in his pew, his part in the ritual completed. She heard Bruno whisper, "What's the matter?" Then her eyes met Aldo's gaze. He stared at her, and the look was fierce and without mercy. She turned back to her bridegroom. It was too late.

Too late to have scruples. She conquered the fear, the impulse to turn and run all the way down the aisle and out into the street so she wouldn't see it happen. She had been abandoned, betrayed. The man she had loved had left her for his first love. For a woman who had given him a child . . . And the Falconis had known it, connived at his desertion, put his ring on a dead man's finger and then cut it off to prove their good faith. When the recessional pealed from the organ, Clara took her new husband's arm, and with a nod to her father, she walked firmly past the congregation to the open doorway.

Photographers were waiting. Bruno held her there, posing for them, resisting her efforts to hurry him to the waiting car. He was smiling, enjoying it. He kissed her for the cameras. She saw Aldo come out onto the steps behind them. "Bruno," she insisted, "Bruno, that's enough. Let's go!"

"What's the hurry?" he demanded. He was smiling, looking ahead of him. She didn't hear the shots. The cameras were snapping, and suddenly there was a great splash of blood all over her jacket, and he was falling backward, dragging her down with him. She heard screams, and more screams. She was on the ground, entangled with him. Blood was pouring through the back of his head. Someone was trying to help her up. Then she screamed and screamed and fought them off because she had seen her father lying sprawled halfway down the steps with a small round hole in the middle of his forehad and a long scarlet trickle creeping toward her. In the confusion, two of the photographers disappeared. They weren't taking pictures anymore.

8

Ralph Maxton liked reading the newspapers in bed. Madeleine was lying beside him, running her fingers down his thigh to attract his attention. Newspapers bored her, except for the gossip columns.

"Stop it, darling," he said absently. "You can't bring the pitcher to the well again."

"Oh, yes I can." She giggled. *She's got a point,* he thought, and smiled at his pun. Then he saw the news item. MAFIA MURDERS AT WEDDING, shouted the headline in bold black letters. He looked closer, skimming through the story, studying the photographs of the carnage on the church steps. A clear, full-face portrait of the bride widowed on her wedding day—Clara Falconi Salviatti, widowed for the second time. Her first husband, Mafia boss Steven Falconi, killed in a burned-out car, and the new bridegroom gunned down at her side. "Bride of Death," the caption screeched. Maxton was staring at the picture. His memory had never failed him. It was his trademark: faces, names, instant recall. The dark, obsessive girl on her honeymoon with her husband, touring the casino, watching the now dead German princess gamble a fortune and win. He had been told to watch them, to shadow the man and see where he went and whom he talked to.

Steven Falconi and his bride, Clara.

They had talked and had a drink together. . . . He threw Madeleine off him.

She protested angrily, and then, seeing his face, she said, "Ralphie— what's wrong? What's the matter?"

"Shut up, shut up, for Christ's sake!"

Pulling on a flimsy negligee, she pouted sulkily. "You don't have to shout at me. I'll take a shower then." He didn't even hear her.

Old Dr. Drummond, confiding over a last pipe of tobacco while they sat together at the villa one evening, had said, "I wasn't too struck by him at first. . . . Too foreign . . . Italian. I suppose it was because of the name . . . Fal-something-or-other."

Maxton held the newspaper clenched in both hands.

Falconi. Steven Falconi, who'd changed his name to Lawrence and sought him out years afterward. No wonder he'd felt they'd met before. . . .

He'd been fooled by the beard and the now mature face of a man in his early forties. . . . Steven Lawrence was the Mafia gangster Steven Falconi. A new name, a new identity, a faked death.

He smoothed out the crumpled newspaper. He read and read again the account of the shooting of gang boss Aldo Fabrizzi and the man just married to his daughter, Clara, widow of top mafioso Steven Falconi. The police investigation talked of a gangland vendetta by the Fabrizzi succession.

Maxton got out of bed. He phoned down and ordered all the American papers. He looked again at the photographs taken outside the church. Mercifully they weren't very clear. Someone had thrown a coat over the corpse in the foreground; only a pair of feet protruded. Blood stained the area black. A second body was lying halfway down the church steps, partly obscured by people crouching over it.

Maxton sat down, the newspaper on his knee. The shower was switched off in the background and Madeleine appeared, partly wrapped in a towel.

She said, "Chéri, what's wrong? You look dreadful."

Maxton looked up at her. "The bastard," he said slowly.

"Who? What?" She came and sat with him. She looked at the headlines. "It's this murder in America? Why do you care about it? Who are you calling a bastard?"

He said half to himself, "She's not even married to him—it's bigamy."

"I'm getting dressed," Madeleine announced. "We'll be late."

He didn't say anything more. He bathed and changed into ski clothes, and they weren't late after all. But she knew the holiday would be cut short. Women who made their living off men had an instinct for shifts in mood. And Maxton didn't even try to hide his.

He was very nice about it; he softened the blow by taking her on a shopping trip. They went their ways, and at the airport she kissed him.

"I'm fond of you," she said. "And we've had fun, haven't we?"

"A lot of fun," Maxton assured her, waving her off to her Paris-bound plane. He could have put his fist in the emptiness where her heart should be.

That evening, on his flight to Nice, he read the full story in the American papers, and if he needed confirmation, there was another picture of Clara Falconi in the *New York Times*.

Steven had lied to Angela; Maxton didn't doubt that. The sudden trip to Morocco had been opportunistic, just when this bloodstained bombshell was about to burst over the media. He must have known; his father was mentioned among the guests who had seen nothing and recognized no assassin.

Omertà. The silence enjoined upon them to deny justice under the law. One report said briefly that the bride had collapsed by her dead husband and been taken to the hospital.

Maxton went to the casino, where he supervised the construction of a grander suite of cloakrooms. Nothing suggested the turmoil inside him.

Now he could admit the truth to himself. For a long time he had hated Steven Falconi, because he possessed the only woman Maxton had ever loved.

But Steven had married her under false pretenses. Angela didn't belong to him. She was his innocent victim. He had cheated her as he had cheated and abandoned the woman of ill omen in the photographs.

Maxton knew he couldn't do anything or plan anything until her child was born. Now he had hope, though, and hope bred a fierce determination. He would play along with Steven Falconi. He would earn his big salary and justify Steven's reliance upon him. And he would wait. He knew all about patience and nerve. It had made him one of the best poker players of his generation.

It was afternoon in Aldo Fabrizzi's house in New York.

"You're looking better, Clara," Joe Nimmi said. "We were sorry to hear about your mama. But maybe it was better for her that way." They were gathered in Aldo's front room. They had come to pay their respects to his daughter. Only out of the hospital a month herself, she had been doubly bereaved by her mother's recent death.

She didn't look well, but what else could Joe Nimmi say? She was white as a sheet, and so thin you could see through her. She was back in her parents' house, sitting in her father's chair. Everything about her was black, except for that white face and a garish slash of scarlet lipstick. It looked as if she'd been sucking blood. Nimmi didn't think she should have worn makeup on such an occasion. He'd led the deputation to see her and offer help if she needed it. And to give advice. Sound, sensible advice to a woman without a man to guide her. Advice she had to take, because they didn't want trouble. The goddamned newspapers had become sick of writing about the gang war about to break out on the streets. There hadn't been a war. It was all settled peacefully. Fabrizzi territories had been parceled out while Clara was in the hospital. Everything was running smoothly. Her mother had had a stroke; she was paralyzed and unable to speak. They were all sorry about that. They'd all visited her in the hospital, sent flowers. Then she'd died.

They had given Aldo a proper funeral, and the relatives of Bruno Salviatti had buried their son along with him. A few Fabrizzi cousins had been found in the old country to sit in the chief mourners' car, since the wife and the daughter were too ill to attend. The flowers had been magnificent. They had all gathered in the church and at the graveside, the heads of the families, representatives from Florida, Chicago, Detroit, and all the New York bosses. They had wiped the tears from their eyes as the coffins were lowered, and had scattered holy water into the graves. It had been done well, with the respect and solemnity a man of Aldo's standing deserved. It was a pity he had to be gotten rid of, but he'd had only himself to blame. It was a business necessity, nothing personal, no one felt any sense of satisfaction. But it had to be done; they all knew that.

Clara sat with her hands folded. She looked at them, one by one: Joe Nimmi, her father's old friend from the early street days; his niece had been given refuge in Aldo Fabrizzi's house. The Guglielmos, Bruno's bosses; the heads of the smaller families. Lucca Falconi hadn't come. He was sick, they told her. The brother hadn't come; he was out of town on business. Only the cousin, Spoletto.

She said, "It's good of you all to come. My mother's better off; she didn't suffer. For myself, I've come to terms. I've lost a father and a husband. Two husbands. I've had my share of grief."

There was a genuine note of sympathy. "You have, Clara," Joe Nimmi said. "God knows, you've had it hard. We all feel that. And that," he said, raising his voice a little, "is why we're here. We're all your friends. We want to help."

She waited; she looked expectant. They'd all been party to it. They knew that she was lying, that the bullets had originally been meant for Lucca and his absent son, and for Spoletto. They knew, and so did she, that this was a charade, but it had a purpose. The purpose was the reality. She was now going to be told what it was.

She said, "I'll be glad of help, Joe. I'll be grateful for it."

"That's what we all hoped," he said. He smiled warmly at her. "We want you to be happy, Clara. To make a new life for yourself. Without your mama to take care of, you have that opportunity. Your papa's business is in safe hands. There's been no trouble; and we've allocated a portion to you. You'll see it's very generous."

"Thank you," Clara said. They'd split up Aldo's interests like carrion crows picking over a corpse. "I know you've all done your best for me, and I know you won't rest till you find out who killed my father and my husband."

They were expecting her to say that. Guglielmo said, "We'll get them. We'll get them for Bruno too; he was a good guy. We knew him since he was a kid." There was another mutter of agreement.

Joe Nimmi leaned toward her, hands clasped in front of him. He spoke gently, like an uncle. "For now, you'd best leave everything to us. It's our business, Clara. Don't you think about it anymore. If my old friend was here this day, I know what he would want you to do. I knew him like my brother."

"You tell me," Clara asked him. "What would my father want me to do?"

The scarlet mouth disturbed him; he kept looking at it. In the old country, when a man was killed his women kissed the wounds, before they cried out for vendetta. "He'd want you to go away," he said. "Leave the house; forget the grief. You've been a sick girl. You need a nice long vacation. Six months; a year maybe." He smiled persuasively at her, his head a little on one side. "Believe me, Clara. It'll be best for you."

She smiled back at him. The red lips parted slightly and then closed. She said very quietly, "You give good advice, Joe. My papa always said so. You're right; he knew you like a brother too."

Someone offered his place in the Bahamas. "One helluva nice villa, Clara. All the help you want, for as long as you want. It's yours."

She thanked him for the offer. "You're good to me," she said. "I appreciate everything my papa's old friends have done for him and for me."

Victor nudged his brother in the ribs. He whispered, "She getting at something, or what?"

Roy nudged him into silence. He said, "Anything we can do, Clara. We don't own properties outside the city, but anything else . . ." He let the sentence die away. She looked around at them and quietly moved out of Aldo's chair and onto her feet. The black mourning dress hung loose on her. "I have a place I can stay. I guess it's far enough away."

They came up and embraced her, those old friends of her father's; others, who weren't on such close terms, shook hands. They all promised anything she needed.

Tino Spoletto made a little bow. "Don Lucca says, anything you want, just say the word." He was thin and pale, with spectacles and a wide forehead that signified incipient baldness. He stared for a moment into Clara's eyes, his own eyes distorted by strong lenses. He had never been afraid of a woman in his life, and had feared very few men, in spite of his lack of weight and inches. But she filled him with fear.

"My thanks to Don Lucca," she said. "Tell him to get well soon." She turned away.

She didn't come to the door; she said goodbye, and one by one they filed out and got into their cars, the engines running. She stood behind the shelter of the curtains until the last of them had gone. The street was empty. She was alone in the house. She had offered wine and the traditional olives. Some of them had smoked, and the haze was visible in the artificial light. It was a wet, overcast day in March, and the heavy curtains were not fully pulled back. It was a house of mourning, of darkness. Clara found a cigarette and lit it; she opened a cupboard and poured herself a straight Scotch on ice. "Clara, Clara," her poor dead mother had protested, "you drink like a man."

They had agreed on the murders. They had gone back on their oath to Aldo and reprieved the Falconis. The men her father had hired had been assigned different targets. So simply done. And they'd all come with their sympathy and their offers of support, and told her to get out and stay out and not try to cause trouble. She sat down, not in her father's chair—that had been a gesture—but on the sofa, where the two of them had usually sat together. She drank the whiskey and finished her cigarette. She was off the dope now. No more tranquilizers. The rest and sedation had let her heal. She had played the part expected of her, because she knew, as they knew, that she was helpless. She couldn't strike back. They were men of power. She was just a woman, and no one would go against them for her sake. Not even for all the money she could offer. There was nothing left for her but exile and obscurity. The villa in the Bahamas . . . She laughed aloud at that: somewhere she could be watched, where the Mafia had influence and friends. Paris. She'd thought of it in the hospital, as she came out of the haze of shock and medication. Paris, where the apartment she'd bought in secret lay empty and dust-sheeted. Unused all these years. The apartment she'd planned as a retreat for Steven and herself, a place in which to recapture their honeymoon happiness. She'd go to Paris. She'd throw off the black drapery of mourning.

She'd let them all think they were safe, that the terrible cry for vengeance wouldn't be uttered. She had painted her mouth symbolically, daring them to read the sign. They would pay for Aldo. For her mother, struck down through grief. For Bruno, falling backward with half his brain shot out. But Steven Falconi would pay first.

She had Mike O'Halloran to thank for that. The file on Steven was locked in her father's desk drawer.

Joe Nimmi was going to the opera that night; he was anxious to get home in time to change his shirt. He loved opera; Verdi was his favorite. He had a fine collection of records and thought Tito Gobbi was the greatest baritone in the world.

Victor and Roy were going home. They lived on the same street, in houses two doors down from each other. Their children played together, went to the same school. Their wives were related. Every two years they took their families on holiday to Naples, where the Guglielmos had lived two generations back. Victor said to his brother, "I still feel lousy about Bruno."

"Yeah, me too. But it had to be. Bruno would've made trouble; she'd have seen to it. He was her husband. And he had honor. He wasn't just a punk."

"He was a good guy. Roy, I guess she knows. The way she said, 'I appreciate all you've done for papa and me.'"

"Sure she knows," Roy said. "But what the fuck can she do? She brought the whole goddamned mess on herself. Her and Aldo. She knows what's expected. She'll take her ass off someplace. Forget about her. Why don't we all go to Gino's for dinner tonight? We'll bring the kids, make it a party."

Victor brightened. "Why not? I got an idea for setting up Bruno's old lady. There's a nice little grocery over on Twenty-first. The guy's a real schmuck. We could move Bruno's mama and the kid brother into the business. It'd give them a good living."

"Why not," Roy agreed. "We owe them. Okay, we go to Gino's and then maybe take in a movie. Find out what the kids want to see."

Clara had closed up her parents' house. She let the maid stay on as caretaker. The woman had two sons and a lazy husband who pretended to have a weak heart if anyone suggested work. Clara would have thrown him out years ago, but her father had a soft spot for him. He'd been a good man once, Aldo used to say, refusing to hear any complaint against him. Clara left the family there out of respect for her father.

She hadn't been back to her own house since she left to go to her wedding. That was going to be a real test of nerve. She didn't mind sensing her father in the familiar rooms, seeing her mother's sentimental mementos of her early life and marriage—the silver-framed photographs of dead grandparents, the picture of Clara as a child, robed in innocent white for her first communion like a tiny bride in veil and flowery headdress—none of this frightened Clara.

But if she went home and found Aldo there, waiting for her as he had on the last morning of his life . . . waiting to take her down the steps to the limousine dressed in silk ribbons . . . What was she thinking? Must be her nerves, that was all. A brief death rattle from the old nightmares that had her screaming in the hospital.

She swallowed a very strong Scotch and drove herself uptown. She opened the front door. It was very quiet inside; the blinds were drawn. There was no one to greet her and make a cheerful human sound. The maid had left after the tragedy. She didn't feel she owed anything to Clara, who had done nothing but shout at her. It was quiet, Clara thought. But no Aldo. No shade in the corner. The Scotch had chased him away.

She laughed, and heard a funny echo that scared her. "You go on like this," she said out loud, "and you'll be back in the hospital instead of Paris. For Christ's sake take hold of yourself and don't go looking for a drink. They warned you about that, didn't they?" She opened the blinds; immediately the sunshine flooded in. The magazines on the table were two months out of date. She drew a finger over the tabletop; her finger tip was smeared with dust. She took a deep breath. No ghosts.

Only memories, and all of them bitter as gall. Her life there with Steven in the early years. Her dashed hopes of having children. Month after month ending in tears. The loveless coupling in the end, when she was desperate for him and he only performed as a duty. The fights, the walkouts when she knew he had gone to some other woman. Her self-inflicted torture of jealousy. The last insane act of spite, when she refused to go to dinner with him, and he went alone and found the woman whose name he'd gasped out on their wedding night as he climaxed inside her. "Angelina."

She put a hand to her cheek as if she'd been struck a blow. He had struck her, she remembered. As she told O'Halloran, he'd slapped her when she called the woman a whore. She took the detective's report from a desk drawer. It was Angelina who was the cause of what had happened. Like some malignant figure in a Greek tragedy, she had drifted onto the stage of Steven's life and out again, and blighted Clara's happiness from the wings. Only to return from the dead and claim him. The bloody cycle of betrayal, vengeance and, finally, death began with her. It would end with her. and Clara would be there to see it. Not like the woman who had taken Steven from her for a night in Monte Carlo.

She hadn't thought about that since it happened. The memory made her smile. Clara felt suffused with a cruel sense of power. That woman had paid a price for having Steven Falconi in her bed. Clara's papa had seen to that. All it had taken was a telephone call and a sob in her voice to cause a woman's disfigurement and near death. But she'd had only a newspaper clipping to soothe her jealousy.

Now that Aldo was dead, she had to deal with such problems herself. She was so rich she could pay any price to get what she wanted. And the money was flooding in. The agency was her operation, staffed by people who owed favors to no one except the frontman who paid them. O'Halloran had been a good choice. She thought about him. He was as rotten as she had suspected he might be. As corrupt as she had made him. A cop gone bad was the worst. Thank God. He was efficient; he'd recruited people outside the families.

She hadn't spoken to him since he got back to New York. He'd sent flowers to the hospital. Someone had told her afterward, when she'd begun to return to awareness.

Now, at last, she was ready to act. She'd read his report and begun to make plans. She reached over and picked up the phone. His assistant answered.

She said, "Mr. O'Halloran, please. . . . Never mind who's calling. Put him on! . . . Mike? . . . Yes, it's me. . . . I'm fine now. . . . Yes, I've read it. You did a good job. How's the blackmail business?" She laughed, hearing him swear in surprise. "Are we doing all right? . . . I'm sure. You must bring me up to date. I'm flying out tomorrow. . . . Paris. . . . Yes, Paris. I'm going to live there for a while. And I want you to come out. I'll be staying at the Crillon. Get there by Thursday, will you? We've got a lot to talk over." She hung up. The silence came down on her like a shroud.

I'll sell this place, she decided. *I'll get good money for it. When I come back, I'll live in Papa's house. I can do it over.* She had deliberately said "when," not "if." They had written her off, Nimmi and the rest of the old friends who'd sentenced her father to death. Let them. All she needed was time. And to settle the first of her debts of honor.

O'Halloran had never been to Paris. He hadn't been to Europe till he took the trip to Sicily. The flight had been via Naples. He had heard that old adage about seeing Naples and dying. He wasn't sure what it meant. He thought the city was sprawling and dirty; he got acute indigestion from some shellfish. Sicily was cold and dry like a desert, with powerful colors that appealed to him and a sparse landscape dominated by mountains. He had to take an interpreter to the village where the Falconis had originated. The interpreter talked to the young priest for him. How strange he should be asking about Signor Falconi. Everyone knew about him. He was the village benefactor. Their protector. Yes, he had been married there during the war. It was in the church registry.

O'Halloran copied down the entry. He wrote it in English, with the interpreter's help. Stefano Antonio Falconi. Angela Frances Drummond. The date in 1943 and their signatures.

The priest saw them out, smiling. He didn't even ask why the American wanted to see the evidence of the marriage. He was a simple, trusting man.

From Sicily, O'Halloran flew to England. That was the worst part of the trip. The weather was vile, raining dull and cold. He stayed in a comfortable little hotel in London, made his contact with David Wickham over the telephone, using a careful cover story.

Wickham was cagey but polite. O'Halloran was amazed at how polite the English were, with their thank yous and pleases. He didn't like them any better. His old man had been a fervent Irish Republican. He'd brought up all his children on the iniquities of English rule in Ireland over eight hundred years.

Wickham made Mike feel clumsy and out of place in the elegant office, as if he'd left his fly undone. But he took the bait about Angela Drummond, being sought in connection with a legacy from a distant American relative and traced to an apartment in New York lent her for a vacation.

Yes, he knew Angela Drummond, Wickham said. She'd been engaged to work as his assistant. It was his bad luck that she went on her New York vacation; it was he who had got her the loan of the apartment. The bad luck, he explained to O'Halloran, was her meeting a man and getting married, without taking up her job. Wickham's dislike of the bridegroom loosened his tongue. O'Halloran was getting the picture: a man honored as its protector by a Sicilian village; an Italian-American whom the Londoner was sticking his knife into. He could have painted Falconi's portrait from those two descriptions. He'd seen a number of such men during his years in the Department. Older men, men with expensive suits and gold watches, who'd earned their place in the hierarchy the hard way. With guns and knives and ice picks. They had brains, and they went on to sit behind the desks and let others bloody their hands.

And then his picture of Steven Falconi went out of focus in a two-bit English village, as different from the hilltop cluster of houses in Sicily as a pothole on the surface of the moon: Haywards Heath, a village with a sodden area of grass surrounding a stone cross on a plinth commemorating the war dead; with old houses, almost too picturesque, standing behind little walls and railings and front gardens, all bare and dripping in the godforsaken winter weather. He'd found the house with the brass plaque, and they told him in the pub, as he forced down tepid beer, that the old doctor didn't practice anymore. He gave the same story he'd told Wickham, with a different ending. He was ninety percent certain that the Angela Drummond he was looking for was not Dr. Drummond's daughter, but he was just drawing a line across all the old leads. He expected to find the young lady in Scotland. He said Scotland because he knew Drummond was a Scottish name.

The old man was not overfriendly at first. But Mike O'Halloran had a way with him. He wasn't Irish for nothing, as his father used to say about himself. He could be good company, and the old doctor offered him a cup of tea and started talking. A lot about his grandson. Mike

[262]

had to pry him away from the subject of how well the boy played cricket and rugger, and how he was passing everything at school. Drummond was nice about the daughter, in a noncommittal way. He was far more enthusiastic about his son-in-law.

"Of course, I would've preferred an Englishman—no offense meant by that, you understand; it was only natural to hope she'd settle down with someone here. But I must say she's lucky. Very lucky. He's a damned good chap. Loves her, marvelous with the boy too. Even changed his name to Lawrence. That's my daughter's name. Said it made them more of a family. Always makes me feel welcome. Even wanted me to live with them in France. Not that I would, mind you. Too hot for me. Can't stand that sort of heat...."

He'd come out to the front door with O'Halloran, shaken hands and apologized for jabbering, as he put it. "Old man's disease, talking too much. Not the one people think you mean, though," and he'd chuckled at his own joke.

And now Mike O'Halloran knew where to find them. Falconi, alias Lawrence, had opened a casino. The doctor seemed rather proud of it. He'd filled in a lot of details, seeing that his listener was interested. Time to go home. Time to write up his report and pick up a fat check. He bought English cashmere for his wife and a lot of souvenirs for his children.

"Darling," Angela asked anxiously, "are you sure this is wise?" Steven put his arm around her.

"I'm sure," he said.

They were preparing for a gala night early in the new season at the casino. He was planning to show a higher profile this time. It worried her, and she said so.

"Why don't you care now? Last year you made such a point about being incognito."

He made her sit on his knee. "You're getting to be quite a weight," he said. "You know, I'm really excited about this baby already."

"Don't change the subject," Angela said. "Why are you taking a chance, Steven? As for shaving off your beard, you must be crazy!"

She's got to know sometime, he decided. *It's old news now. I can soften it, make it less shocking.* He said gently, "Clara can't hurt us now. Her father's dead. The family's business has been divided up. I've talked to my brother, and we don't have to worry anymore."

"Why didn't you tell me?" she asked.

"Because it all happened while we were in Morocco. Her father got it wrong. People didn't like what he was planning to do to us."

She said, "So they killed him?"

He nodded. "Don't think about it. It's got nothing to do with us."

Angela said, "What's happened to her?"

"Nothing. She's gone on a long vacation. It was made clear to her. No trouble. She understood." He held her close to him. "I didn't tell you," he said, "because I knew you wouldn't like it. You were just three months pregnant. I'm not glad about it, I assure you. It's not part of me anymore. I made my choice at Christmas, and I'm never going back, not even in my mind. We have our life here, our son, and the new little one. And let me tell you something, my darling—I'm going to make it up to you for having the boy all on your own last time. You're going to be a princess with this baby."

Angela let him hold her. No danger, no need to hide anymore. But at a price. *I can't think about it,* she said to herself. *I don't know and I don't want to know any more than he's told me. Of course that's easy enough to say, while we're like this and I feel how much he needs me. It's when I'm alone, or wake at night, that it's going to be difficult.*

She said, "I wish I could have it at home."

"No way." He was adamant. "You'll go to the hospital, you'll have the best doctors, the best attention. We're not taking any chances. Now you should go and take your rest. And don't worry about a thing. Promise me?"

"I promise," Angela told him. He held on to her for a moment longer.

"I love you very much," he said. "Now go on, put your feet up. I'll wake you when I get back."

She slept in spite of herself, longer than she meant to. Nature was making it easy to keep her promise to him—not to worry, not to think.

When she woke, it was late in the afternoon, and the telephone beside her bed was ringing. She answered it sleepily. It was a call from England.

Her father's physician was calling. He told her as gently as he could that Hugh Drummond had died of a heart attack. Mrs. P. had found him in his chair after lunch and thought he was asleep. It had been a peaceful and painless death.

* * *

"I should have gone to the funeral, Ralph!"

"No, you shouldn't," Maxton said. "You nearly lost that baby. Steven was quite right, Angela. Your father wouldn't have wanted you taking any risks. The only reason I've remained behind is to make sure you stay in bed and do what you're told."

The pains had begun within hours of that telephone call. She had become so upset at the suggestion of being moved into the local hospital that the doctor left her at home overnight in the hope that the spasms would stop with medication. Any sign of bleeding, he told Steven, and she was to be rushed in immediately.

He had sat up with her while she slept under sedation, watching over her till she woke in the morning.

"It's all right," she'd murmured to him. "The pains have stopped.... Oh, poor Dad ..." And she'd cried out her grief in Steven's arms.

No question of traveling, the doctor had insisted. No emotional upset. At less than seven months, she'd lose the child. Maxton had volunteered to stay with her. Steven had agreed, provided he moved into the villa.

"I don't trust her not to get up, or do something crazy like trying to fly out at the last minute," he'd told Maxton. "Janine couldn't stop her, but you could. It's just because he died so suddenly, sitting up in a chair.... If she'd had any warning, she wouldn't be taking it so hard."

"She wouldn't risk the baby," Maxton had reassured him. "She'd never do anything so irresponsible."

He hated Steven so much, he wondered how he managed to conceal it. He didn't understand the fear for her and the child that made Steven sound harsh.

"You watch over her," he'd told Maxton. "The doctor's visiting every day. I'll be bringing Charlie back with me. I'll get everything settled over there. She's not to be worried with goddamned wills or what happens to the house or Mrs. P. I've told her. She's got to leave it to me and just take care of herself and the baby."

After he'd left for the airport, Maxton went upstairs to Angela's room. He'd brought flowers and a translation of a new French novel from the English bookshop in Cannes.

Sitting up in bed, she looked white and wan. He had never been encouraged to be demonstrative. He had never before wanted to put his arms around a woman and just comfort her. He sat on the edge of the bed and allowed himself to hold her hand.

"You've got to be good," he told her. "Otherwise I'll ring up old Martineau and tell him you're doing the twist round the bedroom, and he'll whisk you off to his hospital in no time!"

She smiled at that. "I can't even do that when I'm not pregnant," she said.

"Nor can I," he admitted. It was the latest dance craze sweeping Europe from America. "The osteopaths are making a fortune out of slipped disks," he said.

"Thanks for the flowers." Angela picked up the novel. "And for this. I ought to be able to read it in French by now. It's said to be a very good book. . . ." She wiped at a tear that had slipped down her cheek.

"I can't stop doing this," she said. "I feel so awful not being there. . . . And I've stopped you from going too. He was so fond of you, Ralph."

"I was very fond of him. You wouldn't try not to cry, would you, Angela? Just for me?"

"All right. I don't want to upset you too. You know, it's funny, I wasn't all that close to him. Or to my mother. But when she died, I missed her dreadfully."

"I'm not surprised," he said. "Being left with a child and having to cope on your own. It must have been bloody awful for you."

She didn't say anything for a moment. She let him go on holding her hand. She thought, *He's so kind, just like my brother Jack would have been if he hadn't been killed.*

"Now why don't I get Janine to put the old bouquet into water and see about some tea for you?" he suggested. "And I've brought some cards. We could play gin rummy if you like. I could do with winning a few quid."

He used to let Hugh Drummond win when they played cards. She said, "I don't really feel like playing anything. Let's have tea together instead."

His smile could be charming; it quite transformed his face. "Let's," he agreed. "That would be very nice."

O'Halloran had been airborne on his way to Italy when the massacre took place. His wife had raised hell about his taking off on such short notice. The flowers hadn't won her over. He had called on the telephone, but the lines were full of static, and by the time he was in

London she was missing him and asking when he'd be home. He hoped she would like the cashmere sweaters he'd bought her, in three different colors.

Anxious about Clara, he called the hospital. "Severe shock" was all the diagnosis he could get out of them. Not surprising. The papers showed the carnage on the church steps; reporters dwelt on the bride in her blood-drenched clothes, being taken from the scene by ambulance.

If she didn't get over it, what the hell would happen to his agency? Then he quieted down. Clients were coming in all the time; money was coming in with them. If she ended up at a funny farm, he could just keep on going till someone came along and asked about her share in the business. But she was tough. He had to admit that. She wasn't out of the hospital a week before she asked for his report. In a way, he felt relieved. He couldn't have felt sorry for her—he shrugged off that idea. She wasn't the type to be pitied, though perhaps she could be admired for her sheer guts.

And now, O'Halloran was telling his wife he'd be flying to Paris, but this time it would be a short trip. And he'd bring back something really special for her.

She met him in the bar at the Crillon. *Christ!* he thought when he first saw her. Her face was so gaunt that all you could see were big black eyes like burnished jet. She was desperately thin, yet eye-catching in a scarlet suit. They shook hands. He said, "It's good to see you, Mrs. Falconi. And you look great." He meant it.

She said, "Let's sit down, Mike, and have a drink. And it's Mrs. Salviatti. I did get married to him. Just barely."

"Sorry," he said. "I wasn't thinking. I'll try and remember the new name. What can I get you?"

"Scotch," Clara said. He didn't look as out of place as she'd expected. But of course she chose his suits. She'd picked Bruno's clothes for him too. Made him look less like a street-corner Romeo. . . . She put the memory of him away. It was odd the way he crept into her mind when she wasn't looking. She often woke up at night, thinking he was touching her. His spirit hadn't settled, as Aldo's had.

O'Halloran came to the table she'd taken. "They're bringing the drinks."

Clara said, "Before we get down to my business, how's our business?"

She could be very disconcerting: rude one minute and then relaxed, almost pleasant. You never knew which way she was going to jump.

She didn't play around with the Scotch. She finished ahead of him and signaled the waiter. "Another," she said.

"Me too," he said. Then he unlocked his briefcase and handed her a folder. "I brought these to show you. Just a few figures on our take since you've been sick. And some names. One or two are pretty interesting."

She read very quickly and took everything in. Her questions were always to the point. She repeated one of the names and cocked her sleek black head to one side. Her hair was like polished silk. A thick knot of it was twisted up at the back. *It must hang a long way down when the pins are removed,* Mike thought. She was smiling over the prominent U.S. senator with presidential ambitions who was among the clients of a prostitute with very special sadomasochistic talents. "A pillar of the church!" O'Halloran commented wryly. "I never trusted the son of a bitch, with all that holy yap."

Clara closed the folder. "I guess his family will want to keep his name off that lady's list. Have we done anything about it yet?"

"I've put out a few feelers. But we've got to go easy. They play rough, and they've got friends who play rougher."

"I know they have," Clara said. "But not when they know there's a copy waiting to be mailed to every major newspaper. They'd be able to stop one or two but not half a dozen, in different states. We'll get to work on this. At last count, his father was worth around eighty million dollars."

Their glasses were empty and he said, "Do you want to talk about the other business now, Mrs. Falconi?"

"Salviatti," she reminded him. "If you can't remember my god-damned name, why don't you just call me Clara?"

"Okay." He was taken by surprise. "Okay. Clara. Thanks."

"We've got a lot to talk about," she said. "I guess you'd better stay for dinner. I don't want to rush this. And I'm going to need you, Mike. I hope you're not planning to go back home for a while."

After a pause he shook his head. "I left it open," he said. "Till I knew what you wanted."

He'd seen it coming. The same old warning signals were flashing, just as they did when she asked him to work for her. And again he switched them off.

"It beats me," he said, "how any guy could want to leave you." The black hair was as long as he'd imagined. He draped it over her, covering each breast, and traced the outline of her navel with a forefinger.

She was too thin, but the lean body was like whipcord. She lay back on the pillows with her arms above her head. He leaned over her, stroking downward. She sighed and raised her pelvis to meet his questing hand.

She was the most exciting woman he had ever met, and he'd been a keen sack man from his early teens. Animal images flitted through the pace and intensity of his lovemaking. Something strong and supple, suddenly, amazingly, under his control. Just to satisfy her made him feel like a giant. She pulled him down and closed her eyes. He wasn't Bruno. He wasn't Steven. But he was good; he seemed to know what she wanted without being told. He had a male identity of his own, and she was surprised at how much she liked it. And needed it. She didn't want to be alone. Too many things waited for her in the silence; she submerged herself in the renewed pleasure he gave her, drowning in the sensation, willing it to go on and on. No Bruno in her dreams tonight, no nightmare about a creeping snake of blood inching down the steps from her father's dead body, threatening to stain her.

He was a sentimental man; he wanted to hold her afterward, to tell her she was wonderful. *I bought him with money first,* Clara thought. *Now he really belongs to me.* And in the sleepy interlude she asked him, "You'll help me, Mike? I need you. I hate to say it, but it's true...."

He promised, not thinking or caring what she would ask of him. She said, "We make a good partnership. I want you out of that crappy hotel and right here with me." He didn't argue. He liked the idea.

He moved into the Crillon the next day. When Clara told him to fly down to the south and scout out where Steven Falconi and his family were living, he went without remembering to send his wife a cable. It was Clara who reminded him. The last thing she needed was trouble from that quarter.

O'Halloran checked out the casino. He'd driven up to where he thought the Falconis' villa was, but he didn't want to make himself conspicuous. He called Clara. When did she want him back in Paris?

She noted he hadn't mentioned going home to the States. "Not yet," she said. "Stay down there, see what you can pick up. I've got things to do here. When you get back, Mike, we'll go out on the town."

"You know where I want to go," he said. "I get hard just talking to you."

She had a low, suggestive laugh. "Just you keep it for me. I'll be moving out of here soon. I'll call you."

When she hung up, she put him out of her mind. She was going to see the apartment on the Rue Constantine that morning. It would be a test of nerve and resolution to go there and relive the barren hopes of the early days with Steven.

"She's going to be all right, isn't she?" Charlie found Steven waiting for him when he came down from his mother's room. He had rushed up to see Angela as soon as they arrived after Hugh Drummond's funeral.

"She's going to be fine. I've just spoken to Dr. Martineau; he saw her this morning, and he's not worried anymore. So you mustn't worry either." He put an arm around Charlie's shoulders.

"You were awfully good, Dad; you got everything organized so quickly. But I do wish he hadn't left everything to me. Mum doesn't seem to mind."

"I'm sure she doesn't. Your grandfather knew she didn't need anything. He did the right thing; he wanted you to have whatever there was. I'd like to talk to you about that a bit later. But there's no hurry. When you finish your exams and leave school, we can have a talk about the future. Now I'll go up and see your mother. Martineau says she can get up at the end of the week."

"Dad?" Steven paused at the foot of the stairs. "Dad, when is Ralph moving out?"

"I haven't thought about it. Why?" Then, sensing something, he frowned. "Charlie, what are you getting at?"

"I don't like him much," Charlie said.

Steven came back into the hall. "You don't have to like him," he said. "What's this all about? He's here because I asked him to look after your mother while I went to the funeral. He's been very helpful; she told me so."

"He's a bit too helpful, if you ask me," his son said quietly. "I shouldn't say this, but I don't like the way he hangs around Mum all the time. And I know he doesn't like you."

It was the last thing Steven wanted to hear. He said roughly, "Don't talk balls, Charlie." But to his surprise, his son stood his ground.

"It's not balls. I was there at Christmas when things weren't too good with you and Mum. You should've seen his face when you walked through that door!" He paused. "Anyway, I've said it."

"Yes," Steven acknowledged, "you sure have."

"I'm not a fool, Dad," Charlie said. "I know you're pissed off with me about it, but I don't like him, and I don't trust him either." He walked away before his father could say anything.

Steven went upstairs to see Angela. Outside the room he paused. He could hear voices. Maxton was in there with her. He hadn't waited long after Charlie had left.

Steven opened the door quickly and went in. Angela quickly sat up in the bed and held out her arms to him. Ralph Maxton was on the other side of the room. It was foolish of him to have expected anything unusual.

"I don't like him, and I don't trust him," Charlie had said.

Steven sat on the bed and took his wife's hand. He said, "When Angela's able to come down, you must come over for dinner, Ralph." Was it his imagination that Maxton looked angry? It was such a fleeting impression that he dismissed it. Instantly the man was all charm, making light of the dismissal. He even preempted Steven by saying that he really had a lot of details to work on for the spring opening, and he hoped they wouldn't mind if he slipped away immediately and got on with them. Angela thanked him warmly.

He made light of that too, mocking himself. "My dear lady, all I did was sit around having tea with you and enjoying myself. Now that you're back, Steven, it'll be plain sailing!"

When he had gone, she said, "Darling, weren't you a bit abrupt? You didn't have to get rid of him so quickly. I thought he looked rather hurt."

"He'll get over it," he said. "I just wanted you to myself."

The shutters were open; the concierge had dusted and swept the parquet floors. Clara stood in the middle of the long drawing room. The Beauvais tapestry had been covered. The concierge had apologized for not removing the dust sheets. "It was difficult for me, madame. I didn't know what might happen if I pulled them."

It was smaller than Clara had remembered; there was a musty smell in spite of the windows flung wide to let in fresh air. What plans she'd made, walking through it all those years ago with Steven! What parties she'd imagined giving when they came over for a visit! They'd been happy in Paris. She was a girl of twenty, newly fledged into womanhood and marriage. Her hope of early pregnancy was disappointed, and she'd fastened on the apartment as a compensation. There was plenty of time, she had insisted; they were going off to Monte Carlo to end their honeymoon. Prophetically, she hadn't wanted to go. She thought of the apartment as a kind of talisman and bought it out of her settlement without letting Steven know. He had never known. By the time they arrived in the States, their marriage was already on course for disaster. The secret Parisian love nest! She laughed aloud in bitterness. No cooing doves had settled there; it was as empty and barren as her life. She lit a cigarette. It needed furnishing; the decorations could wait. She had to move out of the Crillon, leaving no trace of herself. She walked across the floor, her steps echoing on the bare parquet, and on an impulse took a corner of the sheeting that covered the tapestry. It had been brilliantly colored, if she remembered, a typical eighteenth-century pastoral scene with lovers dressed up as shepherdess and gallant. She pulled, and the cover came away. The glowing colors were fresh and beautiful. The lovers dallied, and a whiff of subtle eroticism was in their woven faces and sly eyes. She stood and stared. Not love as she understood it, no visceral torment of desire and jealousy; no passion. They fondled each other in a floral bower, with cupids spying on them from the clouds. A bloodless sensuality, a concept of love that was no more than scented dalliance. Clara reached up and caught the tapestry by the corner. She wrenched with all her strength; the backing tore a little, but the tapestry resisted her. She couldn't pull it down. The lovers went on simpering and eyeing each other, watched by the lascivious siblings of the god of love. She turned and hurried out of the room.

Clara didn't waste time. She toured the shops in the Faubourg Saint-Honoré. She ordered Savonnerie carpets, sets of comfortable chairs and sofas, an expensive and elaborate modern bed, and some fine pieces of early French furniture. She sold the tapestry, and the price gave her a morbid satisfaction. It paid for most of the furnishings.

The concierge, smelling a very wealthy patroness, found her a suitable maid and the services of an Algerian cook. The activity kept Clara going; she gave herself no rest until the miracle was accomplished and the apartment ready to walk into. She told herself she had killed the memories of Steven when that hated tapestry was taken down. The gilded mirrors and a fine flower painting made the whole room look different. She could be happy in it. She might even settle in Paris permanently. But the fantasy didn't last long. The reality was O'Halloran phoning from Valbonne to say that there was a gala evening planned for Steven's casino in May. And he'd found out quite a lot about the man who ran the place. A man who might be approachable. Clara told him to come back to Paris. She had canceled his room at the Crillon when she moved out. But she wouldn't ask him to stay at the Rue Constantine. He'd come by appointment and stay the night by invitation. She wanted no misunderstanding. She might delude him when they were between the sheets, but outside the bedroom she paid the bills and called the shots. That way she kept control.

She wondered what he had found out, what kind of man Steven had trusted who Mike thought might not be trustworthy. Not like Steven to make a mistake, she thought. Always so shrewd, so ruthless in detecting a phony. She smiled in hatred. Maybe he had slipped just once. And once might be enough.

It must have been the boy, Ralph Maxton decided. And not so much a boy anymore. At six feet two and growing into a man, he was the mirror image of his father. He'd come out of the lanky stage. He was a very mature eighteen. It was the Italian blood, Maxton judged. Like the women, they grew up fast and faded early. He had never liked Charlie; at first he'd been jealous because his parents doted on him, but increasingly he found that the teenager grated on him. He wasn't the nice middle-class English lad, about to leave public school and begin life in the adult world; he looked like it and talked like it, but Maxton had always wondered how deep you'd have to scratch to find a very different animal. Now he knew. Charlie hated him. Charlie, with an intuition sharper than his years, knew that Maxton was in love with his mother. And he didn't try to hide his hatred. He wasn't rude; he knew that wouldn't have been tolerated. But he conveyed his feelings to Maxton very clearly. And it was he who must have said something to Steven to change Steven's attitude. They might be subtle and deceptive, but the Falconis and their kind couldn't hide their feelings for long. Poker wasn't their game.

The change was almost imperceptible, but not to Maxton. A coolness in Steven's eye, a reserve when they were all together. And a watchfulness that warned Maxton to be very careful when he was with Angela. Careful to hide the little intimacies that had grown between them when they had spent time alone. She didn't see it, of course. She was too open, too straight in her attitude to people. She was generous with her affections, loyal and trusting to the people she loved. And he believed that he was included in that love. As a friend, as a confidant. She didn't see him as he hoped that one day she might. She wasn't ready for that yet. Maxton didn't know when it would happen, but he was certain it would. Falconi would shipwreck himself. He'd almost done so last Christmas. There would be another time.

Maxton worked prodigiously and waited for his young enemy to go back to England. And he kept a little distance between Angela and himself. The need to do so made him hate father and son even more.

They had planned a spectacular fireworks display for the gala. Steven managed his money carefully but spared no expense on this second opening. This was going to be the season that firmly established them on the coast. They wanted to lure the clients back and get them to become regulars; above all, the heavy gamblers were Steven's quarry.

He spent a lot of money on advance publicity and harassed Maxton about a new batch of celebrities. "We need some big-name movie stars."

It gave Maxton pleasure to debunk that suggestion. "The big movie stars wouldn't be seen dead at a casino gala these days. You're thinking of Monte Carlo in the fifties. The Brandos and that lot are into meditation. But I'll see what I can come up with."

He consulted Madeleine. They met at the Hôtel de Paris in Monte Carlo. She was in high spirits, bubbling over, in fact. The faithful Bernard had been replaced by a younger, richer man.

"He's fabulous," she confided to Maxton, who wasn't the least bit jealous of this paragon, the more she talked to him. "Persians are so generous—look what he gave me last time." She held out a smooth arm encircled by a Bulgari bracelet set with emeralds and rubies. He'd given her some bruises too, she admitted, but she was quite philosophical about a few punches as part of foreplay. Provided that the rewards were big enough.

"I was so bored with that old fart Bernard," she said, pouting. "He was talking about losing money too; that really bothered me. So when Mahmoud came along, I thought, Adieu, Bernard." She giggled delightedly. And then she gave Maxton a celebrity for the gala opening who would raise eyebrows all along the coast.

"I'd like to help you, Ralphie darling. My friend is very close to the Shah; he's got signed photographs and personal presents all over his apartment. I was telling him about the gala, because I want him to take me. But he said it was a bad date for him. The Shah's sister's on a visit here, and she wants him to take her to Monte Carlo. Guess what I said?"

Maxton didn't spoil it for her. It wasn't often she did anyone a favor. "No idea," he said. "Tell me."

"I suggested he bring her along to your casino instead. And he said yes! Isn't that wonderful? She gambles like a lunatic—so does he. And they're so rich, you can't even imagine it."

"You're a clever girl, darling," Maxton told her. "This is going to please my charming boss. He's been climbing on my back about bringing in talent."

"You mean that handsome man I saw—the one who changed his name? Why don't you like him anymore?"

"I never did like him much," Maxton said. "Gangsters don't exactly grow on one. On the strength of this, I'm going to order some champagne for us. And what time do you have to be available for your rich Iranian friend?"

"When does your boss, Mr. Falconi, expect to see you?" she retorted. Her voice had risen; it always did when she was excited.

"Shush," Maxton said. "Keep it down, darling. . . . Sometime to-morrow morning. I've booked us a room, in case you were free."

She smiled at him, punching the loose skin on the back of his straying hand. "Not that nasty little attic room again?"

"No. A nice double on the second floor. Why don't we have them send up champagne?"

"Why not?" They left the bar arm in arm. She looked over her shoulder and whispered to him, "My God, there's that freak! She's still here, sitting in the same corner."

"What freak?" he asked.

"That women with the dreadful face. You know, the one who lives here. Ugh—she ought to wear a yashmak."

"Now I know you're sleeping with a Persian," he said, and their laughter drifted back behind them into the bar.

Pauline Duvalier didn't move. She had her pack of playing cards set out for patience, and the daily bottle of champagne leaning in its ice bucket. She kept herself in shadow; the corner table was reserved for her. She spent most of her day there, drinking and playing patience, but at night she ate a solitary dinner in her suite, fashionably dressed and bedecked with jewels. Nobody saw her but the floor waiters.

The niche in the dimly lit bar was her foray into the outside world. If she wanted to buy anything, the goods were sent to her in the hotel.

[275]

Sometimes she listened to other people's conversations, but not often. She'd seen the Englishman and his French whore on several occasions. She hadn't forgotten the girl's reaction the first time she'd got a clear view of Pauline. The intake of breath, the grimace of revulsion. It had happened often enough over the years. She'd had a lot of plastic surgery, and they'd repaired what was left with great skill. Her eye was gone, but the little silk patch covered that. There was no pain anymore; they'd rebuilt her shattered jaw and done what they could to reshape her nose. The result was hideous, but she had grown used to it. Champagne sustained her. When her doctor warned her of the effect on her liver and kidneys, she dismissed him. When they gave out, it would be time to stop.

Robbery, they'd said. A petty thief surprised in her bedroom. But Pauline Duvalier knew better. She suspected that the police knew better too, but there was nothing they could do about it. She hadn't been robbed; she'd been punished. She hadn't surprised the thief; he had surprised her. She had gone into her bedroom to change for lunch, and then there was a blow and total blackness. He must have watched her, crept in after her when she entered the house. And then systematically beaten her. In all the years that followed, she had never understood why. And then she'd read about the murders at a Mafia wedding. Sitting up in bed with her breakfast tray, the array of newspapers spread out, she'd seen the name. Falconi. Steven Falconi's widow. She had read the details, studied the gory photographs. Falconi. That was the name of the last man she had slept with. The handsome American on his honeymoon in that same hotel.

Widow. He was dead, then. Had she known he was a big name in the Mafia, it might have made her think before picking him up in the bar. Or it might have intrigued her, added extra spice to the liaison. She hadn't been afraid in those days. She was confident then, confident in her looks and her wealth. He had been a very satisfactory lover. An angry man making love to a stranger while his bride slept alone.

She never saw him again. And a week later she was attacked and maimed for life. Almost killed.

Her friends had been very loyal; people who had known her late husband offered help and hospitality when she came out of the hospital. But when she looked in the mirror, she knew what the answer must be. Flowers from the manager and staff at the Hôtel de Paris had given her the solution. She could never live in a house alone, or be left alone again. She went from the hospital to a permanent suite at the hotel, and she had been there ever since. It was her home, and she was free to live there until she drank herself to death. It was taking a very long time.

Falconi. She mouthed the name. She had just heard it, the brittle voices only a few feet away, discussing a gala at some casino . . . and then the shrill young woman: "your boss, Mr. Falconi . . ."

And the nasal English answer: "Shush. Keep it down, darling."

Her heart had begun beating too fast. She'd been warned about that too.

She knew the Englishman by sight. He used to be one of the publicity people at the Monte Carlo casino. That was a long time ago; he'd been there when her husband used to gamble.

She watched them leave arm in arm, to keep their tryst in the "nice double on the second floor."

Falconi.

She could remember him vividly. Their cool formality. Madame Duvalier. Monsieur Falconi. Never Steven or Pauline, even in the lazy aftermath of lovemaking. Falconi. The Mafia. "Gangsters don't exactly grow on one." She called the barman over. He'd been there for three years. He looked after her. Nobody ever got her seat in the corner, even on the days when she didn't feel like leaving her suite. He was almost a friend: he looked at her so kindly.

"Madame?"

She said, "Who were those people—the couple that just left?"

He leaned toward her. "Monsier Maxton and the lady? I do not know her name; I think it is Madeleine. He brings her here sometimes. Why—did they disturb you?"

"No, no. But they talked so loudly. He works for the casino, does he not?"

"Not for some years now, madame. He runs the new one down at Antibes. It is a big success, I believe."

"Ah," she said. "And who owns that? I heard him talk about someone called Falconi. . . ."

"Not Falconi." The barman shook his head. "It is an American, Steven Lawrence, who is the front man. Nobody knows for certain who is behind it. There have been rumors that it is the Mafia." He spoke very quietly. "This is the only place where they can't get a foothold. Maxton could not ever come back here if he's mixed up with them." Then he said, "You're not worried, are you, madame?" He was genuinely sorry for her. She had her odd ways, and she could be irritable and demanding. But she was generous, and she never carried a complaint to the management.

"No, I'm not worried. Why should I be? I was just interested, that's all. Eugène, I want you to do something for me." She opened her handbag and began taking out franc notes.

"Find out about this casino. They talked about a gala evening." She pushed the money toward him.

He shook his head. "That's not necessary. I can ask for you." He lifted the champagne out of its nest and checked the level.

Pauline Duvalier thrust the money into his pocket. "Don't be stupid, take it. And pour me the rest of that. Let me know about this gala."

"Yes, madame. Thank you very much."

He went back to the bar. It was very strange. She hadn't left the hotel for nearly twelve years. Maybe she was going off her head. But the tip was a big one. The questions were easy to answer. At lunchtime, he crossed the room to help her up from the table. It was a sign of courtesy since she was actually steady on her feet. She gave him the pack of playing cards. "Keep them for me for this evening," she said. "And one more favor. Find out what this Steven Lawrence looks like."

O'Halloran had been living in Valbonne for six weeks when Clara summoned him back to Paris. He looked around the apartment in the Rue Constantine. He'd never seen anything like it. "This is one helluva place. And you've fixed it up so fast!"

Clara shrugged. "It's all right. It needs doing over properly, but that can wait."

"You're going to stay here alone?" he asked her. She'd met his flight from Nice at Charles de Gaulle Airport. He hadn't expected her, and it pleased him. She had moods. Moods when she felt sexy, moods when she behaved like a bully, and other, softer moods, which made him feel he was important.

"I've got a maid," Clara answered. "She sleeps down the hall. I got your old room back in the Place de l'Opéra."

"Thanks." No invitation to move in. But perhaps an invitation to stay the night; he badly wanted that. She seemed on edge, smoking too much, moving about with restless energy. He said, "Clara, why don't you relax? Stop burning yourself out."

"Why don't you get us both a drink and then get down to business. I want the details, everything."

"Okay, okay. Scotch coming up, followed by progress report. Just try and sit still, for Christ's sake. You'll wear out the floor."

She bit back an angry retort. She'd taken him into her bed; he'd naturally presume on that. She needed him too much to slap him down. She threw herself into the deep sofa, watching him move across the room, getting the drinks. He moved well; he was fit and light on his feet. He was a crack shot with a revolver. He told her he had trophies for marksmanship at home.

"He's going by the name Lawrence. The name she uses. He bought this place a couple of years ago. Spent like crazy and turned it into the smartest casino outside of Monte Carlo. He employed this guy Maxton to negotiate and set it up for him. They rented a villa and then bought it last year. Her old man died recently in England. The son is around eighteen years old and in school over there. You want to see pictures?"

"How did you find out all this? Where did you get the pictures?"

"From the maid. It's pretty much a village up there. I took a room and hung around. I said I was an artist. Set up an easel and painted by numbers. So long as I spent money and bought wine, nobody gave a damn what I was doing. The maid came to buy groceries, and the old dame behind the counter couldn't wait to tell me what a good job she and her mother had, working for the rich American who owned the casino at Antibes. So I picked her up in the café, and we went on from there."

Clara was not really listening. He had an envelope, and the photographs were sticking out of the open flap. She reached forward and took them. O'Halloran went on talking.

"It wasn't too difficult to get her to gossip about them. She was full of yap. I got the feeling she didn't like him much. I had to pay for those," he said, pointing at the pictures. "They sure know the value of money."

Steven was smiling up at her, with his arm around a tall, dark boy, his double. She felt as if she were being knifed. In another photograph, a woman with blond hair was laughing at the camera, wearing a sundress that showed her to be full-breasted, smooth-skinned.

O'Halloran leaned over. "That's her. Jesus, you really had it figured. I didn't believe it until I went to see her old man in England."

"She's nothing," Clara said slowly. "She looks like nothing." He could see she was going to tear the picture to pieces. He took it away from her and put it back in the envelope.

"Like I said," he reminded her. "How could any guy want to leave you? She's nothing, you're right. Just another blonde."

"He threw everything away for her," Clara said slowly. "He could have ended up the head of all the families. My father would be alive today if he hadn't run out on us. It must have been for the son. That's what got to him. That's what I couldn't give him. And there was no reason, no goddamned, fucking reason, why he never got me pregnant."

She was on her feet by then. He didn't try to stop her. He had never imagined she could cry.

"I went everywhere. Every specialist, every quack practitioner promising miracles. I made him take a test; I thought it was him. I thought she must have cheated on him, and I said so. He hated me for that. He hated me for being jealous—he hated me period! His test was okay. He had his pride in his dead wife and baby, and I had nothing! You know what happened on my wedding night? He was screwing me, Mike, and he yelled out her name. 'Angelina!' "

O'Halloran said, "Jesus," under his breath.

She stopped in front of him. "I was crazy about him. He went with a woman on our honeymoon. I wanted to kill him, kill myself. . . ."

There was a moment, as he watched and listened, when he recoiled. He had his soft side; he was a fond father, and he loved his wife, even if he did get between the sheets with other women now and then. He didn't like this kind of savage self-exposure. He felt as if she might tear at her clothes, claw at her skin. It wasn't love as he understood love. The word "evil" came into his mind. He was very close to getting up and getting out while the going was good.

"I'll pay half a million dollars," she said.

He stayed where he was. He said after a pause, "What are you buying with it, Clara?"

She sat down beside him; she reached for her drink and sipped it. She was suddenly cool. "My peace of mind," she said. "My family's honor. I want them dead, Mike. All of them. I'll pay half a million dollars to the man who fixes it. Or does it."

He reached for his own glass. His hand wasn't quite steady. "You could get the President of the United States knocked off for that."

"For less," she corrected him.

He still didn't get up and leave. "With your contacts, that shouldn't be too much of a problem," he said.

"I can't use them. No one from back home would touch a contract for me. The word's gone out. No trouble. That's why I'm here. That's why I need you, Mike. I need you to find someone for me. But we won't talk about it now. Tell me about the man my husband hired. What was the name?"

"Maxton," he said. "Ralph Maxton." He was finding it hard to concentrate. It wasn't the Scotch. He had a head like a rock.

"Tell me about him," Clara insisted. Her voice was soft. She laid a hand on his knee. She had long red nails and very white skin.

Half a million dollars. And she meant it. She had the money. "He's English," he said. "His old man's some kind of lord. They kicked him out for stealing and gambling. He was into every kind of shit before he came out here. He worked in Monaco; they caught him playing the roulette wheel, and he was out. Then your husband picked him up. He sounds the kind who'd do anything for money."

"And where did you get all this?"

"From his old bosses at the casino. They're not too pleased with him in Monte Carlo. He's done too good a job pulling some of their customers into the new place. They don't like him for it. They hoped they were getting him in some kind of trouble."

"He'd need money," she said thoughtfully. "If he gambles, he'd always need money."

"That's what I figured," O'Halloran said. "But we can't rush it. We've got to get an angle on this guy first. He doesn't fit into the picture they gave me up in Monaco."

"Why not?"

"Because the maid Janine talked about him too. He's some kind of family friend, from what she said. Stays at the villa to take care of the wife, goes to England with them at Christmas. He's gotten himself stuck in there."

Clara snapped impatiently, "Then why waste time on him? Why the hell think he'll be any use?"

"Because from what she said, he's got the hots for the wife."

Clara stared at him, then said, "And my husband doesn't know? They're cheating on him?"

"No. That Janine would bad-mouth anyone, but she didn't even try that one. She said Maxton was crazy about her. 'Madame doesn't see it,' she told me. She was smirking all over her face. 'And Monsieur Lawrence must be blind.' She's the kind that gets a kick out of that kind of situation. I guess she looks through the keyhole when they're in bed."

Clara was silent. He waited. He hadn't told her the woman was pregnant. He didn't think she was ready to hear about that yet. He said, "If it was only your husband, this could be the guy. He could have two motives. The money and the widow. But we're speculating, Clara. Nothing adds up till I've made contact with him."

"And you think you'd be able to judge?" she demanded.

"I spent the best part of twenty years with crooks, and I always reckoned I could smell the ones who'd murder. Why don't I go to this gala and take a look at him?"

"Why don't you?" Clara said quietly. "And if you like what you see, Mike, then maybe I should meet with him. I went to the casino at Monte Carlo on my honeymoon with Steven. Maybe he was there. When is this gala?"

"Middle of May," he told her. "I'd have to get an invitation. They're pretty choosy who gets in."

She smiled at him. "You'll fix it," she said. "Show someone a wad, and turn on the charm. Now why don't we eat? You like Algerian food?"

He stroked the back of her neck, feeling the small nape and the silky hair under his fingers. "I've never eaten any," he said.

"It's spicy. I like it. And you'll stay, won't you?"

"I'll stay," he said. He leaned over and kissed her. Half a million dollars. He could really get out from under if he had that kind of money.

Meantime she was writhing under him like a beautiful snake. They didn't eat till very late.

9

"It's a girl," Steven said. "She's beautiful!"

"That's great," Piero said, "Just great! The mother's okay?" He covered the telephone mouthpiece and shouted to Lucia: "Steven's had a girl. . . . Yeah, yeah, I'm here. So what's she weigh?" He was an expert on babies. Lucia was expecting their fourth child.

"Just six pounds," Steven said. "She came a little early, but it was easy, and Angela's fine. Tell Mama, won't you? And Papa . . ."

"I'll tell them," Piero promised. "Mama will be happy. You know how she is about babies. Listen, Steven, maybe we could come out and visit and bring her. How would that be?"

"You think Papa would let her go?"

"I don't know. We could talk about it. Lucia and me and the kids would love to see you. We miss you, Steven."

"I miss you too," was the reply. "How's everything? No troubles?"

"No troubles," Piero assured him. "No Fabrizzis, no troubles." He laughed. "And Clara's gone off on her broomstick! If Papa'd see sense, you could come home and bring the family with you."

Steven didn't answer. Whether his father forgave him or not, he would never go back, and never bring his wife and family. He said, "It's good to talk to you, Piero. Give everyone my love, and I'll send you pictures of the baby. She's beautiful. She's like Angela. . . . I'll call again soon."

For a moment nostalgia clouded his happiness. He missed them. He missed the warmth that was so much a part of his old life. The birth of a new baby was such a celebration in his family. Everyone participated. Cousins and uncles and relatives stretching way back were all involved in the event. But the nostalgia didn't last; by the time he'd left the phone booth and gone back to Angela's bedside, he'd forgotten his regret.

The baby had come early; there'd been a late-night dash to the hospital, and the little girl was born within two hours. He'd held her in his arms and loved her instantly. As he loved her mother. He'd missed the birth of his son; he wept at the thought of that lonely birth in England, without a husband to comfort and rejoice with Angela. And she smiled with the baby in her arms and told him not to be so silly. She loved him more for those tears than for the pride and happiness that followed. "You said we'd have a girl," she reminded him, "in that crazy old bed in the hotel at Palermo."

In the end the nurse insisted he go home and let mother and baby sleep in peace. He came to get them three days later, and drove them back to the villa. He'd filled the rooms with flowers; and in spite of Angela's protests, he'd engaged a nurse to look after the child so she wouldn't get tired.

She telephoned Charlie at school. Steven had already given him the news, as soon as the baby was born. "I wish I could get over," he said. "I'd love to see you, Mum. But it's right in the middle of exams. They'd have a fit if I suggested it. You sure you're okay? Dad said it was very easy."

"I'm fine, darling," she told him. "And don't you think of anything but passing and getting the best marks. . . . You'll love the baby; she's sweet. Looks a bit like a little monkey—Steven goes mad when I say that! . . . No, she's quite fair. She may be dark later, but I don't think so. . . . Yes, I will. You too."

The baby was christened Anna Joy, after her grandmothers. They delayed the ceremony until Charlie came home, his exams over. To Angela's surprise, Steven refused to have Ralph Maxton as a godfather. Two of their French acquaintances stood for the child. They weren't even close friends. But they were Catholics. Steven wanted his daughter baptized, and Angela didn't object. To her, all religions were much the same. She preferred the less flamboyant Anglican services, but that was only because she had been brought up with them. It was a happy day, and they gave a party at the villa afterward. She went among the guests, carrying her little daughter in her arms. Toasts were drunk, and a handsome cake was cut, to applause from the guests. Maxton had been very generous. Too generous, she felt, since he must have hoped to be a godfather. His gift stood on the table with all the other presents: the exquisite baby clothes, the stuffed animals, the silver dishes and spoons.

Maxton's gift was a silver rattle with a coral handle, festooned with little silver bells.

Angela thanked him, the tiny child, wrapped in lace and silk, fast asleep in her arms. "What a lovely present," she said. "It looks very old."

"It is quite old," he said. "I got a chum in England to get it for me." The chum was his younger brother, and the rattle was a Maxton heirloom. It had been passed on by tradition to Ralph at his own christening. "I'm glad you like it,' he said to her. "I hope she'll play with it one day." He touched the miniature closed fist with the tip of his finger. "She's a pretty little thing," he said. "Very like you."

"Darling"—Steven had come up beside her—"why don't we give her to the nurse, so you can join in the fun?"

"I *am* having fun," Angela answered. "Isn't Ralph's present beautiful? What date is it?"

He said, "About 1720. There's the nurse hovering over there—shall I call her for you?"

"Thanks," Steven said. He was pleasant, but there was a note of firm dismissal in the word.

Maxton gave a crooked smile. "At your service—as always," and he moved rapidly away through the crowd.

"You should have thanked him for the lovely rattle," Angela said.

"I thought I did," Steven answered. "Here, give her to me for a minute. *Bellissima*," he murmured to his tiny daughter, and kissed her gently on her downy head. "Here, go to Natalie." He handed her over to the nurse and took Angela by the arm. "Stop frowning at me," he said quietly. "You make too much of a fuss over him. He might misunderstand it. And it annoys Charlie. It's even starting to annoy me."

"Then you're both being very silly," she said.

"Maybe, but we love you too much to share you," he whispered. She was angry, and he didn't want the day to be spoiled for her. He regretted saying that about Maxton. He shouldn't have brought Charlie into it. For all her gentleness, Angela could be surprisingly firm with their son. Much firmer than he was, he thought. But then why not spoil him? He was a son to be proud of—so handsome and sure of himself. And he was certain to do well on his exams. He was talking about going to college. That was something, Steven exulted. Oxford or Cambridge—the best there was. He talked about the prospect with such enthusiasm that he refused to listen when Angela suggested that perhaps Charlie wasn't exceptional. There were other universities, prestigious

[285]

enough for most young men. "Not for my boy," was all he said, and that was that.

"What a charming party . . . what a beautiful baby. . ." The compliments flowed like the champagne. It was all so different this time, Angela thought, so different from that other christening, in the village church. Her parents there, the few friends gathered at the house for tea. And dear Jim Hulbert, the good man they'd hoped would marry her one day. He'd left the practice long ago. She'd heard he'd married a widow and set up practice in the Midlands. She could hardly remember what he looked like.

"Are you happy?" Steven asked her. "It's been such a good day, hasn't it? She never even cried when the priest baptized her."

"I'm very happy," Angela answered. "I just wish Mum and Dad had been here with us."

"I was thinking the same thing," he said. "How my father and mother would love to see her. My mother is crazy about my brother's kids. But I'll send pictures."

The barman at the Hôtel de Paris couldn't believe it. The manager couldn't believe it either. Madame Duvalier was going to the gala at the Casino Poliakoff. Going out for the first time in all these years. The manager was so concerned he went to see her.

"Madame," he said gently, "do you think it's wise? It's a big occasion, crowds of people. Won't it be too much for you?"

"Don't worry," she said. "I'll hide my face. Oh, don't be embarrassed—I know that's not what you meant. . . . You're a good friend. You've taken good care of me. I shall need a car and a driver."

"That'll be arranged. I was thinking, wouldn't you like someone to escort you? Someone to look after you for the evening?"

She laughed. "You're not suggesting some boy, are you? I used to pick my own men. Maybe I wouldn't be like this if I hadn't."

He didn't know what she meant by that. She could be very eccentric at times. "One of the staff would be glad to go with you," he said.

"No, thank you. I can order my own drinks and take myself home when I get bored. It's good of you to think of it. It should be an interesting evening. Won't you join me in a glass of champagne?"

He excused himself. He thought she was insane to contemplate such an excursion after twelve years of seclusion. Cover her face. How?

When he had gone, Pauline Duvalier picked up her glass. He *was* a good friend and not just because she was a permanent source of income. The hotel didn't need her that much. He was kind, protective. She appreciated that; he'd be surprised how much she did, when he learned after her death what she had left him and Eugène and the staff who looked after her.

"Steven Lawrence." She said the name aloud. It didn't sound very Italian. But then Eugène had said he certainly had Latin blood. He was very tall and very dark; he could have been French from the south, or Monégasque, by the look of him. Nobody knew much about him, except that he had an English wife and a son.

He'd employed Ralph Maxton when he was destitute and unable to get another job. He seemed very rich, judging by the way he'd restored the old Palais Poliakoff.

Eugène had been able to find out so much because his sister's niece worked at the casino as a waitress. Pauline knew the web of relationships that stretched throughout the families along that coastline. His description could be made to tally. Or it could prove false and misleading. Steven Falconi the gangster was dead. The newspapers said so. His widow had just remarried when the massacre began. Minutes after the ceremony, the report had said. On the church steps.

There was no Falconi working at the Poliakoff; Eugène was positive. Maxton worked for Steven Lawrence. But she had heard them, Maxton and his French woman, in the bar, sniggering together: "your boss, Mr. Falconi . . . Gangsters don't exactly grow on one. . . ."

She finished the champagne and touched her face with her fingertips. "I'm going," she said aloud. She often talked to herself. "I'm going and I shall know if it's the same one. Then I can ask him the question. I'll show him this, and then I'll say, 'Tell me, was this done because of you?' "

She dressed for dinner as usual; she put on her fine rings and a ruby necklace.

When the floor waiter arrived with the trolley, she was sitting on the sofa, a heavy black veil over her head. "Come in," she called out to him. "Come in. Set it up over there, please. Don't you think this suits me?"

He went out, followed by her low, self-mocking laughter.

May 28 was chosen for the gala; it had been widely publicized, and to Steven's gratification, there was a scramble for invitations. Maxton had carefully leaked a rumor about the Shah and his empress, and nobody discouraged it. When the time came, they'd have to make do with Princess Ashraff. She was glamorous enough.

They'd been open for business since April, and the casino was well attended, with some serious gamblers visiting regularly. There was an air of excitement among the staff as the gala evening drew near. Steven worked as long and as hard as anyone, supervising the smallest detail, poring over the menus, working out the firework displays and the timing. Flowers were Angela's province, and he told her to be as lavish as possible.

"This is going to make us or break us," he insisted. "We can't afford to do this every year, so we've got to make a big splash that will be remembered."

Ralph Maxton called the staff together. The croupiers and dealers gathered in the *salon privé* for a final briefing. Everything was ready; the roulette wheels were polished, the green baize tables brushed to perfection.

Maxton said, "Gentlemen, tomorrow's the big night. We've got to make it a bigger success than our opening. I don't have to remind you that all our jobs depend upon it. You've had the list of names; you know who should get star treatment, and one or two that shouldn't."

A few people laughed.

The dealers knew who tried to pay with bad checks. They would find it very difficult to get into the play.

Someone called out, "What about the Save the Soul rule? Do we still apply that?"

Maxton shrugged. "Those are the orders. The boss says no one's to be allowed to play beyond his limit." He made a joke of it. "The only thing we want hanging from the trees around here are fairy lights!"

They didn't understand this philanthropy. Suckers were suckers; the more compulsive the gambler, the better for the casino and the profits they all shared. But when Mr. Lawrence made a rule, nobody broke it and kept his job. The staff dispersed, and Maxton went to his office to take a breather. He needed one. They'd all been working overtime for days.

Angela would be coming to the gala. He still dined at the villa once a week, and she went out of her way to be friendly with him. She was trying to make up for Steven's reserve. It was even harder for Ralph not to respond. But that way lay dismissal. He knew Steven Falconi. He'd stopped thinking of him as Lawrence since that morning at Val d'Isère. He called him by the name that denoted what the man really was: a hood, a fraud.

Maxton couldn't chance being fired. He had to keep his feelings tied up tight. He tried not to look at Angela too often, not to talk more to her than to Steven or anyone else who happened to join them. If he lost his job, he'd lose his opportunity. And that would come. He knew it.

"Remember our first gala, when we opened?" Steven asked. "This has something more—no rough edges this time!"

"There weren't any then," Angela said. "You're a perfectionist, that's the trouble. It looks marvelous, and you're right, darling—there's a very special atmosphere tonight. It'll be a huge success."

"It had better be," he muttered. "I've spent a fortune on the fireworks alone. Did I tell you how beautiful you look?"

"You said the same thing last time," she reminded him.

"You chose the dress to match the necklace," he noted. "Blue always looks good on you. Wait a minute, sweetheart. I just want to check something."

Angela could see her reflection in the big gilt-framed mirror that hung in the casino's entrance hall. He'd given her a sapphire-and-diamond necklace after Anna's birth. It glittered as she turned. Too expensive, too generous, especially since he admitted he had stretched his resources for the gala. She had stopped him from giving her jewelry, because she felt uncomfortable wearing it. This time he hadn't listened. He wanted to deck her out in a visible sign of his gratitude and love. She would sooner have had a single string of pearls. She had kept her slim figure, and the dark-blue dress fitted snugly. She looked very good in it. In spite of her dislike of ostentation, the gleam and flash of the jewels around her neck was exciting. It was going to be a very special evening. A huge success.

Then she saw him hurrying toward her, and they were side by side, waiting to greet the first guests as they arrived. Photographers began snapping, flashlights popped. He wasn't hiding anymore. Steven Falconi was truly dead and gone. Steven Lawrence was in his place, alive and free of danger.

It was nearly midnight when the Iranian princess arrived. By that time the reception was long over. They came to the entrance and onto the steps to meet her. Steven conducted her upstairs for a private supper party before the fireworks began. After that, she could play a little baccarat if she wished. And she did wish. Twenty minutes after the multicolored stars and rockets began to blaze into the sky, the pièce de résistance—the Iranian royal coat of arms—rose and exploded in a million colored lights, then finally sputtered and died. The princess hurried to the *salon privé* with her escorts. When she was settled at the table, with cigarettes in case she wished to smoke, and a waiter ready with champagne in case she wished to drink, Steven was able to go up to his office with Angela and watch the TV screens. And Maxton decided he could slip away and join the friendly American O'Halloran for a drink at the bar.

"How does this compare with Monte Carlo?"

Maxton didn't see why he should be tactful. "It doesn't. It's well done, very spectacular, but it's all a bit new. The old Queen invented the gala night; here we're looking for gimmicks."

"Who's the Queen? I thought Grace Kelly was a princess," Mike said.

"Oh, how confusing for you—that's the name we all call the casino. The Queen. The Queen of the Coast. You'd better go up and see for yourself."

"How come you're advertising the opposition?" Mike finished his Scotch. "Let me buy you another, Mr. Maxton. Waiter?"

Maxton accepted. He was adept at not drinking drinks if he didn't want them. The trick was not to annoy a client by refusing. "I'm only suggesting you take a look," he said. "I've got a soft spot for the place. I worked there for ten years."

"Were you a manager there too?" Mike asked. He sounded interested. So many of the people Maxton entertained talked only about themselves. He mustn't keep him talking too long. He should lead him to the tables, suggest a modest flutter. What the hell . . . Mike O'Halloran wasn't a rich fish to hook. He'd got the invitation through the Carlton Hotel at Cannes. He'd booked in there especially to come to the new casino.

"I managed the PR," Maxton said. "The celebrities who got drunk, welshed on their bets, felt up ladies at the baccarat table. I told the press the right thing about the wrong people, and I made sure nobody made any trouble. It was a fascinating job. Didn't do much for one's opinion of the human race, though."

"I guess not," O'Halloran agreed. "So why did you leave? Or was that why?"

"I'm afraid not." Maxton had his own brand of charm, and the self-deprecating smile was part of it. "Nobody leaves a well-paid job in a paradise like Monaco just because he doesn't like people. I was offered something better here. Let's say I needed a challenge."

"Starting up here from scratch must have taken a hell of a lot of nerve. But your boss looks like he's got plenty. Quite impressive when you meet him. I only shook hands and got passed on, but all the same . . ." He left it open for Maxton.

"He's got plenty of nerve. He knows exactly what he wants, and he goes out to get it. It helps to work for someone like that. You always know where you stand. You deliver the goods, or you're out on your ear. Now, why don't I stop boring you, Mr. O'Halloran. Let me take you over and see whether you can get back some of your ticket money. Do you play roulette?"

"I've always wanted to; my game is craps back home."

"Then let me introduce you. It's very simple. You put your money down, and we win it back!" Maxton brayed with laughter. He ushered Mike over to the roulette tables and presented him with a thousand francs of chips. "On the house, Mr. O'Halloran. Once you've lost that little lot, then you have to start writing checks."

O'Halloran grinned. "Is this casino policy?"

"Not in this casino. Others, yes. In fishing terms it's called baiting the hook, but we don't do that here. These chips have absolutely no strings attached to them. I shan't encourage you to go on playing if you lose. That was only my little joke. We run a very straight ship. I am getting nautical, aren't I? It must be your whiskey."

"Must be," Mike agreed, though he had noticed that Maxton avoided drinking too much of it.

"There's a high moral tone you won't find in many casinos on the coast. Or anywhere else. Which has its funny side. Now, if you're a real beginner, why don't we start with a simple bet on *rouge et noir* and see how we get on?"

Angela had kicked off her shoes. It had been a very long evening, and very few people had gone home. The rooms were full of gamblers and onlookers. Steven was watching the Iranian princess playing at the top baccarat table. He was concentrating, absorbed. Angela closed her eyes for a moment. It had been a triumph, surpassing their first effort. Crowned by the attendance of one of the biggest and richest gamblers in the world. Even Steven had to give Maxton credit for that particular coup. . . . She had drifted to sleep, because she woke suddenly when there was a knock on the door. Steven switched off the screen.

"Come in."

"Pardon, Monsieur Lawrence. There's a lady asking to see you." It was Louis, one of the assistant managers. He saw Steven frown and said quickly, "I couldn't see Monsieur Ralph anywhere, and I was afraid she'd make a fuss. She's insisting. She's come up here with me; I couldn't stop her." He lowered his voice.

Steven said, "Did she give a name? What does she want?"

"I don't know. She just said she wanted to speak to you in private. Monsieur, she's wearing a veil so you can't see her face. . . . I don't know how to get rid of her." He glanced behind him at the closed door. "She's been sitting in the bar all night. Alone."

Steven made up his mind. All casinos had their share of eccentrics. If she was veiled, as Louis said, she might be connected with Princess Ashraff's visit. Gambling was forbidden to Muslims. The last thing he wanted was someone making a scene about that.

"Take her to Monsieur Ralph's office," he said. "I'll see her there. Tell Gérard to send up a woman from the cloakroom and one of his men from the door. Just in case she causes trouble. They can wait outside."

"What is it?" Angela asked him.

"Just some nut, I expect. Don't worry. I won't be long." He opened the door to Maxton's office. A woman was sitting in one of the armchairs, a veil covering her face completely. A handsome diamond comb kept it in place.

"Good evening, madame," he said. "You wanted to see me?" She didn't speak; she sat there and stared at him from behind the floating tulle. He came toward her. "Madame. What can I do for you?"

It was a husky voice. "Hello, Monsieur Falconi. It's been a very long time."

Falconi. Steven said slowly, "Who are you?"

She got up; she was not very tall.

"What do you want?" he said. There was something, something familiar about that voice. Something from the past he had hoped to bury.

"I knew it was you," she said. "I saw you downstairs, and I was sure. I knew you, even though we spent only one night together."

He said, "Take that thing off! I don't play games."

"If you wish," she said. "But I don't think you'll recognize me." Slowly she lifted the tulle and looked up at him. He couldn't stop the shocked intake of breath. "It isn't very pretty," she remarked. "I was a rather good-looking woman before it happened. I'm Pauline Duvalier. We slept together at the Hôtel de Paris. You were on your honeymoon. Do you remember?"

"Yes, yes," Steven said. "I remember. I remember you. I'm so sorry. Sit down, please."

"Thank you. Do you have any champagne? I could do with a glass."

"I'll get some," he said. Pauline Duvalier. The night he'd slammed out of their suite, leaving Clara alone. The elegant older woman who'd picked him up in the bar when he was getting drunk, trying to come to terms with himself and the nightmare of Clara's jealousy. They had gone up to her suite, and he'd made love to her. For a few hours he'd forgotten his anger and despair. He remembered it only too well.

Maxton kept a supply of drinks for hospitality. Steven opened a bottle of champagne. He poured a glass and gave it to her. Her hand trembled a little. She had lost an eye. Her face was a travesty.

He sat beside her. "What happened to you?"

She sipped the drink. "A robbery," she said. "That's what they called it in the newspapers. But the police had a different idea. I never saw anyone. I was knocked out and beaten. Only my face, Monsieur Falconi. I think he took a gold watch and some trinkets. To make it look like theft. They even asked me if I'd had any dealings with the underworld. It happened exactly a week after I spent the night with you."

"Oh, Jesus," he said slowly. "Jesus."

"It was because of that, wasn't it? Who could have done it, Monsieur Falconi? Who had me beaten almost to death?"

He covered his face with his hands. There was a long silence. Then he raised his head and looked at her. He reached out and took her hand and held it. "I know who did it," he said at last. "God forgive me. I told her, and this is what she did."

"Told whom?" Pauline Duvalier asked him. He was gripping her so hard it hurt.

"My wife Clara. I told her I'd been with someone else. She'd been accusing me, driving me crazy. She must have found out who it was. Oh, God, what can I say to you? What can I do?"

"Is she the woman whose husband was shot in New York at their

[293]

wedding? It said she was your widow. Are you hiding from her, Monsieur Falconi?"

He said, "Yes, madame, I am. I have a wife and a family. You saw my wife with me tonight."

"A blond woman, very pretty," Pauline Duvalier said. She held out the empty glass. "I live on this," she said. "Do you know this is the first time I've left the Hôtel de Paris since I came out of the hospital? I live there all year round. Everyone knows me; they don't look at my face anymore. The surgeons did their best, but there wasn't much left for them to work on."

Steven said, "You were beautiful. I remember that well. Tell me, what can I do? Is there anything, anything at all I can do for you?"

She smiled. It was a painful sight. "Nothing. You've been kind. I appreciate that. You have a manager here; I saw him. An Englishman?"

"Yes. Ralph Maxton. Do you know him?"

"By sight. He comes to the Hôtel de Paris; he has a woman he brings there. That's how I found you. He talked about you, Monsieur Falconi, and the woman said your name out loud. Perhaps you should speak to him about it?"

"Thank you. I will."

"I must go now," she said. She drew the tulle down over her face.

Steven helped her to her feet. "I would like it very much if you'd come here again," he said. "As my special guest. I'd like you to meet my wife. We would look after you."

"Thank you, but I don't think so. I'm happy enough. I just wanted to be sure of why it happened, that's all."

"I'll take you to your car," he said. People paused as they walked through the entrance hall. The woman with the veil intrigued them. He waited with her till the car and driver came to the front steps.

"Good night, Monsieur Lawrence," she said. She held out her hand, and Steven brought it to his lips and kissed it.

"I want you to know one thing," he said. "If I'd known, I'd have killed her."

He closed the car door and stood on the steps, watching till it had driven out of sight.

Two days after the gala, Maxton went to the Carlton for drinks, in response to an invitation from the genial American.

O'Halloran clapped him on the back. "Great you could spare the time."

"Nice of you to ask me."

"Least I could do after the great time I had!" O'Halloran had certainly been lucky. He'd never played roulette in his life, but it hadn't taken him long to calculate the odds, and by the end of the evening he'd come away twenty thousand francs ahead.

Maxton looked edgy, Mike decided. Nothing ruffled the exterior, but there was tension underneath. The laugh was an ugly cawing sound, with nothing humorous about it. "Well, you sure had a big success the other night! All that publicity about the Persian princess—what's her name?"

"Ashraff," Ralph supplied. They were drinking whiskey. Champagne would have been sour in his stomach that evening. The American was right. The gala had been a smash. His reward had been a summons to Steven's office and the bald statement that after the summer, he wouldn't be working there anymore. He kept going over the conversation in his mind, absently saying inconsequential things while O'Halloran talked on about himself.

Steven's words resounded in his head. "You've done very good work, but you're through here. I'm not firing you; I'm telling you to look someplace else. And I'll give you a reference that'll make it easy."

He had been shocked. Had Steven discovered his true feelings for Angela? Or was it something else? After a pause he'd said, "Is there any reason, or aren't I to know?"

Steven had looked at him. "When I hire staff, I expect one thing: loyalty. You don't have any." He turned away with a gesture of contempt.

"That's a sweeping accusation," Maxton had said. "I think you owe me more than that."

"You're owed nothing. You were on the skids when I employed you. I'm calling it quits." Steven hadn't turned around. Maxton walked out of the office.

Nobody knew. He'd gone back to work as if nothing had happened. He hadn't seen Falconi since.

O'Halloran leaned forward and tapped him on the knee. He'd been so lost in his thoughts that he jumped.

"What's wrong? What's eating you? Come on—maybe I can help."

"I've lost my job." Maxton said it before he could stop and consider the consequences of making it public knowledge. But O'Halloran was an outsider. He was a fly-by-night friend, gone in a few days. He had to tell someone.

O'Halloran looked surprised. "Jesus," he said. "I guess you weren't expecting it. Any reason, if you don't mind me asking?"

"No reason I know of; certainly not the one I was given." There were two red spots on Maxton's cheeks, like dabs of paint. He was naturally pale and sallow, and it made him look ill.

"I'm sorry," O'Halloran said. "It sounds like you've been given a real bum deal."

"I think that's a fair comment," Maxton said. "You were rather impressed by my boss, weren't you? But you only shook hands, of course."

"I'm not so impressed now," was the answer. "What kind of a shit is he, to treat you like that?"

"A very special kind," Maxton said slowly. "I built that place up single-handed. He knew nothing about running a casino. He didn't know anyone on the coast, whom to employ, how to get the press interested—nothing! All he had was money. I did the donkey work, Mike. And now he thinks he's got it in the bag, and he kicks me out. With a good reference, of course." His eyes were bright with rage.

O'Halloran watched him closely. The man could be nasty, he decided, very nasty, if you crossed him. He decided to press a little further. "Listen, Ralph—don't take this wrong....I made a bit of money thanks to you. If you need anything, I'd be only too happy..."

"Thanks," Maxton said. He wasn't grateful, Mike realized that. There wasn't room in him for anything like gratitude; he was brimming over with his rage. "I don't need money immediately; he always paid well."

O'Halloran decided to make sure. "You'll get another job?"

"Oh, yes, I'll have to eventually. I have expensive tastes. I don't have the piggy-bank mentality. I'll go to another place. I could try Italy."

Mike let a silence grow between them. Finally, he said, "What a bastard! Listen, why don't we have some dinner? I'm doing nothing tonight; I'd really like it. You know, I just might be able to think of something for you. I've got a few contacts. Unless you've got some girl waiting . . ."

Maxton shook his head. "My girl's busy tonight." *My whore is being kicked around by her rich boyfriend. And the woman I love is sitting down to dinner with that self-righteous crook.* "I'm free," he said. "And just because I've been so boring, dinner's on me."

*　*　*

In the Paris apartment, Clara answered the telephone. She sounded impatient. "What the hell have you been doing? You haven't called me in a week!"

"If you want me to foul it up, then I'll rush," Mike said. He was bolder over the telephone than face-to-face. "I've made contact with this guy Maxton, and I think luck's running our way."

"Why? What's changed?"

"He's just been fired, and he's sore as hell about it. I spent this evening telling him what a crap deal he's been handed."

"Will he do it?" Clara demanded. "Where's your goddamned instinct you bragged about? I'm not interested in grievances—I want someone who'll take on the contract!"

The week had made her edgy. She was sleeping badly, mentally abusing O'Halloran for wasting time, for not getting on with it. "I've got someone," she heard him say. "Wait, before you start bawling me out. Just get ready with the half-million dollars."

She swore in Italian. "Maxton? You don't even know—"

"Not Maxton," he interrupted. "Me, Clara. I've got it all figured out. Just trust me." He hung up.

He waited for the phone to ring again. It didn't. He could imagine that bloodthirsty temper erupting. He grinned to himself. She could yell at him, but there wasn't much else she could do. There was no one else she could trust to commit three cold-blooded murders. She'd taken him on, and they'd ended up as partners.

And she'd pay. He sat back, sipping Scotch, thinking how he could cash in the agency, take his wife and his kids and buy a place in Mexico. Live in comfort for the rest of their lives. They'd taken a cheap holiday down there some years ago and loved the place. The sun, the easygoing tempo. It was cheap too. They could live it up, have anything they wanted. He could work when he felt like it. Half a million dollars.

He'd thought about it carefully, testing his nerve. He'd shot men, and on two occasions women, during his time in the Department. He knew what it felt like to pull a trigger, see them arch up and then fall. He'd smelled blood and the death stink of human excrement. This could be a lot easier. He was a very good shot. He'd taken a sighting on Falconi that night at the gala. A matter of psychology, they were taught during their training. You aim at the targets without really seeing them. They could be cardboard cutouts, dummies set up on the range. You dehumanize them, and from then on it's easy. Because you've dehu-

[297]

manized yourself. Falconi wouldn't keep him awake at night. As for the blond wife, she was a target, not a breathing woman. He couldn't have described her face, but the part of him that needed to identify her could have picked her out of any crowd.

He could smell the ones who'd kill, because he recognized them. It was a brotherhood that went deeper than any uniform or any oath sworn to uphold the law.

Maxton had gone home, obviously feeling worse after Mike had finished being sympathetic. And Mike had made a judgment: Maxton would knock off Steven Falconi for nothing. That was the irony of it.

Steven was in his office. He spent every night at the casino, greeting guests, watching them play; keeping an eye on his staff. He had already seen Maxton briefly that evening, had spoken equally briefly about something concerned with the casino. He wasn't expecting him to come to the office late at night.

"Can I see you for a moment?"

"Sure. Come on in. Anything wrong downstairs?"

"Nothing. You're making a lot of money as usual."

Steven didn't rise. He knew that mocking tone, the supercilious twist of the thin mouth. "So what brings you up here?" he asked.

Maxton had a habit of standing with both hands in his pockets. He said, "I've been thinking about our conversation the other day. Wouldn't it save a lot of trouble if I just resigned?"

Steven hesitated. It sounded like a dignified way out for them both. No explanations to Angela. That was something he'd dreaded. And put off. The act of a gentleman. He didn't know why he thought of it like that. He saw the cold and bitter hatred lurking in Ralph Maxton's pale eyes. "Who are you getting off the hook, Ralph? Me or yourself?"

"Me," was the answer. "One should never remind someone of what they've said in anger. Some pompous ass said that to me one day. I thought it was rubbish at the time. You told me you didn't owe me anything. Not even a proper explanation for throwing me out. So don't fool yourself I'm thinking of you. It suits me to go early. Then I don't owe you anything either. And it makes it easier to say goodbye to your wife. Unless you've told her what you wouldn't tell me—why I'm being fired."

Steven looked at him. He'd trusted Maxton, welcomed him into his family, paid him beyond the claims of generosity for what he did, considered him a friend. And Maxton had been snooping behind his back. It was a chilling thought that only a few months ago, his revelation of the name Falconi could have been fatal to Steven. How had he discovered it? Now, luckily, it didn't really matter. A chance word had been spoken, and no enemy had heard. He had been tempted to face Maxton with the truth. But that was to admit it, to involve Pauline Duvalier. He couldn't risk that. She had suffered enough. He thought, *My son was right. He hates me; he hoped to find something he could use against me. Because he loves Angela...*

He said aloud, "I've told you all I'm going to tell you. When I don't trust a man, he doesn't work for me. Anything else?"

"No," Maxton said evenly, and turned away. His walk was nonchalant, hands thrust into his pockets, insolence in every line of the tall, angular body.

He opened the door and looked back. "You know, Steven, you remind me of those gentlemen in Las Vegas who let my poor friend drown himself for a couple of thousand dollars. What a bloody fool I was to think you were any different!" He closed the door quietly behind him.

That evening, Maxton was lying on his bed, his shoes kicked off, his shirt sleeves rolled up. He'd made the gesture, salvaged something of his self-respect. Falconi had winced at that parting shot. It helped, but only a little. He'd forced himself to be practical, reminding himself of those hungry days after he'd left Monte Carlo—the dwindling money, the borrowing, the move to cheaper hotels, which ended in a single room in a mean boardinghouse. He got out his bank statements and calculated. He had enough to keep him comfortably on the coast for at least six months, while he looked for a job.

But six months could pass very quickly; inertia was always at his elbow, urging him to wait in times of trouble for something to turn up. He wasn't going to risk it again. Italy, he'd said to Mike O'Halloran. There were rich resorts on the Italian Riviera, fine casinos. Italy meant losing touch with Angela, though. Out of sight, out of mind. He'd been so sure that he would be in place, ready to step forward when the inevitable happened and there was a second crisis between her and Falconi. A repeat of the near miss at Christmas. But the cards had run against him. Falconi had found an opportunity to get rid of him. In Maxton's view, he'd been waiting for an excuse ever since that little bastard Charlie had put in a bad word after Hugh Drummond died. He owed the kid for that. He didn't even think of him as Angela's son. To Maxton he was an enemy, a clone of his father.

He was sunk in bitter thoughts when he heard the telephone ring. It was that ubiquitous friendly American. He almost cut him off with a curt excuse.

"Come on over, Ralph," he heard him say. "I think I've got a proposition for you. Can you make it right away?" But he sounded different, not friendly, not so hail-fellow-well-met. He was cool and businesslike. Maxton considered for a moment. Why not? What did he have to lose when the alternative was an evening spent alone in fruitless longing for someone who was now even further out of reach.

He said, "I guess there's no harm in a drink and a chat. I'll be along in half an hour." Then he tried to probe: "What kind of proposition is it?"

O'Halloran answered, "See you in half an hour," and hung up.

In spite of the air-conditioning, the room was hot and smoky. As soon as he opened the door and saw O'Halloran sitting there with his feet on the coffee table, Maxton knew everything had changed. The American *was* different. No tie, crumpled shirt, cigarette butts and a half-empty bottle of Scotch, a glass on the floor beside him. At first he thought, *He's drunk,* and could have kicked himself for bothering to come. But he wasn't. He had simply shed a skin. "Come on in, pal. Take a glass and help yourself. Found another job yet?"

"No." Maxton was cautious. He didn't take a drink. "I haven't looked. It's early yet. I'm not rushing anything."

"You see much of that bastard Falconi?" It was delivered straight, like a blow. Maxton prided himself on taking the unexpected in his stride. He managed very well, considering. "Sorry," he said. "Who did you say?"

Mike shook his head at him. He had shrewd eyes and a mouth that could set like a trap. Not the same man at all. He'd put on a very convincing act, Mr. Mike O'Halloran.

"Cut the crap, Ralph," he said. "I know who he is, the same as you. As a matter of fact, that's why I'm here. You're not the only one he's screwed up. And you're not the only one who hates his guts. It's my guess you've got the balls to do something about it. How would you like to earn yourself half a million dollars?"

Half a million dollars. Maxton didn't try to sleep that night after he left O'Halloran. He took his car and drove along the coast road, all the way past Juan-les-Pins, past the casino at Antibes in the palace where his great-uncle had dallied in the palmy days before the Russian Revolution; on through Nice itself, still pulsing with life in the restaurants and bars. He drove through Beaulieu and the little fishing village of Villefranche and up onto the Moyenne Corniche above Monte Carlo. When he stopped the car, there was a magical view of Monaco itself: the yachts in the harbor, all lit up, the pleasure palaces of the rich, the casino complex in all its extravagant glory. The sea was like black satin, streaked by moonlight. A light breeze fanned his face as he stood by the side of the car, looking at the mirage that had been his life. Half a million. Five hundred thousand dollars. For the life of Steven Falconi.

He lit a cigarette. He'd tried to take it as a joke at first. But the American wasn't amused. He'd gone on talking, overriding Maxton when he protested. There'd been an option, of course. All he had to do was turn around and walk out. He didn't have to listen to the proposition when it became a matter of murder. He didn't have to pour himself a drink and stay. But he had done so. And O'Halloran had known he would. The man had judged him and come up with an answer Maxton would not have thought possible. He was prepared to listen.

He remembered saying: "Why so much money? It's a fortune. You could hire someone in Marseilles for a few thousand francs."

And then O'Halloran had known he was ready to talk business. No criminal connection. Nothing that could lead back to his client. A clean killing, the payoff, and a ticket on the next plane leaving Nice. The gangsters in Marseilles, the Mafia in Nice, would be obvious suspects in any crime connected with gambling.

And then the next questions, drawing him further in.

"Who's paying for this?"

"A client," O'Halloran had said. "Who is none of your business. You want time to think about it?"

Maxton had tested him—or perhaps himself. "How do you know I won't tell the police?"

The American had grinned. It was a sneer he didn't try to hide. "You won't even think about it; you've made your mind up already, pal. I'll call you at home tomorrow. Don't try contacting me; I'm checking out right now."

Maxton had one last try. "If I say no?"

"No sweat," O'Halloran said. "Someone else'll do the job and collect the dough." He'd got up and opened the door for Maxton.

A fortune. Enough money to start all over again. To change his way of life. A house in England, a stable future. Angela would need him. She would turn to him, as she had done before. He was in the best of all positions. The faithful friend, ready to comfort and protect after a tragedy. All he had to do was nerve himself to just one desperate act, and he would scoop the pool. He would be truly happy. Conscience wouldn't be a problem. He had never had one. He prided himself on regretting nothing except when it turned out badly for himself. If he did what was needed, it wouldn't haunt him. He'd break the bank and walk away for the only time in his life, and without a backward glance. He threw his cigarette over the side of the road, into the abyss below. Starting the engine, he drove very carefully back down the dangerous road to the safety of the coast.

Angela and Steven were eating breakfast out on the terrace. They were waiting for Charlie to join them, and they talked about the success of the gala.

"It was great!" Steven exclaimed. "Full house, some big spenders. "We're home, sweetheart, home and dried, as your father used to say."

"He did, didn't he. It sounds so funny when you repeat his expressions. I often think how kind you were to him. He was really fond of you."

"I liked him a lot," Steven said gently. "Is Anna coming down?"

"It's too early." Angela smiled at him. "The doting father will have to wait till she's had her bath and is ready to go out in the pram. I'd better go and call Charlie; he's overslept again. I'm afraid we'll miss him when he goes back to school." He was leaving the next morning.

"We will," he confirmed. "But he'll be back with us for good in a few weeks. I'll have to talk with him about his future." He paused. "Angela . . ."

"Yes?" She was on her feet, ready to run up and wake their son.

"Ralph's given notice," he said. "He's leaving."

She came and sat down again. "Oh, no! Why? When did this happen?"

He didn't lie to her. "I've known he was going for a while. He told me last night he didn't want to see the season out."

"But didn't you try and persuade him?" she asked.

He hesitated for a moment. Then he looked up at her. "No, I didn't. I think it's best he goes."

"Steven, it's not because of all that nonsense Charlie started? Don't tell me you really took any notice...." She looked distressed.

He said quickly, "No, darling. Maybe he was a bit soft on you—so what? It was nothing like that, I promise. I guess for some reason he's gone sour on me. We haven't been getting along for some time; he wants out. So you see, it's better this way."

"Yes," Angela said. "I suppose it is. But it's sad, all the same. We were all so happy, and we worked so well together. What will you do now?"

"I'll give Louis a trial; he knows the running of the business. I'll find someone to do the PR by the end of the year. We've had so much coverage we don't need anyone for a while."

"I expect he'll come and say goodbye," Angela said. "I'm so sorry it had to end badly. There was something pathetic about him; I always felt it."

"Who's pathetic, Mum?" Charlie stood there, smiling and looking cheerful. A good-looking young man, brimming with confidence in himself and his world.

"I was talking about Ralph," she said. "He's leaving."

"Good," her son said. "And he's not pathetic. He just put that on to get round you. I'm starving. Any coffee left?" Charlie sat down and started eating breakfast.

"I'll go and see how Anna's doing," Steven said, getting up. "Darling, why don't you drive down and I'll take you out to lunch today."

Angela smiled up at him. "I'd love to. Where shall we go?"

"Leave it to me." He bent and kissed her. "I'll surprise you." He strode away.

Angela looked at her son. "Why do you hate Ralph?"

Charlie set down his coffee. "Because he hates my father," he said calmly. "I haven't liked him smarming round you, either, and playing up to poor old Grandpa. It's all been part of the process.... But it's the way he looks at Dad. He never thought I noticed. I never liked him or trusted him. I'm glad he's going. Don't be too sorry for him, Mum. He's a nasty piece of work. Can I have another croissant?"

"I didn't realize you were so implacable," his mother said. "You're very young still, Charlie. Don't judge too harshly." She got up and left him.

He finished his breakfast. She was too softhearted for her own good. If you have an enemy, why treat him like a friend? It didn't make sense. He went off to pick up his tennis partner.

Steven found a charming little restaurant in the hills above Mougins. It was an old farmhouse, imaginatively converted, with tables set out on a terrace, shaded by olive trees, that had a commanding view of the valley. The food was simple but excellent; it was remote enough not to attract tourists. He was in a happy mood, holding her hand as they sat under an umbrella and ordered lunch. He looked at her, and his heart was full of contentment.

Life had been good to him, he thought. His wife, his son and his little daughter. The child was growing visibly, smiling, developing into a person in her own right. He had everything he could desire, and he owed it all to Angela. "You know something?" he said suddenly. "You're as good as you are pretty. And I mean good."

She was embarrassed. "Don't be silly, darling. I'm not good at all."

"I think so," he said. "You've made sense of so many things for me. You've brought up a fine son too. And I've never known you to do or say a rotten thing to anyone. I wonder what I've done to deserve you."

"I wonder." She made light of it. "You're in a funny mood today."

"Happy," he corrected. "It's all come right for us, hasn't it?"

"It certainly has."

"Maybe I shouldn't say that. In Sicily, you don't boast about good fortune. It makes the gods jealous."

"We're not in Sicily," she reminded him gently. "So we don't have to worry."

He stroked her arm, catching her fingers, playing with the wedding ring. The same ring he'd been given by a frightened jeweler in Palermo all those years ago. "You're right," he said. "We don't. Here comes our lunch. Maybe we might slip home for an hour or so afterward...."

"Why not? The afternoons were always our best times."

The villa, when they returned, was very quiet; it was the siesta hour. Charlie had gone off with his friends for the day. Janine and her mother were resting, as were the nurse and the baby. It was the hottest part of the day, even in the cool hills. The sun throbbed in the brazen sky about them. The air was still and heavy with heat. As they walked through the gardens, he said to her, "Remember the first time? When I took you into the hills? It was hot like this."

"You talked about the gods," she reminded him. "I poured some wine on the ground."

"And we made love out there. Why don't we just walk and find a place. . . ?"

There was shade beneath the olive trees; the earth was cushioned in soft grass.

Afterward, it was Steven who put it into words. "It wasn't the same, my darling: it was something new—different from any other time. Or any place." She reached out and kissed him. "When will I ever get tired of making love to you? It's always different. It's always the best."

They swam naked in the warm water of the pool and dried each other lazily in the hot sun. He liked to look at her, to touch the firm breasts and feel the texture of her skin. He told her how beautiful she was and how she made him feel. She had learned a little Italian, and now when he spoke in his native language she understood more than just the music and rhythm of the words. The time passed; the siesta was over. The household would soon come back to life. They covered each other, tied on their robes and walked back into the villa. He caught her from behind and lifted her against him. "Upstairs," he whispered. At that moment the telephone began to shrill. He let her go.

"Nemesis," she said, laughing, and went to answer it. It was Ralph Maxton, asking if he might come over and see her that evening to say goodbye.

"You fixed it?" Clara demanded.

"He said yes, about an hour ago. I even gave him time to call back if he wanted to rat on the deal, but he didn't call." At the other end, he heard Clara's excited laugh.

"Clever Mike," she exulted. "When? When's it going to be?"

"Sooner the better, I guess," O'Halloran answered. "I don't want the bastard going cold. It's tomorrow night."

Clara said, "I want to be there, Mike."

He was thrown by that. "Don't be crazy," he protested. "You stay right where you are. You'll hear about it as soon as I can call you."

"I'm not sitting here waiting," she said. "Don't argue with me. I'm flying down there today."

He almost shouted in exasperation. "For Christ's sake, Clara! You want to stand and watch?"

"That," she said, "would make it perfect. I said don't argue. I've waited a long time for this. I want to be close by when they all get it!" The line went dead while he was still talking.

She packed; she threw clothes into the suitcase. Her hands were trembling. She told the maid in her preemptory way that she was taking a trip and wouldn't be back for some days. No, she snapped back, she didn't know how long. . . . As long as it took, she said to herself. Steven first. Then that whey-faced blonde and the boy. "Oh, Papa," she said out loud, "Papa, you'll rest easy when I've finished. They'll pay for what they did to me. And then I'll go home and I'll get Nimmi and the rest of them for what they did to you. It'll take a little time, but I swear it, I swear I'll get them all. . . ." She smiled as an idea came to mind. Where should she stay? O'Halloran had left the Carlton. He was holed up in a small pensione inland, in case Maxton tried to trace him for the wrong reasons—he took precautions, her clever Mike. Good; cops learned precautions from criminals. He'd get his money. When he'd done what she wanted. You never welsh on a contract; Aldo had impressed that on her. They deliver, you pay up.

He could go back to New York, back to his wife and his children and his agency work. She didn't much care what he did once it was over. Where should she stay? The only place she knew. The honeymoon hotel. Romantic Monte Carlo, where her husband had betrayed her with a woman for the first time. The first of so many times, just as he had promised while she wept and pleaded, choking on that woman's scent, Joy.

The Hôtel de Paris. She got the number and made an open-ended reservation. Then she called the airport and booked herself on the afternoon flight to Nice.

"You know how to use a gun?" O'Halloran demanded.

"I know how to use a shotgun. For pheasants, not people."

He glared at Maxton. "Cut the crap." He took out his own automatic, laid it on the table. He unloaded it, loaded it, gave it to Ralph. "You do it," he said. Maxton was surprised at how nimbly he handled the weapon. O'Halloran pulled a pillow from the bed and upended it on a chair. "Now aim at that and pull the goddamned trigger."

Maxton had a trained eye, for he had participated in the annual grouse and pheasant slaughter at home, though it had bored him. He leveled the gun, aimed at the center of the pillow and fired. It made an alarmingly loud noise. The hole was directly in the center. A few feathers fluttered in the air and then drifted to the carpet.

"Aren't you worried someone might hear?" he remarked.

"No. They're in the kitchen. If you hit a man with that caliber bullet at that range, you'll blow a hole big enough to put your fist in. You want to try again?"

"How do I know it'll be that close?" Maxton demanded. "Make it a smaller target. If you're sure no one's going to come rushing in with the noise." He examined the automatic. The standard Smith & Wesson: high-caliber bullets indeed. He watched O'Halloran.

It was a room rented in a small hotel. An empty room, not where the American was staying. He marked the man's caution. His lack of trust.

"Try this," O'Halloran suggested. He marked the same pillow with a ballpoint pen: a circle the size of a man's head. He set it up again. "Okay," he said. Maxton hit within the circle.

O'Halloran took the pillow and stuffed it under the bedcover. More feathers were floating about. He said, "You don't need to worry. I'd say you were a natural. Now let's get down to the details." Ralph handed him back the gun. "Let's get down to the money and how it's going to be paid."

Pauline Duvalier had not been feeling well. She'd spent a lot of time in her room resting after the gala night at Antibes. Nothing wrong, she assured the manager when he called to inquire. Just tired. The excursion had been too much of an excitement. She didn't plan to sally into the outside world again. Eugène the barman came up to see her. He brought the patience cards. She thanked him, but she didn't feel like playing. She was sure she'd feel up to going to her old corner in the bar tomorrow and watching the world go by.

The next day she was late going downstairs. It had been an effort to get up, to let the chambermaid help her dress. She had fought off the lethargy that told her to stay in bed and let the hours drift by. Her champagne was on ice; her cards were ready for her to play.

But someone was trying to sit at her special table. She saw the woman's back, and the stubborn stance Eugène had assumed in front of the table as he told her he was so sorry, madame, but that place was always reserved. The woman's voice was American and loud.

"It doesn't say so. There's no sign on it. If it's reserved, why doesn't it have a sign? I'm sitting here anyway. Bring me a Scotch and water and plenty of ice." Eugène didn't move. Pauline stayed back, just outside the entrance to the bar. She felt weak, and began to tremble.

Her place, her safe corner in life, was being taken from her. She had to hold on to the doorframe. She heard Eugène's voice. It wasn't discreet anymore. It was raised, and it was angry. "I'm sorry, madame, but that table is always reserved for one of the hotel guests. She lives here, and that is her place in the bar. If you will kindly move somewhere else, I'll bring your order."

The woman said in a furious tone, "Goddamn you, you'll bring me the manager!" Eugène had been hoping for that. "I was going to call him anyway. And don't swear at me, madame!" He was in a rage as he hurried to take the woman at her word and bring Monsieur Jacques himself to deal with her.

He was shocked to find Pauline standing at the entrance. He led her away, taking her arm. "Don't worry, I'll get rid of her. I'll see you to the lift, and when Monsieur Jacques has told that one where to get off, I'll ring you and you come right down, eh? Here, let me get someone to go up with you. . . . Take Madame up to her suite." He surrendered her to a young waiter and hurried off to the manager's office.

In her room, Pauline sank down on the bed. She meant to take off her shoes, then she forgot and kept feeling her face with her hands instead.

She wouldn't go down. She'd never risk that again. If she had only been a few seconds earlier, the woman would have seen her, seen the special guest Eugène was protecting. She would go back to bed, where she was safe. There was a knock on the door. It was the manager himself. He was shocked. She looked so old suddenly; the eye patch was awry, showing the corner of the empty socket. "Madame Duvalier, I've come to apologize. That most unpleasant scene downstairs. The lady has left the bar. Your place is waiting for you. I've come to escort you myself."

"No," she said. "Not today. I won't come down today." He was a kind man; he had admired her courage for many years. He came and sat beside her. "Madame," he said gently. "You must come to the bar as usual. If you don't, you may never leave this room again. Do you

understand me? And all your brave efforts will be wasted. Now give
me your arm, and we are going down in the lift together. I shall join
you for a glass of champagne to celebrate, if I may. Allow me." He
reached out and moved the eye patch into place. "Now," he said. "We
are going."

At the door of her bedroom, she hesitated. "You say she's left the
bar?"

"She won't be going there again. She said so. I did suggest she
might be happier in another hotel. When guests here aren't welcome,
madame, they don't stay long."

She drank a lot of champagne that morning. The bar filled up,
but the woman didn't return. She had only seen her back and heard
her voice, but Pauline felt she would have recognized her. She was
feeling less tired; she'd played out three games in a row, smoked half
a pack of cigarettes and got her confidence back. Someone had shielded
her still further with a large vase of flowers, strategically placed. Eugène,
most likely. He was kind, she thought, the champagne melting her
perceptions into a benevolent blur. She had been weak-willed, foolish
to behave as she did that morning, because an outsider had seemed to
threaten her secure routine, her safe little world. She despised herself.
When the trade slackened at lunchtime, she called the barman over.
"I've had a good morning," she announced. "Three games in a row!
Do you know how difficult that is? Three games. Who was that creature
shouting at you this morning, Eugène? Monsieur Jacques said she was
staying here."

Eugène leaned toward her. "You ought to have heard her, madame.
These rich Americans think they can buy their way in anywhere. 'I
came here in the old days,' she shouts at him. 'When you had staff that
knew how to treat important guests and a manager that made sure of
it! I wouldn't be seen dead in this lousy little bar.' And she swept out.
She's taken the best suite, that's the trouble. I asked about her afterward.
Her name's Salviatti. Mrs. Salviatti. When my father worked here, we
never allowed rubbish like that into the hotel!"

Pauline stayed on till long after lunch. When she did go upstairs
she was rock steady, despite the bottle of champagne she'd drunk, and
its half-empty companion in the bucket of melting ice.

She slept that afternoon, waking in time to dress as usual and
choose her jewels for the solitary dinner in her suite.

What had Eugène said? Salviatti. Why did she think she knew
that name? She hated her lapses of memory. It only happened when

she was upset, like this morning. The waiter came in to take her order, and she put it out of her mind. If you didn't force it, memory readjusted itself. It would come back to her.

"It's such a lovely evening; why don't we have a drink outside?" Angela suggested. Ralph had brought her flowers. It was sad and touching to have to say goodbye.

"He hates my father," Charlie had insisted. Did he? she wondered—but even so she pitied him.

He followed her out onto the terrace. The beautiful evening was the aftermath of another blistering day, almost too hot. A pleasant breeze stirred the trees overhead; that was the joy of living in the hills. The coast was merciless in such weather.

"You're looking very well," he said. "I'm sorry I haven't been up before. I thought you might come down to the casino tonight."

"I won't be coming tonight," she said. "I like to spend time with the baby, and Steven is always so busy there. . . . Ralph, I'm sorry you're leaving."

"Do you really mind? I rather hoped you would." No mockery, no light touch this time. He had pale eyes, a watery color that changed from green to gray-blue. He was looking at her intently.

"You know I do," she said. "We've always been such friends. All of us. Steven'll miss you too."

"I doubt that," he responded. "We've come to the end of the road. He doesn't need me anymore."

She rose quickly to his defense. "You shouldn't say that, Ralph. It's not true."

"No, I shouldn't say it," he agreed. "Certainly not to you. Forget it; don't let's spoil our time together."

"What are you going to do now?" Angela asked. The exchange had made her feel uncomfortable.

"Take a short holiday, look round for another job. I thought I'd see what Italy has to offer. I need a break from the coast; I've been here a very long time."

"You wouldn't go home," she asked him.

"No." He shook his head. He smiled at her and said, "It's not home to me. Except when I stayed with you that Christmas. I'm going to miss you, Angela. You've been very special to me." He was going further than he meant, urged by the gambler's need to try his luck.

Flying a kite to see if the wind would lift it even for a moment. She poured them each a glass of wine, saying nothing. No wind, no flutter of the kite as yet.

"I hope I mean something to you," he said. She knew then that her son was right. Right about Ralph's feelings for her.

She had blinded herself to what was happening, leaning on him, encouraging him to think he meant more to her than a friend. A brother almost, like the one killed in the war. "Dear Ralph," she said gently. "Of course you mean a lot to me. I had an older brother—I told you about him, didn't I? That's how I look on you. I often said to Steven, if only you could meet a really nice girl and get married, settle down. I hope you haven't misunderstood...." She left the rest unsaid. The long, thin face was a mask when she looked at him. No reaction, no expression. "I'm making such a mess of this," she said desperately.

"Oh, I don't think so," he said. "I'm the one who's made a mess of it. But you'll forgive me, won't you? We'll go on being friends?"

"You know we will. This isn't why you're leaving, is it? Please—"

"No. Nothing to do with it. Can I ask you just one question before I go?" She nodded. "Are you really happy? I've wondered sometimes."

"I'm happy," she said. "He's the only man I've ever loved or ever will. From the moment I met him, Ralph. There'll never be anyone else for me but Steven."

He got up, and she rose with him. "That's clear enough," he said. "I hope he knows just how lucky he is. Goodbye, Angela."

She said, "Goodbye, Ralph. Keep in touch, won't you? And look after yourself." She reached up and kissed him on the cheek. He didn't touch her; he didn't respond. His skin was quite cold. "Throw the poor dog a bone," he said, and he laughed his high-pitched, mirthless laugh as he turned and walked away.

"Ralphie." Madeleine's voice was plaintive. "I *can't* get away this evening."

He said into the telephone, "I've got to see you. Make an excuse— think of something. Just get down and meet me.... No, darling, there won't be time for bed. This is money. Lots of money for both of us." There was a pause; he knew her so well. Death and disaster wouldn't motivate her; she'd only risk her rich protector if more money was in prospect.

"All right, I'll manage somehow. He's such a pig about letting me go out without him. Where shall I meet you?"

"The bar at Eden Roc," he said.

She gave a delighted giggle. "Ooh, Ralphie, you must be feeling very rich."

"Seven-thirty," he said, and rang off. He had an hour to spare. His bags were already packed; the ticket from Nice to Paris on the early-morning plane was in his pocket. He had spent the afternoon saying goodbye to the staff at the casino before he traveled up to the villa at Valbonne. He had gone out of his way to present a cheerful picture, praising Steven, saying how sorry he was to leave them and the old place, but he'd had such an outstanding offer. He managed to avoid saying where it came from. Poaching wasn't popular, so no one pressed him. He was especially friendly to his successor, Louis, making jokes and offering tips on how to deal with certain clients. They had waved him goodbye in an atmosphere of good wishes and goodwill. The impression was important. A disgruntled ex-employee would certainly come under suspicion.

He looked around his apartment. He'd lived there on the Croisette since Steven had put him in charge. He felt no twinge of nostalgia for the place. Just rented rooms, like all the other rented rooms he'd lived in for so much of his life. He sent his baggage down to his car. That could wait at the airport till he sent someone for it. He closed up the apartment and left the keys with the concierge. The rent was paid till the end of the year. He said he was going away but might be back from time to time. He gave her extra money to keep an eye on the place. Driving off through the heavy traffic of Cannes, he headed up the coast road to the beautiful Eden Roc hotel.

He had to wait for Madeleine. He bought himself a glass of Pernod. It raised the barman's eyebrows; it wasn't a drink his customers usually ordered. The bitter, cloudy drink burned on his tongue.

"Oh, darling Ralphie, I'm so sorry." She came hurrying up to him, bestowing a light kiss on his cheek as he greeted her. She was looking especially attractive. Beautifully, expensively dressed, with some new jewelry. People were admiring her. Wondering what she was doing with such an ugly man, he thought, savaging himself. For money, of course. What else had he to offer? "Now tell me, what's this about our being rich?" she questioned. She looked at the glass of Pernod and made a charming little grimace. "Only workmen drink that filthy stuff!"

"I've got very common tastes," he said. "That's why I'm so fond of you. You want champagne, of course."

"Of course," she said. "Don't be nasty, Ralph." She knew him in this mood. He could be cruel, insulting. Sometimes she put up with it, sometimes she didn't. She was used to being ill used by men. And Ralph could be very generous and rather sweet. "Now tell me—what's happened? I'm so curious, I'm dying!"

He sipped his Pernod. He tantalized her, keeping her waiting. So greedy. Licking her lips already at the idea of money. "I've had a bit of luck," he said at last.

She jumped in eagerly. "Gambling? You've won a lot?"

"Not gambling. I never did win, actually. Not as often as I lost. No, my sweet, someone has died and left me a fortune. What do you think of that?"

"I think it's wonderful," she said. She laid her hand on his upper thigh. "How much?"

It amused him to watch her face. "Half a million dollars," he said. "You're catching flies, sweetheart; you'd better close your mouth." The hand on his leg began to grip. He pushed it aside. "Not in public," he chided her. "You're not in one of your old haunts now." She'd started in the red-light district in Marseilles. A very superior type of brothel, where the girls were able to come and go. Madeleine had formed an association with one of the clients and gone. Her career took off after that.

She ignored him. He was trying to hurt her, to goad her. Something had upset him. She smiled, showing her lovely white teeth, and wet her lips at the same time. "I'm so happy for you," she said. "What are you going to do with it?"

He summoned the barman. "Another of those. And champagne for Mademoiselle. . . . I'm going to spend it. I'm going to book myself into a nice cruise, where I might play a little bridge or poker if I get bored. I shall spend the winter in the Caribbean. I've always wanted to go there. I may even buy myself a permanent house on the coast here when I've got sick of traveling. I just wondered whether you'd like to come along."

"Ralph! Oh, darling, you really mean it?"

"Why not? We've always got on. We have fun when we're together. And at least you won't have to be a punching bag for that Persian boyfriend of yours." She looked down and then shrugged. "What do you say, then?" he demanded.

She looked startled. "You mean you want me to make up my mind now. This minute?"

"No. But in, say, the next ten, while we finish our drinks."

"Why such a hurry?" she asked, her eyes suddenly narrowing. "You're telling me the truth? You haven't stolen it? Somebody died?"

"Somebody died," he assured her. "But I'm leaving for Paris tonight. Either you come with me, or you don't come at all."

She hesitated. But not for long. He could be sweet. He was a very active lover. And straight. The Persian got too enthused by his fantasies. She was becoming scared that one day he would carry them too far. "To hell with the pig!" she declared. "I've decided. I'm coming with you, Ralphie. You know, I think I'm a bit in love with you."

"Madeleine," he mocked, "you love me as much as I love you. For as long as the money lasts. Now you get your things together and meet me at the airport for the eleven o'clock flight. *Au revoir,* my sweet."

She turned at the little flight of steps leading out of the bar and blew him a kiss. It was a charming gesture. He paid the bill and left.

The waiter muttered under his breath. English pig. Hadn't even left a tip.

Clara was early. She'd arranged to meet O'Halloran at Beaulieu. There was an unobtrusive little fish restaurant with a bar. She ordered a drink. She felt conspicuous in her smart clothes. She was irritable at being kept waiting and on edge. When he hurried through with an excuse about the traffic, she snapped at him. "Where the hell have you been? You're late!"

Even though he'd slept with her, felt a transitory dominance because of that relationship, she could still overawe him. "I'm sorry," he said, and sat down.

She said, without preliminaries, "Well? Is it tonight?"

He looked at her. "It's tonight," he answered.

She felt short of breath suddenly. After a moment she controlled the rush of excitement. It had left a deep flush on her pale face. "Tell me," she demanded. "I want to know everything!"

He had made up his mind not to give too many details. She was quite capable of getting herself there to watch. "Maxton gets him on his way to the casino," he said, lowering his voice.

"And then you go to the villa," she breathed, "and you get *her* and that son." He hadn't mentioned that there was a baby girl. He had a gut feeling that she might ask for that too.

"With the same gun that shot the husband," he went on. "The maid told me the staff go off duty at nine. After dinner. There won't be any witnesses. Just the shots and the sound of a car driving off. I'll make it sound real panicky—squealing tires, the works."

She smiled slightly, savoring it. "You're Maxton," she said. "You've just killed the husband. You have a fight with the wife; the son interferes. You go haywire and shoot them both."

He nodded. "So, haywire I drive myself over that hundred-foot drop afterward." They had talked it over and over, planning the details. The talkative Janine, with her compulsive curiosity, had given them the motive, the motive that would explain three murders and a suicide— Maxton's love for his employer's wife. She hadn't confined her spiteful gossip to the American who'd stayed in the village, painting bad pictures. Everyone knew about it. The café owners, the couple who ran the patisserie, the old grocery woman.

Maxton had been dismissed from his job, and the cycle of revenge and ultimate despair was set in motion. It would fit into the pattern of crime that the French had made their own. The crime of passion.

"All neat and tidy," O'Halloran said.

"When will I know?" she demanded.

He calculated quickly. "Around eleven o'clock. I'll go back to my hotel and call you from there. Don't worry. It'll work out exactly like we planned it. You just relax."

She gathered her bag, her cigarettes and lighter. "You do it, Mike," she said softly. "You do it for me."

And for the money, he said to himself, *and for the chance to get out from under you, before it's too late.* "Consider it done," he said.

Ralph Maxton drove up toward Valbonne. He knew every twist and turn of the road, he'd driven it so often. Taking Angela there for the first time to see the villa he'd rented for them: she was shaken after a bad flight over from England. Dinner every Friday night. Thinking to himself, *By God, you've fallen on your feet at last. He needs you, and she likes you. All you've got to do is be your witty self, my friend, give him what he wants with Great-uncle Oleg's white elephant on the seafront and make up amusing stories for the dinner table.*

It hadn't stayed like that, unfortunately. He'd gone there too often, allowed himself to indulge in the ultimate folly: falling in love. He'd even enjoyed playing piquet with her old father. The trickster tricked, he murmured, watching the empty road ahead. But in the end, it led to riches. Considerable riches. Enough to make a very different dream come true. Not the original one, of course.

"There'll never be anyone else for me but Steven." The kind little kiss on the cheek. "Keep in touch . . . look after yourself." She wouldn't be sitting with him in the candlelight. Madeleine would. He deserved Madeleine. They deserved each other.

He pulled the car onto the shoulder of the road and checked his watch. Steven left home at the same time every night, arriving at the casino at nine-thirty sharp. A very punctual man, our mafioso. Never late for an appointment. He'd be on time for this one, though he didn't know it. Unless he'd brought Angela with him. Maxton hadn't warned his American about that. He'd made sure that evening. "I won't be coming tonight." He didn't have to worry about stopping the car and finding her sitting next to Steven Falconi, saying, "Oh, Ralph, have you had an accident?" He looked at his watch again. The hands had hardly moved.

He shook his wrist, thinking, *It must have stopped. I've been here God knows how long.*

They'd go to the Caribbean for the winter, he and Madeleine. She'd drive him wild with the tricks she'd learned since she was a little whore at age sixteen. They'd dine and dance to steel bands in the lovely warm evenings. They'd have the best suites in the best hotels. He'd wear her like a lucky charm, showing the world what a delicious woman he could get for himself. But he'd forgotten about the cruise.

Where would they go to? The Far East? Hong Kong? He'd often thought of going there. The Chinese were mad gamblers. He might even make some money. It had a marvelous racetrack. Madeleine would love it. He would take her shopping. He'd heard that you could get a suit made up in a day. As good as Savile Row. Well, not quite as good, perhaps. People exaggerated. His father had ordered him a suit from his own tailor when he was eighteen. His father had all his suits made there. His grandfather too. They said the suits lasted for thirty years if you kept your shape. They wouldn't be able to guarantee that in Hong Kong. What a bloody idiot to think he could settle in some pretty English village, with a wife and possibly a child of his own. He must have been out of his tiny mind.

He could see headlights rounding a corner high above. Falconi, due in a few more minutes. He switched on the engine and eased the gear into place. The big Peugeot glided past him, with only Steven in the front, behind the wheel. Maxton pulled into a little side road, not more than a track, that would bring him out onto the main road ahead of the car, with time to swing half around and block the way. The Smith & Wesson, fully loaded, was on the car seat beside him. All he had to do was get out and fire through the window at close range. It was a thousand to one against another car following in that isolated place.

O'Halloran was to meet Maxton at the turnoff to the *autoroute* to Nice. Nine-thirty. He'd driven very carefully on account of the big drop at the bend of the road. He had the bank draft in his pocket. A blackjack nestled in the other one. A cosh didn't break the surface of the scalp like a blow from something made of metal.

Nine-thirty passed. He wasn't worried. A few minutes either side to allow for Maxton's maneuvering his car back on the road. Maybe Falconi had got out of the car when he was forced to stop.... A few minutes was okay.

Nine thirty-five. "Hell," he muttered. Where was the son of a bitch? He heard the car before it came into view. A sports model, as you'd expect with that type, the top folded back, the driver easily recognizable as he slowed down and stopped. O'Halloran opened his car door and got out. He walked quite slowly toward Maxton. Not hurrying, not seeming edgy. Like a cop on his beat. His hand was locked around the cosh in his pocket.

He stopped by the side of the little car. He looked down at Maxton. Maybe it was the moonlight, but he looked a ghastly color.

"You got him?"

"Yes. Where's the money?"

"Right here," Mike O'Halloran said. He had the draft in his left hand. He held it out to Ralph Maxton. "No trouble?"

"No trouble at all."

He saw the glint of the gun and opened his mouth to yell. The bullet knocked him backward before he could make a sound. He spun and then collapsed facedown. Maxton got out. The American had been right about the damage that caliber could do. There was a gaping hole in his back.

He looked at him for a moment. Nothing moved. A lot of blood was spreading over the road like spilled ink in the silver light.

"Sorry about that," he said. "But you'd only have found someone else." He climbed into his car. The bank draft was lying on the seat. "Sorry about you too"—he looked at it—"but I can't cash you. After all, I have my standards." He tore up the draft and laughed as he threw the pieces into the air. The breeze caught them, whirling them down and out of sight into the valley below. He began to drive, taking the corners at his usual speed. He was a first-class driver, eyesight like an eagle's, reflexes lightning fast. He reached the coast road in less than ten minutes. He stopped at a bistro on the outskirts of Juan-les-Pins.

He bought himself a brandy. The proprietor said he could use the telephone at the back if it was urgent. For five francs.

"Mr. Lawrence, please," he said. He'd brought the brandy with him. He sipped most of it while he waited.

"Steven Lawrence."

"Good evening," Ralph Maxton said. "It's me."

"What do you want?" Steven's voice grated on him.

"Just to tell you there's a dead man lying in the road on the intersection to the *autoroute*. The shortcut to the airport. He was offering half a million dollars to anyone who'd kill you. You'd be amazed how close I came to doing it. If it wasn't for your wife, I'd be a rich man now. Give her my love." He put the receiver down, finished his drink and left a twenty-franc note on the counter. The proprietor stared after him in amazement. But he didn't rush out to give him change.

Steven came down the grand staircase at a run. He pushed past anyone who was in the way, rushed outside to where the car was parked. He heard Louis calling after him. He turned and shouted back through the open car window. "I'm going home. Take over for me!"

He drove faster than he had ever driven. Maxton's voice was ringing in his head: "a dead man lying in the road . . . half a million dollars to anyone who'd kill you." Angela, Angela and his son and baby daughter, unprotected in the villa, unsuspecting of any danger.

Twice he almost hit another car; he didn't hear the furious honking of horns and the shouts that followed him. Up into the hills, around the dark, twisting little roads, approaching the turnoff to the *autoroute*. He saw lights flashing, police cars, an ambulance. Someone had found the dead man, whoever he was. . . .

He put his foot down and went faster. He saw the lights on in the villa, in the ground-floor drawing room, where his wife and son would be after Angela had given the little girl her late feeding.

He raced inside, throwing the door open. They were sitting together; the TV was on, and Angela had been reading. He saw they were safe and forgot momentarily about everything else. He heard her say, "Darling, what's the matter? What is it?" He saw Charlie staring at him. Both were on their feet, alarmed.

He said to Angela, "Maxton called me. He said there was a contract out on me. It's Clara—it has to be."

Angela went white. "Oh, my God—"

Charlie interrupted. "Contract? Dad, what are you talking about?"

Steven said quietly, "A contract to kill me. It failed. The man's dead. But there could be another one—on you and your mother. It's a long story, and this is one hell of a time to tell you—"

"Steven—no!" Angela cried out.

He held his hand up to silence her protests. "It's no good, darling; he's got to know the truth." He turned to his son. "Charlie, I want you to listen to me. Don't ask questions, just listen. . . . Your father wasn't killed in the war. I'm your real father." He paused, seeing the shock on the boy's face. He said, "I loved your mother the first moment I saw her. I married her in Sicily, but we got separated. I thought she'd been killed in that hospital bombing. Years later I married someone else.

"Then I found her again in New York. And I found you, my son, who I'd thought was dead too." There were tears in his eyes.

Angela came and stood with her arms around him, facing Charlie. She saw her son's pain and confusion. "I lied to you, Charlie," she said. "We both lied to you, but we did it for the best of reasons. Your father gave up everything to be with us and make a new life for all of us together. He's been in terrible danger ever since. I hope you'll forgive me, but you mustn't ever blame him!"

Charlie looked at them. "I'm not blaming anyone." His voice wasn't quite steady. "I don't know what to say. . . . I can't believe it's happening."

"I love you, Charlie," Steven said. "You're my son, and I love you. That's the only important thing right now. And I want you to do what I tell you. I want you to take your mother and the baby and get the hell out of here. Just drive. Drive as far away as you can go."

"Not without you!" Angela insisted. "I'm not going without you."

"Yes, you are," Steven told her. "So long as I know you and the kids are safe, I can take care of myself. I'm through running away, my darling. It's between me and Clara now. Charlie?"

"Yes?"

"Come here, my son."

For a moment he hesitated. A long moment, an eternity to Steven and Angela. Then Charlie rushed forward to be clasped in his father's arms. They didn't speak, just held each other, and then the boy looked up at him and said, "I'm glad. I love you too." His cheeks were wet.

"We haven't time to talk now," Steven said. "But we will. I promise. No more secrets between us. Now you get the car, and I'll bring your mother and Anna."

It took Charlie some seconds to fit the key into the lock, to start the ignition and back out of the driveway. His hands were shaking. He saw the light go on and off in the nursery, and then Steven and his mother were outside, the baby still asleep in her arms. Steven opened the door and helped them inside. He laid a hand on his son's shoulder.

"I'm relying on you, Charlie. Take good care of them. Call me tomorrow and let me know where you are. And stay put till I tell you."

"I will. Don't worry. And, Dad—you'll be careful, won't you?"

Charlie heard Angela's anguished whisper as she said goodbye: "Oh, Steven darling." And Steven's reassurance: "Don't worry; we'll be together soon."

He looked back quickly as he drove away, and saw his father wave once from the doorway, with the lights behind him. In the back seat, cradling the sleeping child, Angela was crying.

It was a lovely night. A perfect night for a drive on the splendid road up to the Moyenne Corniche, and then there was the great panoramic view from the Grande Corniche itself, carved out of the topmost lip of the mountain. Bright moonlight, a little cold up there, a constant breeze that sang around Maxton as he drove. He found a place to stop, reversing carefully back from the edge. It was eerily beautiful to be so high, with the pygmy towns below, their lights reduced to twinkling dots, the black sea spread out around the silver path of moonlight that was supposed to beckon suicides. Like that of his old friend all those years ago. Swimming out because the sharks on land had eaten his heart out. *What a waste my life has been,* Maxton thought. *Worthless.* And so nearly doomed to years of yet more waste. He and his soulmate, Madeleine. No cruise to the delights of the Far East now. No steel bands and limbo dancers in Jamaica, with someone as rotten as himself to share it. And all because he had known what it would do to Angela. It wasn't scruples or a sudden rush of morality that had stopped him; he'd never known the meaning of either. He was rather proud of that.

He just couldn't make her so unhappy. Love, not conscience, had made a coward of him. Poor Madeleine, waiting at the airport. She'd be so furious, so disappointed. Thank God he wasn't going with her. What an appalling prospect!

"You'll come to a bad end if you don't mend your ways." He could hear his father thundering away at him. Such a Victorian his father was; never quite at home in the modern world. His mother kept hoping against hope that it was just a phase and he'd grow out of it. He'd stolen the jewelry from her bedroom. That was her reward for her faith. He hadn't mended his ways. But he hadn't come to as bad an end as he might have.

He switched the engine on and put the car into first gear. The nose was aimed at the black chasm in front of him. He didn't like the idea of that plunge downward very much. He set his foot on the brake, holding the engine in thrall. Then he put the American's revolver into his mouth and pulled the trigger. A few seconds later there was a distant tinkling crash and a flare of flame that licked upward as the car began to burn.

Steven stood in the darkness for some moments. It was very quiet. Angela, Charlie and the baby were out of reach; if danger threatened, he could meet it alone. He drove his car into the garage, locked the doors and went inside. He was calm, not afraid of what the next few hours might bring. He had never been afraid for himself. He knew the routine by heart; it had been part of his early life experience.

He shuttered every ground-floor window; drew the curtains; doused the lights inside and out; double-locked the doors. At home there was bulletproof glass, fine steel-mesh shutters to ward off a fire bomb or a grenade. Here, in the peace of the villa, nestling in the French hills, there was nothing but locks and bolts to stave off an attacker. Steven checked everything, even the tiny larder window.

He made the place as safe as possible and walked up to the second floor with a flashlight. Darkness would be his friend. If the man found dead on the *autoroute* had failed to recruit Maxton, then he must have hired another killer.

In the bedroom he shared with Angela, he drew the curtains and latched the windows, closing shutters that were designed to keep out nothing more deadly than the afternoon sun. It was Clara. Clara seeking him out, putting a king's ransom on his head. "She's gone on a long vacation," his brother, Piero, had said. But where? How close was she? Not too far, if he knew her. She'd want to be near, to exult over her vengeance.

He felt cold and, for the first time, felt a sense of fear. She should have been broken, disarmed, but the deaths of her father and her luckless husband were not enough. So long as she lived, he and, more important, Angela and his children would never be safe. A long vacation... He knew with certainty that she was in France. Nearer perhaps, than he dared think. If nothing happened during the night, he would start by checking the hotels. He knew her taste. Only the best would be good enough. First find her, and then face up to what he had decided to do. He settled in a chair to wait out the night.

He fell into a light doze while it was still dark. The dawn chorus of shrilling birds awoke him. He was stiff and weary, and sick inside. Opening the shutters, he saw the lovely glow of the sunrise in the sky. Only yesterday he would have wakened with Angela beside him, his children asleep down the hall, another happy day ahead.

He rested his head on his hands in private anguish. Out of consideration for Angela, he had never kept a weapon. Now he would have to get one. And use it. He went downstairs into the darkened kitchen and made coffee. They would be safe somewhere, out of reach of the Fury that was Clara. Charlie had promised to telephone and let him know where they were. He went back to the bedroom to wait for the call.

It was midmorning, and he still had no word. He switched on the radio to pass the time. It was the first item on the morning news bulletin.

"You're sure?" Madeleine demanded, "You're certain there's no message for me?"

The girl at the departure desk look bored. This was the third time the woman had been back to ask. "No, madame. No message."

Madeleine turned away. She cursed under her breath. She'd phoned the apartment. No answer. She'd tried the concierge, who was sleepy and ill-tempered. Monsieur Maxton had gone a long time ago. The flat was closed up.

There she was at the airport, all her luggage, her jewelry, the loot of five years on the coast, waiting with her. The last of that night's flights had gone. Something must have happened. An accident? He always drove like a maniac. She wondered for a moment whether he hadn't played a vicious practical joke. He'd been in such a strange mood that evening.

She couldn't return to her Persian friend. He would be very angry. Very angry indeed. She didn't want to risk it.

She went back to the information desk. To her relief, a man was on duty. He told her the next plane to Paris was at seven in the morning. Did she wish to go to a hotel? No, Madeleine decided. She wasn't risking her luggage, her clothes and her precious jewelry in some strange place. He directed a porter to bring everything to the VIP Lounge, which he unlocked specially for her. She was so attractive and charming, and he was aware of her distress.

She smiled at him, thanked him. If something had happened to Ralphie, what could she do about it? She'd stay there for the night. Only a few more hours. They boarded at six-fifteen for the early flight. She'd be quite comfortable. She settled herself on a sofa with her baggage piled up around her. Maybe it was fate. Time to leave the coast and start afresh. She had a big savings account. Paris was as good a place as any. There were lots of rich men to be picked up there. She slipped off her shoes, made herself comfortable and dozed off.

That night, Clara had dressed for dinner. She chose carefully, for an occasion known only to herself. A long cream dinner dress, part of the trousseau for her honeymoon with Bruno Salviatti. The ruby earrings Steven had given her for a wedding present. She'd worn them in this same hotel. She had twisted and turned before the looking glass, assessing her appearance. This was her night, her moment of triumph. She would walk into the restaurant alone, making an entrance. The last time people had stared at her, seeing her as beautiful, desirable, her handsome husband at her side. No husband this time. She looked at her watch. Eight-thirty.

The hours had dragged since she'd come back from Beaulieu. The hairdresser, the beautician, had served as diversions, but not for long enough. She had adjusted her left earring. It had always pinched, in spite of the new fitting. Then she'd gone downstairs in the elevator and into the restaurant. The headwaiter showed her to her table; he hovered deferentially. She had the best suite in the hotel. She wasn't hungry, but she ordered just the same. Some champagne, she decided, and looking coolly at the sommelier, she mentioned that she was celebrating.

It was difficult to eat; she picked at the courses, smoking between them. She took her time drinking the champagne. She had wanted to enjoy every moment, to let her imagination wander to the isolated road where Steven Falconi would meet his just end. How she had worshiped him all those years ago, when they had come here, dined in this same restaurant together.

And how she had suffered, impaled on the sharp stake of her own jealousy, all through that miserable marriage. Misery had made her barren. There was no other cause. He had rejected everything she had to offer. Her love, her sexual passion, the family traditions that bound them together.

Rejected her for the woman she'd seen in that photograph. A pale, bloodless image of a blonde like any other blonde. A nothing, Clara had called her, and O'Halloran had echoed it. How lucky she had been to find him. How wise to approach him with her proposition for the agency, instead of the ex-policeman with the Italian name. She was a shrewd judge of people, like her father, Aldo. She smelled corruption in that dingy office. The Ace Detective Agency. It made her smile. Fate had directed her that day. The fate that had overtaken Steven Falconi, even as she saw the time in the glitter of ruby on her wrist. He was dead. The woman and the son she had borne him were dead too. She'd lingered long over her coffee, dreaming of vengeance. It was a quarter to eleven. She thanked the headwaiter for an excellent dinner and made her way back to her suite.

A good-looking man with a much younger woman gave her an admiring look as he passed. She smiled provocatively at him. She was free. Free at last. She went into her suite. The bedroom door was open, her bed turned down, the satin nightgown draped across it. She kicked off her shoes and lit a cigarette. Eleven o'clock. She curled up in an armchair by the telephone to wait. The earring hurt a little. She unscrewed it, put it on the table. It rolled back and forth for a moment, glittering under the light. She reached up to undo the other one, when there was a knock on the door. "Mike . . ." She jumped up. He'd come instead of phoning. She called out, "Come in," and hurried to meet him.

It was the worst day in the history of the hotel. Worse than the fire of 1937, which had destroyed one third of the building, though without loss of life.

It started at seven that morning, with a commotion on the second floor. The manager was roused out of sleep. He came hurrying up to the suite. He was a man used to dealing with crises.

The young floor waiter was shaking uncontrollably. "I stumbled over it," he kept repeating. "I opened the door and nearly fell on top of it." He had dropped the breakfast tray. The manager crouched down beside the body of Clara Falconi Salviatti. She was lying on her back, and she had been stabbed to death with one of the hotel's own sharp-pointed steak knives. Right through the heart. The handle was sticking out of her chest. The dead woman's face was twisted in a grimace of such naked horror that the manager hurriedly covered it with his handkerchief. He stood up; he spoke kindly to the trembling boy and sent him downstairs. But on pain of instant dismissal, the waiter was ordered to say nothing. Nothing at all until the police arrived. He sidestepped the body. Thank God he didn't have to look at her face. And only God knew what she had seen that terrified her so much at the moment of her death. He went to the telephone and dialed the private number of the superintendent of the Monaco police. He was aware, just before the call was answered, of a strong smell in the room.

He recognized the distinctive scent of Joy.

Pauline Duvalier's funeral took place at the end of the week. She had died peacefully of a heart attack in her sleep, but the murder of the woman in the suite on the same floor overshadowed her passing.

Pauline's possessions were locked up. The old newspapers she'd hoarded were thrown away. Her will was found, addressed to the manager. She had repaid their kindness and care over the years by leaving everything to him and his staff. She was buried in Monaco, as she'd requested, and old friends like Eugène wept at the graveside. Among the mourners was Steven Lawrence, owner of the Casino Poliakoff.

"Oh, darling," Angela said, "I'm sorry I didn't come with you. I just couldn't face it." Steven put his arm around her.

"You've been through enough," he said. "I wanted to go; I owed it to her. For all she'd suffered," he added. And more. Much more.

She had found Clara before he did. He knew immediately who had plunged the knife into Clara's heart. Mercifully, Pauline had died the same night. He looked anxiously at his wife. She was pale and exhausted after the flight with Charlie and the baby.

They were together in the villa, and for the first few days they had stayed close as if some danger still threatened them. He was worried about his son. He seemed so quiet, almost in shock, after the emotional reunion upon his return with his mother and sister. Steven had rushed out to embrace them all and bring them inside. There had been tears, tears of joy and relief, but then reality had intruded. When Steven came back from Pauline Duvalier's funeral, he had already made up his mind what had to be done. He said gently to Angela, "Darling, where's Charlie?"

"Upstairs," she answered, "playing with the baby. He'd spend all day with her if he could."

"Go and call him," he said. "I've got things to talk over with both of you. And don't worry, everything's going to be all right."

He went into the kitchen and brought out a bottle of wine and three glasses. Wine was the gift of the gods; it eased pain and enhanced pleasure. They would drink wine together in the old tradition, and they would talk, as a family should when decisions had to be made.

He embraced his son. "Pour for us, Charlie," he said.

And the boy said simply, "Yes, Dad. Mum says you want to talk to me. You don't need to; she told me everything while we were away."

"I know she did," Steven answered. "But you and I must talk about it too. I promised you that now we have no secrets. I will explain everything to you, as a father to his son. But not today. Today I went to a funeral. I buried more than a friend. I buried my life here. All our lives here." He paused, waiting for Angela to speak.

"You mean you want to leave?" she asked.

He said simply, "I want us all to leave. This villa will never be a home to us again. I will never forget seeing you drive away, and spending that night here waiting. I don't want to live on the coast."

"What about the casino?" Charlie asked him.

The answer was prompt. "I will sell it. I don't want to live by gambling either. I'd like to start again. A clean business: hotels, restaurants . . . a new home and a new life for us. That's what I'd like. But I want to hear from your mother and from you."

Angela put down her wine glass. She looked at Charlie and then at Steven.

"Nothing would make me happier," she said. "I see Ralph around every corner here. I couldn't bear to go near the Poliakoff again. I would like to get right away and forget everything that's happened. Even the good things, the happy times . . . they've been blotted out for me now."

"Charlie?" Steven asked quietly. "What about you? Everything I've built here would have been yours if you wanted it. I can't guarantee the same success if I try again. I won't do this if you don't want it too."

Charlie finished his wine. He set the glass down. "I don't know what I want to do, Dad," he said. "Hotels and restaurants sound pretty good to me. I just want us to be a happy family and be together. I never want to live through another night like that last one."

"Then it's decided?" Steven asked them. "We make a new start somewhere else?"

Angela got up and put her arms around him. "That's what we'll do," she said. "Charlie, come here, darling."

She drew him close to them and said, "You have a wonderful father—you know that, don't you?"

"I know," he said. He reached out and gripped Steven's shoulder. "Don't worry about making a success, Dad. Whatever you do, it'll be great. Any idea where we'll go?"

"We could fly over to Biarritz and take a look," Steven suggested. "Take a break while this place goes on the market."

"I could look up some timetables," Charlie suggested.

"You do that." Steven nodded.

When his son had left them, he turned to Angela. "He's a good son," he said gently. "And you're the best wife in the world. *Io ti amo, amore mio*—remember, darling?"

"I remember," she said, and kissed him.

DATE DUE
